My Kendall...

Better than Expected

My Kendall

Copyright © 2022 Kendra Martin

ISBN-13: 978-1-7332290-2-9
Library of Congress Control Number: 2022910315

Cover image by: Randi Wadsworth

Kendra Martin LTD.
teamkendra16@gmail.com

Acknowledgments

Going through the pandemic and many other changes the last few years has many of us grappling for normalcy. I, too, have struggled with trying to find my way. But one thing has been a constant. I continue to be overjoyed with God's Grace and His never ending Love for me. Lord, I'm unable to properly thank You for all You do, but I pray my gratitude and praise reaches into the Heavens, and is a sweet, sweet fragrance for You. Thank you, Father…

I'm forever grateful to my husband, my children, and my entire family for always being there for me and always supporting my work. I love you all with all my heart.

I believe without 'Sisters', no woman is complete. Thank you TeamKendra and my forever sisters for pouring into me without measure. I love you all dearly.

And thank you to my friends, for not only supporting me, but for answering my endless questions. You know who you are. Thanks guys!

Thanks to Miss Randi Wadsworth for another fabulous cover. Your artwork is as beautiful as you are! Love you!

I thank you my dear LaMonda. You create the most beautiful work with my scrambled puzzle pieces. You put it all together and make me look marvelous! Love to you always!

Thank you to each and every person who found it 'not robbery' to support me and my work. I'm so thrilled when I get the chance to meet my supporters.

A special thank you to 'Sista-Love Book Club' for their enthusiasm in the 'Exes Series'. And a big thank you for participating in my book review.

To honor the beautiful sisters in my life, I dedicate this book to you... With Love

From the very first book, to this very day, my sisters have encouraged me in ways that make me continue to put pen to paper.
I'm blessed to have women in my life that have been there since childhood. Some came along during my early adulthood. And some I've only known since relocating to North Carolina. But each one of you has been a nugget God allowed me to encounter along the way. And those encounters morphed into lifelong 'sisterships.'

You Rock!

Love amongst women is unmatched by any other kind. Of course, trust, loyalty, and integrity MUST be your middle name. You trust me with your secrets when I need help writing about something I've never experienced. You literally SCREAM your joy when it's good, and you tell me when it's not. You all are as much a part of 'Exes' as my characters are.

My Sisters Rock!

Losing my one and only sister during the publication of 'Embracing Shiree' was absolutely devastating for me. But the women in my life carried me and held my arms up in battle. They pushed me over the finish line and celebrated me. Gosh, how I love you all!

YOU. ABSOLUTELY. ROCK.

Character List

FELICIA BENSON - MAIN CHARACTER
FELICIA'S CHILDREN – TODD JR (TJ), MARCUS, ALYSIYA (ALEECE), HAROLD III (BENNY)
CALVIN PIERCE AND BARBARA PIERCE - FELICIA'S PARENTS
HAROLD BENSON II – FELICIA'S HUSBAND
HAROLD BENSON SR AND JACQUELINE BENSON - HAROLD'S PARENTS
HAROLD'S FIVE SISTERS:
TARA - MARRIED TO BARRY, DAUGHTER MYA
DANIELLE - MARRIED TO CLIFF, DAUGHTER CHEYENNE
KAREN, MELISSA AND TAMMY
ANNETTE FRAZIER - FELICIA'S (SISTER) FRIEND
TONY FRAZIER SR – ANNETTE'S HUSBAND, SON TONY JR
CARLA SUMMERS - FELICIA'S (SISTER) FRIEND
EARL SUMMERS SR – CARLA'S HUSBAND, SONS EARL JR AND EVAN
SIMONE LAWSON – FELICIA'S (SISTER) FRIEND
VERONICA - SIMONE'S SISTER, - SHAYNA, SIMONE'S DAUGHTER
TODD WILSON SR. - FELICIA'S FIRST HUSBAND – BROTHER TO CARLA, COUSIN TO ANNETTE
GINA WILSON - TODD'S SECOND WIFE, DAUGHTER ANGEL
SAM MCELROY - FELICIA'S LOVER WHILE SHE WAS ENGAGED TO HAROLD
JONATHON - SAM'S FRIEND AND FELICIA'S LOVER WHILE SHE WAS ENGAGED TO HAROLD
LENORA - FELICIA'S SUPERVISOR
TRINA - FELICIA'S CO-WORKER
LINDA – FELICIA'S PREVIOUS CO-WORKER
DELISA – FELICIA'S HIGH SCHOOL FRIEND
ROBERT COVELLO - SAM'S COWORKER, HIRED BY SAM AND HAROLD TO SPY ON FELICIA.
BENNY – ANNETTE'S EX LOVER AND PRIVATE INVESTIGATOR USED BY FELICIA
DR. KENDALL MONTGOMERY – FELICIA'S CHILDREN'S PEDIATRICIAN AND HER LOVER
DR. JUANITA MONTGOMERY – KENDALL'S WIFE

YVONNE – JUANITA'S LOVER
SANDY – KENDALL'S NURSE
DR. STEWART GREER – KENDALL'S BEST FRIEND AND SIMONE'S LOVER
TOM – THIRD MEMBER OF THE JAZZ TRIO (DRUMMER)
GARY – ANNETTE'S LOVER
CARRIE – HAROLD'S BUSINESS ASSOCIATE AND LOVER
PHILLIP – FELICIA'S CHILDHOOD FRIEND WHO CRUSHED ON HER
PAT – KENDALL'S FRIEND
KELLY – KENDALL'S SISTER
TERRELL – KENDALL'S NEPHEW
KEENAN SR. AND LORRAINE – KENDALL'S PARENTS
KEENAN JR. – KENDALL'S BROTHER

Prologue

He was very calm. I tried to figure out if that was a good thing. He opened a folder. "That guy I used to find Robert, I called him. He tracked you for a month. I've known for weeks. I can't imagine that this has happened again."

He removed two photos from the folder and handed them to me. Both were of Kendall and me. One was of us going into the movie theater last month. His arm was around me and he was kissing my forehead. And the other one was us eating afterwards. In Syracuse.

The room started spinning. My mind went back to that night when I called him Kendall. *Of course,* he heard me say it. I knew it would send him spiraling. That's when he hired the PI, just like I suspected he would.

He got up and stood over me. He had his hands in his pockets and a smug look on his face. "So, is it true? You're actually *fucking* Kendall Montgomery??"

Chapter One

November 2012

My life had become something I no longer recognized. For the majority of the last three and a half years, I'd spent it being a wife to two men.

Looking back, as crazy as it sounds, I would've only changed one thing. I would *never* have married Harold Benson.

The door opened and Doctor Morales walked in. She was a kind and patient woman who seemed genuinely concerned and anxious to resolve my issues.

This was my third and final session with her. She'd taken me through several exercises, and it seemed we discussed everything except the obvious.

She concluded that amongst other things, I had low self-esteem and an unhealthy need to be perfect.

After pleasantries, she looked in my file. "Mrs. Benson. The time has come to deal with what brought you here. I'd like to know the details about the last couple of weeks, and every key detail you recall about the evening of November first."

I told her everything. We discussed it thoroughly, and she smiled while I exposed my painful truth.

Before leaving, she assured me she wouldn't need to see me for anymore sessions. She would send me a report by mail soon, and we'd get together one last time to go over her findings.

It was a cold November day in Rochester. After my appointment, I went home. No one was there, so I made a cup of tea and sat looking out at the deck.

I closed my eyes and could still hear Harold's voice when he asked that chilling question. "So, it's true? You're actually *fucking* Kendall Montgomery??"

I knew the memory of that night would forever be etched in my brain...

I looked up at the second mention of Kendall's name. I closed my eyes and put my head back down. I didn't answer him. But I reached for the armrest, with the intention of getting the hell out of there.

He put his hand under my chin and raised my head, which prevented me from getting up. "*This* time, Felicia, I *will not* fight for you. *This* time, it'll be *your* fight."

He released my chin. I put my head back down and he put his hands in his pockets again. "What do you have to say, Mrs. Benson?"

Kendall told me not to respond. I couldn't, even if I wanted to. Without waiting for a response, he said, "Since you seem to be tongue tied, I'll say this. If you decide your family is enough for you, I'll forgive you. But I'll *never* accept this shit again. On the other hand, if you decide we are *not enough*, then you're free to do whatever you want. But not with my children. We'll move to Detroit, and you can have your life. They'll see you on vacations and holidays."

He walked out and went downstairs.

My breath caught in my throat. I couldn't even cry. I was so used to being the one who was wronged, I didn't know what I was supposed to do. The men in my life always begged me to take *them* back.

I couldn't move. I wanted to run behind him and beg his forgiveness. But something stopped me.

my kendall...

I suddenly had this vision of a puppy that had been caged. And unexpectedly, someone left the gate open. She was finally free. She was wagging her tail and looking back. Then she looked at the open gate.

She knew it was time to go, but she was afraid to leave.

I still hadn't moved. I *couldn't*. So, I sat there. For what seemed an eternity, but it was actually only about five minutes.

I suddenly felt all alone. I did this. I could blame Harold for many things, but I stayed in this charade we called a marriage.

And I knew it was about to blow up. But I thought, *hoped,* I could wiggle my way out of it. But I was wrong. And Harold was going to humiliate me.

Unless I stayed.

If I stayed, I'd have to give up Kendall. How could I survive that again? But if I left, Harold would drag my name through the mud, and...

I'd have to give up my babies.

I tried to get a glimpse at what my life would look like if I stayed. He would absolutely never trust me again. *Never*.

And I would have to live day and night tortured by Kendall's memory. Again. And life with Harold would be awful because Kendall would always be in bed with us. In *my* mind, and *certainly* in Harold's.

Not to mention the fact that Harold would probably insist we move to Detroit, and I would have to leave my family. *And my Kendall.* And I'm sure he would hire someone to spy on me permanently.

But there was something else. Something I never thought I'd ever see. The look on his face told me he didn't give a shit what I decided.

And he spoke to me like he'd been treating me for years. *Like I was worthless*. But he wasn't subtle like in the past. This time venom dripped with every word.

Kendall told me to leave. I wish now I'd listened to him.

I finally got up. I was dizzy, but I made it to the shower, and I sat on the bench. I finally cried. I spent so much time worrying about how it would end with Kendall that it never dawned on me to consider that it was my marriage that would end.

I made up my mind. I went into the twins' room and gently kissed each of them. Then I got my Kendall phone, went back in the bathroom and locked the door.

I knew Harold would never allow me to leave with the twins. But if I left without them, he would accuse me of abandonment. I was damned either way.

I looked at my reflection in the mirror and was again forced to see the me I had become. The woman I saw had no redeeming qualities or value. She'd become...

I turned the water on in the shower and looked in the medicine cabinet. I got the pills Harold had for his back...and I took all of them.

I sent my K a text telling him how much I loved him. And that I couldn't live without him...

Not again.

I put the phone in my pocket, got in the tub and laid down fully clothed.

I didn't want them to find me naked.
Or looking like what I'd become...*worthless*.

Chapter Two

When I woke up, I screamed because I never wanted to wake up again. Mom and familiar voices behind me held me and begged me not to fight them.

The voices belonged to Simone and Carla. Then I watched my father walk away with tears in his eyes. I'd never seen him cry before. I screamed again. *"Daddy!"*

He turned toward me, and I reached for him. I said softly, *"I'm sorry, Daddy."*

He walked out. I closed my eyes and wailed again. Then I turned to my sisters. "Please, Simone. I can't go back. I can't face him. Carla, Harold knows about...my...*Kendall.*"

Mom said, "We know, Baby. He told us."

"What did he say, Mommy?"

"Just that he suspected something was going on, and..."

I looked around. "Where is he?"

Everyone was quiet. I looked back at my mother. "Mommy? Where are my kids?"

They all looked at each other. I screamed, *"Where are they?!"*

Simone closed her eyes and rubbed my arm. "He took them to Detroit. But he swears he's coming back."

I wanted to die again. I was certain I'd never see my babies again. I prayed silently, *"Please, God. Wake me from this nightmare! Or please, God...kill me!!"*

How could he leave me, and not even know if I survived? I really thought he loved me...*more than that.*

He took my babies to add insult to injury. He clearly didn't care what happened to me. Felicia Pierce got up. Mom said, "Felicia, get back in the bed. You need to rest, Baby."

I tried to walk away from the bed, but I was attached to an IV. I snatched it out and asked Simone for her phone. "Felice..."

"*Give me your fucking phone, Simone!*"

Mom grabbed a towel and immediately put it around my arm. "You're bleeding, Baby. Please…"

Simone went in her pocket and took out her phone. Carla left the room. I watched her leave and Simone asked, "Who do you want to call, Felicia?"

"I want you to call Harold."

She glared at me, and I watched as she began her search for his name. I asked her, "Have you talked to Kendall? Where is *he?*"

Simone looked at Mom. Then she said, "He was here, but…"

She put her phone on speakerphone, and I could hear it dialing. I grabbed her phone and walked away. He answered quickly. I said in a voice even I didn't recognize, "Bring my children back or I *will* kill you."

"Once you're better…"

"*Now, Harold!* Or I'll come and get them, and I won't be alone."

I hung up and gave Simone her phone back. "Where are my clothes?"

Carla had apparently gone to get the doctor. They both came in, and the doctor approached me. She said, "Mrs. Benson. I'm Doctor Morales. How are you feeling?"

"I'm fine. I accidentally took too many pain pills."

"Your husband said you did it intentionally."

"He's a liar. He said that so he could get custody of our children."

Daddy walked back in, and it took all I had not to cry again. I hated that I disappointed him. "I have pressing business to take care of, so I'm going home now, Doctor. Thank you for all of your help."

"We need you to stay for a few days. Just until you're…better."

I got right in her face. "I don't have a few days. I need to get my children from their kidnapping father. Right now. I'll make an appointment and see you later."

I walked over to the closet, opened it, and saw my clothes. Mom said, "You can't leave, Felicia. You have to stay a period of time when you…attempt that."

She began to cry. "Mother. It was a mistake. I didn't *attempt* anything!"

I looked at the doctor. *"My husband* has convinced my family that I did something crazy. Look at what this has done to my mother. I assure you it was an accident. I'm leaving."

My father said to the doctor, "Let her go. I'll take responsibility for her."

I turned to him. "How did he leave so fast, Daddy?"

"He left this morning. I told him to leave the kids, but he insisted he didn't want them to witness any of this. You've been here since last night."

I said almost to myself, "I swear I'll make him pay for this. Or I'll kill him."

Daddy convinced them to release me around two o'clock. But they insisted I make an appointment for the next day. And Daddy insisted I stay with them.

Daddy dropped me off at my house with the condition that I handle my business and come to their house within an hour. Once inside, I noticed Harold had obviously gone through my purse.

My iPhone was no longer in my pocket, so I ran upstairs and went in my bathroom. It wasn't there. I called Mom and asked if she'd seen it. She said no, but Harold gave her my other phone.

I had no choice but to call from the house phone. When he answered, I said softly, "I'm sorry, Kendall."

"Are you okay, Baby? I was just about to come and get you. Simone told me you were released and that he took the kids."

I cried. "It's over, Kendall. He hired someone and he followed me for a month. He's got pictures of us together."

"What do you mean, *it's over?*"

"I don't mean us, Baby. And I can't find my, your phone. I think he has it."

"I'm coming to get you. I didn't go into the office today. I'm at our place downtown."

I thought about that. "No. I'll come there."

"No, Shiree. You shouldn't be driving."

"I'm fine."

I hung up, took a shower, and left. I stopped to get my other phone and I told Mom I'd be right back.

During the drive downtown, I called my supervisor. "Len. I don't know how to say…"

"Harold called me this morning. What the hell happened??!!"

"What did he tell you?!"

"That you were in the hospital, but he wouldn't say why."

"Harold and I have struggled a lot lately. I think it's over, Len. Just know that I'm all better now and I'll be back Monday. Okay?"

"That bastard didn't hurt you, did he?"

I couldn't help but laugh. Lenora was always an undercover thug. "No, Girl. I promise to sit down with you soon and tell you everything."

When I pulled into the garage, Kendall and Simone came out at the same time. Simone asked, "What the hell are you doing driving, Sister? You should be taking it easy."

"Probably. But Harold has pissed me the fuck off, taking my kids."

Kendall held my face and looked in my eyes. He said, "She's right, Shiree. You need rest."

He kissed my forehead and reached for my hand. When we went inside, I put my head down in embarrassment. "I'm so sorry for what I did. I didn't…"

He touched my lip. "You don't have to explain. I understand how it feels. Just promise me you'll *never*…do it again."

"I need to call my mother."

He again held my face and looked in my eyes. "Shiree? Did you hear me?"

"I promise, Kendall. I'm sorry."

I looked in his eyes, and what I saw was a different kind of fear. The kind that said of all the things in the world, I never thought you would do *that*.

And I believe what scared him most of all was that he had no control over it. He brought me in his arms. "Don't move or fuss. Just let me have this moment."

He held me so tight. I realized how scared he must have been. I felt terrible for putting my loved ones through that. What was I thinking?

When I called Mom, I put her on speakerphone. She was *not* happy. I paced, chewed my lip, and respectfully listened as she unleashed on me. "Your father is gonna have a fit. He's already mad as hell because he knows I've known about Kendall. He's coming in here now. I don't want..."

Daddy picked up the other phone. "Where are you, Felicia?"

"Daddy, I just needed..."

I paused. "Are you with him, Daughter?"

Still chewing my lip, I looked up at Kendall. Daddy yelled, "Answer me, Little Girl!!"

I almost jumped out of my skin. "Yes, Daddy."

"I want you back here in the morning. Let me talk to him."

My heart almost stopped. "Kendall. My dad..."

Kendall reached for my phone. "Yes, Mr. Pierce?"

"Do you really love my daughter, or are you just...*enjoying* her?"

I almost fainted. But Kendall was cool. "Mr. Pierce. I'm *enjoying* the fact, that I've found the woman I want to spend the rest of my life with. And yes, Sir. I love her *very* much."

Daddy paused, but then said quietly, "She's my only child. And like I told you earlier. I will kill *you*, and *any man* that's a threat to her. Do you understand me, Doctor? I'm too old for this shit!"

I looked at Kendall with my mouth opened. "Yes, Sir. I understand. And I assure you that I share your sentiments. It'll be my priority and privilege to make sure she's protected and well taken care of, Sir."

"My wife says you're a gentleman. I expect you to make sure she's back here in the morning. No excuses."

"I will make sure, Mr. Pierce."

Mom chimed in. "Kendall?"

He smiled and answered. "Yes, Mrs. Pierce?"

"Please take care of her. Keep an eye on her, Honey. Okay?"

He smiled again. "Yes, Ma'am. I promise not to let her out of my sight. And I'll make sure she rests and gets plenty of fluids. Please don't worry."

Daddy asked, "Felicia, are you still there?"

"Yes, Daddy."

"No later than ten. If he doesn't bring the children by noon, I'm going to Detroit. And then you won't have to kill him. Because I will."

I'd never heard my father talk like that. Kendall brought me water and tea. "You must drink all of it. Okay?"

"Kendall. My dad…"

"Shiree. I expected nothing less from your father. I was at the hospital most of the night, and your father wouldn't let me near you. He told me if I took one more step, he'd snatch my heart out."

"Dear God, Kendall. *My* father said that?"

"Yes, Shiree. And believe me, I backed the hell up. And I knew I'd have to face him again. He's seen men hurt his daughter. My father beat Terrell's dad to a pulp, then dared him to hit him back. Real men cover the women in their lives."

He shook his head and smiled. "Your mother… Umph. She is something else. I really love her. She's always been so sweet to me."

"She adores you, Kendall."

He smiled again. He got up, poured himself a drink and more water for me. I watched him while thinking about my life. How in a moment, I no longer wanted it. But when I learned Harold had taken my babies, I needed to live for all of them.

I looked up and thanked God for sparing my life.

Nothing was the same. I was full of sadness and anger and fear. I don't know why, but I never thought Harold would hate me.

I knew he was hurt, but I didn't think he'd be so cruel. Or leave me. I said almost to myself, "He wanted me to choose, Kendall. You or my kids. If I chose my kids, I'd have a life of misery with him. But if I chose you, he threatened to take them, Kendall. *Just like I feared. He took my babies*…"

I cried and he took me in his arms. He held me until I fell asleep.

I woke up with him carrying me up the stairs. He put me down in the bathroom. "Get rid of some of that water, Baby."

After using the bathroom, I came out and he was sitting on the bed. It was only six o'clock in the evening, but I was so sleepy. I guess it was from the pills. "Come on. Let's lay down and rest, Shiree."

"Are you sleepy too?"

"I'm a little tired. I was up all night worrying about you."

He undressed me, and as soon as my head hit the pillow, I was asleep again.

About nine o'clock, I woke up. Kendall was gone and I heard voices. I dressed and went downstairs, where I found Annette, Carla, and Simone in the kitchen.

Kendall, Stew and Gary were in the garage. I smelled food, and I was suddenly so hungry. Carla smiled and asked, "Licia, you feeling better? I was about to go up and check on you."

I nodded yes. Annette said, "You sit. We'll fix you something to eat."

I asked, "What smells so good?"

Carla said, "Vegetable soup. Stew made it for you."

I smiled. It warmed my heart how much he loved me. Kendall came over and kissed my cheek. "Shiree. I need you to come upstairs with me for a minute."

"Okay. Is something wrong?"

"Nothing at all. I just need a minute, okay?"

We went upstairs and sat on the bed. "I need to say some things to you, Sweetheart. And they need to be said now."

I put my head down. I wished I'd thought it through before I took those pills. I wondered if everyone thought I was nuts. Maybe I should have died. "Shiree?"

I looked up and said, "I didn't think I could live without you, Kendall. I couldn't choose you over my babies, but I couldn't live with him without you. *I couldn't live*."

"Felicia, I didn't ask you up here for that. Did you hear what I said?"

"No, what did you say?"

He laughed and touched my nose. "I really adore you, you know that?"

"You don't think I'm nuts, do you?"

"No, Baby. You were devastated. What I said was that you'll be staying with me now. I promised your father I'd take you back in the morning, and I will. But I'm staying with you so I can speak with your dad. If Harold is there, so be it. We'll face him together and you will now live with me."

He stood up and extended his hand. "Kendall, I..."

"I said what I needed to say, Shiree. You're staying with me."

"When he brings my babies, I have to be with them, Kendall."

"*We* have to be with them, Shiree. We'll move into my house and bring the children. He can fight us for them, but he can't take them. I'll whip his Black ass. Which is next on my agenda anyhow."

I suddenly felt so empty. And I felt sorry for Harold. I'd devastated him again. Why did I do this to him again? "Come on, Shiree. You need to eat."

"Please don't beat him up, Kendall."

He grunted, took my hand and we went downstairs. I quietly ate while the others drank and laughed and had fun. My sisters were very attentive, but I began to feel sadder and sadder.

And after a couple spoons of soup, my stomach wasn't happy either. I excused myself and went upstairs. I barely made it to the bathroom before I threw up. I rinsed my mouth and looked in the mirror.

I was so tired. Life had finally beat me up.

I opened the cabinet for the mouthwash, but what I saw was me reaching for those pain pills again. Maybe this time…

All I could find was Advil.

I decided to check the other bathroom. I turned and Kendall was standing there. "Shiree. Please tell me what will make you feel better. If you would've died, I would've laid in that grave with you. Please don't leave me."

I covered my face. "I can't face this, Kendall. I can't face *him*. He gave me everything and I… I was so terrible to him. He never deserved to be treated that way."

Kendall embraced my face. "Look at me, Shiree. Look at the man who adores you. If he'd given you *everything,* you wouldn't be *here!*"

I opened my mouth but couldn't speak. I knew he was right, but…I couldn't seem to get over hurting Harold. And now Kendall was planning to hurt him more.

He grabbed my arms and looked in my face. He said quietly, "I didn't have the strength to do what you did, Shiree. So, before you kill yourself, you *better* kill me first. Don't you *dare* leave me!"

I was horrified. "Oh, *Kendall…I'm so sorry.*"

"I mean it, Shiree. Remember what I did when you were pregnant? And when you caught me with that woman? No matter what I said or what I did, I couldn't change any of it. We can't *change* it, Baby! I tried repeatedly to get you outta there. It's killing me that you're crying over him."

"Kendall, I…"

My phone rang. I went in my pocket and saw that it was Harold. I answered on speakerphone. "Are you back with my babies?"

"Felicia, your mother said you were released. Are you okay?"

I frowned and didn't answer him. "Felicia, where are you?"

"You left me in a hospital, not knowing or caring if I was dead or alive. You took my babies halfway across the country, without any regard for how much *more* that would devastate me. Not only did you take them from *me*, but my parents feel like their own *children* have been kidnapped. No, Motherfucker! I'm *not* okay! And if those children are not back here in the next twenty-four hours, I will make life for you far worse than you could ever imagine."

"Don't talk to me like that, Felicia."

"I will talk to you anyway I please! I admit I've done some foul things. But I *never* did anything to *intentionally* hurt you. You did this to hurt me, Harold. I endured a lot for the sake of our family. But this…I will *never* forgive you for this!"

Kendall reached for the phone, and I pulled away. Harold asked, "So you've chosen him over me? Over our family? Why? Because he made you feel good? It's just sex, Felicia. If that's the case, I would've left you a long time ago."

"Until you bring my children home, I have nothing more to say to you."

"We're a family. Don't do this. I believe we can iron out our differences."

"Bring me my babies!"

I hung up, and Kendall walked away and turned toward me. He was rubbing his chin and clearly not happy. "Are you going back to him?"

"No. I just need him to bring my kids back. And for the record, I wasn't crying over him. I was crying for myself. Because the truth is, it's me I can't face. I'm such a fucking coward."

We eventually went back downstairs, and the fellows went next door. I finally told my sisters everything. We talked while I tried to eat again.

Simone was pissed. "Curtis is so low down. I bet he also told Tony and Earl."

Carla asked, "You think so, Simone?"

"Of course. Curtis wants everybody to be miserable with him. He would say he was doing the guys a favor. I never should have married him."

Annette had been quiet. Without looking up, she said, "Felicia, don't do that again."

I turned and looked at her, and she had tears on her face. Carla gasped and Simone put her hand over her mouth. Annette looked up and said, "There's no problem that bad, Sis. Please promise you won't do it again."

We all had a moment. I promised them I'd never do it again. I held Annette in my arms a long time. It was rare that she cried.

I finished my soup, and we talked a while longer. Eventually, Carla said, "Annette and I are leaving soon. Is there anything you need us to take care of, Sister?"

I answered, "Thanks, Carla. I can't think of anything."

She kissed my cheek and smiled. "We love you, Sis. We'll talk tomorrow. Okay?"

I nodded, kissed my sisters, and thanked them. I watched them leave and I thanked God for giving me such loving sisters.

Chapter Three

That evening as Kendall and I were putting things in order, out of left field he asked, "Do you love me, Shiree?"

"Of course, Kendall."

"Are you done giving me a hard time?"

"A hard time?"

"Yes. I've waited a long time to be your husband. I need your assurance that your wall of resistance is gone now."

"I gotta make sure my kids are okay first. And I expect Harold to be *my* wall of resistance. I don't think he plans to let me or the kids go easily."

He came closer to me. "That, I can handle. I need you to let me be a man here, and trust that I'll take care of this. Okay, Sweetie?"

I stared at him. He leaned his head, waiting for an answer. "Are you done with Harold, Felicia?"

"Yes, Kendall. I just…"

"I will not share you with him any longer. And you know me well enough to know that I expect you to be completely honest with me. Do you or do you not want me as your *only* husband?"

"Yes, Baby. But…"

"No buts, Felicia Pierce. It's important that you trust me with this. It's over, Baby. You still love me?"

I turned away from him. I was scared. Not of him, but of leaving Harold. He was calling my name. "Shiree? I asked if you still love me?"

I turned back. "Yes, I love you. And yes, I trust you. But you have to trust me too. I've done some foul things, Kendall. So…for me, for *my sake*, I must do this properly. With decency. Do you understand?"

He smiled. "I expect nothing less from you, Baby. The problem is, neither does he. And because of that, he knows he can manipulate you."

I stared at him. "Are you saying I'm dumb?"

"*Dumb?* Did you forget which of your husbands you're talking to?"

"What? No, but…"

"Have I *ever* called you or treated you like you're dumb, Shiree? *Have I?*"

"No, Kendall."

"*Has he?*"

I felt like the answer blazed like a neon sign on my forehead. "Shiree. Being decent and being dumb are two different things. He took your decency and misused it. Whereas I treasure it."

I smiled. And without warning, he came after me. I was on one side of the sofa, and he was on the other. "Stop, Kendall. I'm too tired to run from you."

"Then stop running."

He slowly walked toward me. I heard the double meaning, and once again, anxiety rose up in me. I was back at that place wondering what and who to choose.

I couldn't bear the thought of not choosing Kendall. He said he would make sure we got the kids. He said we'd fight for them. But what if we lost?

Would Harold actually take them from me? Kendall embraced me. "We'll be fine, Shiree. I can't promise it'll be easy, but it'll be worth it. Okay, Baby?"

I nodded and he kissed my forehead. Then he carried me to our room and held me all night. I dreamed of my babies.

The next morning I was up early, and I decided to call my buddy. It was about six forty-five and he answered right away.

Kendall never asked much about our relationship, but he knew we were close. He went to the bathroom, and I was on speakerphone. "Good morning, Todd. You got a minute?"

"Yeah, I'm on my way to work. What's up?"

I was putting my socks on and paused. "How are my babies?"

He laughed. "*What* babies? Your *sons* are fine."

We both laughed. "Harold and I are kind of separated."

Kendall walked in from the bathroom. "What the hell happened, Licia?"

"That's not important. But I..."

"Tell me what he did. Is it another woman? Licia, you have to stop running..."

I laughed. "No, Todd. I...sort of have another man."

He was actually speechless. I looked up at Kendall, and he was smiling. Todd eventually said, "Licia! What the hell?! *What* man?"

"Stop being nosey, Todd. Isn't that what you always tell me? Did you ever stop seeing Miss Thing?"

"That girl was after my little bit of money."

"And you were after her ass. Are you still seeing her?"

"Stop changing the subject. When did this happen, Licia?"

"A couple of days ago. I can't talk now, but soon we'll sit and talk. Okay?"

"Yeah, okay."

Kendall was standing there with his arms crossed. I'm sure he thought it was bizarre. "So, you can help me out?"

"Yeah. I gotchu. Always, Licia."

"If he calls you, don't mention it. Let him tell you. Okay?"

"All right. And I know, don't tell the boys, right?"

"Right."

"Should I tell Gina?"

"Yeah, you can tell her. And, Todd?"

"Yes?"

"I sort of took too many pills and ended up in the hospital the other night. I thought you'd rather hear it from me."

"*Nooo,* Licia. Come on ex-wife of mine. Please tell me that's not true."

"It's true. But I promise one day soon, we'll have one of our lunch dates and I'll tell you everything. Okay?"

"Umm-hmm. You okay?"

"Yes. I'm fine now."

"You know I love you, Girl. Call me if you need *anything*."

"I love you too. And thanks, Todd. Keep my secret."

"I always do. Let's go to Unkl Moe's next week. It's been a while."

"Okay, ex-husband of mine."

When I hung up, I looked at Kendall and laughed. "I know. It's weird. But we're like brother and sister now. We've always been able to talk like that."

"Why didn't you tell him about me before now?"

"Because he never asked. The only reason I know about Lisa Raye is because I asked if he was cheating on Gina."

"Lisa Raye?"

I laughed. "That's what he calls her. She reminds him of her."

"Damn, I need to see her."

I laughed again. "Let's go out for breakfast, Shiree. Take it easy today."

"I'd prefer to cook, Kendall. I'm not ready for that yet."

He sat down next to me and held my hand. "Shiree. When I got that text from you, I smiled and thought you were sending something sweet. When Simone called me, my heart stopped. She was hysterical, but I convinced her to let me drive her to the hospital. I went back to the text and reread it. I couldn't believe the love of my life was back in a hospital because of me. Again. Three times, Shiree. Never again."

He got up, walked across the room and back to me. "I can't deny that I'm thrilled he knows, Shiree. And didn't I tell you he knew?"

"I know, Kendall."

I confessed to him what Lenora told me. He paced again. "And *I confess,* that when I told you it was absurd we weren't together, I was planning to confront him."

I pretended to be surprised. "*You were?*"

He stared at me. "Yes. I knew it was risky, but he beat me to the punch."

He knelt in front of me. "This is our time now, Shiree. Are you with me?"

I closed my eyes, trying again to escape it. I put my head on his and sighed. "I spent an hour watching you sleep this morning. You've made me so happy, Kendall. But I'm not ready to get married again right now. Does that bother you?"

"Yes, but I understand. As long as we're together, and that our *goal* is to marry. We *will* be together, right?"

"That's my plan, Kendall. I just can't say when until I can see my situation clearer. I have no idea what Harold has up his sleeve."

"My fist, if he's not careful."

While eating breakfast, I rubbed his arm. "Kendall, please promise me you won't beat Harold up. Please."

He looked up at me. "Um-hmm."

"That wasn't very convincing."

"Listen, Shiree. I will not allow *anyone* to misuse you. I don't care who it is. You do plan to discontinue sleeping with him, don't you?"

"I hadn't thought about it. I assume he'll never want to touch me again."

"Just the opposite, Shiree. He said he wants to iron out your problems. That means sex. I will never allow that."

"Can we talk about something else? I can't deal with that right now."

He glared at me so hard, I dropped my bacon.

While Kendall was checking on things at the office, I began to replay that conversation with Harold. I knew he was cheating, but I never thought he would admit to it so easily.

I was trying to figure out how I felt about it. I decided to say I did it because he was doing it. Then I realized that wouldn't work either. Because in *his* mind, that wasn't enough to end our marriage. He wanted to work it out.

I needed another escape plan.

When we pulled up at my parents' house, I was nervous as hell. I was sure Harold would walk in. We both drove, so when we reached the porch, I asked him one more time not to stay. "I need to speak with your father. Then I'll leave."

"Why, Kendall? You already spoke with him."

He reached for the door. "I'm staying until I've talked to him, Shiree."

When we walked in, I was stunned. Aleece and Benny were there. My *babies!* They ran to me, and then their father walked out of the kitchen.

My parents followed him. When I looked up and saw him, my heart sank. I couldn't help but remember my dream. I silently prayed, "Lord, please don't let Kendall kill Harold in front of his children."

I felt my body shaking and the air seemed to stop circulating. I watched them look at each other. The only sounds were the kids talking to each other. Until Harold said, "Dr. Montgomery."

Harold extended his hand. Kendall said, "Good morning."

I moved closer to my father. Kendall reached for his hand and shook it. That handshake seemed to last an eternity. Aleece went over and looked up at Kendall. She smiled her big smile. "Hi, Dr. Ken!"

He touched her head and smiled too. "Good morning, Alysiya."

Harold crossed his arms and looked right at Kendall. "I see my children aren't the only Bensons you've had your hands on. Doctor."

I stopped breathing. Kendall paused and glared at him. I saw that look once before. In my dream. That look that was foreign to me.

I closed my eyes and moved almost behind Daddy. I held his arm because I was certain Kendall was gonna *kill* Harold. But he turned to Daddy and said, "Good morning, Mr. and Mrs. Pierce. Mr. Pierce, may I speak with you?"

Daddy motioned for Kendall to follow him in the kitchen. Harold looked at me. I closed my eyes and was sure that I'd never felt so low.

Harold walked over to me. "I hoped we could work this out."

"I'm not going to discuss that right now, Harold."

I was dreading facing him, but I pulled my big girl panties up high. Mom took the kids downstairs and I looked up at him. "How could you leave me like that, Harold?"

"You've been sleeping with this man, and you wonder how I could *leave you?*"

"I thought you at least cared about me."

"Whether it means anything or not, I *do* care about you. As a matter of fact, even after all of this, I still love you. Like I said, I'd like us to work through this."

"I never wanted to hurt you, Harold. And you may not believe this, but my love for you has always been genuine. That's why I...stayed."

"That's why you *stayed?* Because you *love* me? That's a helluva way to show someone you *love them*, Felicia."

"About the same way you showed love for me, don't you think? The humiliation, treating me like I'm worthless. The imprisonment. Should I go on?"

We simultaneously turned away. Neither of us could face the other. While I was looking out of the window, he came up behind me. "I admit I took the kids to hurt you. I've spent the last month in pain, Felicia. I've been grieving and fearing what you would do."

Again, I closed my eyes and put my head down. I stepped away from him, not wanting Kendall to walk out and see us so close.

He came close again and whispered, "I watched you leave the house to fuck another man. It was horrible, Felicia. But like before, I couldn't face you with it. I almost hit the ceiling when I found out it was him. How long has this been going on? The PI said he thinks about six months. Is that true?"

"I'm not sure, Harold. Something like that."

Kendall came out of the kitchen and went toward the door. Harold whispered in my ear, "I forgive you, Babe. Tell him it's over."

Kendall said, "Felicia, may I have a word with you please?"

He glared at Harold, then he stepped outside. I also looked at Harold. I went toward the door, and Harold grabbed my arm. "Who the hell does he think he is? And did you hear what I said?"

I looked toward the door again and Harold held my arm tighter. Kendall would've whipped Harold's ass for doing that. I noticed my parents were also absent. I pulled away and he released me. "You better remind him that you're *my damn wife!*"

I went out the door and Kendall turned to me. "Shiree, I... What's wrong?"

"Nothing."

"What the fuck did he say? I'll go back in there and..."

"He didn't say anything. You must know this is stressful for me, Kendall."

"I know that, Baby. Which is why you *cannot* allow yourself to be charmed by him. Don't let him fill your head with crazy ideas. I expect you to stay with me now. I mean it. Either you leave the children with him or bring them with you. Understand?"

"Kendall. Please give me a chance to work through this."

"Work through what, Shiree? Get them now and..."

"Not now, Sweetie. I don't want my parents to witness any mess. Please, just give me a little time."

He reached for my hand, and we walked over to his car. He raised my chin to kiss me. "I can't kiss you in front of them. Please understand."

He sighed and got in his car. He was not happy. "I need your patience, Kendall. Okay?"

He bit his lip, and I leaned in and kissed his cheek. "You want too much too soon, Kendall. I need you to trust me too. Okay, Baby?"

He nodded. Then he laughed. "It took all I had not to break his jaw."

I shook my head. "Kendall..."

"He's fucking with the wrong one, Shiree."

Just to change the subject, I asked him what my father said. "He appreciated me coming and facing him. He said that's what a real man is supposed to do. Then he laughed and said he thought I was gonna knock the shit out of Harold. He told me not to let his arrogance rile me."

"That's my daddy. So, what did you say to him?"

"I assured him again that I have the best of intentions regarding you and the children. I also told him that I plan to make you my wife when you're ready."

I smiled. "I need to go back and finish my fight. I'll call you soon. Okay?"

Again, the intense glare. "Stop pouting, Doctor. You're my man, right?"

He chuckled and put his head down. "You're damn right I am. I expect you and the kids to move out of there soon. I don't trust him."

I went back in and went downstairs instead of up. Of course, Harold came down too. Mom went back upstairs, and he motioned for me to come over to him. "You're in love with him, aren't you?"

"What are you talking about, Harold?"

"You spent the night with him. I was at home when I called you last night."

I didn't respond. "I never thought this would happen to us, Felicia. While watching you with him, the realization that I'd lost you hit me like a ton of bricks."

"This isn't because of Kendall, Harold."

"Well, he's not innocent here, Felicia. What does his wife think of this? I'm sure she doesn't appreciate the fact that you befriended her, and then slept with her husband. Isn't that what you accused Carrie of?"

"How long did you date Carrie, or are you still dating her?"

"I never dated her. However, I did sleep with her. Once. She was awful."

I tried to pretend I wasn't shocked. "How many others?"

"Two. They were all awful. I'll never find another you."

"You only slept with three other women? I figured it was more."

"How many did *you* sleep with?"

I sucked my teeth and didn't answer him. I was amazed we were talking like that. "Do you hate me, Harold?"

"I wanted to, Felicia. My manhood took a helluva beating, which is why I behaved the way I did. But I was no better. I needed to believe I was the victim, but I was as guilty as you. Do you hate *me*?"

"No, but I was delirious when you took the twins. I wanted to kill your ass."

He laughed. "I'd like us to continue to live together. For the kids."

I didn't know where to put that. "Harold, what would that look like?"

"I know you're in love with him. And he's clearly in love with you. I'm still trying to figure out something. Does Juanita know?"

"Yes. She's known from the beginning."

"What the hell is that about?"

"She and Kendall had an open marriage. They're now divorced, but publicly, they behave as though they're still married."

He came closer to me. "You're kidding?"

"When she learned about us, he told her the truth. And it worked better for she and I to be friends."

He looked at me like he didn't believe me. "Come here, Felicia."

We went over to our children. "They adore us, Babe. You're their mother, and it would be wrong of me to fight you for them. So, let's not disrupt their lives. I admit I selfishly don't want to divorce, and I don't want to leave the kids or my job."

We were hand in hand, watching our babies. "And I'll give you free reign to see him. I promise. But that also means I'll date too. We'll both use discretion."

I was shocked. I asked quietly, "You want me to agree to an open marriage?"

"Yes. But I still want my rights as a husband."

"Kendall will never agree to that."

"Why would you tell him?"

I realized he was giving me a way out. Except Kendall would have a fit. "Let me think about this. I'll give you an answer in a day or so. Okay?"

He said okay, and we went upstairs with both kids on their daddy's shoulders. Mom and Daddy were sitting in the family room, trying to pretend they weren't worried.

I sat next to my father and smiled. "Daddy. We've decided to try and work this out, so the kid's lives won't be disrupted too much."

Harold said, "Yes, and in the meantime, we don't want to involve anyone else. Especially my family."

My parents insisted on keeping the kids, and Harold and I went home. Dr. Morales' assistant called when we pulled into the garage, confirming my appointment for one o'clock that afternoon. I assured her I'd be there.

Harold began removing food from the refrigerator, and said, "How about I fix us a great dinner. It'll be my way of apologizing to you for taking the kids. I'm sorry for upsetting you. And the truth is, I never went to Detroit. We went to a hotel."

"I wondered about that. I couldn't imagine you telling them...the truth."

"I know, right. I have to figure out how and when to tell them. Would you like me to go with you to your appointment?"

"No. I think I need to go alone. And...I'm sorry about doing that. I panicked."

"Let's not talk about that. So, dinner sounds good?"

"I need to...talk to him. Maybe I can have dinner with you and then go and talk to him afterwards."

"Are you staying with him tonight?"

"I think so. He would..."

"It's okay, Felicia. At least you haven't left me…yet. And if you decide to live here, I assure you I'll understand when you need to stay with him. Just please try to convince him it's best for the kids."

My session with Dr. Morales went well. She smiled a lot and asked me several questions. I thought most of them were irrelevant to my situation.

For instance, she wanted to know about my childhood and my first marriage. I answered as best I could. She took tons of notes, and I felt intimidated by it. She recognized my discomfort, so she assured me I was doing fine and not to worry. She also said this line of questioning was normal.

Afterwards, I had an early dinner with Harold. He insisted that I consider not moving out, and he was adamant about receiving his marital rights.

What was that about???

By the time I pulled into the garage on East Avenue, I was still confused. He hadn't wanted me in so long. Why now? And why was he so calm?

Before the garage door went down, Kendall had the door opened and Simone had hers opened. Kendall asked, "Moni, what do you want?"

Her mouth was opened. "Kendall, what the hell did you call me?"

"Moni. Isn't that your nick name?"

I got out of the car and Kendall kissed me. "Hey, Baby. Everything all right?"

"Yes. Couldn't be better."

Simone asked, "Felice, you told that Negro my old nick name?"

"Simone. I happened to mention it. I never thought he'd use it."

Kendall was cracking up and Stew came out. He asked us, "What the hell is so funny?"

Kendall asked Stew, "Did you know her nickname is Moni?"

Stewart tried to contain his laughter. He asked Simone, "Baby, were you in a gang? That sounds like a gang name."

We all hollered, and Simone looked at me. "Felice. I can't believe you told him that. That was wrong, Girl."

"I promise you. It just slipped out."

Kendall went over and hugged her. "I like it, Moni. I think I'll call you that from now on."

She rolled her eyes and took my hand. She pulled me into her kitchen and closed the door. "Curtis called me. I cussed his ass out and told him he could forget *ever* talking to me again!"

"He's the kind that wants to be right, no matter who it destroys."

"Don't I know it. Your text said you and Harold resolved your issues. What happened?"

"You will not believe what he said, Simone. I was so scared when I walked in with Kendall. And he walked out of the kitchen, they had words, but it was brief."

I told her everything. "What did Kendall say about Harold's proposal?"

"I haven't told him yet. I'm praying he agrees it's..."

"An *open marriage?* You know there's no way in hell Kendall will agree to that, Felice."

She laughed and I shook my head. She was about to say more, but Stew came in, so I said my goodbyes and went over with Kendall.

I went in the kitchen and grabbed a Pepsi. Kendall reached for it, and I handed it to him. He asked, "What have you had to drink today, Shiree?"

"Water and wine. At dinner."

He glared at me. "No soda and no alcohol, Baby. Just water and clear liquids. Understand?"

I laughed. "Do you remember that night I first saw you at the club, and you and Stew told me to drink cranberry juice?"

He laughed too. "Um-hmmm. That night was magical. I couldn't believe I looked up and saw the woman of my dreams. It was inconceivable."

"It *was* magical, Kendall. I felt I needed to *run*, not walk out of there. I was mesmerized by you."

He laughed at that. "I was hoping to talk you into spending the night with me at the Hyatt."

"Until you saw *the husbands.*"

His smile disappeared. "I remember wanting to punch his ass then. He rubbed your ass and my blood pressure went through the ceiling."

We both laughed. We looked at each other and he kissed me. He embraced my face and looked in my eyes. "Shiree, are you staying with me tonight?"

"Yes, Kendall."

He seemed surprised. Then he suddenly picked me up. "But we need to talk, Baby."

He carried me up those stairs again. "Kendall..."

"Shush...undress and let's get in bed."

I did as he asked. He also undressed and brought me close. "Kendall, I need to..."

He shushed me again. We made love for two hours. When I woke up, it was after one o'clock and he was watching me. "What do you have to tell me, Shiree?"

I began to sit up and he stopped me. "If you have to get up, it can't be good."

I laughed. "I think you'll be surprised, Kendall. It's not what I expected."

"Please tell me you haven't agreed to anything yet."

"No, I haven't. I wanted to speak with you first."

He brought me closer. "Okay, Shiree. Tell me."

"First of all, he and I were open and honest. He wasn't mean or nasty, and he admitted to cheating with three women. One was Carrie."

"I knew that woman was trouble. Is he still seeing her?"

"He says no. He also said she was awful in bed."

"Tell me what I need to know, Shiree."

"He doesn't want to get divorced."

He began shifting. "But he's accepted that we're in love, Kendall. He even said..."

"You told him?"

"No. He said it was obvious. So, he's willing to compromise if I am."

He sat up. "Shiree. I will not share you with him. I'll never agree to that."

"He suggested an open marriage."

"What?"

"I think it's a good compromise. Don't you?"

He got up and walked around the bed. "Kendall..."

"Does he expect you to sleep with him?"

"No."

He glared at me. "I *do not* believe that, Shiree. I believe you'll do what you think will keep us both happy. Please tell me the truth."

"Kendall, he said he would give me free reign to see you as often as I want to. I assure you, it's just so the kid's lives won't be disrupted. So they can still have both of us. I promise not to touch him. I promise, Kendall."

He was furious. "No, Shiree! *We* will raise the kids and *he* can visit. No way!"

"He told me he has no interest in me, and we both agreed to date discreetly."

"That's his way of *keeping you there, Shiree.* Don't you see?"

"Why would he do that?"

He didn't answer. His glare was piercing. And by the look on his face, he needed something to punch. "Baby...please come back over here."

He didn't move. "I always come to you when you ask me to, Kendall."

He bit his lip and eventually started toward me. I watched him in his nakedness, come across the room like a panther. His beauty caused me to take pause. He was still the most gorgeous man I'd ever seen.

When he was close enough, I touched his thick thighs and laid my head on them. "I was willing to die, because I love you so much. Now I'm willing to do this to have my babies *and* you. Please, Baby. I no longer want him."

He sat next to me and sighed. "Juanita told me you'd put a bullet in Harold's head, *and mine,* to protect your children. She said don't ever make a woman choose where her children are concerned. So believe me, I get it. But it's too much, Baby."

"I've done it for three years. If anything, it'll be easier. I won't have to sneak and lie anymore. Or keep him happy. That was exhausting, Kendall."

"I'm still waiting for you to trust me, Shiree. I can take care of this much easier than you. And I can certainly take care of him better than you."

"This isn't about him! It's about my kids, Kendall. *They're* my priority. Please understand that."

"You *and the kids* are *my* priority! No, Shiree. I'll never agree to this."

The following morning, I went downstairs to cook his breakfast when there was a knock on the garage door. Assuming it was Simone, I opened it.

Stew was standing there, and I was in a nightshirt. I quickly closed it. "Sorry, Stew. I thought it was Simone."

"No problem. I'd like to run something by you."

"Okay. Give me a minute."

I ran up, put on a robe and came back down. I let him in and immediately asked, "Is something wrong, Stew?"

"No, I'm just concerned about Simone and I need to ask you something."

I started making coffee. "Okay."

"I think I should start bonding with Shayna, but Simone is worried about her becoming attached to me. Because Shayna was so close to Curtis, Simone's concern is understandable. Shayna's really close to her dad too, but he's so far away."

I thought about that and wondered how I'd feel if it were me. "I think with Curtis' departure so recent, I agree with Simone. She said she accepted your proposal with conditions. I never asked what they were. Is Shayna one of them?"

"Yes. And, that we wait at least a year before getting married, which will give me time to bond with Shayna. But soon, she'll get Shayna from her sister and they'll be in their own place. That *is not* sitting well with me. I want them here."

Kendall walked into the kitchen. He apparently overheard our conversation, because he said, "I understand your position very well, Stew. Harold wants Felicia to continue to live there, even though he now knows we love each other. I told her I want her and the kids with me and he can visit."

Stew said, "I agree with Kendall. Men know how to wear women down to get what they want, Felicia. It sounds like he's playing you."

Simone walked in and looked at us. She asked, "What's going on?"

I looked around at everyone and said, "You guys get comfortable and I'll cook breakfast. Do you have eggs? I forgot to get some."

Stew said, "Yes, we have plenty."

While cooking, I asked Stew, "Why do you think Harold is playing me?"

"Because the average man would be ready to kill somebody. Instead, he's trying to woo you. Not necessarily because he wants you, but possibly to get back at Kendall. By preying on your kindness and your love for him. And your guilt."

I looked at Stew with my mouth opened. I couldn't believe he said that. Kendall said, "You need to be careful not to be drawn in by manipulation, like him wanting you there for the kids. Or he might use money to persuade you. I think you and the kids should move into my house, and you and Harold can share custody. There's no reason for you to be there anymore. You need to be with me now."

"Okay, Kendall. What do you suggest as a fair counteroffer?"

"I just gave it."

"A *fair* offer, Doctor."

"What does that mean, Shiree? The pretense is over. Tell him you're leaving and walk out."

For some reason, I couldn't do that. I felt I needed to part with Harold amicably. Kendall was getting frustrated and Stew said, "This isn't normal, Felicia. I don't trust him. I think you should get out of there too."

I looked at the guys and told them, "My kids are my priority right now. Once Harold and I settle on an arrangement, I plan to leave."

I began scrambling eggs and Kendall got up. Simone was flipping the pancakes and Stew was pouring the coffee. Kendall began pacing. Simone said, "You're always exempt from helping. Your ass is so spoiled, Kendall."

"Moni, mind your business. Shiree doesn't like me in her kitchen. She enjoys cooking for me. It makes both of us happy."

I smiled at him. "That's very true, Kendall. That's why I need you to be more understanding about this. There's nothing I won't do for you, Baby. I don't want you worried that I'll sleep with him. I only want you."

Stew and Simone both looked at Kendall. They knew and *he* knew I'd hit the nail on the head. So he said, "We'll try it, Shiree. But I have a condition."

"What is that, Doctor?"

"You have to agree that you and I will move into my house, and you will spend your nights with me. We'll create a space for the kids to play, and you can turn one of the guest rooms into a bedroom for them."

I thought about that. "That's fair. Okay, Kendall. I just have to get him to agree to me being away at night."

"You don't need his permission, Shiree. It's time for your thinking to change."

After breakfast, the guys went to Stew's side and Simone and I cleaned the kitchen. She whispered, "Did he really agree not to touch you?"

"No. I told Kendall that to calm him down. He still wants to have sex with me because he said no one else satisfies him. I gave him some yesterday."

"Felice. You know you can't keep that up. They can smell when another man has been there."

"Yeah, a different man. But Harold has always been there. Plus we used a condom. My problem will be getting Harold to agree with me staying with Kendall."

We heard them coming back. "I need to go and see about the kids, Kendall."

"When will you bring them here?"

"Kendall, Sweetie. They're not ready for that yet. They're too young to understand any of this. I need your patience, Baby."

Stew asked, "That's what you were trying to tell me earlier, right?"

I smiled. "Yes. Shayna has endured a lot of change in her young life. She needs some calm for a moment. Besides, you're worth the wait, Big Brother."

He smiled, and Simone said, "I don't know when that conversation happened, but I sure am glad it did. Thanks, Sis."

Once I got home with the kids, Harold was in his office. It was a cold Saturday morning, and the house was chilly. I walked up to his desk and asked, "Aren't you cold, Harold?"

"Good morning."

"Good morning."

"Yeah, but I wasn't sure if I'd see you this weekend. And I've been playing with the idea of going to an island. To clear my mind and maybe have some fun."

"Where are you going? On that bogus cruise?"

"To Jamaica. How did you know the cruise was bogus?"

"After the alarm company trick, I began to suspect you might know about...you know. So, I figured the cruise might be a ruse too."

"I'm sorry for being a jerk, Felicia. By the way, I told my parents we temporarily separated."

I closed my eyes. "The kids are in the playpen, so let's go in there."

He turned up the heat, and we went into the family room and sat down. He looked at me and said, "I decided to tell them the same thing I told them before. That I cheated and you left. That way, when you're not here, I won't have to explain. Like this morning."

"How did they take it?"

"Mom took it better than Dad. I haven't talked to any of my sisters yet."

I cleared my throat and said, "Kendall expects me to move in with him. But I have no immediate plans to divorce you or marry him. So, if you want to stay here, the kids and I will live ten minutes away at his house."

"What do you mean he *expects* you to move in with him? That doesn't sound like something you would do, Felicia. You're gonna live with that guy?"

"Well, I mean..."

"Is he forcing this on you?"

"No, Harold. This is what I want. I can't stay here any longer."

He exhaled and seemed sad. "I hoped we'd *both* continue to live here, Felicia."

"Harold. Why do you want *me* here?"

"Because of the kids. I want my kids to stay *here*. I suppose it's inevitable, but I'm not feeling my kids at his house right now. Not yet."

"They need to be with me, Harold."

"I disagree, Felicia. I think they can stay with your folks if I'm away. Or, if I'm out for the evening, you can keep them here."

He reached for my hand. "I'm perfectly capable of taking care of them. They're all I have. Don't take them from me yet. Please."

I looked at him and decided he was right. For now. "I don't want to be away from them either, Harold."

"That's why it's better that we're both here. You can…"

"I'll stay here Tuesdays and Wednesdays. Those can be your nights out. And for now, the kids can stay here with you. I'll see them during the day."

"That's better, but…"

"And if you're out of town, they'll stay with Mom or I'll stay here. For now."

"Okay, Felicia. There's something else we need to discuss."

"What?"

"Money."

I cringed. I was hoping Kendall was wrong. "What do you propose?"

"We can each begin to get our pay in our own personal accounts, and I'll continue to pay the bills here, unless you want child support."

I exhaled and felt better. "That's fine, Harold. I don't need any support."

"The support, or home maintenance is for the *kids,* Felicia. Not you. So, you *will* get support. But if you sell the house, I'll support them some other way.

"Okay, Harold. I'm sure you'll be fair."

"Secondly, effective November first, all of my assets are mine and you'll keep yours. But all assets gained during our marriage, we'll divide in half. Your stock in Benson Holdings can be sold back to us, or you can just keep it. I figure you should have over two million in other investments. But your stock in Benson's is over three million. And we'll also split our savings."

I just looked at him. I again thought of Kendall. "No. I can't take anything. Just give me my portion of the savings. I don't want or deserve anything else. Do something kind with the rest of it. Please."

"*You* do something kind with it. It's yours, Felicia."

I stared at him a long time. I didn't know how I'd ever forgive myself for what I did. I didn't forget what Kendall said, but I believed he was genuine.

He added, "The money we're currently investing for the kids will continue. I mean, I'll continue it. For all the kids. Are you still listening, Felicia?"

Harold always gave me things. But I always felt his giving came with a price. He was calling my name. "Let's discuss it another time, Harold. I need to...do something."

He laughed. "Why don't you go. The kids will be fine."

I leaned over and kissed his cheek. He embraced me and kissed me back. Then he rubbed my thigh. "Could you stay an hour longer?"

On my way to our place, it became clearer to me I had a new problem. I was taking two, sometimes three showers a day. Trying to clean one man away so I could satisfy another one. Halfway there, I called Kendall. "Are you downtown?"

"Yes, Shiree. But I'm at the club."

"Oh. Is something wrong? It's so early."

"No. We're watching the football game with friends. Did you talk to him?"

"Yes."

"It doesn't sound good. Did you have a fight?"

"We came to a compromise. I don't want to fight with you either, Kendall."

"Where are you, Shiree?"

"On my way downtown."

"Come here first. Okay?"

"Alright. I'll be right there."

He let me in through the back door because I insisted I looked a mess. "When will I be able to introduce you to my friends?"

"Not today, Kendall."

I laughed. "You look cute in your ponytail and sweats. Why did you change?"

"Because I played with the kids outside on the swings. He needed to grocery shop, so I stayed and played with them. Then we cleaned up."

He looked at me like he didn't believe me. "What compromise, Shiree?"

I told him everything except the part about the money. "I allowed him to keep the children for now. He would be alone without them."

"Two nights a week he wouldn't be."

I smiled and kissed him. "I love you too."

"Okay, Shiree. We'll try this."

He brought me in his arms and removed the rubber band from my hair. "Why is your hair wet, Shiree? Did you sleep with him?"

"Kendall, I bathed the kids and got my hair wet."

He didn't respond, but he looked as if he was disappointed in me for lying to him. He reached for his phone and asked, "Would you like to go out for dinner?"

"Not yet, Kendall. I'll fix dinner and then we can come here. Okay?"

"You're staying tonight?"

"Yes, Kendall. What's the matter?"

He didn't answer me. "Oh, by the way. Harold said he might be going away for a week or so. But he's not ready for the kids to be at your place."

He glared at me through slanted eyes. "But soon, they *will* be with us, Kendall. Are you ready for that?"

"I love your kids. Why would you ask me that?"

"How many times have kids wrecked your house?"

I laughed as I watched his face change colors.

I went to our place and went over to see Simone. She was watching TV and twisting her hair. "I wish my hair would twist up like that. You wear the hell out of those twists, Simone."

"I love them. All natural and easy to do."

I sat closer. "Simone. I had to screw him again today. I realize he's playing me, but what's gonna happen when I say no?"

"You give in way too easy, Felice. Are you still in love with Harold?"

"No, Simone. I just feel so bad about what I've done to him."

"That's funny, because he seems okay with how he treated you."

She got up and went in her kitchen. She appeared to have gained weight. "You want something, Felice?"

"Your ass looks wider. Have you gained weight? Them jeans are screaming."

She laughed and turned back. "I know, right. Ever since Stew proposed, we've both been eating like fiends. I gotta bring it in, Girl."

I laughed. "Do you have any white wine in the fridge?"

"Yes. Come in here. I wanna show you something."

Her kitchen has a window that faces the garage. She looked out and then she turned and faced me. "I needed to be sure neither of their cars was here."

She went in a drawer, pulled out an envelope and handed it to me. "Ken asked Stew to keep this so you wouldn't find it. And believe me, the only reason I'm showing it to you is because it's time for you to make a decision."

I opened the envelope and removed a receipt. It was from a jeweler. And he paid fourteen thousand dollars for *something*. "My God, Simone. What did he buy?"

"That's irrelevant, Felice. But it's for you, so I'm sure you can figure it out. You need to decide who you want. You can't have both of them."

"What?"

"There's something about having both of them you don't want to let go of."

I never thought of it that way. Is that the reason I never left him? "Do you really think I want *both* of them?"

She sucked her teeth. "The average woman would've left Harold years ago, Felicia. He's crazy. Even I stayed with Curtis way too long."

"I didn't wanna tear up my family, Simone. That's why I stayed."

"Okay, Felice. If you say so. So what's your excuse now? Is it over?"

I picked up the wine and began pouring it. "Is it, Felice?"

I didn't know. *I knew*, but I wasn't completely sure. "Of course, it's over. But I feel so guilty. I can't seem to say no to him."

She rolled her eyes. "And he's preying on that. He knows he can use you."

I chose to ignore that. I turned back to her and changed the subject. "Now there's something else. He told me my share of our money comes to well over five million dollars. Please don't tell anyone, Simone. I will not be taking that money. Especially after what Kendall said."

"Hell yes you are! That man put you through hell! You earned that money!"

I thought about that too. "I just left Kendall at the club. He took my hair down and it was wet. Then he asked if I'd slept with Harold."

"Felice, you know how crazy he is. He's gonna go to your house and whip Harold's ass. You better stop, Girl."

My eyes got big and I realized she was right. And suddenly, my dream danced through my head. When Kendall told Harold he'd kill him if he touched me again.

"Simone, this guilt is killing me. I destroyed our family. And he doesn't know that I've been with Kendall for over three years. He thinks six months."

Simone laughed at that. "Stop trying to justify this, Felice. With time, you'll handle this better. I suggest you stay away from Harold for a while. Because if you continue to sex him every day, he'll convince you you're in love with him, not Ken."

"You think that's what he's doing?"

"Absolutely. Realistically, do you think Harold would give you up this easily? He told you he's known for weeks, but he couldn't confront you with it. Stew's right, Sis. I don't trust him either."

My phone vibrated. It was a text from Harold. It read: Pls call me.

Simone was livid. "This is what I mean, Felice. What the hell does he want?"

I shrugged and called him. He was cheerful and seemed excited about something. "Hi, Babe."

"What's up?"

"Are you busy?"

"I'm at Simone's. Is something wrong?"

"No. I just wanted to let you know that I booked reservations for Detroit. I decided to go home and just relax for a week. And we didn't talk about the house there. It's yours, so you need to decide if you want to keep it or sell it."

"I'd rather discuss it later, if you don't mind."

"Okay. Would you consider going with me? I was thinking..."

"No, Harold. We're separated, and we need to stick to our arrangements. Neither of us can think clearly if we're sexing each other."

"Didn't you enjoy our lovemaking?"

"That has nothing to do with our issues, Harold."

The garage door went up and Simone looked out. It was Kendall and he asked Simone if I was with her. She told him yes. I told Harold, "Let's discuss this later. Privately."

"Okay. I'm leaving tomorrow afternoon. Should I take the kids to your folks?"

Kendall walked in. "That's fine, Harold. Text me when you know what time you'll drop them off, and I'll let Mom know."

"Will I see you?"

"I don't think so."

Kendall came over and put it on speakerphone. Harold said, "I'll be there until next Sunday. If you want, I can put the house on the market while I'm there."

"I'll let you know in a few days. I really need to go."

"Okay, Babe. I'll send you the text."

"Okay, bye."

"Bye."

I hung up and knew I was in trouble. I looked up and asked Kendall, "You hungry, Baby?"

He never answered me. The look on his face spoke volumes. His dimples and the cleft began warring with each other. "Come on, Shiree."

He extended his hand, and I took it.

Once we were on our side, he went to the bar and poured himself a drink. He poured me a shot of vodka and smiled at me. "Are you okay, Shiree?"

"I guess so. He wants me to make decisions at a moment's notice, and it's getting on my nerves."

He handed me my drink and walked toward the window. He stood there looking out. "What decisions?"

"He bought me a house that's minutes away from his family. I don't need…"

"What else?"

He was clearly pissed. "Our house was a wedding gift from his parents, but he gave it to me. It's in my name and paid for."

He emptied his glass and came toward me. "What else?"

"Money. He said I'm entitled to my share from our savings, investments and stock in Benson's."

He was in front of me. "What else, Shiree?"

"That's it."

"How much money did he offer you?"

"I've never cared about his money."

He slammed his glass on the table, and yelled, "How much, Felicia!"

I almost jumped out of my skin. "Kendall! Stop that. You scared me."

"I asked you a question."

"He just said I'm entitled to half of it. And stop calling me Felicia."

He went back to the bar and poured more cognac. "He's going away?"

"Yes. Tomorrow."

My phone dinged and I saw where he sent the text. "I need to let Mom know he's taking the kids to her at ten o'clock tomorrow morning."

He came back over to me and reached for my phone. I gave it to him grudgingly. He read the text. It read: My flight is at noon. I'll take them around ten. Call me soon. Love u.

He glared at it so hard, I thought he was gonna crush my phone with his bare hands. He again emptied his glass and slowly walked back to the bar. He poured another shot of cognac and drank that too.

He pointed the phone at me. "When I learned Juanita was in love with Yvonne, I admit it threw me. I knew how much she loved me, so I couldn't for the life of me imagine her loving someone else the same way. My love for her was a gentle love. But as deep as I'd *ever* loved. And I knew I would always love her."

He poured more cognac and he glared at me as though he was looking through me. I had that familiar feeling like when my grandmother was in front of me with a switch. The closer he got, the more I wanted to run.

He sat next to me and kissed me. Then he said almost in a whisper, "I understand his love for you. But I will *kill him,* if he doesn't soon stop playing on your sensibilities. I'm sure you still love him. I still love Juanita. We all love each other. But you must understand that your days of having it all are over, Shiree. You can't have both of us anymore. I love Juanita from a distance. You must learn to do the same. *And so must he!"*

He held my hand, and we got up. "We need to open up the house and buy food. We're going home, Shiree. I've waited a long time to say that."

He smiled. I wanted to cry. *"I'm sorry, Kendall."*

"It'll get easier. I promise."

He brought me closer in his arms. "I'm hurt that you've lied to me, Shiree. It's disturbing for many reasons."

I tensed and was about to respond, but he stopped me. He looked in my eyes, caressed my face and kissed me. "Kendall..."

"You asked me to be patient, and we promised to never lie. If you don't want me to beat his brains out, *do not* sleep with him again. Because if I even *think*...that he's touched you again, I will clean this fucking city with his Black ass."

Chapter Four

I'm not sure if it got easier, but it definitely became interesting.

That night marked the first time I spent the night in his house. After Juanita gave me her blessing, I began meeting him there periodically.

He bought another new bed about six months ago, so it was now *my* bed. I still wasn't completely comfortable being in her house, but I was trying to adjust.

We finally got in bed after working all evening cleaning. He played in my hair and stared at me. "My family wants to meet you. I'm thinking of having Thanksgiving dinner here."

I cringed at the thought of it. I couldn't imagine what they must think of me. "Kendall, what did you tell them?"

"My mom knows everything, Shiree. She was beside herself when I was sick. And my dad masked his worry with humor. He told me to hurry up and get better so Mom could resume taking care of *him*."

I laughed. "Then Dad asked me if I could still get an erection. I laughed and told him yes. He said he could still get one too, and he would like to use it."

"Kendall, he did not!"

"Yeah, he did. Then he told me to get the hell out of his house. He said your mother won't come near me when you kids are around."

I cracked up. "Why did you tell me that?"

"My father is a trip. All he talks about is sex. It's just a warning."

"I'm not ready to meet your family. They probably think I'm a slut."

"That is in no way true, Sweetie. Mom wants to meet you. I told her you would be horrified. Keenan couldn't care less. He's broken so many married women's hearts, my story is a yawner to him. Now

Kelly, she's tickled by it all. She said everyone talks about how devoted and gorgeous Felicia Benson is. How did you snag her?"

"Kendall, you didn't! You told her who I am?"

"I love you too, Baby."

He smiled and kissed my nose. "Tell me how you're doing, Shiree?"

"I'm fine."

"I'm sure that's not true. I know this isn't easy. And I'm sorry I've been so tough on you. But it always bothered me that he takes advantage of you. No longer will I sit back and let him do that. Not anymore."

"He doesn't do anything I don't allow, Kendall. If anything, it's my fault."

"Shiree, listen to me. Your kindness is not a license for motherfuckers to use you. Stop making excuses for him."

I closed my eyes. I knew he was right, but… "And I'm sure, like Stew said, he's using your guilt to his benefit. You're a good woman for the right man. But the wrong man is incapable of seeing your value."

I didn't respond. It was hard to hear, but I had to admit his words conjured up painful memories. Not only of Harold, but of Sam and Todd too.

And hidden in his frustration was the sweetest compliment. Kendall always had a way of making me feel better. Not just about the situation, but about myself.

"Shiree. Talk to me, Baby. I wanna help you through this. Remember, I promised to help make your transition easier. So, let me."

I sighed. "I admit I'm uneasy about the uncertainties, Kendall. For instance, Harold said he wouldn't fight me for the kids. But I don't think I should relax knowing that. Maybe he's setting me up. He's notorious for doing that."

"I think we need to get you an attorney and get some of these things documented. That way, he can't go back on what you've agreed on."

I didn't want to do that, but I nodded my head yes. "These uncertainties. Do any of them involve me, Shiree?"

"Not really, Kendall. I'm mostly concerned that Harold might humiliate me. Or that my loved ones are disappointed in me…"

"Shiree, please don't do this. Don't beat yourself up over this. We're not *criminals*, Baby. We fell in love."

He brought me into his arms while I grieved the loss of my virtue. He soothed me by making love to me, just for me.

Once he was asleep, I laid there and wondered how on earth I ended up here. Again, my life was a mess.

I still didn't know what to do. What I *did* know was that I adored Kendall. I decided I needed to allow time to help me feel better about it, like Simone said.

When we went in my parents' house this time, I was more at ease. We waited until after noon to be sure he would be gone. I still had a hard time facing my dad, but otherwise it was okay.

I told Kendall I needed to stop at my house for a few things, so we went there first. He was still moving a bit too fast for me. For example, he insisted we take my new car. Which was no longer new.

He pulled into the driveway and I used the touchpad to open the garage. I was relieved to see Harold's car was gone. We went into the kitchen, and I asked him if he wanted a drink. "Get what you need. I'll be okay."

"You want a tour? It's a big house."

"Sure."

We started the tour down in the playroom and media room. We went through the French doors and I showed him the pool. We toured the first and second floors and the kid's rooms. Then we were in front of the master. "You wanna see it?"

"It's not weird, is it?"

I punched him and opened the double doors into our room. "This house is really big. How many bedrooms did I see? Six?"

"Yes. Six bedrooms and six baths. A lot of work."

We went into my dressing room and both closets. He saw the bathroom and settled on my chair in front of the fireplace.

I went into my closet to grab a few things. Then I looked at the armoire. I didn't realize how heart wrenching it would be when I opened it.

Tears filled my eyes as I completed the task. I inserted my wedding rings in there and closed the door. Kendall asked, "What about Todd and Marcus? When will you tell them?"

I wiped away my tears and came out of the closet. I turned away from him and retrieved a few things from my dresser. "I plan to have lunch with Todd next week and we'll decide how to tackle that. Maybe you and Gina can also come along."

"Okay. I like that idea. Then I can get to know them casually, not just as their kids' doctor."

I shook my head at the enormity of this. My whole life was changing. *And* his. But mostly my kids. Lord, my kids.

Daddy came over and kissed my forehead. I thanked them again for allowing the kids to stay. "Daughter, you know we love having them. With so much going on, your mom and I feel better with them here."

Mom said, "You two can come by in the evenings and we can all have dinner together. You can spend time with the kids, and that gives us a chance to get to know you better, Kendall."

He smiled. "Thank you, Mrs. Pierce. That's very kind of you."

Mom said, "Felicia says you're vegetarian, but you eat fish. Is that right?"

"Yes, Ma'am. We'll bring dinner some nights, and that way you..."

"Nonsense. I love to cook. What are your favorites?"

"I love all vegetables, Mrs. Pierce. Thank you."

Daddy said, "Then it's settled. We'll see you two tomorrow around six. Okay?"

We looked at each other, and Kendall said, "We'll be here."

Once outside, Kendall said, "I'll be right back."

He went back inside, and I went to the car. I checked my phone and Annette sent me a message asking me to call her. I looked at the door, and he was still in there. I called her and chewed my lip. "Can you talk, Nette?"

"Yes. You okay, Licia?"

"I'm fine."

"The husbands know almost everything. Curtis told both of them. That dirty bastard. I never liked him once I got to know him."

"Me either, Nette."

"So now, the assumption is that Carla and I *must* have boyfriends too."

"I'm really sorry, Nette. I'm sure Simone and I are now the worst people in the world."

"I hate that we talked her into staying with him last year."

"He would've done it then. He's a prick."

Kendall came out and I asked Annette if Carla was okay. "She's fine. She told Earl to kiss her ass, and that if you were cheating, you must have had a good reason."

I hollered laughing. "Girl, I need to go. By the way, Harold is in Detroit for a week. Hopefully, things will quiet down for a while."

She and I both laughed. I told her Kendall was waiting for me, so we hung up and I turned to Kendall. "Why did you go back?"

"I just needed to confirm that they have my contact info. And I put three hundred dollars in your mom's hand. I know how much food costs. She fought me and I had to run out."

I smiled. "We have the day to ourselves. What should we do?"

He pulled me into his arms. "Let's make love all afternoon, have a great dinner, and you can come and hear me play tonight. Something just for you."

I could forget about spending once a month with my sisters again. Their husbands think I'm a whore, and I guess I am. I don't feel like one, although I'm not real sure how one feels.

I *feel* like, I fell in lust and then in love with a man who happened to be married, and I'm also married. They also believe Simone is one, and again, I don't feel she's one either.

We were both wrong. There's no denying that. But we had husbands who were unbearable and drove us to do things because of *their* insecurities.

I don't believe anyone should have to live under those conditions. Speaking for myself, I clearly handled my situation terribly.

That evening Simone and I were having a drink while the guys prepared to go to the club. We were feeling some kind a way about our sisters. Simone said, "I'm gonna call Tony. I'm gonna tell him what *really* happened.

"He's not gonna talk to you, Simone."

"Oh, yes he will. Especially when he hears what I have to say."

Simone called Tony's cell phone and I called Annette's. I told her what Simone was doing. Annette ran downstairs. Simone said, "Hi, Tony."

"What's up?"

I stood there waiting to hear what she would say. They were on speakerphone. "I know Curtis told you what happened between us. And I admit he drove me to do some things I'm not proud of."

"Simone, why are you telling me this?"

"Because I thought you'd be interested in some of the things he's said and done. And since he's still with the company, I felt you should know."

"Listen. I'm sorry about what happened with you two. But honestly, I'm not sure I'm interested."

"I think you'll be interested in knowing how he threw you under the bus for that promotion last year. He and I fought because he bragged about it. That's when I slept on Felicia's sofa for two nights, remember?"

"What are you talking about, Simone?"

"He told your manager you really didn't want or deserve the responsibility. I slapped his ass when he told me what he'd done. Curtis wasn't qualified, and he couldn't stand the fact that you were. I was so glad when you got the next one. You do remember he didn't come out with us to celebrate, right?"

Tony was clearly upset. "I hope you're not saying this to get back at him."

"Actually, I am. But it's still the truth. I'm ashamed to say I was married to someone like that. In hindsight, I wish I'd told you sooner."

"I'm not sure I wanted to know that. But, I guess I *needed* to know it."

"That's not all, Tony. I apologize for disappointing you guys. I tried really hard to make it work with him. He was mean and hurtful, and impossible to live with. Please don't punish Annette for what I did. Me and Felicia lived in hell. Especially Felicia."

He was quiet. "I appreciate you taking the time to hear me out, Tony."

"Simone. I have something to say."

"Okay."

"Annette is standing here next to me. I've heard some terrible things over the last few weeks about you, Felicia, and now Curtis. And the truth is, it *was* disappointing. But I admit I've learned something here. Felicia kept saying the reason you all would leave us would be because of us. And she was right. We drove you all to do things. Some of you went further than others, but I have no right to judge either of you. Is Felicia okay?"

"Yes, we're here together. We wanted to call you and apologize. We don't want you to think that Annette and Carla played a part in any of our wrongdoing."

"Tell her she'll always be my little sister, and you too Simone."

I said, "Thanks, Tony. I love you too."

"Hey, Licia."

"Hey, Tony."

"Bring my niece and nephew back over. We enjoyed having them here. Are you guys okay? You need anything?"

I smiled. Then I said, "We're good, Tony. Thanks. For everything."

When we hung up, Stewart and Kendall were standing in the doorway. Stew asked Simone, "What was that about?"

"We needed to let Tony know our actions were due to our crazy ass husbands. And, that Annette and Carla had nothing to do with it."

I said, "We don't want to lose our sisters over this."

Kendall said, "He sounds like he's okay, Licia."

"Don't call me that, Kendall."

He laughed. "Come on. We need to go."

"We're not dressed yet. You two ride together and I'll drive my car."

Simone said, "Make sure you reserve our table, Dr. Greer."

Stew winked at her and said, "Will do, Mrs. Greer."

When we arrived, the place was packed. More so than usual for a Sunday. Our husbands looked so handsome in their tuxedos. They sometimes wore them when they performed.

Out of the corner of my eye, I saw a woman that looked just like Carla. I looked again and she was gone. "Damn, Simone. Did you see that woman? She looked just like Carla."

"Girl, you need another drink. I didn't see anyone that looked like Carla."

She poured me another glass of wine and motioned for the waitress to bring us another bottle. The guys began to play, and they were great as usual. During intermission, they came over to our table.

Kendall kissed my cheek and sat next to me. Once again, I saw someone I recognized. Except this time I wasn't happy about it. She came over and Simone asked her, "May I help you?"

Carrie asked her, "Do I know you?"

"I'm Felicia's sister, and she's not interested in talking to you."

I said, "It's okay, Simone. What can I do for you, Carrie? Are you planning to call my husband again?"

She smiled. "No. I just wanted to inform you that you are *not* the only woman he fucks. *Sweetie.*"

My blood began to boil. I slowly stood up and faced her. Kendall said, "Shiree…"

I ignored him and stared at her. "Maybe not. *You,* however, are the only *hound* he fucks. *Sweetie!*"

"*Excuse me!?*"

Simone stood up too. Carrie backed up, and I said, "If memory serves me right, he shook his head and said you were the worst piece he'd ever had."

Kendall and Stew's heads went down. I got right in her face and said, "Until you're at least *half* the woman I am, don't you *ever* roll up on me again, Bitch!"

The guys quickly got up and escorted her out. They informed her she was no longer welcome there.

I went to the ladies' room and I was shaking like a leaf. Simone came in screaming laughing. "Girl, I can't *believe* you called that bitch a hound!"

Kendall came in a few minutes later and asked if I was okay. "Yes, I'm fine. I'm sorry about that. I can't believe I called her a bitch."

"I can't believe you called her a *hound*. Damn, Baby."

He cracked up and said, "There's five minutes before our next set. Come on."

During the next set, just before the last song, Stew sat his sax down and walked up to the mic. "Tonight is a special night. She doesn't know it, but we're about to celebrate Felicia's birthday."

I looked up at Stew and couldn't close my mouth. "Her birthday is Tuesday, and I'm told she doesn't normally celebrate it."

I turned toward Simone, and my mother and father walked in. They sat at the table next to ours that had been empty all night. Annette and Carla also came in. They sat with us.

Many of our friends from school, and even poor Phillip was there. When Todd and Gina walked in, I almost fell out. I suddenly wondered who had my kids.

Then I heard that voice. I turned back toward the stage and Kendall was looking at me. "We all wish you a Happy Birthday, Felicia. This song is dedicated to you. It's from the man who will never stop loving you."

He looked at me with so much love, I put my hand over my mouth.

The song was Kem's, *I Can't Stop Loving You*. I thought to myself, "If he starts singing, I'll lose it."

I looked back at Simone. "You knew about this?"

"Yeah, you got a problem with that?"

I glared at her and she laughed. Carla and Annette were laughing too. I turned back and Kendall was in front of me. He reached for my hand and Ashley began to sing. She's a local singer who joins them sometimes.

He brought me up in his arms and whispered, "Happy Birthday, Shiree."

"I don't like surprises, Kendall. How many times do I have to tell you that?"

He brought me closer. "You better smile and act like you're enjoying it. I'm told Annette and your dad both have guns aimed at me."

I laughed and he did too. "That's the sound I want to hear, Shiree. I love to hear you laugh."

He twirled me around and brought me close again. Ashley was singing so beautifully. He knew I loved that song.

I looked up and saw my dad watching us. I smiled at him and he smiled back. Then I saw Gary. I guess everyone was hiding. "Kendall, who has my kids?"

"They're in the back asleep."

I almost stopped dancing. "They're fine, Shiree. Your parents were with them and we've all been taking turns checking on them."

"I'll get you back for this."

He smiled and brought me close again. He leaned down close to my ear and sang in his beautiful baritone voice, "I can't stop loving you. I can't help myself."

I laid my head on his chest. "No you won't, because I won't let you."

When the song ended, everyone applauded the trio and Ashley. Then Stew announced it was time to toast the birthday girl.

Annette came out with a big cake, and it had thirty-two candles on it. Todd went over and helped her. I was kind of sad that Earl and Tony weren't there, but I was delighted that my sisters were there.

Kendall escorted me back to our table, and everyone came over to sing Happy Birthday. Annette said, "Licia, make a wish."

I looked around at my friends and family. Kendall was across from me helping the waiters and waitresses with champagne. But he kept his eyes on me.

I looked down at the beautiful cake I recognized as one of my mother's. The candles were begging to be blown out, so I closed my eyes and wished that Harold would have a life filled with love and joy. I blew out the candles, and corks popped all over the building.

Simone and I couldn't wait to tell our sisters the latest events. But it would have to wait because I needed to help my parents with the kids. So, after the champagne, I told the girls I'd be right back.

We met in the lounge and I said to my parents, "Thank you both so much for all you do. I have no idea how I would've made it without you guys."

I hugged Mom, and then I turned to my father. "Daddy, I'm sorry you got caught up in all of this. Will you ever forgive me?"

"I feared at some point Harold would drive you away. I prayed he wouldn't, but he went too far. I just want you happy, Daughter. And I'd like to see you wait a while before getting married again. Take your time and get to know this one."

"I've known Kendall for over three years, Daddy. But I did tell him I'm not ready for marriage again. Not yet."

"Are you sure? Because he asked for my blessing. Did you know?"

"What did you tell him?"

Mom said, "We need to get the children home. We'll see you tomorrow for dinner, Daughter."

Mom clearly wanted us to end our conversation. I nodded and said, "Okay, Mommy."

Kendall and Stewart walked in, and Kendall introduced Stew to my parents. I went in the bedroom to put the twin's coats on, and Kendall came in and undressed. "I'm gonna help your folks get the kids in the car."

I smiled and thanked him. Mom walked in and Kendall was in his boxers. She yelped and turned around. Kendall laughed saying, "It's okay, Mrs. Pierce."

He put his slacks on and picked up Benny. Mom opened the door for him while I put Aleece's coat on. "Was that Simone's Stew, Felicia?"

"Yes, Mom."

"He's so handsome. I'm happy for her."

I smiled. "Me too, Mommy. So, what did Daddy tell Kendall?"

She laughed. "He told him to ask him again in a year."

"He *did?* What did Kendall say?"

"Your dad said he smiled and said okay. But then Calvin told him, realistically, you were gonna do what the hell you wanted to, and that he's always respected your decisions."

"Did he really say that, Mommy?"

"Yes, Daughter.

Stew came in, and I hit him and told him, "Stew. You guys are in trouble for surprising me. I'm gonna get you back."

He laughed. "By the way, Stew, my mom thinks you're cute."

He actually blushed. He smiled at her and thanked her. Then he turned to me. "This is the first time I've seen your kids in person. They're adorable."

He reached for Aleece and she screamed. Loud. He stepped back and looked at her. "Felicia. She screams just..."

"Stewart?"

He looked at Mom and smiled again. Aleece got away from him and ran to me. Kendall came in, and when she saw him, she ran to him. "Dr. Ken!"

He picked her up. "Mommy, look who it is!"

She put her arms around his neck, and it was obvious they loved each other. Kendall asked, "Why aren't you asleep, Alysiya?"

"I woked up. Can I have a treat?"

He shook his head and laughed at her. "Not now. Maybe tomorrow, okay?"

She smiled and hugged his neck again. Stew reached for her and she screamed again. "Dr. Ken, don't let him get me!"

Mom and I cracked up. Kendall was clearing his ear and Stew asked, "Are you thinking what I'm thinking?"

Kendall nodded vigorously. *"Yes!!"*

I said to Aleece, "Dr. Ken is gonna take you to Grandma's car, okay?"

She smiled. "Okay, Mommy."

I kissed her. "Mommy will see you tomorrow. I love you, Sweetie."

"I love you, Mommy."

Carla came in. "What are you doing? We're waiting for you."

"I had to help get the kids out of here."

When I finally made it back to the table, I was able to catch up with the girls. Phillip spoke to Kendall and I saw them shake hands.

Everyone was sending me drinks and Kendall came over and sat with me. Todd and Gina came over and were out of breath. I asked, "How long have you two been dancing?"

Gina said, "This fool won't sit."

I laughed and got Todd's attention. "I know you know Dr. Montgomery. I want you to meet Kendall."

"Man, it's nice to meet you. Again."

Kendall said, "Same here. And Mrs. Wilson, it's nice seeing you again too."

"Me too. And Kendall, please call me Gina."

Another song came on and Todd said, "Come on, Gina. That's my song!"

We all laughed, and Kendall said to me, "You have to remember to set up that lunch date."

"I know. You're right."

Annette whispered, "Kendall. I need to use your back room. I haven't seen Gary in a week."

"Hell no, Annette!"

"It's your fault, Kendall. You and Licia caused my ass to be on lock down."

Kendall and I laughed. I said, "Go on, Nette. You can use it."

I looked at Kendall and smiled. He shook his head and stood. "Damn! I'll tell him where to find you."

He went toward the bar and Annette went to the back. When Kendall came back, he said, "They're turning my place into a damn sex club."

"What does that mean?"

"You haven't noticed that Carla and Tom are gone?"

I looked at Simone and she laughed. I asked her, "Where the hell is Carla?"

"Tom whispered in her ear, and five minutes later she went with him."

Kendall said, "He doesn't even have a bed. It's just a dressing room."

We laughed and he said, "They'll probably have the most fun."

After we drank more and danced more and ate more, Carla and Annette finally came back. I looked at Carla and she asked, "What?"

I shook my head and laughed. "Where were you, Sis?"

"Mind your business. You too, Stewart. I see you laughing."

We all laughed at Carla's expense. A few minutes later, Tom and Gary came over. We put three tables together, so no one knew who was with who.

Todd came over and asked me, "Did I see some guy whispering in my sister's ear? And did she leave with him?"

Annette heard him and said, "Todd. Mind your business, Cousin. You're lucky we're letting you hang out with us."

Gina asked from the other end of the table, "What are you all talking about?"

I said, "We're planning a lunch date for next week, Gina. I'd like you to come with Todd. What day is good for you?"

"Tomorrow is my best day."

Todd said, "Tomorrow is good for me too."

The next day was Monday, so Kendall and I both said yes too. Then I said, "Okay. Unkl Moe's at noon?"

Everyone agreed. I whispered to Todd, "You owe me."

Kendall started laughing, and Todd said quietly, "Man, she knows *all* my damn business. I always owe her. But I see she kept *something* from me. How come you didn't tell me, Licia?"

"Because you didn't ask. Gina knew."

"What the hell you mean, *Gina* knew?"

"Gina busted us years ago."

He looked stunned. "*Years* ago? This has been going on for years, Licia?"

"Yes, and don't you dare say anything to her."

Todd said to Kendall, "Man, when she told me, I almost drove into a wall."

We all laughed, and Todd said, "We need to go. Mom has the kids."

"How is Mom?"

"Ornery as ever. But doing well. I'll tell her you asked about her."

Todd got up and shook Kendall's hand. He said, "We'll see you tomorrow."

He kissed my cheek. "Happy birthday ex-wife of mine. Love you."

"Thanks. Love you too. And kiss my sons and Goddaughter for me."

"I'll kiss Angel. The boys don't allow me to kiss them anymore."

Gina came over and kissed and hugged me. "I had a great time. I'll see you tomorrow. Bye, Kendall."

Kendall and Stew soon left the table too. Simone told the girls about Carrie, and Carla asked, "You mean to tell me while I was in the back watching the kids, *that* happened?! I always miss the good stuff. I would've whipped her *ass* if I was out here."

We all said, "We know."

I was drunk as hell and still had drinks on the table. I asked, "So how did you guys get away tonight?"

Carla said, "We told them we were coming. We invited them, but of course they didn't want to come. Tony would've come, but Earl feels some kind a way because you all didn't call *him*."

I turned to Simone. "We must do that as soon as possible."

Simone said, "Yes. First thing tomorrow."

We went to our place on East Avenue instead of Kendall's house. I was so wasted, he had to help me up the stairs. I said, "Alysiya loves her some Dr. Ken."

Kendall laughed while shaking his head. "Man, that girl has stolen my heart. For real. *And* my hearing. She screams just like her mother."

I laughed and remembered Harold saying the same thing. When we were in bed, he snuggled up to me. "Baby, don't go to sleep."

"No, I can't Kendall."

"You love it when you're drunk."

"Um-hmm..."

"Shiree?"

No answer. He turned me over and kissed my stomach. "You're about to be an old woman. Did you enjoy your birthday celebration?"

I started to cry. Out of nowhere, I wept pitifully. He pulled me up and began to panic. "What is it, Baby?"

I couldn't answer. I was feeling sorry for myself, but I didn't want him to feel like he was to blame. "Answer me, Shiree. What's wrong?"

"Kendall. When will I stop feeling so guilty? I know I don't want him anymore, but I do care about him. What's he gonna do without me?"

Of course, I wished I hadn't said any of that out loud. I looked up at Kendall and his mouth was opened. "I'm sorry, Kendall. I didn't mean..."

He sighed. "Shiree. I fully expected you to feel bad about this. I also understand why you're worried about him. That's your nature, Baby. And why I love you so much."

"Are you okay, Kendall? Have I upset you?"

"I'm fine, Baby. I'm thrilled we're finally together. And like I told you before, let me handle this. I need you to concentrate on our future, and I'll take care of *you*. Please stop worrying."

He kissed my forehead and held me close. I exhaled and relaxed in his arms. He laid me back down and informed me I wasn't allowed to speak or move.

He opened my legs. "And by the way. I'm not *old*, Doctor."

"Didn't I ask you to not to speak?"

I giggled. "I don't know, Shiree. You can't hold your liquor anymore."

He kissed me there and I reached for him. I remained silent and caressed his Locs. I raised my legs and pulled him closer.

He sent me into orbit and turned me over. He entered me and held me captive. "This is for you. Don't fight me, Shiree. Relax and enjoy it."

"I love you, Baby."

"That's the one that makes me hard, Shiree. I love you too, Baby."

Over the years, I learned to enjoy and appreciate his unselfish, just for me, treatment. Not only did it magnify the experience, it also magnified my love for him.

When he finally stopped, he straddled me and massaged my shoulders and back. He kept saying, "Go to sleep, Baby."

But I refused. I turned over and felt his erection. "Are you better, Shiree?"

"Yes, I'm much better. But I now need you to lay down, Kendall."

He glared at me, but eventually obeyed me. I kissed him all the way to his manhood. He was thoroughly enjoying it. And the way his stomach muscles were contracting, his need was obvious.

His breathing was labored, and he began to moan. His joy and pleasure overwhelmed me, and I was dizzy with desire for him. So I straddled him.

My whole body was aflame. When I inserted him, I wondered yet again what I would do without him.

I finally found my strength, so I got on my knees and I was determined to experience every inch of him. He held on to my hips and wanted me to move faster. "No, Baby. It's my turn to pleasure you. And *your turn* to be quiet."

I closed my eyes and moved slower. He moaned again and moved with me. My hands were in my hair and my head was back.

Once he relaxed, we danced a slow, sensual waltz. It was amazing. I eventually moved my hands to his abdomen, and I held on to his six pack.

Our dance became a sexy salsa, and he was beside himself. *"Oh, Shiree..."*

I felt so full of him. We both knew what was about to happen, and he went deeper and he held me tighter. We erupted into each other, and...

I screamed like Alysiya.

The following day was a busy one. I went to my house to work a couple of hours and then I met him at the house in Gates. He asked me about setting up my workstation at his house. "I'm all set up there, Kendall."

That's when he actually said, "Shiree, maybe it's best that you start preparing to quit that job. You don't need the money. I can take care of you."

"Kendall Montgomery. I don't work just for the money. Don't start that."

"Harold's reason for not wanting you to work is very different from mine, Felicia. You have a lot on your plate right now. And Stew and I have been discussing the advantages of you and Simone helping us at the club. Are you aware of how much money we make there?"

"No."

"The money Stew and I make pays all of our bills. All of them. With a lot to spare. I rarely touch the money I make as a doctor."

"Listen at what you're saying. You're blessed to be able to do the things you love and get paid for it. I also want that. And stop calling me Felicia."

He raised his hand to argue. Then he lowered it. "You're absolutely right, Baby. I don't wanna take that from you."

"I'll gladly help at the club. But that's not my passion. It's yours."

"I know, but your presence will also stop women from bothering me."

"I think you made it clear that you love me. Everyone heard that last night."

He smiled. "I got some nasty looks last night. Pat told me I might need a bullet proof vest."

"Who *is* Pat? She's always in your face."

He laughed. "We went to school together. She's also a doctor. We're like you and Todd, except we've never slept together. She's like one of the guys."

"Why didn't you tell me? I would love to know her."

"Pat's biggest problem is that she talks too much. She'll tell you about every woman I've ever dated."

"Really? I think I'll talk to her."

He laughed and went into the kitchen. My phone was in there. It rang and he answered it. I heard him say, "Sometimes. And sometimes I do other things for her too."

I grabbed the phone and saw it was Harold. Kendall walked away laughing. "Harold, what is it?"

"I would appreciate it if he didn't answer your phone. The one I pay for."

"What do you *need, Harold!?*"

"Would you kindly call me when we can talk privately? Doesn't he work?"

"I'll call you tomorrow. What time should I..."

He hung up.

I turned and Kendall was smirking. Then he put his hands up. "He started it."

I glared at him. "This is far more difficult for me than for you, Kendall. I need you to be nice. I even need you to take his shit for a while. What did he say?"

"He asked me if I now answer your calls. I told him sometimes, and that I sometimes do other things for you too."

I shook my head. It felt like I was dealing with a mischievous child. "There's no reason for him to call you two and three times a day, Felicia. He's doing it to rattle me. But I know how to stop him from fucking with me."

"You're choosing to be rattled."

"Felicia, I'm..."

I grabbed his crotch. "If you don't stop calling me that, Felicia will make sure you're out of commission for a week."

He leaned forward and froze. Our noses were touching. "Are we clear, Doctor?"

He nodded. I slung my hair in his face and walked off. He followed me, picked me up and threw me over his shoulder. He headed toward the stairs and I screamed, "Put me down!"

He carried me up the stairs, into our room and dropped me on the bed. "Do you think you're my mother, Shiree?"

"Only when you act like a child."

He stared and smiled. "You're so hot when you're mad. Come here and be sweet to me."

I rolled my eyes. He went inside of his pants and removed it. He massaged it and moaned, "Don't you love it? Like I love your pussy? Kiss it, Shiree."

I walked over and squatted in front of him. I never took my eyes off of him. I took him in my mouth, and he closed his eyes.

After enjoying it, he brought me back to the bed and undressed me. I gave him what he wanted quickly, because we didn't have much time.

Once we were on our way, I shared my plans regarding the boys with Kendall. Then he raised my hand and kissed it. "I'm anxious for you to be my wife, Shiree. And I promise to be a good father."

I smiled, but I didn't respond. I remembered what Simone said and the receipt she showed me. I knew he wasn't gonna stop until I was Mrs. Montgomery.

When we pulled up at Unkl Moe's, it was really crowded. Luckily, Todd and Gina were already there and had a booth. We all spoke, and I sat next to Gina. Kendall said, "I'm not sitting with a man in this booth."

Everyone laughed and Gina got up and sat with Todd. After ordering, Todd said, "Okay, Licia. Business first. Then I wanna know some shit since my wife won't answer my questions."

He turned to Kendall. "Man. Can you believe she's more loyal to Licia than to me? I hit the damn ceiling."

Kendall laughed. I said, "Todd. I recall telling you not to ask her about it."

He sucked his teeth and waved me off. Kendall and Gina were dying laughing. I said, "Todd, for the sake of the kids, I've decided to give you what you asked for. They can live with you for now, but we continue to share custody. Okay?"

He looked at Gina and they both smiled. "We think that's best, Licia."

Gina added, "We'll make sure they spend plenty of time with you."

I smiled and continued. "We'll talk about their financial needs later, but I'll continue to pay for everything I've been paying for. And by the way, Harold insists he still wants the boys in his life."

Todd said, "I'll work it out with him, Licia. So, it's over? You and Harold are finished?"

He looked at Kendall then back at me. I said, "Yes. He hired a private detective and found out about us. He admitted to cheating too."

Todd leaned back, appearing to be absorbing it all. "Should we tell the boys?"

Gina said, "I don't think it's necessary right now. For the time being, we'll just make sure the boys visit when you're there, Felicia."

I asked, "What about Angel? She now has separated Godparents."

Todd said, "We know you love her, Licia."

Gina said, "If not for you, we wouldn't have her."

Gina and I both had tears. Todd said, "Hell naw. I can't have you doing that in public, Gina. Stop it. Damn."

Kendall put his arm around me. "Baby, this is supposed to be a fun lunch. Let's tell Todd our story."

Todd said, "Yeah. I still can't believe this."

I laughed and said, "Todd. When you first went to Kendall with Angel, he was chasing me then."

"Um… Excuse me? Angel is over three years old, Licia."

He looked at Kendall again, and I said, "I know. We've been seeing each other for over three years."

Kendall said, "Gina, that day you busted us was the first time we…you know."

She smiled. "I already know, Kendall. Felicia told me everything three years ago. Like you going to Jamaica. She and I are like sisters."

Todd asked Kendall, "You were in Jamaica?"

Kendall smiled. "Yes, I was. That's where we fell in love."

Gina said, "I knew that too."

We all laughed and enjoyed our meal. I was pleased that Kendall and Todd got along so well. Gina winked at me and we both smiled.

Later while at the apartment, Simone reminded me we needed to call Earl. We went over to her side and took care of that right away.

Afterwards, she whispered, "Have you decided to stop sleeping with Harold?"

"I have to work that out, Simone."

"Yes, you do. I overheard Stew telling Kendall you would need time to work through your guilt. He was talking Ken out of beating his ass, Felice."

"What am I gonna do about Kendall and his temper, Simone?"

"For starters, stop fucking Harold."

When I went back over to our side, he was watching TV. He tapped the sofa wanting me to join him. "You okay, Shiree?"

"Yeah. But I'm concerned about you. Are you planning to beat Harold up?"

He shook his head and laughed. "I told you I wouldn't do that unless..."

"Kendall. You told me you wouldn't kill Sam either."

"That's true. And I *didn't* kill him. I also recall telling *him* that if he contacted you again, I'd pay him a visit. He needed to understand that I'm a man of my word."

I picked up his hand and kissed it. "Please, Kendall. For the sake of peace and harmony, please be patient. I'm certain Harold will continue to do and say things to piss us off. In his mind, we've taken everything from him."

He pulled me closer and kissed me. "I promise, I promise."

I looked in his face and hoped he meant it. "Maybe you should count to five before responding to him."

"What happened, Shiree? Did he call you again?"

"No. I'm just concerned about your temper."

"Didn't I do well at your parent's house?"

"I have to admit, Kendall. I thought Harold was history."

He laughed out loud. "It's good we were there, because if we were anywhere else, I probably would have knocked him on his arrogant ass."

When we walked in my parent's house that night for dinner, the kids were in the kitchen on the phone with their father. I stood there with my arms crossed watching them. Benny said, "Daddy! Grandpa gave me a watch!"

Aleece was jumping up and down. "Benny, my turn!"

They finally saw me and Aleece ran to me. "Mommy. Benny won't let me talk to Daddy."

She started pouting. I told her, "Wait, Aleece. He'll finish soon."

I walked back in the living room, and Kendall and Daddy were talking sports. Daddy told Kendall that the Knicks were his favorite basketball team, and Kendall laughed. Daddy said, "I know they stink, but what can I say. I'm a fan for life."

Benny ran in and Aleece was behind him. I was sitting next to Daddy, and Benny said, "Mommy, Daddy wants you. Here, Mommy!"

I took the phone and gave it to Aleece. Benny said, "Hi, Dr. Ken. Why are you here?"

I picked my son up and sat him on my lap. After kissing him, I said, "Hi, Sweetie."

He put his arms around my neck. "Hi, Mommy."

"Did you have a good day?"

"Yes. Grandpa gave me a watch, Mom!"

"Wow, that sounds exciting! Where is it?"

"I'll get it."

He jumped down and ran to get it. Aleece was twirling her hair and talking to her father. I looked at Kendall. He smiled while watching her, and then she looked up and saw him. "Dr. Ken! Daddy, Dr. Ken is here!"

I closed my eyes and sighed. Kendall smiled, and Aleece said, "Bye, Daddy!"

She gave me the phone and ran to Kendall. "Hi Dr. Ken! Did you bring me a treat?"

He smiled. "No, Alysiya. No treats today."

She looked at him pouting. "But as long as you're a good girl, you'll get them sometimes. Okay?"

She smiled and shook her head yes. Mom said, "Aleece. What did I tell you about shaking that head? We can't *hear* your head."

Aleece turned back to Kendall, and said, "Yes, Dr. Ken."

That's when I realized the phone was in my hand. "Hello?"

"Felicia. I thought you were going to call me back."

"I told you I would call you tomorrow. And I will."

"I'm feeling pretty shitty that first my wife, and now my daughter prefers him over me."

"I'll call you tomorrow. This is not the time, Harold."

"Goodnight, Wife."

"Good..."

And for the second time in the same day, he hung up right in my face. I gave Daddy the phone and exhaled. Daddy said, "I'm sure that didn't go over well."

While shaking my head, I said, "Not at all."

Aleece was still talking to Kendall. She was now on his lap and counting his buttons. Benny came back with his watch. I asked Daddy, "Why a watch?"

"He likes to fiddle with mine while it's on my wrist. It gets on my nerves."

I laughed, and Mom said, "Dinner's ready."

That night I was in the shower and Kendall walked in the bathroom. "What can I do to convince you to leave IBM? I'm not asking you to stop working, but Harold being with the company might prove to be a problem."

I stepped out of the shower. "I admit, I've thought about that too. I'm hoping Harold will eventually leave Rochester, so maybe I'll take a leave until he does."

I put on my robe and walked in the bedroom. After brushing his teeth, he came in too. "Why don't you look around for other opportunities in case he stays here?"

"With so much going on, it's not a good time to start a new job. Besides, I don't want a new job. I want *my* job."

I walked out and went downstairs. He came behind me. "I feel terrible for you. How can I help you through this?"

I didn't answer. I was still trying to get used to his kitchen. After opening several cabinet doors, I finally found the tea bags. He turned me around. "Shiree. Just keep working until it becomes impossible. I'm sorry."

"Let's talk about something else. I've been here before. It's not your fault."

I made the tea and went into the family room. Kendall followed me everywhere I went. He sat next to me. "How much do you make?"

"Why? I don't want money, Kendall."

He laughed. "You are the *only* woman who has *ever* said that to me. What the hell is wrong with you?"

I laughed too. "About seventy-five thousand. You gonna write me a check?"

"Yes. Damn, you make *that* much?"

He and I both laughed. I asked, "How much do *you* make?"

"Over four hundred last year between my practice and the club. And more this year. And I've saved and invested well."

"Damn, you make *that* much?"

He laughed again. "Isn't that enough to take care of you?"

"Kendall, you know I don't need much. Of course, it is."

He smiled and said, "It's funny that we've been together all this time and never knew how much the other one made."

"I remember when you asked me if I knew my net worth. I didn't even know I *had* a net worth. At least not one worth talking about."

We both laughed. I added, "He never got over the fact that I didn't care about his money. You need to know I don't care about yours either. I've always worked so I could take care of myself, Kendall. My daddy taught me that."

"I understand that, Shiree. More than anything, I want you happy, Baby. Please don't be sad. I hope you'll think about it and do what you feel is best. Okay?"

"I will, Kendall. Let's go to bed. It's been a long day."

The following day I left work at eleven. I called Kendall and he had a full load of sick children. I went to my house and looked around. The sounds of a happy family were missing.

I realized I hadn't checked the mail since Harold left. After collecting it, I noticed a large manila envelope from Dr. Morales.

Inside was my report, an appointment card for the following Tuesday, along with a note asking me to confirm the appointment. I confirmed it right away.

Then I sat in the family room and began to read the report. My cell phone vibrated and indicated I had a text from Harold. It read: I thought you were gonna call me.

I sighed and called him. "I didn't think you'd ever call me."

"Harold. I had to work. Did you expect me to call you from work?"

"I'm trying hard to deal with this. It's a lot, Felicia."

I said quietly, "I know. Me too."

"I'd rather forget it ever happened, Babe. Could you do that? Just forget about him? We could leave Rochester and begin anew."

"Then what? Go back to prison? Harold, this is about more than Kendall. Way more. It's about *why* I accepted his indecent proposal in the first place. Besides, if I chose to forget, you certainly wouldn't. As a matter of fact, you'd make sure I remembered for the rest of my life. I couldn't bear living like that again."

"Are you blaming me for what you did?"

"I'm blaming you for *why* I did it. And Sam and Kendall too. You're all to blame for who I am now."

I hung up and went in the kitchen. I opened the wine fridge and grabbed a bottle. I wondered if anyone remembered it was my birthday.

The phone rang. It was hard hearing his sadness. "Felicia. Can we talk? I mean really talk. I'd like us to just open up and say it all. And hear it all."

"I'll try, Harold. But there are things that neither of us is ready to hear."

"You said we're to blame for who you are. Explain that. Because I feel you share in the blame too. You made the decision to do what you did."

"You're right. In part. But I am not the same person you met at that Christmas party. I was proud of that woman. I'm not proud of her now. You gave me sexual fulfillment I'd never experienced. I don't regret that. I regret the pain it's caused."

"What was the real reason you slept with Sam?"

"I told you the truth about that. From the day I saw him, I thought he was handsome and funny. I had no idea he was interested in me. But that day I thought I'd lost you, was as Kendall says, the perfect storm."

"And Kendall? What happened there?"

"Kendall began chasing me the day we met. I ran fast and far from him."

"How long have you known him?"

"A few years."

"He's been chasing you for a few years?"

"Yes, Harold. And I told him I was committed to you, but it didn't stop him."

"So, what was your turning point? Why did you finally give in?"

"Because…the truth is I was so unhappy. I felt like a prisoner. You were so overbearing and unreasonable. I tried everything imaginable to keep you happy. I continued to fail."

"You know that's not true, Felicia. You made me happier than anyone."

"But not happy enough! You expected perfection. I could never give you that! And I couldn't change what happened with Sam. No matter what I did, you wanted to know where I'd been, who I saw, why, when, how, what, and on and on and on. That woman from the Christmas party was destroyed."

"I'm sorry, Felicia."

We were both quiet for a while. "Harold. We need to resolve so many things. But we can't do it all now. Let's talk again later."

"No. No, I'm fine."

"Are you sure?"

"I should have been a different husband. I always felt I was a *good* husband, but I was so consumed with not losing you, that I drove you away."

"I pray that God will send you the woman of your dreams. I don't think I'm that woman. I tried, Harold, but I can't live in a cage. I finally said yes to Kendall as a means of escape."

"You've never admitted whether or not you're in love with him. Are you?"

"I don't know, Harold. I know I love certain things about him."

"Would you be willing to try and salvage our marriage?"

I thought about how to answer that. I finally said, "Before these recent events, I might've said yes, Harold. But too much has happened. I believe this would always define me in your eyes. And I would always feel like…damaged goods."

"I wouldn't do it again, Felicia. I would give you all the freedom you need. We could relocate and start over. And I promise I'll make your life much easier."

"I've heard that promise for years. I don't think you're capable of keeping that promise. But unless you want a divorce, I would like to remain as we are."

"Will you continue to make love to me?"

"Harold..."

"I need you so much, Felicia. I can live with everything else. But I would die without you in my arms...sometimes. Just *sometimes,* Felicia."

"I'm confused, Harold. You haven't wanted me for months. Why..."

"I never stopped wanted you. You no longer wanted *me*. Why, Felicia?"

"That's not true. I just..."

"I'm not asking for much."

Through my tears, I whispered, "Okay, Harold. *Sometimes.*"

After talking to Harold, Lenora and I met for a late lunch. I told her everything. She sat there with her mouth opened. "I don't know if I should say I'm sorry, or congratulations. Are you happy, Felicia?"

"I'm not sure yet. But my job is my joy, Lenora. Help me work it out."

"And you are *our* joy, Felicia. Losing you would destroy our groove. We're the Trouble Shooting Trio. I'll call you in a few days. In the meantime, allow yourself some down time. You damn sure need it! Happy Birthday, Felicia!"

While going to my mom's, I continued to hear Lenora in my head. *Down time.* She was right. I needed some *me time.*

I went to my house, packed a few things and called Lauren. I asked if she had any rooms available. "Yes. I would love to see you guys."

"It's just me, Lauren. We're going through something right now. And please book me in a different room."

"Of course. Come. I'll take care of you."

While on Interstate 90, I called my mother. I told her I needed a respite for a couple of days. "Yes, you do. Stay as long as you need to. And Felicia?"

"Yes?"

"Happy Birthday, Baby!"

"Thanks, Mommy."

I called Todd. "Of course, Licia. I gotchu. And mums the word."

I called Annette. "Happy Birthday, Sis! I'm mad you went without me. But I understand. I'll hold it down here, and I'll tell Carla."

I asked her not to tell Simone or Kendall.

When I was settled in my room and drinking a glass of wine, I finally called Kendall. It was twenty minutes to five and I knew I was in for a fight. He picked up and I swallowed hard. "Hi."

"What's wrong?"

"Why do you think something's wrong?"

"Because you always...what's wrong, Shiree?"

I began to panic. "Kendall. My life feels like a tangled mess. I decided not to quit my job. I spoke to Lenora today and she agreed to work with me."

"That's great news, right?"

"Yes, but..."

I started to cry. "I'm not in Rochester, Kendall. I left this afternoon."

I heard something fall and I closed my eyes. When I heard the door slam, I almost jumped out of my skin. "Felicia. Are you in Detroit? Tell me!"

"No! What the hell made you think that?!"

He said quietly, "Tell me where you are."

I closed my eyes again. "Kendall. I need a short rest, Sweetie. Not from you. Honest. But for me. This has been so overwhelming. I'm tired, Baby, and I need a moment without kids and work and everyone pulling at me. Please understand."

He was quiet for a moment. "Please tell me where you are. I won't be able to rest until you tell me. I'll think you're with him. Please, Shiree."

"I'm one hour away, Kendall. I swear, Baby. I wouldn't lie to you."

"Shiree. We've always said we're each other's soft place to land when the world gets hard and cold. Please, Baby. I have nowhere to land."

I heard him start the car. "Please, Shiree. Please, Baby. You're scaring me."

"Kendall..."

"It's your birthday, Shiree."

I sighed. "I'm at Geneva on the Lake. It's peaceful here. The owner is a wonderful friend and she promised to take care of me."

He was quiet again and I heard him turn off the car. In a very stern voice he said, "*I*...will take care of you."

I opened my mouth, but I was unable to utter a single word. He then said, "Happy Birthday, Baby. I have your gift and I want to give it to you. Today, Shiree."

I paused and finally said, "Give me a few days."

"No! *No*, Felicia! *I'll take care of you!*"

I closed my eyes and inhaled. I sighed again. "Okay, Kendall. I'll come home tomorrow."

I hung up, left my room, and walked along the lake. I cried for an hour. There was no rest for the weary.

After returning to my room, Lauren knocked on my door. She brought another bottle of my favorite wine. "I watched you outside in your sorrow. I'm a really good listener."

She smiled. This woman had been kind to me for years. I'd never been close to a white woman before, but I always had a blast with those I knew.

I told her the truth. She reminded me of my mother because she seemed to be pondering something. "Love and lust are like siblings. They're a lot alike, but different in the important ways. Similar to perennials and annuals. Most people don't know the difference between perennials and annuals. They see something beautiful and bring it home. They enjoy it that year, then stand there waiting for it to reappear the following year. Usually nothing appears or sometimes weeds come up. They never knew what they had was designed to be temporary."

She and I laughed at her analogy. We were drinking wine and she reached for my hand. "Being the owner of a place like this, I see a lot of things. Unfortunately, some of it is a bit kooky. But I know what I saw in Harold was love. And in you. But some people can't separate love from control. It can be narcissistic. But..."

"No. He *is* narcissistic. Nothing I do is good enough. And he has to know everything I do and say and think. He's impossible. And believe it or not, you're right about the annuals. I never should've married Harold."

She seemed to be taking it all in. "And the other one? Are you sure you're in love with him?"

"I am. We've been seeing each other for over three years. He's amazing."

She was surprised. "Sounds like you probably are. Tell me about him."

I told her a lot about Kendall. "You'll probably see him soon. He can't seem to breathe without me either. If not tonight, tomorrow. He'll be here."

She got up and looked back at me. "Are you sure you're not trading in one narcissist for another one?"

I laughed. "It probably sounds that way, but Kendall's ex-wife described it perfectly. Kendall is possessive, whereas Harold is obsessive. Harold loves me, but Kendall adores me."

She seemed surprised that my man's ex-wife would say something like that. I laughed and explained that Juanita and I were friends.

We talked a little more and she left. When I hung up on Kendall earlier, I turned off my phone. I turned it back on and saw three calls and a text from him.

I opened the text and it read: I'm sorry, Shiree. I want you to be happy, Baby. Not sad like this. I'm so worried. Please respond to me.

I replied and told him I was fine and that I'd be home the next day. Afterwards, I went in my overnight bag and took out the report. I sat back and read it.

In a nutshell, Dr. Morales explained that Harold's control issues, and his and my insecurities, contributed in large part to my infidelity. And, that my lack of self-worth is what led me into that tub, which Harold greatly contributed to over the years.

She recommended that I commit to at least six months of counselling. She also recommended that I do two other things; Divorce Harold and suspend my relationship with Kendall for those six months.

How did this happen to me? As painful as it was to admit, she was right about so many things. I finished my wine and thought more about her recommendations.

There was a knock on the door. I opened it, and Lauren was standing there smiling. "He's here, Felicia. He's so handsome. And a *doctor*."

I smiled too. She added, "He has his own room. He asked me to tell you he's here, but for you to take all the time you need. He was afraid for you."

I told her about the pills. She surprised me and told me she'd also done that after leaving college. "Everyone feared I'd do it again, and they followed me around for months. They'll stop. Are you okay?"

"Yes. And thanks, Lauren. I no longer have any interest in doing that."

She smiled, gave me his room number and left. I hid the report in my bag and went to his room. He opened the door and embraced me. "I'm so sorry, Baby."

"You didn't do anything, Kendall. It's me. I'm tired."

I stepped in and walked toward the sofa. "I'm not him, Shiree. I was just so scared, Baby. I promise not to be like him."

"I know that. I just hope you aren't worried about other men. Are you?"

"That's a loaded question, Shiree. At first, I worried he begged you to come back to him and talked you into joining him there. But no, worrying about *other* men is exhausting."

"You're here because you fear I'll take more pills, right?"

He closed his eyes. "I *fear*, I'll wake up without you. Some way or other."

"I'm not gonna do it again. I felt trapped, Kendall. Between guilt and being exposed. But mostly I felt I had to choose between you and my kids. And I couldn't imagine my life without them or you again."

He ran his fingers through his Locs and closed his eyes. "For that alone, I wanna kill him."

"Kendall..."

He embraced my face. "About the guilt, Shiree..."

"Right now, I feel like I'll always have the guilt. But now that it's exposed, I realize that I underestimated my loved ones. Like you said."

"Of course, Shiree. You're the kindest, sweetest person I know. You're not a bad person."

With tears in my eyes, I looked up at him. "I saw my daddy cry, Kendall. In thirty-two years, I'd never seen that. I couldn't believe I'd done that to him. And…after you confronted me in the bathroom, I realized how selfish I was. I'll never do that to you all again."

He embraced me. "Do you recall telling me you're made soft?"

"Yes."

"You were right. That's why you're so special. And why we're always protecting you. It's not a flaw, Baby. It's what makes you Felicia Shiree."

I smiled and kissed his hand. "Have you unpacked, Kendall?"

"Not yet."

"Get your bag and come on down to my room."

"Are you sure? You know I can't resist you."

I rolled my eyes at him and he followed me.

We had a quiet dinner, and afterwards I laid in his arms. We watched TV and I fell asleep. He carried me to bed and undressed me. I watched him undress and get in beside me. He embraced me, kissed my neck and shoulder, and went to sleep.

The following morning, Lauren called and said she was sending breakfast up. She asked, "For one or two?"

I laughed. "Two."

"If you'd like, I can send all of your meals up. Would you like that?"

"That would be great. Thanks, Lauren. He's vegetarian, but he loves bacon."

"I'll do a wonderful omelet for him. Rest, my friend."

I smiled and hung up. I saw something on my finger. It was another pink diamond. This time on my left ring finger.

I looked at it and smiled. "Do you like it, Shiree?"

I turned toward him. "I love it, Kendall. Thank you."

He reached for my hand and kissed it. "Will you wear it? I know we can't marry yet, but…will you be my wife? And will you allow me to be your husband when you're ready?"

"That's a lot of questions, Kendall. Yes, Baby."

It was a pear-shaped pink diamond. "How many carats is this? It's too much, Kendall."

"It's only one and a half, Shiree."

He went in his bag and pulled out a ring box. "Open it."

Inside was the matching wedding band. Another pink diamond eternity band. But this one was designed to interconnect with its pear-shaped companion.

While admiring them, I remembered how much they cost. I asked him, "Do you plan to wear one that matches these?"

He laughed. "If you want me to. But I'm hoping you won't ask me to do that. Happy Birthday, Baby."

"Thank you, Kendall. It's a beautiful gift."

I kissed him and smiled at him. He smiled back and said, "Stay in bed and I'll feed you when the food comes, Shiree. Are you feeling better?"

"Yes. Thank you for coming."

He got up and went in the bathroom. When he came out, he asked, "Would you like me to bathe you first? Before breakfast?"

I smiled. "That would be nice."

After I got in the tub, he got in behind me. He knew I enjoyed bathing with him. "You didn't answer the other questions, Shiree."

"Yes, Kendall. I will."

He looked at me through slanted eyes. We soon rinsed off, and he put my robe around me and a towel around his waist. "You will *what*, Shiree?"

I laughed and turned to him. "Once this is over, yes, I will be your wife."

Ten minutes later, I was back in bed and squeaky clean. The waiter brought our food and asked Kendall, "Is there anything else, Sir?"

I heard Kendall ask the waiter if he would bring a bottle of champagne. I smiled. He came back in and set the food up for me. Soon there was another knock and Kendall returned with the champagne.

He poured two glasses and gave one to me. We both smiled and he toasted our engagement. "Shiree, I wish I could put into words how happy I am. There's no way I could've known my fascination with you would turn into the best thing that's ever happened to me. You have far exceeded my wildest dreams."

I smiled. "Kendall. I wish I'd met you first. You're the best thing that's happened to me too. I'm looking forward to being your wife."

"Is that true, Shiree?"

"Yes, of course it's true, Kendall."

He smiled and kissed my hand. "Are you ready for me to be your husband?"

I laughed. "You're already my husband. Right?"

He glared at me, then shook his head and laughed. "I love you so much, Shiree."

"I love you more, Kendall."

He kissed me and we drank our champagne.

He was so happy. I felt happy too. But admittedly, I was also scared and concerned about Harold for several reasons.

I didn't trust him. I found it really hard to believe that he would let us go without some sort of fight. Especially his children. I prayed he wasn't setting me up again.

When Kendall and I finished our meal, he got in bed and laid his head on my lap. "Shiree. I can be a prick sometimes, but I have the best of intentions."

"I'm not ready to meet your family, Kendall."

"I know. I promised them I would come home. You should know that Mom insisted I bring you with me, but I'll understand if you don't go."

"I need to be with the kids, Kendall."

"And she's excited about meeting the kids. I would love for us to bring them."

"Sweetie, we need to slow down. Just a bit. Okay?"

He stared at me. Then he sat up and kissed me. "Okay."

"Kendall. Why do you think I'm here?"

He didn't answer at first. Eventually he said, "Shiree. Your mom told me not to smother you. I tried really hard not to. But I clearly failed."

I played in his hair, and asked again, "Why am I here, Kendall?"

"Like you told me, you're overwhelmed and need to think without my influence. And I admit I'm scared that you'll decide...to stay with him."

I smiled and looked into his beautiful face. "Kendall. I'm not going back to Hell. I know I should've left a long time ago. I'm here because I'm tired. You don't listen. Sometimes people need *me* time. You can't do to me what Harold did. I can't do that again."

He came closer and kissed me again. "I've wanted this for so long, Shiree. I tried patience, but it didn't seem to work. But I promise you…I'll be your soft place to land. No more mania. Unless someone is a threat to you. Or us."

"How do you define that?"

He laughed. "I know Harold will be a thorn. I'll be most patient with him. Okay, Shiree?"

"Okay, Kendall."

He laid back down, and we both slept most of the day.

Chapter Five

Thursday morning, I got up early. After going into the bathroom, I slipped out into the living room.

I looked out at the lake and wondered what I was gonna do about Harold. Everyone said he was playing me. Not to mention what Dr. Morales said.

Even so, I still cared for him. And from where I sat, I didn't think he was asking a lot. If he had something brewing to undermine me, he was playing the role very well. Especially since he seemed to be handling this much better than I thought he would.

Simone and Kendall both accused me of wanting both of them. Could that be true? I could easily live happily ever after with Kendall, without Harold. But I was having a hard time living with the reality that I'd hurt him like that.

What was the big deal if I slept with him periodically? I never gave Kendall a hard time when he and Juanita were having sex. And I hated to admit it, but it was great having sex with Harold again.

I closed my eyes and prayed for peace and harmony. I walked over to the fridge, got a bottle of water and Kendall came out of the bedroom. "I saw you daydreaming. Do you feel rested?"

I smiled. "Good morning, Doctor. Yes, I do."

He smiled too. "Good morning, Wife."

He reached for my hand and brought me back into the bedroom. "If we make love, will it destroy your respite? I've slept next to you for two nights, and I fear I'll have to go back to my room. I'm dying, Shiree."

I smiled. "What do you recommend, Doctor? Maybe I can help."

He laid me down. "One of you every four hours. Can you make that happen?"

Later we walked along the lake. It was chilly, but the sun was out, making it bearable. "So, have you talked to Harold anymore?"

"Yes. On Tuesday. Remember I told him I would call him back?"

"How did it go?"

"I guess it depends on who you ask. I told him why I cheated."

We sat on a bench. "What did you say?"

"I told him he was overbearing and controlling. I also told him that nothing I did was ever good enough, and that we no longer have a future together."

I stood and looked at the lake. Then I looked back at Kendall and said, "He wanted to know about you. So, I told him."

He gave me that glare he was so notorious for. "What did you tell him?"

I heard a splash and turned back toward the lake. "I told him you chased me for a long time. And if I wasn't so unhappy, you would've never caught me."

I turned back toward him. "He never let me forget Sam. Now it'll be you. I guess I decided to be who and what he saw when he looked at me."

Kendall walked over to me. "Shiree. Don't start."

I looked up at him. "If I was your wife, and you watched me sneak out to fuck another man, I think you would have an adjective or two for me too. Right?"

He stared at me. Then he looked away and sighed. "I don't want to discuss that, Shiree."

"Would you ever beat me up, Kendall?"

He laughed. "Are you crazy? I would never lay a hand on you, Baby. You know those times when sex is painful for you, and how it upsets me?"

"Yes."

"I can't bear the thought of inflicting pain on you. That tears me up."

"Kendall. You're delusional if you think Harold hasn't called me a whore or worse. It's unsettling."

I looked at the lake again. "I told him that he, Sam and you share the blame. I refuse to take it all."

He laughed again. "What about Todd? Didn't he start it?"

"Actually, I blame him most of all. If not for him, I'd still be virtuous."

"I can't speak for the others, but because your kids were patients at my practice, I would've still worked hard to snag you. Our meeting was inevitable."

"I wouldn't have given you the time of day."

He came closer and whispered in my ear, "Then you would never know the thrill of having your pussy sucked. Or the ecstasy of orgasms that make you scream and cry. Or giving me the kind of pleasure that makes me scream and cry."

I bit my lip. "I've never made you cry."

He smiled. "You've made me cry, Shiree. More than once."

He kissed my forehead and looked in my eyes. Then he raised my chin and said, "I need you to understand something. Sam and I were wrong for disrupting your life. But that *does not* make you a *whore*. It makes *us* the *bad guys*."

He caressed my face. "A whore is not particular. You are. A slut...fucks anything. You don't. You refused me for a long time, Shiree. Believe it or not, I almost stopped chasing you."

"Really? Why?"

"It was exhausting. I'd never begged like that before in my life. What kept me coming was that conversation when you climaxed on the phone. I had to have more than just that seduction in my office."

"I did not seduce you. You seduced *me*, Kendall. You offered me a fortune to watch me nurse Aleece."

"You didn't do it for a fortune. Only a whore would have done that, right?"

I glared at him. "You never paid me."

He embraced me and looked in my eyes. "I think I did. I can still taste it."

Later that night he asked when I planned to go home. "Probably Saturday. Why don't you go on home tomorrow, and I'll see you the next day?"

We were sitting on the sofa, with my feet on his lap. "I'll stay with you, Shiree. Have I destroyed your rest?"

"No, Kendall. But when you're around, I feel the need to take care of you. I need some quiet *me* time. Why don't you understand that?"

"Okay, Shiree. I'll go back to my room, and..."

"I told Lauren to give it away. We'll both go tomorrow."

He smiled. "We'll go Saturday. We haven't done this since Jamaica. I'm enjoying spending this time with you."

"I am too, Kendall."

He leaned back and smiled. "Stew and I are sending you and Simone away. Another birthday gift."

"What? Where?"

"Friday after Thanksgiving, the two of you are booked at a spa in Miami. You'll come back Monday."

I stared at him. "Are you planning to crash us?"

He laughed. "Not a chance. I wouldn't dare do to you what I saw Harold do. I'd lose you for sure. Besides, my mom would kill me if I cancelled or left early. Stew is also going home. To Pittsburgh."

I had a feeling that he and Stew were up to something. I couldn't wait to talk to Simone. But I smiled and thanked him. In many ways.

The following day, I went in my bag and took out my phone. I put it there so I wouldn't have to deal with anyone. Especially Harold. I had several voice and text messages. I checked the texts first.

Harold's texts read: I'll be home Friday instead of Sunday. Are you still staying Tuesday and Wednesday? I didn't know you were going away. The children miss us. We need to communicate better. On and on and on.

I didn't bother listening to the voice messages. Kendall saw the look on my face. "What's wrong?"

I shook my head. "Nothing new. He's complaining because I didn't tell him I was going away."

"That's no longer his business. It's time he understood that. You too."

I put the phone back in my bag. "By the way. He's coming back today."

Kendall sighed. "This shit is getting on my nerves."

Tuesday morning after going over her recommendations, Dr. Morales closed her file and smiled at me. "Mrs. Benson, you seem better. How do you feel?"

"I'm not sure. I mean, I still feel like I'll never get over devastating my husband. But at the same time, I fully understand that he's not good for me."

"I asked how do *you* feel?"

"I'm relieved it's finally over. I had sleepless nights worrying about how it would end. And although the weight of him finding out is gone, it's the uncertainty that has me on edge now."

"That's normal. Just stay focused on what's best for *you*."

I nodded and she asked, "What about Dr. Montgomery?"

I put my head down and thought how to answer her. I finally said, "I'm so in love with him, Doctor Morales. I feel foolish saying it out loud, because I know you want me to stop seeing him, but..."

"That isn't entirely true, Mrs. Benson. I believe you need to understand your worth and be less dependent. You allowed both of these men to control your life. The difference is, because your husband is narcissistic, he didn't have your best interests at heart. He was, and still is more concerned with his own interests. I've spoken to both of them."

I was stunned. "You *have?*"

"Yes. Over the last week I've talked to Mr. Benson twice and Dr. Montgomery three times."

She opened her file again and continued. "I asked both of them about the pills. Your husband dismissed it, whereas Dr. Montgomery was very concerned. I believe Mr. Benson is avoiding it because he doesn't want to face the fact that he's the reason you got in that tub."

There was irritation in her voice and her body language spoke volumes. She clearly wasn't fond of Harold. "Neither of them mentioned talking to you, Doctor."

"I asked them not to. Listen. I believe they both love you. But this isn't about them. It's about you, and your unhealthy need to be perfect. What you've done these last three years is somewhere between insanity and being Superwoman. Which tells me you're capable of a lot more than you think you are."

"What does that mean?"

"It means you've *never* needed validation. It was a façade your husband created to destroy your confidence. But it backfired when you met Dr. Montgomery, because he showed you unconditional love and reinforced your faith in yourself."

I was slowly absorbing what she said. "Mrs. Benson? Are you okay?"

"Yes, I'm sorry. Please continue."

"I believe Dr. Montgomery's love is genuine, but I also believe you feel you're not good enough. You continue to be plagued with needing to be perfect, mostly because of Mr. Benson. Although, I'm sure your first husband's infidelity devastated your self-esteem too."

I nodded and agreed. "Mr. Benson's need to control you only fueled your determination to continue your affair. Being with your lover was a means to an end. At first. But I believe you're truly in love with Dr. Montgomery. My recommendation that you suspend your relationship with him is for *you*. You need that time to validate *yourself*, by taking care of *you* and depending only on *you*."

That same afternoon, I was preparing a few meals for Kendall before going to spend a couple of days at my house. I was still reeling from the doctor's recommendations when Kendall came and sat in the kitchen. He was a basket case.

He grabbed me and pulled me down on his lap. He kissed my neck and held me tight. "Shiree. You're not going."

"It'll go by quickly, Sweetie. I promise. And I'll see you every day."

"You don't understand. I, um...I called him."

I slowly got up and faced my *husband*. "Kendall. What did you do?"

My cell phone rang. Harold was calling me, and I watched it vibrate on the table. I pressed decline and turned back to Kendall. He had his head down and his hands on his forehead. "If you get mad, Shiree, please let it be for a short time."

He looked up at me. "I told him you would not be staying there anymore."

I closed my eyes and tried to stay calm. "What did he say, Kendall?"

"He said he wanted to hear that from *Felicia*."

Kendall was so angry. "I told him from now on, where you sleep, *I* sleep."

I turned toward the stove and stirred the food. "So, what was his response to *that*, Kendall?"

"He laughed at that, and asked me what I was more afraid of? You choosing your *husband*, or that he knew more ways to make you come?"

I dropped the spoon. "*Oh my God*, Kendall! *What?!*"

He stood in front of me. "Kendall, what did you say?"

"Well...I laughed at him. Then I told him I wasn't afraid of any of those things, because you chose your *husband* when you chose *me*."

My heart was beating a mile a minute. "And...I made it very clear to him that making you come has never been an issue. I also informed him that since his reach can't compare to mine, he might want to reexamine the notion that he *might* be superior to me."

"*Kendall!*"

"Did you think I didn't know? A man knows, Shiree. Then I told him if anyone should be afraid, it was him. Because frankly, you've been *my* wife, and screaming in *my* arms for over three years."

"*Kendall!* You *promised!*"

I was so upset with him. I turned off the stove and grabbed my phone. I left the kitchen and picked up my purse. I went toward the garage and he grabbed me. "I'm sorry, Shiree. Please..."

"You've become my worst nightmare! Let me go!"

I ran out and got in the car. After raising the garage door, I realized the Lexus had me blocked in. I got out of my car and got into the Lexus to move it. Kendall came running after me, so I drove off.

I didn't know where to go. I realized Carla was only minutes away. I pulled up in front of her house and sat there. I couldn't go in.

I drove to Mom's and parked. My phone rang and I jumped. It was Harold again. I shook my head and answered it. "You really *are* a piece of work, Felicia!"

I closed my eyes and decided to handle him calmly. "What is it, Harold?"

He yelled, "You've been fucking him for *three years?!*"

"Harold..."

He yelled again, "We just had our fourth anniversary. What the fuck, Felicia!"

"I'm coming home."

He was suddenly quiet. "I'll see you in a few minutes, Harold."

When I walked in, he was in his office. I asked about the kids. Without looking up he told me they were napping. "Why are you here, Felicia?"

"We have an arrangement. I plan to keep it."

He looked up. "Your man has informed me that he will not allow you to sleep here. Alone with me. Is that resolved?"

"He had a moment of jealousy. This is between you and me, Harold. Not him. These are *our* children."

He got up. "Three *years,* Felicia? Is that even true?"

My mouth was opened, but I was at a loss for words. "I've been sitting here remembering certain things that were weird to me. Especially those two times you were in the hospital. I always felt like part of the story was missing."

I sighed and told him the truth. "The car accident happened when I left his house. And the real reason I didn't tell you about the pregnancy, was because I assumed Kendall was the father. But honestly, I didn't know which one of you was the father. That's why I went to another doctor."

I left his office and he followed me. "So, we were *both* fucking him! You didn't use protection?!"

Again, I didn't answer him. He sat on a barstool with his arms crossed. "Would you mind telling me the rest. I have all night, Felicia. I would appreciate not being surprised anymore by him."

I sat on the arm of the chair and looked down at the floor. "I first started seeing him just before we went to Jamaica. The reason I was so upset when you showed up there is because he was there. He surprised me too."

The color left his face. "He was in Jamaica?"

"Yes, but I didn't know he was coming."

He stood up and began to pace. "You mean to tell me your friends have known all along about this?"

"Yes, Harold. We saw each other for about two years. Most of that time we met at his place on East Avenue. After the miscarriage, we ended it."

I walked in the kitchen and poured myself a glass of wine. "That's when you were so depressed. I always felt there was more to that. You were…"

He shook his head and his anger was obvious. He grabbed my arm and shouted, "You had a broken heart, didn't you?!"

I turned away without answering him. He released my arm, but I was clear he was mad as hell. Still yelling, he said, "Along with your disinterest in sex. You obviously started seeing him again. When did that happen?"

"Hold your voice down, Harold. The kids…"

"I asked when you began seeing him again?"

"Earlier this year. After we saw them at dinner, he called me."

He went into the kitchen and poured himself a glass of wine. "I hate this, Felicia. I hate that I drove you to this, and I hate that you did it."

"Honestly, I hate it too. I really don't want to do this anymore."

"So, our plans are squashed now? I trusted you, Felicia."

I sat down. "No. I want to come home. And live together like you proposed at first. Open marriage. With marital rights."

I got a visual of Dr. Morales and the disappointment on her face. He came over to me. "Okay, Felicia. But what marital rights are you referring to?"

Confused, I watched him walk into the family room. I followed him. "The ones you asked for."

He turned and looked at me with disdain. "That is no longer necessary."

"What does that mean?"

"Whose red Lexus is that?"

"What?"

"You drove up in a red Lexus. Is it yours?"

"No, no it's Kendall's. I left quickly, and my car…"

He yelled, "Why does the license plate read FSM?!"

I'd never seen him so angry, so I didn't answer. "If you want me, you'll come to my room and get it. With a condom. And you will remove that ring on your finger. I'm not gonna fuck another man's wife!"

I watched him go upstairs. I looked at my ring and hung my head.

After the kids woke up, I let them wash the cherry tomatoes and tear up the lettuce while I cooked dinner. Harold came down an hour later and joined us.

We pretended all was well. After getting the kids settled, I went into the guest room on the first floor and Harold went out. He was pissed. After what Kendall said to him, my confessions, the ring and the car, I didn't know what he would do. Would he spiral even more???

I never responded to any of Kendall's calls or texts.

After listening to my voice messages, I learned Lenora offered me a position where I would be on call full time.

I would need to report to the office twice a week for meetings, but I would no longer be a supervisor. I was okay with that. For now. I called her and accepted the position. I told her what happened, and that I'd start in a few days.

The following day I took the kids to Mom's and I told her everything. "Do you think you'll end it with him?"

"I love him more than anything, Mommy. But I loved Harold too. Why do I get men that do this to me?"

"You have great taste in men. They adore you. Too much, unfortunately."

"I thought I would die when Harold asked about that car."

"I can't believe Kendall bought you a car and you didn't tell me. And that ring is...wow, Felicia. Is he richer than Harold?"

"Not even close. I don't think."

I began to wonder just what *his* net worth was.

Afterwards, I drove to Kendall's practice and saw his car. Assuming the coast was clear, I went downtown to our place. Stew's car was there, but otherwise, all was quiet.

I went upstairs and gathered some of my things. I wasn't going to let what happened before happen again.

I quickly put my stuff in a bag. I took off the pretty pink diamond ring and put it on the dresser. I went downstairs and looked around. I knew there was a chance I wouldn't be back for a while.

I feared Stew would call Kendall, so I knew I had to hurry. All of a sudden, a wave of sadness washed over me. I went toward the kitchen and heard the garage door go up. Too late.

I hoped it was Simone, but in case it wasn't, I threw my bag in the closet. I went back in the kitchen and he ran in. He called my name. "I'm in here."

He came in behind me. "Please don't be mad at me for too long."

I didn't say anything. "Please, Shiree."

I turned around. "Okay."

"Listen to me, Shiree. Harold is playing games. This is no longer about you. Harold is more concerned about winning than he is about you."

Dr. Morales said the same thing. And I began to wonder if the same was also true about Kendall. "And you can't get mad at me for standing up for you, Baby."

I walked out of the kitchen without looking at him. Then I turned to him. "You will not tell me what to do or how to feel, Kendall. I suppose some women would be flattered by your heroics, but I'm not."

"Shiree…"

"I saw a monster, Kendall. A two-headed, fucking monster. You and Harold. One fucking body. Mine. I will never have peace with either of you. So, I've decided that I'll get my own place and you and I can spend time together there. And nobody can tell me where the hell to sleep."

I grabbed my purse. He reached for me and I stepped back. "I totally understand, and I insist on paying for your place. Okay, Shiree?"

"I will pay for my *own* place. *No,* Kendall! I will *not* be your property. I will give my mother a key. Not you or Harold. You're both like a couple of children."

I went back in the kitchen, and he went upstairs without responding. He came right back down. "Where is your stuff, Shiree?"

I didn't answer. "Are you leaving me?"

"I told you I can't live like this. I'm going home."

I turned and he embraced me from behind. I closed my eyes and felt his pain. "Please don't do this. I need you here, Shiree."

He picked me up. "No, Kendall. *No!*"

He ignored me, took me upstairs and sat me on the bed. "Listen to me. I know the last time you were there, you…you slept with him. I don't doubt you love me, but I fear he'll turn your guilt into something beneficial for *him*. Did you…"

"No, Kendall!! I *did not!*"

He closed his eyes and sighed. He reached for my hand and noticed the ring was missing. He looked in my eyes. "No, Shiree. Where is it?"

I motioned toward the dresser. He went over and got it, and I stood. He picked up my hand and put the ring back on. "Kendall…"

He held me and wouldn't let me go. "I need to get home, Kendall."

"*This* is your home, Shiree. Everything here is yours. You *are* home, Baby."

"I'll be back, Kendall. I'm not leaving you."

"Yes, you are. If you aren't staying, you're leaving me. I need you with me."

"No, you *want* me with you."

"Yes, I do. But I also *need* you here. I'll never rest with you under the same roof with him, Shiree."

His vulnerability moved me. "Kendall. This is the last time I will forgive this. I will not accept having someone trying to control my life again. I was in Hell for *years!* Please don't do that to me again."

"I have no interest in controlling your life, Baby. There's a difference between someone trying to control you versus someone looking out for you."

"You must promise to never call him again."

He paused. Then he glared at me. "Shiree. How would you feel if you *knew* I was having sex with someone else?"

I watched his dimples move around his face. "You slept with Juanita, and I never gave you a problem. He's not *someone else*. He's…my husband, Kendall."

"*HE IS NOT YOUR FUCKING HUSBAND!!! KENDALL MONTGOMERY* is your husband! You no longer *have* two husbands, Felicia! You must accept that!"

I don't believe he'd *ever* yelled at me like that. And if I didn't know him like I did, I would've thought he was gonna knock the shit out of me. But I refused to be afraid of him. "When you slept with Juanita…"

"When I had sex with Juanita, it was out of need. That was different. If you need relief, I have plenty of what you need. Right here. I have *never* denied you!"

He grabbed his crotch. I was shocked at how demonstrative he was. "Stop that, Kendall. I don't understand why..."

"*Because he is not Juanita!* I need you to see that he will do whatever necessary to destroy us, Baby. And even if he *has* lost interest in you, he would sleep with you just to come between us. I believe you've underestimated his ruthlessness. Do not fuck that man again, Felicia!"

I put my head down and closed my eyes. "Listen to me. I *always* knew when you had sex with him. That hasn't changed. I know you've slept with him at least twice since I forbade you to do it."

I opened my mouth, but his eyes pleaded with me not to lie. "Kendall, you don't believe you're all I want?"

"Yes, but I also believe you would do whatever necessary to keep peace."

He leaned against the dresser and looked at me. "There are times when I look at you, and I pause at the depth of my love for you. I never in a million years would've believed I could love *anyone* like I love you, Shiree."

My heart melted a little more. He was so sweet. He paused again. "I kept hoping... I thought, if I loved you *sweeter* and *better*. Or bigger... I really thought that one day you would leave him. But you never did. I needed you to *show* me, that you loved me more. I needed you to...choose *me*."

He ran his fingers through his hair. I hated that he was right, but he was. But he *wasn't*. "Kendall, Sweetie..."

He stopped me. "Although I realize the kids played a major role in your decisions, I always felt he somehow trumped me."

I kept shaking my head no, and my eyes filled with tears. He crossed his arms and looked at me. "Is he still holding those children over your head? Is that why you're doing it?"

"No, Kendall. He's not doing that."

"If I learn he is, Felicia, I'll whip his ass. I'm telling you right now."

"I would've told you, Kendall. And...for years, I loved you more. So much more. Please believe that."

He moved closer to me. "I'm going to ask you a question, Shiree. And you *must* be honest with me."

We were facing each other, and I looked up at him without responding. He stared at me like our lives depended on it. "Do you prefer him? Sexually?"

I pushed him as hard as I could. "Absolutely *not*, Kendall! Why would you ask me that?"

"Because I need to know if you're having sex with him out of guilt, or because you want or prefer him. If you still want him sexually, Shiree, then we have a bigger problem. I *will not* allow that."

"No, Kendall! No, no, no!"

I kept shaking my head no. He began to pace again. "No more, Shiree. If you don't want me to hurt that man, you better stay away from him."

"Kendall. He told me the only way he would have sex with me would be if I got in his bed. I'll never do that. I've preferred you since the first day you touched me."

"Honestly, Shiree. I don't believe a word that bastard says."

I stared at him. I couldn't understand how he knew I'd slept with Harold. Looking back over the years, he knew then too.

But I dismissed it then, because he also said he assumed we had sex daily. But there were times when he *did* know. How? Simone said they could smell another man. Is that true?

He walked over to me. His cleft looked crazy again. I stood there looking up at him. "You asked me to promise I wouldn't call him again or whip his ass. I promise *none of that!!* Because you are now *my wife,* and I will not allow him or *anyone* to take advantage of you. I will *beat his ass* if he touches you again. You *and* Harold need to be clear about that. You might feel sorry for him, but I don't."

I said nothing.

He raised my chin and said quietly, "When we fell in love, two things became mine. Your heart...*and* your body. My heart and body became yours too. I understood I had to share you then, but I will *not* share you with him now. And I will no longer sit on the sidelines like some punk, Felicia. I can't do that anymore."

I was *very* clear he meant business. He'd called me Felicia several times.

I sat down and motioned for him to sit next to me. I held his hands and looked down at them. "I'm sorry, Kendall. For the pain I caused you by staying with him. I hate to admit it, but I didn't leave because I was too scared to. And he kept saying..."

I shook my head and sighed. "He kept saying he couldn't live without me. And...because of my kids. And honestly, I didn't know how to. I know it sounds ridiculous, because I left Todd without a second thought. But it's true."

I looked up at him and touched his face. "That night when Harold confronted me about us, he gave me a way out. He told me to choose. And although you weren't there to witness it, when I took those pills and sent you that text, I chose *you*. And since this happened, he's begged me to come back. I continue to choose *you*."

I began to cry, but I continued. "I hope you know now, that I can't imagine my life without you. To me, you are the sexiest, smartest and sweetest man alive. And no man could *ever* trump you. In *anything*. *Ever*."

His face softened. "And...I'm sorry for...you know. I won't do it again. I promise. Okay, Kendall?"

He raised my chin and smiled at me. "You still love me?"

"With all my heart."

He smiled again. "You still mad at me?"

"No, Kendall. Yes. I mean, I..."

"Shiree, always remember. Your heart and body belong to me. But your mind is your own. I would never try to control you, Baby. I'm possessive. I admit that. But I will not tell you what to do. Except...I don't ever want to see that ring anywhere but on your finger."

I realized once again he meant business. He looked in my eyes and embraced me. "Shiree. I'm sorry for calling him when I promised no more mania. But I'm just not comfortable with this arrangement. The time has come for you to walk away. You just said you chose *me*, so trust me and allow me to handle this."

After we had dinner, I called Harold and told him I wouldn't be coming. "No problem, Felicia. I'll get the kids settled. We can talk tomorrow."

Kendall heard our conversation and was surprised. "That was easy."

"Don't be impressed. He assumes you're listening."

While loading the dishwasher, I asked about Stew and Simone. "I think they went out to dinner. She brought Shayna over yesterday. He already adores her."

"That's great to hear. I'm happy for them."

He kissed my neck and I walked away. "When will I be off punishment?"

I rolled my eyes. "In a week."

"Shiree, I already cried all of last night. Please give me some pussy."

"You are a filthy mouthed man. Goodness, Kendall."

He laughed. "I know how to get it, Shiree."

"I could always go home, Kendall. You don't scare me."

"Sweetie. I told you earlier. You *are* home."

"Did your mother have to whip you?"

"All the time. And when I got taller than her, she slapped the shit out of me many times. I was a straight A student, but very mischievous. I was also a star basketball player, but I only played to get a scholarship for school. Once, she slapped me because I got caught with two girls on the bus after a game."

"*Two* girls, Kendall?"

I walked past him and out of the kitchen. "They each offered me their pussy, Shiree. What was I supposed to do?"

I looked over my shoulder at him and shook my head. "I know you love me, Shiree. Wanna know how I know?"

"Yes, Kendall. How do you know?"

"Because you and my mother are the only people who have ever slapped me. Remember that night we reconciled, and you slapped me?"

"Um-hmm. I remember."

"Women slap men when they love them. They hit them in other places when they hate them, or really want to hurt them."

"How do you know that, Kendall?"

"My grandfather told me. He saw my mom slap me once, and I later told him how mean she was. But he explained it to me. He said it's their hurt and love coming at you all at once. That's why I kept asking you to tell me the truth that night. I knew you loved me."

I laughed at him, and he laughed too. "Are you sure you don't have any children, Kendall?"

"Pretty sure. I began using condoms at fifteen. I never stopped until I got married. And then I had to start again."

He laughed. "And then I met you. And you've given me more pleasure than I've ever imagined. I've never wanted another woman since I met you."

I rolled my eyes at him. I admit he was all I wanted too. When I got in bed, he had a fit. I had on a nightshirt and panties. "Hell no, Shiree. Take that off, Baby."

I hollered laughing. "Go to sleep, Kendall."

He rolled on top of me. "Felicia. I'm your husband. Stop this."

I could feel his erection, and I reached between us and held it. He held my hand, wanting me to hold it tighter.

As it expanded in my hand, I became anxious for it. I rolled him off of me and I straddled him. "Not yet, Shiree. You're not ready, Baby."

"Oh, I'm Shiree again."

He rolled me over and removed my clothes. "Of course. Felicia gives me what she feels I need, but *Shiree* gives me what I want."

He kissed my thighs and wrapped my legs around his head. He proceeded to do things that made me forget to be mad at him.

He then pulled me up so I was facing him. I put my arms around his neck and kissed him. "You want me to make you feel good too?"

He whispered in my ear, "Umm-hmm."

"Are you gonna be good from now on, Kendall?"

"I'm gonna be your husband, Shiree. And I'll be good at *that*."

That I believed. As a matter of fact, I believed he would be a better husband than he was a boyfriend. Unlike Harold, who flipped in the wrong direction.

I turned and got on my knees with my back to him. He both loved and hated this position because it made him come fast. "Umm… Shiree, you're killing me."

His thickness made it difficult for me to take all of him. So, I leaned back into him and he held me close. And together, we slowly danced our way to that magical place neither of us could get enough of.

The following day I went into the office and got a tablet for my new job. Lenora needed me to bring in the laptop, and she gave me a phone.

Now I had three phones. So I forwarded all of my personal calls to my Kendall phone, which Kendall replaced for me. Of course, the first call was from Harold.

Kendall scowled. I'd sent Harold a text earlier telling him I'd keep the kids that night since I didn't go the previous night. He asked if I was busy. "Not really."

"I understand you've changed jobs. Why did you do that?"

"It's not important."

"Is he there?"

"Yes, Harold."

"Umph. Are you still coming home tonight?"

"Yes. I'll get the kids and fix dinner."

"It's already done. You just need to warm it up. I might need you tomorrow too. Will that be a problem?"

I paused. Then I decided to take Kendall's advice. "Harold. This is why they should be with me. If you need me tomorrow night, I'll bring them here."

"Not to worry. I'll work it out."

"Do you plan to ask my parents?"

"Maybe. I'll call you."

"Okay."

He hung up. Kendall asked, "What's up?"

"He asked me to stay again tomorrow night."

"You did the right thing, Shiree. I know it won't be easy, but he'll take advantage of you if you allow him to."

I rubbed his arm, because I didn't want him getting upset. "You do that when you're happy. Are you, Baby?"

I smiled and kissed him. "Yes, Kendall. I'm better. He was livid when you told him we've been together over three years. That's when I told him everything."

"Everything?"

"Yeah, almost. I told him about Jamaica and the accident. And I told him when we first started dating and how we broke up after the miscarriage."

I began to notice his sadness when the miscarriage was mentioned. So, I decided the time had come to tell him my secret. I also decided to reveal it to him as his Christmas gift. He asked, "What did he say?"

Lost in thought, I asked, "What?"

"What did Harold say when you told him the truth?"

"Not much. The look on his face said it all. He looked at me like he didn't know me. It was unnerving. I really need to sit him down and let him know my plan to move or ask him to."

Kendall walked into the kitchen and picked up an apple. I followed him. "Why are you doing that, Baby? Just move into this house."

"Kendall. I can't handle either of you telling me where to sleep or where to stay. I need to do this."

I went close to him and took a bite of his apple. He smiled at me. "Then you and the kids can stay downtown, Shiree."

I looked at him and laughed. "Why are you laughing?"

"That will never work, Kendall. It would be just like I'm living with you. Plus, he would have a fit."

"That's too bad. No matter where you and the kids are, I'll be around. And you all will be safer there. Near Stew and Simone. That's better, right?"

"I suppose. But the best possible scenario would be for Harold to move."

"The sooner, the better. And as far away as possible."

I looked at him and we both laughed.

Later that day, I called Angie at the adoption agency. She's the one I called to put me in touch with the people to have my eggs removed.

After telling her my plans, she sent me a couple of private agencies that screened surrogates and made the best possible matches. She reminded me the cost was astronomical.

The following weeks were busy. Harold and I talked, and I told him I would not stay overnight at the house unless he wasn't there, because it was causing too much grief. He told me he wasn't ready for his children to be at Kendall's house.

So we amended our arrangement. I would stay at our house only when he was away, and the kids would continue to stay with him. He seemed fine with it.

Hmmm... I had yet to see the devastation I assumed he'd have. Was something brewing? Did he have someone else? I was like Kendall. This shit was getting on my nerves.

The week of Thanksgiving was especially busy. Simone and I were ready to roll, and Kendall and Stew were also preparing to leave.

Harold was taking the kids to Detroit, and each of his sisters called me, trying to offer some solution to our separation. It bothered me that they thought Harold was so awful, when I was the awful one.

Tuesday before Thanksgiving I spent the morning at the salon. Then my three sisters and I got together at The Cheesecake Factory. It seemed like ages since we'd hung out. We went early to avoid the crowd.

Around four o'clock we were all enjoying a cocktail, when Harold and some chick walked in. I heard Carla choking, and I turned in her direction. She motioned to her right, and there they were.

We all had our mouths opened, and I begged them to act natural. We began making small talk, and I asked, "Damn, is she fat?"

Annette said, "Not really fat. She's just thick."

Simone said, "Damn, I can't see shit."

I was next to Simone, so I couldn't see well either. Carla and Annette were on the other side of the table, so they had the best view. I asked, "Did he see us?"

Carla said, "I don't think so. They're at the bar now."

"Is it safe to look?"

"Yes. They're backs are facing us."

We all turned at the same time. She was very pretty with flawless dark brown skin. She sported a short funky hairstyle and was dressed well. I was painfully jealous. I said, "I want to leave, but I know he would love that."

We turned away and Simone said, "Oh, *hell no!* What we *should* do, is go over there and make *him* uncomfortable."

We all laughed, and Annette said, "He's getting up."

He headed toward the men's room. Annette and Carla watched, while Simone and I looked at our menus. Annette said, "Okay, he's gone."

We all turned again, and Miss Thing was on her phone. Simone said, "She looks too old for him. You think she's older than him?"

I kept wondering if he'd slept with her. I asked, "Is her ass bigger than mine?"

They turned toward me and cracked up. Carla screamed laughing. She said, "Hell no! Are you crazy? Your ass is in a class all by itself!"

We all laughed again. Harold came out and looked right at us. We all went back to small talk, trying to act like we didn't see him.

He went back to the bar, and Annette said, "Damn. He saw us."

After we ordered, Annette looked up and said, "Oh, shit. Here he comes."

I said, "Please tell me she's not with him."

Carla said, "No. He's alone."

Carla looked up and smiled. She said, "Hey, Harold. What brings you here?"

He smiled. "Just having a late lunch with an associate. How is everyone?"

We all said fine, and he asked me, "Felicia, can I see you a minute?"

I cringed and asked, "Why? You don't want me to meet her, do you?"

He leaned his head back and laughed. "No, Felicia. Unless you want to."

"No. Thank you."

I got up and we went away from everyone. "I assure you. I'm not on a date."

"You don't have to explain, Harold. It's okay. Really."

"I promised I'd be discreet. I wouldn't disrespect you like that. You're still staying tonight, right?"

"Yes, Harold."

He smiled at me and kissed my cheek. "Pay for the girl's meals on me. And have a great vacation."

"Thanks, Harold."

"Is he going with you?"

"Just Simone and me. For my birthday. By the way, did you find a place yet?"

"Honestly, I haven't had time to look. What if I start looking the first of the year? Is that too late?"

"Harold. I need this now."

"Why don't you find me something?"

"We'll talk about it later. Go back to your...friend."

He smiled again. Then he came closer to me. "I miss you. I might come home later tonight."

I didn't know how to answer. He smiled and whispered, "I'll text you."

He walked away.

My sisters were all staring at me when I sat down. "He told me to pay for your meals, and he also asked me to give him some tonight."

I picked up my drink and looked the other way. Simone said, "Don't you dare! You are *not* fucking up our getaway."

Carla said, "Shit, Licia. Give it to him. It keeps the peace."

Annette said, "Hell no, no Licia. He'll throw it back in Kendall's face."

Carla said, "Miss Thing is looking over here. Do *not* turn around, Felicia. She's really pretty."

I said, "He claims he's not dating her, and that he wouldn't disrespect me like that."

Annette said, "That's bullshit. He didn't expect you to be here."

Carla said, "Maybe he did. Earl talked to him today. I bet he mentioned it."

I asked, "You think?"

Simone said, "Yeah. I believe it. He figured if he grabbed some chick and brought her in your face, you'd be jealous and fuck him."

Annette said, "They're getting up."

We'd already ordered, so I couldn't hide behind a menu. He stopped at our table and said, "Michelle, this is my wife Felicia and her sisters."

We all said hello, and she said, "Felicia Benson. I've heard so much about you. I'm at the Houston office. You work with Lenora, right?"

"Yes."

"You all have quite the reputation. Great work. Keep it up."

I smiled and said, "Thanks, Michelle. Enjoy your meal."

She smiled and they left. Simone said, "Let him fuck *her*. She's *gorgeous!*"

I looked at Simone cross eyed. "Sorry, Felice. But if Kendall finds out, he'll kill us all and you know it."

"Simone. I have to go there anyhow. If I decide to, you know, Kendall won't know the difference. Besides, I agreed to give Harold sex…sometimes."

"You're insane if you think Kendall won't know the difference. Not to mention he told you he'd whip Harold's ass, Felicia."

I thought about that and finished my drink.

Earlier, while under the dryer at the salon, I reflected on a few things.

I enjoyed spending more time with all four of my kids. My older sons were doing very well, and Todd agreed they could spend one day a week with Harold. It warmed my heart that Harold loved them like that.

And I admit, I was taken aback by Harold's reaction to all of this. I was certain for years this would kill him. Was that arrogance on my part? Or was he playing me, like Stew said?

There had to be something I'd missed. It was almost as if he'd finally relaxed now that it was out in the open, and he was right to worry about his wife.

Out in the open? Hmmm?

I never looked at our finances. Harold paid the bills and handled our money. Our paychecks went into a joint account, and he worked everything out.

I never moved my money like he suggested. I just continued doing my thing like before. Harold never said anymore about it, but he did transfer over seven million dollars into a new account for me. I never mentioned that either.

Kendall asked me about my bills and expenses. I told him I didn't have any. He no longer wanted Harold *taking care of me*. He gave me access to all of his money again. I put the checkbook and cards away, and I told him we'd deal with that later too.

Harold seemed too calm. Other than that one moment of anger, he appeared ready to move on with his life. I suddenly wondered, "How long has he *really* known?"

He admitted to knowing for a month in November. Which meant he knew during those anniversary and alarm company charades.

Who does that?

I learned early on something else about Harold. He hated to lose. At anything. I never liked it when he said he didn't want to *lose* me to Sam. It made me feel like he was competing for me. Which Kendall also said.

Both times, he told his family that he'd cheated, making me think he was protecting me from shame. Now I wonder if he was actually protecting *himself* from shame.

Consider this Felicia, I said to myself. Because of his status, looks and wealth, he would be mortified if the world learned another man took his wife from him. Right? And to cover his own ass, he needed them (especially his family) to think he was still that infamous playboy.

Because realistically, if *anyone* was cheating, it certainly wouldn't be me. Because no one would even *consider* cheating on Mr. Harold Benson II. I'm supposed to deem myself lucky to even be with someone like him. Right? Hmmm?

So, if he knew about Kendall before now, why expose it now?

Because Curtis also knew.

He had to pretend to be upset, and he had to expose his knowledge of it. Right? Because Curtis had a big mouth and would certainly tell it. Which he proved by telling Earl and Tony.

That would explain why Harold was adamant about not telling his family the truth. And why he was so nice to me, and gave me so much money. And why he wasn't devastated. It all made sense. I think. I planned to find out.

Chapter Six

That evening, the kids and I finished packing their things. They were excited about getting on the plane. Harold was also packing and talking on his phone.

Kendall continued to text me, and I told him all was well. Harold wasn't supposed to be there, and I struggled over telling Kendall the truth. I decided not to. I promised to call him when I got in bed for phone sex.

At eight-thirty, I put the kids down and Harold was in his office. I went into my closet. Everything was as I'd left it, except the armoire was slightly ajar.

I opened it and saw a new pearl necklace. I looked behind me, and Harold was there. "I bought it for your birthday. I didn't really know where to put it, so I put it there."

"That was very kind, Harold. Thank you."

"And thank you for my card. I appreciate that you didn't forget."

I smiled and went into the bathroom. He followed me. "You do believe that Michelle and I are just friends, don't you?"

"That's not my business, Harold."

He came closer. "I think it's only right that you know something. I *am* seeing someone. Her name is Nikki."

"Harold, I really don't need to know anymore. We agreed to be discreet, so...I'm good with that."

Again, he came closer. "Did I upset you?"

I walked into the bedroom and wanted nothing more than to change the subject. "I'd rather not know. If we..."

He came up behind me and embraced me. He whispered, "But she does nothing for me. Not like you."

I could feel his hardness behind me, and he kissed my neck. His hands were under my breasts and I allowed myself to enjoy him.

He picked me up and placed me on the bed. He laid beside me, and he began kissing me and removing my clothes. He went to my breast, and I unzipped his pants.

I got up and freed him from his clothes. He came up to face me. "I'll always love you, Licia. Even if I have to share you."

He kissed me again, and then kissed me all the way to my legs. He kissed me there, and then he opened my legs. He buried his tongue in me, and he wouldn't stop until I gave him what he wanted.

He got a condom and crawled up to face me again. He watched me as he entered me. "I always loved watching your face during sex."

I moaned and closed my eyes. For some reason, he was incredible again. I came quickly and he turned me over. I had two more orgasms before he had his.

After a while, I moved to get up. "He's not gonna know, Felicia. Stay here."

"I need to prepare for tomorrow, Harold."

I got up and walked toward the doorway. "Tell him I said hi."

I kept walking, but I stopped at the stairs. I went back in and I looked at him. "Have you always thought of me as dumb, Harold? Or is it just recently? Because I believed we just enjoyed a moment of love making."

"You're clearly not dumb, Felicia. You played me...like a fiddle?"

"I didn't play you, Harold. If anything, you played me. All of those promises. You never had any intention of letting me forget about Sam. Do you hate *me* or *yourself* for driving me to do what I did?"

"What I *hate* is what your precious doctor did. If he was a stranger, I might feel differently. He saw your beauty and your innocence, and he took it. And by the way, only a *snake* would fuck a man's wife and smile in his face."

He sat up. "And I *hate*...I hate that you chose him over me. I admit I wasn't perfect. I cheated too. Actually, more than I admitted."

I sat down on the bed. "What are you saying, Harold?"

"I've been unfaithful our entire marriage. And while you were pregnant. But none of them, not even one...made me feel like you do."

"Is that why you hate me? Because you can't get past *that*? *Sex?*"

He laughed. "I do not *hate you*, Felicia. I hate that he's now the recipient of everything I taught you. I'll never find that again."

"Because we had love, Harold. Don't you think that makes a difference?"

"*You* had love. *I* still have it."

"You competed for me then, and you're competing for me now. Stop saying you love me. You don't know the meaning of the word."

"Did you ever love *me*, Felicia?"

I sighed. I didn't want to fight any more. "I feel terrible about all of this, Harold. I always loved you. If I didn't, I wouldn't have stayed. And I would *not* have gotten in this bed with you."

"But you love him more. That's why you're *leaving* my bed. But I believe he can't compete with me sexually. That's why you never left me. Right?"

"I'm not going there with you, Harold. I admit I love him. Because his love is easy. He's *easier*. He became my soft place to land in an unbearable existence with you. Your love was hard. Soften it for Nikki or whoever. If I hadn't felt so sad and imprisoned, I would never have done it. I ran from him for so long. And more than anything, I wanted *you* to be what I needed."

He put his head down. We were both at a loss for words. He finally said, "I *am sorry* for making your life so difficult. I wish now I'd done things differently. I had no idea...never mind."

"What, Harold?"

"I thought if I made life *too* easy, you'd change. But I was wrong. You *deserved* to be pampered."

"I never wanted pampering, Harold. I wanted to be treated with dignity and respect. I just wanted to be loved."

With tears on my face, I stood up. He did too. "Can we be friends, Felicia?"

"Of course. But I'm not gonna sleep with you anymore."

He kissed my cheek and I went downstairs.

It was after ten o'clock, and I knew I was in for a fight. I checked my phone and no calls or texts from him. But two from Simone. I called her first. "Yes. I'm all packed and I have Shayna's stuff ready too."

"He's there?"

"Yes, Veronica. I told you she needs a larger size now. I'll get you some money, so if you see something larger, you can get it for her. Hold on a minute."

I heard her talking to them. She apparently went in the kitchen and whispered, "He's pissed! Fit to be tied! Call him! He's talking about coming over there!"

She began talking to them again. When she came back, she said, "Now!"

She hung up.

I waited five minutes before calling him. As soon as he answered, I pretended Benny was in the bed with me. "Benny, it's okay. Lay down with Mommy. Kendall, I'm sorry. Benny has been out of sorts all evening. I have him with me. You okay?"

"Let me call you back."

I waited and chewed my nails. I looked at them and got mad because I'd just gotten a manicure. I went in the kitchen and poured a glass of wine. He finally called back. "Are you in your car?"

"Yes. I was at Stew's, but now I'm on my way to Gates."

"I can't wait to tell you what I learned tonight. I…"

"He called me, Shiree. I heard you fucking him."

"What?"

"You fucking heard me! I heard it all."

He hung up.

I looked at the phone. I closed my eyes and wanted to go up and kill that bastard. But, my first priority was to fix this with Kendall. He said he was on his way to Gates. Oh shit! He's on his way here!!

I showered quickly and dressed. I went out onto the front porch. He wouldn't answer my calls. It was close to eleven o'clock, so the neighborhood was quiet.

I heard a car after about five minutes. I prayed it wasn't him. It was slowing down. It was a black Lexus, and it pulled up in front of my house.

I ran off the porch. He turned off the ignition and got out. "Where is he, Shiree?"

"He's asleep. Let's go home, Kendall."

He glared at me and reached for the back of my neck. At first, he scared the shit out of me. He brought me close to him and looked in my eyes. "Oh, we're going home, Wife. Right after I whip that motherfucker's ass!"

"Be quiet, Baby. Somebody might call the police."

Another car came down the street. Kendall turned and I did too. It was Stew. I felt like my prayers had been answered. Until he got out. I ran over to him, but he totally ignored me. He turned to Kendall. "Where is he?"

"In the house. Go on home, Stew. I got this."

Stew laughed. "I know that. Come on. Let's go in."

I panicked and grabbed Stew. I whispered, "*NO, STEW!* Please, Brother. Please don't do this."

It was my dream, but to the tenth power! The front door opened and Harold was standing there. Stew said, "Come on out, Benson. We have something for you."

I prayed Harold wasn't stupid enough to come out. I looked over at Kendall, and he had that look on his face. The one that was foreign to me.

Kendall walked toward the porch and I turned to follow him. Stewart picked me up and carried me toward his car. I fought him at first, but of course, I was wasting my time. Stewart sat me in his car and stood in front of the door.

Kendall started up the stairs and said to Harold, "That little stunt you pulled meant nothing to me because you can't begin to compare to me. And after I whip your ass, I'mma prove to you how deep I can go."

Before Kendall reached the top step, Harold smiled and closed the door.

I wanted to go to my parent's house, but I knew Kendall wouldn't allow it. My heart was beating faster than ever. I didn't know what he was gonna do or say to me. Stew walked over and spoke with Kendall. I just sat there.

Eventually, Kendall came over and told me to get out. I shook my head no. "Shiree, get your ass out of that car! We're going home."

I looked straight ahead. Kendall laughed at me. "Baby, you can't possibly think I would hurt you. I'm mad, hell yeah! But I know you're not scared of me. Get out of the damn car."

I decided he was right. If ever there was a time for him to beat me up, this would be it. This was my chance to know for sure. So, I got out and got in his car.

The guys talked for a few minutes, then Stew left, and Kendall got in the car. He raised my chin and kissed my forehead, and we rode to his house in silence.

When we got there, he filled the tub with Falling in Love and warm water. He got in and he motioned for me to join him. I was shaking like a leaf.

While cleaning me, he asked, "Do you believe me now, Shiree?"

I nodded. "Do you now see the difference between him and Juanita?"

I nodded again. Tears were streaming down my face. "Kendall..."

He rose out of the water and turned on the shower. He reached for my hand and we stepped inside. He kissed my forehead again. While wiping away my tears, he said, "Honestly, Shiree. I expected it to come to this. Although he didn't deserve it, you've always been loyal to him. That was his only means of retaliation."

"Kendall, I..."

"Don't, Shiree. I don't want to hear why you did it. Let's just..."

"I promise you I'll never *ever* do it again."

"I know."

We rinsed off and he gave me my toothbrush. Now I knew why he only kissed me on my forehead. I was embarrassed, and he knew it.

We brushed our teeth, and he went into the bedroom. He checked his phone and I came in and prepared for bed. I felt tainted. "You want me to sleep in the guestroom?"

"My wife will never sleep in the guestroom. I admit I'm mad. But not at you. Come here, Baby."

He sat on the bed, and I walked over to him. He kissed my stomach and squeezed my behind. I closed my eyes, and silently vowed to never betray him again.

The following morning after using the bathroom, I sat on the bed and watched him sleep. I became misty eyed and I began to cry. He woke up. "What's wrong, Baby?"

It was only six o'clock and he got up and embraced me. "He told me he's cheated our entire marriage. Did you hear him tell me that?"

"No. He hung up after telling you to tell me hi. What else did he say."

"He told me my actions were nothing compared to how he cheated during my pregnancy and throughout our marriage."

"Do you believe him?"

"What? Why would he lie?"

"Many reasons. So you don't show him up, for one. Or, to make you think that many other women want him. To make you jealous. Are you jealous?"

"Absolutely not, Kendall. But you know what? I've been wondering why he's so calm. I think there's something going on I'm not aware of."

"Of course there's more. But I also think he wants you to believe he cheated better than you."

"That's sick, Kendall. Something is seriously wrong with him."

After feeding Kendall, I drove to my house. I drove my Lexus because I refused to allow Kendall to drive me and be that close to Harold. On the drive over, I thought more about what Kendall said.

It all made sense. I was sure that Harold, like me, had done a lot of lying. Now it was my turn to learn exactly what *he* was hiding.

I planned to play spy once Harold and the kids left, but they didn't appear to be leaving anytime soon. I walked in around eight-fifteen, and Harold was cooking breakfast. "Good morning, Licia."

I glared at him like Kendall does. "What time is your flight, Harold?"

He smiled. "One o'clock. We're leaving about eleven. Why?"

I didn't answer him. I walked into the guestroom, and he came in behind me. "Get out, Harold."

"Don't be mad. I want a little more. Don't you?"

"I told you we're done with that. And after what you did last night..."

He smiled and left the room. I removed my clothes and put my robe on. He walked back in eating a strip of bacon. "You hungry?"

I ignored him again. He laughed and gave me his bacon. "It always tickled me how little you eat. Yesterday, Michelle ate as much as I did. That tickled me too."

"Did you fuck her too?"

Smiling, he ignored my question and reached for my robe. "Get your paws off of me! It's interesting to me that all of a sudden you want me, Harold. You've barely touched me over the last twelve months, and now you're all over me. And didn't you say you wouldn't come to me for sex anymore?"

"I changed my mind, considering you came to me last night. Right, Licia?"

He went to his knees and I backed up. "No, Harold! And don't call me that."

I tried to walk away, but he held me. "Is he the reason you began shaving?"

He forced me on the bed. "Are you really going to *take it*? That would be the final nail in your coffin, because believe me, Kendall was planning to kill you last night."

He laughed again. "I know you want it. Besides, you're still my wife, Shiree."

I sat up. "What the hell did you call me?"

"Isn't that your middle name?"

I got up. "Why did you call me that, Harold!?"

"Is he the only one allowed to call you that? Does it turn *you* on or him? I would've called you Shiree if that's what you wanted."

"I've tried really hard to work with you through this, Harold. But you just won't stop. How do you know that?"

"The PI told me. Your phone was tapped."

I paused. "You dirty..."

He laughed. "I think *dirty* describes you more you than me. *Shiree*."

I walked around him and went up the stairs. I was convinced something here was not what it seemed. I hadn't talked to Kendall on that phone in months.

I came back down about nine-thirty. The kids and I were dressed and ready for breakfast. "I told you I hired him, Felicia. Why are you so upset?"

"Until you've been violated like you've violated me over the years...

I shook my head, reflecting over the last four years. "I knew I should've gotten our marriage annulled."

He stared at me and I stared at him. I think I actually hurt his feelings. But like Kendall said, he was gonna stop fucking with me.

I wasn't surprised he called me dirty, but I couldn't *believe* he called me Shiree. That really jacked me up. Once they left for the airport, I got myself together and went to the house in Gates.

I still felt some kind a way about the previous night. I walked in the bedroom and he was on the phone. I heard him say, "She just walked in. She's doing good."

When I got closer, he smiled at me. "Hey, Baby. Come here."

I sat on his lap and he kissed me. "Who are you talking to?"

"My mom. Say hi to her."

I'd talked to her before, and he knew it tore my nerves up. I made a face, but he gave me his phone anyhow. "Hello, Mrs. Montgomery. How are you?"

"I'm fine, Felicia. How are you?"

"I'm fine, thank you. I'm sure you're all looking forward to this weekend. He hasn't stopped talking about seeing you all."

She laughed. "Actually, he never stops talking about *you*. We're looking forward to meeting you. Soon I hope."

"Yes, Ma'am. I hope so too. Have a wonderful Thanksgiving."

"You too, Dear."

"Thank you. Here's Kendall."

When he hung up, I punched him. "Why do you do that?"

"She loves talking to you. And she's really anxious to meet you."

"I'm too embarrassed, Kendall. I can only imagine what she must think of me. That won't happen any time soon."

He kissed me. "My mom is not like that, Shiree."

I sighed and sat on the bed. "I cried when my babies left. And I continue to fear that Harold will take my kids somewhere and I'll never see them again."

"Did he say anything about last night?"

"Nothing. He thought it was funny."

He came over and sat next to me. "I'm leaving around one-thirty. I want you to have a good time and stop worrying. Okay, Baby? You good?"

"I'm good."

He went in his shirt pocket and removed an envelope. He motioned for me to take it, but I was hesitant. "There's a thousand dollars in cash and a fifteen-hundred dollar prepaid Visa card."

"Kendall, that's too much. It's just a weekend."

"But it's a weekend in *Miami,* Baby. Don't argue with me on this. Stew gave Simone the same amount. I want you to shop and do everything you want to do. And promise me you'll stop worrying. Okay? Do you need anything else?"

"No, Kendall. You've given me everything I'll need. Thank you, Baby."

He raised my chin. "Not everything."

I smiled. "But there's so much to do."

"I'm done. I just have to get my toiletries."

I went into the bathroom to get his things. He came in and stopped me. "What are you doing?"

"I'm helping you, Baby."

He embraced my hand and put it on his crotch. "This is what I need help with."

I kissed him and walked out of the bathroom. He followed me. I turned and walked right into him. "Kendall. You won't believe what that bastard did."

His dimples enlarged. "What?"

"He called me Shiree. He called me *Shiree,* Kendall! I was devastated."

He chuckled and sat down. A weird, sinister kind of chuckle. Maybe I shouldn't have told him. I wasn't thinking. "Just ignore him, Shiree. I got this."

I sat on his lap. I kissed his forehead and asked softly, "What would it take for you to also ignore him?"

He glared at me. "What are you afraid of, Shiree?"

"I don't want you to get in trouble. Please don't pursue beating him up."

He glared at me again. "How did he know I call you Shiree?"

"He claims my phone was tapped. By the PI. I was so upset."

He began to undress me. "When did he say it?"

"During breakfast. I tried not to show how upset I was. But I'm sure he knew."

Once we were both undressed, I straddled him. He snuggled up to my neck. "I don't smell Philosophy."

"I didn't have time this morning. Wait one minute."

I went into the bathroom and sprayed a tiny bit of Falling in Love perfume on my wrist. I tapped it all over. Then I went back and sat on him, and he was happy.

After we made love, he was dealing with a patient and I was packing his toiletries. I heard him say, "Ms. Thomas, I've faxed the script to the pharmacy. Please make an appointment for her early next week. You're welcome, and please enjoy your holiday. Thank you, but I already have plans."

When he hung up, he shook his head. "She's actually hitting on me. I hoped I was imagining it. Damn."

"Really? What did she say?"

"She invited me over for Thanksgiving dinner. And it's not the first invitation I've gotten from her."

"You want me to talk to her?"

"No, Baby. You'll call her a hound and she'll sue my ass."

I laughed. "Just tell her you're engaged. Maybe then she'll stop."

"She thinks I'm still married, and *that* hasn't stopped her."

"Is she Black?"

"No. Why?"

"Have you slept with White women?"

"Yes, as well as other races. Why, Baby?"

I didn't answer. "Like most men, I wanted to experience other races. But none of them compared to the women who look and love like you. Does it bother you?"

"No. I was just curious, Kendall. I assumed you had."

I smirked at him. He looked at me lovingly. "Shiree. I'm gonna miss you, Baby. I wish you were coming with me."

"Maybe next time. Thanks for giving me such a sweet send off."

He came over and embraced me. "Did I give you enough?"

I rubbed his crotch. "For the record, I never get enough of you."

I showed him my tongue and he laughed. "I'll change my flight if you don't stop teasing me. I love you, Baby."

"I love you more."

"Really? You think?"

"Umm-hmm. I *do* think."

After Thanksgiving dinner with my parents, I took the boys to Annette's, where the entire Wilson family gathered for the holiday. Simone met me there.

I hadn't seen many of them since that infamous cook out, when Gina wore the bikini. Carla pulled me into the den. "You look great, Girl! Are you okay?"

"I don't know yet. It's really hard dealing with Harold and his bullshit. Or Kendall wanting to beat Harold up, *because* of his bullshit."

I'd already told them what happened. The others came in and asked the same question. "I'm fine. I forgot to tell you guys that Harold called me Shiree."

Annette said, "You're kidding. No that fool didn't."

"He admitted my phone was tapped. Luckily, most of my calls were on my Kendall phone. And I only use that now. What a bastard."

We all laughed, and Carla hit Simone on the behind. "Girl, your ass needs a *wide load* sign on it. What the hell?!"

"I know, right! Me and Stew have both gained weight. We've agreed to start a serious weight loss and exercise program after the holidays."

Earlier, I talked Simone into staying at my house. I used the excuse that it's only ten minutes from the airport, but I really wanted to snoop and see if my suspicions were right.

After getting settled at my house, we went into the office and I found the file for the PI. I sat down and looked through it. I screamed, "Simone! Look at this!"

The file showed he'd been paying him for twenty-two months. Consistently. Almost two years!

I looked further and saw pictures of me driving into the garage on East Ave. A year ago. There was a picture of Kendall and me near the ladies' room talking at the Black and White Ball. Over eighteen months ago.

Also, one of Simone, Stew, Kendall and me at the club. And many more.

Simone and I looked at each other shocked.

I looked back in the file drawer and saw two more files. One had the tapes of our conversations. The other one was full of pictures. It was unbelievable!

I saw where Harold paid them recently. They were still watching me. Simone said, "You need to shred all of it."

"I will. Although I'm sure the PI has copies. But I'll shred these after I make my own copies. And I'll leave it here so he can see that I know.

While I went through his credit card files, Simone started making copies. He claimed to only use credit cards for emergencies, but I saw tons of hotel charges. Locally and out of town. Simone said, "That's why he suggested an open marriage, Felice. He's screwing all over the country. All of those supposed business trips."

I thought about his recent trip. I was convinced then it was a lie, and now I had evidence of his whoring. I knew he was with some chick. "He claims none of them can compare to me."

Simone laughed. "Felice, he's full of shit! Nobody has coochie that good. He just wanted to get back at Kendall. I wouldn't be surprised if he taped the two of you having sex. *Do not trust him!*"

My skin began to crawl as her words created a visual of what Harold *really* was. He was a low-down snake, far worse than the snake he accused Kendall of being. She scared the shit out of me and I stood up. "Let's go upstairs."

We went up to the master bedroom and I told her about the security system I had in my apartment. She and I scoured the bedroom.

We found nothing. I thought out loud. "It wouldn't be obvious. It would be somewhere...inconspicuous. Like a..."

I looked up and saw the framed print over the dresser. It faced the bed. My blood began to run cold in my veins, because the creepiest feeling came over me.

Something told me the real man I'd married was hidden there. I looked behind it and gasped. There was indeed a tiny cord coming out of the wall and into the print.

I went into his closet, which was on the other side of the wall. I moved his suits and saw it. It was a camcorder.

I reached up to get it, and Simone came in behind me. She inhaled and held her chest. "That dirty Son of a Bitch!"

I started shaking and couldn't reach it. Simone took it out, and I looked at it. "Dear God, Simone. What if he recorded last night? And if so, where's the tape?"

"Maybe it's still inside."

I looked inside and there was a tape in there. We looked at each other and I asked, "You think there's more?"

"I'm sure he's taped other times, Felice."

We went through his closet and eventually, not far from the system, was a drawer he had created in the wall itself. Inside were eight tapes.

I was embarrassed to let Simone watch me with my husband, so I asked her to step out. I watched bits of each one. Most were of me alone or the empty bed.

Which meant he knew when I wasn't home. Something was very wrong with him. There were only two recordings of us having sex. The one in the recorder from the previous night, and one from seven months prior. They were all dated.

I destroyed all of them, and I smashed the camcorder. My concern was there might be more. I did another check of the bedroom, and then the guest room where I'd been sleeping.

Then I put it all in a box. We agreed to dump it all on the way to the airport the next morning. Our flight was at seven a.m.

I was in tears and Simone was pissed. "Whatever you do, do not let on that you know anything. Remember, he has your babies."

I was still crying. "Why does this keep happening to me?"

She walked behind me and rubbed my shoulders. "Very few people can appreciate your kindness, Felice. Most men see you as an easy piece. That's why we were so upset when you were seeing those guys."

I looked up at her. "What does that mean, Simone?"

"It *means* we were afraid you were setting yourself up to be used. There's an art to hoeing, and you gotta know what you're doing. You're not that girl, Felice. Everyone's not built for it."

That was funny to me. Annette told me that during my Sam days. "What about Kendall? Is he playing me too?"

She laughed and sat down. "That fool would drink your dirty bath water."

I remembered Mom saying that about Harold. "Simone. Remember we thought the guys were up to something this weekend?"

"Umm-hmm. Why? You still think it?"

"I know Kendall's in North Carolina. I spoke to his mom today."

"And I'm sure Stew went home too. Why? What are you thinking?"

When the plane landed the following day, I was nervous but excited. I'd never been to North Carolina. I prayed I wouldn't be devastated by him not being there. Or worse.

Simone went to Pittsburgh and we both agreed that if it was a bust for either of us, we would meet in Miami or come back home.

I took a taxi to the address. The house was large, but simple and nice. The landscape was breathtaking. Kendall told me it was mostly green year-round there, and that his mom spent a lot of time making her yard beautiful. It showed.

I paid the driver, but asked him to please wait. I got out, turned toward the house and I looked ahead of me. It felt as though I was about to walk the plank.

My nerves were frazzled, but I walked the long walkway and I went up the few stairs. The scent of the flowers was wonderful, and they had a calming effect on me. I was admiring the wraparound porch when the door opened.

A man came out who looked a lot like Kendall, but without Locs. I cleared my throat. "Hi. Is this the Montgomery residence?"

He smiled and crossed his arms. "Maybe. Who wants to know?"

I smiled because he glared like Kendall. And I could tell he was just as charming. "I'm Felicia. I'm Kendall's...I'm a friend of Kendall's."

He smiled again. "If you're Felicia, you're more than a friend. It's nice to finally meet you. I'm Keenan, his brother."

We shook hands and he saw the cab. "Stay here. I'll take care of it."

"I left my luggage in case I had the wrong address."

He waved his hand and assured me he would get my stuff. He removed my luggage and gave the driver a tip. When he returned, he set the luggage down and reached for the door. "How was your flight?"

"It was very nice. Thank you, Keenan."

"You're welcome. He didn't mention you were coming. Is he expecting you?"

It occurred to me I might've made a mistake. "No. I'm kinda surprising him."

He laughed. "This is hilarious. He said he couldn't get you to come. I can't wait to see the look on his face."

"Is he here?"

"Yes. He's out back with Dad. Come on in the house."

The inside reminded me so much of my parents' home. He put my luggage down and we went into the kitchen. It smelled like my mother's homemade biscuits and bacon. Keenan got his sister's attention quietly. "Kelly."

She turned around and looked at me. She smiled politely and said hi. Her complexion was lighter than her brothers, but they all shared the same dimples.

She was as pretty as Kendall described her. Before I could respond to her greeting, Keenan said, "This is Felicia."

She got up. "My God. Are you *Kendall's* Felicia?"

I smiled and nodded. "Girl, I'm so glad to finally meet you!"

She came over and hugged me. "I'm happy to meet you too, Kelly."

Keenan said, "He doesn't know she's here. She's surprising him."

Kelly smiled the most brilliant smile. She took my arm and led me into the dining room. When I saw her, I realized this was scarier than surprising Kendall.

I could see her beauty from across the room. She was honey colored, with salt and pepper hair. Kelly said, "Mom."

She turned around and looked at me. Kelly looked a lot like her. At first, she just stared. Then she put her hand up to her chest and said, "Lord! Felicia Shiree."

She stood up. Kelly asked, "Mom, how did you know?"

"That brother of yours sends me pictures of her. Come here, Felicia."

I was shaking in my boots. She reached for my hands and looked at me. Then she embraced me and I hugged her back. "My Goodness! Pictures don't do you justice. You're so pretty! I didn't think I'd ever meet you."

Keenan said, "Um-hmm. She sure is. You better be glad you identified yourself."

I hit Keenan as if I'd known him forever. We all laughed. "Thank you, Mrs. Montgomery. I'm so happy to finally meet you all."

Keenan said, "He's coming in. Stand over here so he doesn't see you, Felicia."

Kendall walked in through the back door and his dad was behind him. They were in the kitchen and his nephew came running down the stairs.

He almost fell over my luggage. Kendall yelled, "Terrell, watch out! Who left this…"

He walked toward my bags and paused. Then he looked out the front door. He came toward the dining room and asked, "Mom, whose luggage is that?"

"Come here, Kendall."

He came in and said, "If I didn't know better, I would think that was…"

He turned and saw me. He closed his eyes and put his head down. We both laughed, and he came over and embraced me. *"My God, Shiree. I smelled your scent and thought I was losing it."*

He held me a long time. Then he picked me up and carried me outside. "Kendall, put me down!"

Everyone laughed and followed us. He put me down and kissed me. He held my face in his hands and looked at me. "I'm so glad to see you, Baby."

"Me too, Kendall. Don't I always give you what you ask for?"

He glared at me and kissed me again. "Um-hmm. You're naughty, Shiree. You've ruined our plans."

"What plans?"

He laughed. "Stew and I were going to Miami on Monday. We have plans to go to Jamaica. But we were not going to interfere with your spa weekend."

He and I both laughed. Then, the second sexiest baritone voice I'd ever heard asked, "So, you're Felicia?"

I turned around and smiled. Kendall and Keenan got their height and brown complexion from him. He was very handsome, and well-groomed for a man his age.

I extended my hand and said, "Hello, Mr. Montgomery. It's a pleasure to finally meet you."

He held on to my hand. "I secretly believed you were a figment of my son's imagination. Or that he was exaggerating. But you really are *quite* beautiful."

I was speechless. But I regained my composure and thanked him. He hugged me, then held me at arm's length. "This one's a keeper, Son. How tall are you?"

I opened my mouth to answer him, but Kendall said, "Tall enough, Dad. Don't embarrass my fiancée. She just got here."

We all laughed, and I remembered Kendall telling me his dad was hilarious. Kendall then turned to me and said, "Shiree. Don't pay any attention to him."

His sister grabbed my hand and brought me back into the house. "It's Black Friday, Felicia. Let's go shopping and get to know each other."

Kendall followed us and began shaking his head. "No, Kelly. She came to see *me*. She doesn't even like to shop. Especially *today*."

I turned to him. "We won't be long, Kendall. I would love to go with Kelly."

He began his pout and stare, and I kissed his lip. "Stop it, Kendall."

"No, Shiree. Go shopping tomorrow."

Kelly asked, "Why does he call you Shiree? Mom said it too."

I looked at him and smiled. "He prefers it because it reminds him of when we fell in love. It's my middle name."

"He's such a romantic. He's always been, Felicia. Making those poor girls fall in love with him, when all he wanted was sex."

Kendall glared at his sister. "Really, Kelly?"

We all laughed, and I turned to Kelly. "I need five minutes to talk to him."

"Okay. I'll freshen up and be right back."

Kendall and I went out on the wraparound porch. The weather was beautiful. We sat on a loveseat and he pulled me in his arms. He kissed me for a long time.

His mom came out and smiled. "Son, she's just as lovely as you said."

I said, "Thank you, Mrs. Montgomery."

She smiled and went into the yard. I looked in his face and played in his hair. "You look beautiful, Shiree. Thank you for surprising me."

I smiled. "I realize I put you in a bad position. I plan to stay in a hotel."

He laughed. "No, you're not. They're not like that, Shiree. We're engaged."

"I will not disrespect your parents, Kendall. You were so disappointed that I wasn't coming, and it seemed so important to you that I meet your family. Even though I was nervous, I'm glad I came. But…"

"Shiree, they love you. Already. And…"

"Please find me a hotel. There's no way I'll do that, Kendall."

"You're not going *anywhere,* Shiree. If you do that, Mom will…"

His parents came around the corner. His mom said, "Felicia. I expect you to stay *here. With us.*"

His dad said, "If you don't want to upset her, you better do what she says. We know what you all do. Just don't let me hear it."

His mom hit his dad, and she said, "He's terrible, Felicia. Don't even think about staying in a hotel. I'm sorry, but I overheard you. We want you here with us."

I felt uneasy about it. Kendall nudged me and I looked back at her. "Thank you both. I appreciate it."

They left, and Kendall asked, "You okay now?"

"It doesn't seem right, but I guess so."

He turned my head and pointed at the house next door. He whispered, "The house is almost done. What do you think?"

It was a beautiful brick house. It was newly landscaped, and new trees lined the newly paved long winding driveway. "What I can see is beautiful, Kendall. When can I see the rest of it?"

"Soon. I think they're going out this evening. I'll take you then."

"Okay. I'm so excited!"

"I'm so happy you're here. Where's Simone?"

I put my hand over my mouth. "Oh, Lord! She surprised Stew in Pittsburgh. I forgot to call her."

He went inside and got my purse. "I've told you to keep your phone on you. In your pocket, Baby."

I quickly called her. "You okay, Felice?"

"Yes. You?"

"Yes. He almost fell off the chair when I walked in. He's very happy."

"Same here. Did he tell you about Jamaica?"

"Yes! Are we going?"

"Let's make it happen."

"Okay. Let's talk tomorrow."

When I hung up, I turned to Kendall. "We cancelled the spa and were able to get you and Stew eighty percent back. Sorry about the loss."

"Don't worry about it. You can go another time."

"Simone and I are going to rearrange our schedules for Jamaica."

"Actually, I already told your parents. Your mom called your supervisor and she got you out of work next week. Stew did the same for Simone."

I kissed him and smiled. "I love you, Baby."

He whispered, "That's the one that warms my heart, Shiree. I love you too."

Kelly came out and grabbed my hand. "Enough of that. Let's do this."

He whispered again, "I put my card in your purse. I want you and Kelly to get whatever you want. Enjoy yourselves. Okay, Baby?"

"Thank you, Sweetie. By the way, I left the money and card you gave me at home. So, I'll need that card."

He laughed. I removed my heels, put on some flats and we did the damn thing.

I brought home six bags. Kendall was shocked. "I can't believe what I'm seeing. You *never* shop like that."

"Everything was on sale, Baby."

He shook his head and laughed. We went upstairs, and he showed me his room. "I brought your luggage up while you were gone. I unpacked for you."

"Thank you, Baby."

I looked at him with my head tilted. "Is something wrong? Did you have plans with an old girlfriend?"

"It's time for us to get married, Shiree."

I ignored him and went to the closet. I put the dress I bought on a hanger, and the shoes on the floor. I bought him a couple pair of boxers and a pair of pajamas. "You need to wear these while we're here. And I'd like to go down and help with dinner. Come with me, Kenny."

He came over to me and smiled. I looked up at him and smiled back. "Why did your dad ask about my height?"

He laughed. "Dad told Keenan and me to marry a medium height, big butt woman, because they're better lovers and give birth easier."

I hollered laughing.

He began to massage my shoulders, and he was suddenly very serious. "No more ignoring me or changing the subject when I bring up marriage. I mean it, Felicia Shiree."

"I know, Kendall. But I can't right now. However, I *do* have plans for us. Be patient for a while longer. Okay?"

He leaned his head and stared at me. "What plans?"

"I don't have all of the pieces put together yet, but soon. Okay?"

He slanted his eyes and looked unsure, but...curious. I laughed and said what I knew he enjoyed hearing. "But in the meantime, can I still be your wife?"

"Of course."

He leaned down and kissed me. Then he closed and locked the door. The look on his face was very familiar. "None of that, Doctor."

He leaned me against the wall and pulled up my skirt. He began to pull down my panties, but I stopped him. "No, Kendall. Not now, Baby."

He squatted and tugged at my panties again as if he didn't hear a word I said. "Let go, Shiree."

I whispered, "*No, Kendall! Stop that!*"

"Haven't you missed me, Shiree? I've missed you so much, Baby."

He was spoiled rotten. And *so* sweet. And yes, I knew what he was doing. While holding onto the dresser, I said quietly, "Please don't make me scream."

He removed my panties, opened my legs, and did things with his tongue that made me lightheaded. While moaning, he told me how good it was. I grabbed his hair and slid down the wall. "I can't, Kendall. I'm gonna make too much noise."

He turned on the music. Loud. Then he turned to me and rubbed his crotch. "It's so hard, Shiree. Only you can make me feel better."

I went to him and massaged it. He led me to the bed and removed his pants and underwear. "Let me kiss you...really sweet, Kendall."

He smiled and shook his head. "No, Shiree. Open them, Baby."

He put his head between my legs again, and I rose up to meet his tongue. I groaned and closed my eyes tight. I came quickly without being too loud. He moved up to face me and kissed my forehead. He was suddenly inside of me and it felt unbelievable. I closed my eyes and groaned. *"Umm, Kendall*... Please hurry, Baby."

He moaned loud and went deeper inside of me. *"I've missed you, Shiree."*

He raised my legs and went even deeper. He held me close and told me again how much he'd missed me. It felt like my insides were boiling over. I whispered, *"My God, Kendall...hurry!"*

But it was too late. I grabbed his arms and moaned louder than I wanted to. He leaned down and kissed me. We both groaned and came so hard...so good.

I was so embarrassed. I couldn't believe I had to face his family after that. And worse, when I went to take a quick shower, Kendall followed me.

I was afraid someone would see us because the bathroom was in the hall. I whispered, "Get out!"

He laughed and got in anyhow. When we went downstairs, his mom was preparing dinner. I walked over to her and she smiled at me. "Have a seat, Felicia. You've had a long day and I'm sure you're tired."

"I'm fine, Mrs. Montgomery. What can I do to help?"

"Not a thing. Kelly and I will take care of everything. You rest."

"I don't mind. I'd like to help."

Kendall said, "Mom. Please let her help."

She laughed. "Okay. I need the bread put on a cookie sheet, and you can preheat the oven for about five minutes at about four hundred."

I smiled and washed my hands. Kendall sat and watched us. Kelly came in and kissed her brother. "Thank you, Kendall. I didn't spend too much."

He laughed at her. "You and my wife are always worrying about my money. You're welcome, Sis."

Kendall opened a bag of chips that were sitting on the table. I said, "Kendall, you know better. Put that down."

He pouted and put them down. I turned back and finished with the bread. A few minutes later I heard crunching. I removed the bag and put it on the counter. He smacked my behind. "Stop that, Kendall. Be nice."

Kelly asked, "Does he ever listen to you?"

"No. Sometimes he pretends to."

He pulled me down on his lap. "I do whatever she asks, and she knows it."

"You do not. I'm gonna tell your mom how you beat people up."

His mother was watching us and smiling. Then she frowned. "Kendall, I hope that's not true. You're still doing that?"

Kelly asked, "You didn't beat up...you know?"

"Not yet. But I did...take care of one guy."

His mom said, "Kendy. You're gonna get in trouble. Don't do that, Son."

I smiled at that. "*Kendy?* I think Simone will be thrilled to hear that."

He began tickling me, and I screamed and jumped off of his lap. His dad walked in and said, "Boy, stop doing that. I heard enough of that an hour ago. I told you two not to let me hear that stuff."

I turned toward the sink. Kendall said, "Dad. You're embarrassing Shiree."

His dad asked, "Why do you call her Shiree?"

"It's her middle name, Dad."

Kelly said, "He started calling her that when he fell in love with her, Daddy."

His dad said, "Shiree, Felicia, whatever your name is. Let me help you out."

He laughed. I composed myself and faced him. "Listen. Put a pillow over your head. That way no one has to hear that noise."

I turned back toward the sink and Kendall said, "Dad. Be nice. I was only tickling her."

Both of his parents laughed. His dad said, "I'm not so old that I don't know what *that* kind of noise is."

Everyone laughed and I covered my face. Kendall got up and embraced me from behind. He kissed my neck and I turned around. "It's okay, Baby. He's just teasing you. He wouldn't do it if he didn't like you."

Mr. Montgomery was sitting at the table laughing. He had the chips and was about to eat some. I walked over and hit his hand. "No eating that crap. It's almost dinner time and you're not supposed to have that mess."

He looked at me with his mouth opened. I took the chips and wagged my finger at him. He finally closed his mouth and laughed again.

I smiled and turned around. "What else can I do, Mrs. Montgomery?"

They were all laughing. She said, "Sit. Everything's done."

After dinner, his parents went out to visit friends. The four of us went next door to see the house. It had three bedrooms and two full baths. They had hardwood floors installed throughout the ranch style home. It was beautiful.

While Kelly and I were shopping, Kendall had gone out and bought my favorite wine. While looking at the new kitchen, he told me to open the fridge. He'd put a bottle in there for Kelly and me, along with a six pack for himself and Keenan.

They had all new appliances put in, as well as a new island with bar stools. We sat and had our drinks, and they told me how they planned to present the house to their parents.

When we returned to their house, Keenan suggested we go out and have a drink. While the guys were upstairs, I said to Kelly, "Your brother is awfully jealous. I don't really like to go out with him."

"We'll take care of him."

"You don't understand. If a man shows interest in me, he'll attack him. He's done it more than once."

"You *are* kidding, right?"

"No. I wish I was. Stew is the only one who can calm him down. I admit he's much better now. But I'm still leery of him."

"Men can't miss that big behind of yours."

We both laughed. "That's why I rarely wear pants."

"I would imagine that Harold is devastated."

I frowned at the mention of his name. "If he is, he's not acting like it. I learned he's been cheating on me since before we were married."

She shook her head. "How long have you and Kendall been...together?"

"Over three years."

"And Harold never knew?"

I shook my head no. I began washing the two glasses in the sink, hoping she couldn't tell I was lying. She asked, "So, how long were you two apart?"

I looked up at her. "You mean..."

"When you guys lost the baby. When my brother...he was such a mess, Felicia. I'm sure you were too."

I closed my eyes. "Yes, losing the babies devastated both of us. We were apart for nine months."

"Babies?"

"Yes. There was two fetuses."

"My God. I'm so sorry you guys went through that, Felicia. But then it got worse, because he insisted it was all his fault. He was sure you would never forgive him, and he didn't want to live without you."

I closed my eyes as I remembered. "I couldn't move on without him either. But Kendall and I shared in the blame, Kelly. I made bad choices too."

I walked across the room closer to her. I looked around and said quietly, "When I miscarried, I had to have a hysterectomy. So, he assumes we can't have more children. But, he doesn't know I..."

"*But?*"

I looked up and cringed. Kendall was in the doorway. He asked, "What were you gonna say, Shiree?"

"Nothing, Kendall. We'll talk about it later."

He came over to me. "Tell me now. What were you about to tell Kelly?"

"There are ways, Kendall. It's a Christmas surprise. Please wait."

"Don't make me wait, Felicia. Tell me."

I rolled my eyes at him. "You called me Felicia."

"I'm aware of that."

"Don't do that, Sweetie. Remember the plans I mentioned earlier?"

He rubbed my shoulders and looked in my face. "What *ways*, Shiree?"

I looked up, and his sister and brother were standing there watching our back and forth. I looked back at him and swallowed. "Adoption."

"Is that the truth, Shiree?"

I turned away as my eyes filled. He made me sick sometimes. "Kendall..."

The tears fell as he turned me to face him. "What is it, Shiree?"

He wiped away my tears. "Please don't cry, Baby. *Tell me*."

I sighed. "When I gave you your birthday gift last year, before the miscarriage..."

He turned and put his hand over his mouth as if he knew (or feared), what I was going to say. He reached inside of his shirt and took out his ring and chain. "When you gave me this?"

"Yes. I also gave you a card. Do you remember?"

"Yes, Shiree."

I paused. "Do you remember what I wrote?"

He nodded slowly. "Right after your birthday, I began the process of..."

He stepped back, as the reality of what I was about to say set in. "...having my eggs removed and frozen...for you. For us, Kendall."

"You *began* the process?"

"I completed it."

He stood there. His eyes glazed over, and he turned to his sister. He turned back toward me and asked in a whisper, *"Are you serious?* I mean, *you did?"*

I sat down and had more tears. "I love you so much, and I wanted you, *us* to have a child. I...I want us to have a daughter named Shiree."

He sat next to me and caressed my face. "You did that for me?"

"Why are you so surprised? That's what you asked me to do, remember? You still want a child, right?"

"Yes, but…"

He brought me close and held me tight. "As much as I love you, I think you *do* love me more. Why didn't you tell me?"

"Because I kept waiting for the right time. Then we broke up and got back together and there was so much going on. I was gonna tell you this Christmas. I've been interviewing surrogates."

He had tears in his eyes. He told his siblings, "Go without us."

Kelly said, "I'll do it."

We all looked at her, not knowing what she meant. "I'll carry the baby. I'll be your surrogate. I read a story…"

We all asked, "You will?"

She started to cry, and then she began fanning herself. *"Please. I'd love to!"*

Keenan said, "Kelly. Won't the child be yours and Kendall's?"

We all looked at Kendall. Kelly said, "I read a story where a mother carried her daughter's child. I assume…"

Kendall said, "You're right. Once the egg is fertilized outside of your body, you would only house it. The fertilized egg will have Felicia's and my DNA only."

Kelly said, "I want to do this."

Kendall looked at me, and I was thrilled. He asked, "Are you sure, Kelle?"

"Absolutely!"

I stood and hugged her. "Kelly, it's a lot. Maybe you should take some time and think about it more. You would have to nurse for six months."

"I don't mind."

She turned to Kendall. "You and Keenan and Dad have been Terrell's dads all of his life, Kendall. I don't know what I would have done without you. Let me do this. I'd be honored to carry the next Montgomery."

Kendall smiled at Kelly, and then he turned to me. "Where are the eggs?"

"At the hospital. Juanita went with me. She's the only one I told."

His siblings were looking at him shocked. And he was looking at me the same way. Then he chuckled and turned to Kelly and Keenan. "It's a long story."

He turned back to me and asked, "What did that cost you, Shiree?"

"Let's talk about that later. Let's go and get that drink and celebrate."

"Don't move, Shiree Pierce. How much?"

"A few thousand dollars. And I have to pay five hundred a year for storage. But with Kelly being the surrogate, she saves us at least twenty, maybe thirty thousand dollars."

"How did you keep it from him?"

"I used Juanita's address. And honestly, she offered to cover the cost, considering my situation. But it was my gift to you, and I was determined to work it out. I get bonuses periodically, and they somehow found their way into my secret personal account, which also has Juanita's address."

"And how were you going to get thirty thousand dollars, Shiree?"

"By then you would have known, and *you* would have paid it. Or I would've simply withdrawn it, Kendall. I do have my own money."

His siblings were watching us like a tennis match. "You have *Benson* money, and I've told you…"

"It's not all his money. I have…millions, Kendall."

"No, Shiree. We've had this discussion. I will not allow…."

"It's *mine*, Kendall. He has his money, and I have mine. My own money I earned and invested."

"Tell him to keep it. I'll take care of this. And you."

"I know, Sweetie. But I had four years of income that was invested for my kids. He's not keeping that."

Keenan said, "If you're having trouble spending it…"

Kendall glared at Keenan and Keenan laughed. Kendall turned to Kelly and touched her arm. "We'll come up with something for you, Kelly."

"I don't want any money. Just pay the medical bills. Okay?"

Kendall kissed her forehead. "I love you, Kelle. We appreciate this."

I hugged her and smiled at all of them. "We have planning to do."

The look on Kendall's face told me he wasn't done with our conversation.

The guys went out and bought more wine. While they were gone, Kelly said, "He adores you, Felicia. I've never seen two people more in love."

I smiled at that. "Your brother means everything to me too."

"Mom said she was horrified when he came home sick. He was a mess. I almost came home myself."

I put my hand up. "Kelly, that's really hard for me to talk about."

"I'm sorry."

I sat and put my head down. "My girlfriend Simone is Stew's fiancée. The four of us are very close. When we broke up, I made her promise not to mention his name around me. So, I never knew he was suffering like that."

She sat next to me. "He was devastated about the baby. But he was *more* devastated about you."

"When we found out I was pregnant, he insisted the baby, or babies, were his. And they probably were."

I looked up and he was there. He said, "Even though she'd had her tubes tied, she got pregnant. It was a miracle, Kelly."

I added, "But about three months into the pregnancy, I miscarried and had to have an emergency hysterectomy. We were crushed."

Kelly said, "Well, thank God we now have another chance."

We drank wine and talked well into the night. The next morning, I got up early and went to the bathroom. When I returned, Kendall asked me not to get dressed yet. "I'm gonna make breakfast for everyone. I want to, Kendall."

"Get back in bed and give me some pussy first."

I whispered, "If you don't stop talking like that... They can hear you."

"Come here, or I'll say it louder."

I sat on the bed next to him. He reached for me. "Get in, Baby. I'm so hard."

I whispered, "Go pee, Kendall."

"No, Shiree. I want you."

"You are not going to have your way, Doctor. I mean it. I've spoiled you long enough. I won't have the time or space to spoil you, *and* your daughter, Kendall."

He opened his mouth, but nothing came out. Then he said, "I still can't believe we're gonna have a child together. I can't believe it."

"Maybe. We have to pray it works, Kendall. Please don't get your hopes up too high. I don't want you too disappointed."

"I'll never forget this, Shiree. And I understand it might not work. So, if it doesn't, could we do something else?"

"Absolutely, Kendall. We'll exhaust all options, even adoption. Okay?"

He whispered, "Thank you."

I kissed him and stood. "Don't leave yet. Make love to me."

"Go to the bathroom. You'll be fine."

He pouted and went to the bathroom. He came back and dressed. He smiled at me. "I'd like to help you."

I laughed as he tried to help me. We went to the store first. Then I gave him simple tasks. "I must learn, right?"

"Yes, Kendall. You need to know how to make a simple meal."

"I'm willing to learn if you don't mind teaching me."

I smiled and changed from giving orders, to teaching him. I taught him how to use the vegetable peeler, and he caught on quickly. He peeled and cut the potatoes and beat up the eggs.

His dad came down first. He looked around the kitchen and said, "You two make the most noise. What are you doing now?"

"I'm cooking breakfast and Kendall is helping me. I'm sorry we woke you."

"You didn't wake me. I always wake up early. I usually make breakfast. What are we having?"

"Sausage, bacon, potatoes and eggs. And I'm making Kendall a veggie omelet. Would you like one?"

"I'd love one. But I want meat in mine."

"Just a little. I'm well aware of dietary restrictions."

He sucked his teeth and Kendall laughed. Dad said, "I'll make you some homemade biscuits. Have you ever had any?"

"Yes. My mother makes them."

"She doesn't know what she's doing. I'll make you some."

I laughed. And then I watched as he performed his magic. Kendall began watching too, so Dad and I completed the meal.

Soon the family strolled in, and once we were halfway through our meal, Kendall said, "Mom. Felicia gave me my Christmas gift yesterday."

Kelly clapped her hands, and Keenan laughed at his sister. Mom asked, "What did you get?"

"Earlier last year, she had her eggs removed for me. I never knew. It's a long story, but I told her I wanted to have a baby with her. Anyhow, she's been waiting to tell me about the eggs. So now we can still have a baby together."

She looked at me. "Felicia, is this true?"

"Yes, Ma'am. I know some people might think it's a little weird, but..."

"No, not at all. He said he wanted to have a family with you. He also said you're the best mother he's ever seen. Next to me, of course."

We all laughed. I looked at him and smiled. He leaned over and kissed me. Kelly was about to bust, so I said, "Tell her, Kelly."

"Mom. Because she can't carry the child, they have to get a surrogate. Guess who's gonna carry your grandchild?"

She looked at us, then turned back to her daughter. "You, Kelly?"

"Yes! Isn't it great?"

Terrell looked up. He seemed to be ignoring us until then. He asked, "Mom, you're gonna have a baby?"

We all laughed. His father asked, "How can you carry your brother's child? That doesn't sound right."

Kendall explained it to them, and then he grabbed his laptop and showed all of us how it works.

Later that day, it was mild enough for us to lounge in the back yard. We were on the patio in the double swing, and he was lying with his head on my lap.

While playing in his hair, I reminded him how far away Kelly was. "I plan to ask her to take a leave once the pregnancy is confirmed. I'll assure her that we'll pay her bills. What do you think?"

"That sounds good. But what about Terrell and school?"

"We'll talk to her about that too."

He tugged my hair. "Shiree. Our child *must* be born a Montgomery."

"She'll be a Montgomery, Kendall."

"And her *mother*?"

"I assure you I'll be your wife before she's born. Okay?"

He sat up and looked at me. "That was too easy, Shiree."

I smiled. "Kendall, I want us to be married too. I just need time to organize my life. And hopefully the hardest part is over."

He was quiet for a moment. "What would have happened if we'd never gotten back together? Would you have told me about the eggs?"

"I was so heartbroken, that I thought to have them thrown away. But even in my pain and anger, I continued to love you. So when it was time to pay the storage fee, I paid it. I think I felt it was my last connection to you. I'm sure Juanita would have told you eventually."

"One thing about Juanita, she doesn't tell secrets. Which reminds me. I thought about what you said about the money."

"Kendall, I don't want..."

"Shiree, listen. I have to admit something. The truth is, I worry people will think I married you for your money. Or, that Harold will throw in my face the size of his bank account compared to mine, and..."

"Stop right there, Kendall. I realize men are consumed with the size of things, but I love you because of the size of your heart. And Harold knows that because I told him."

He stared at me lovingly. I leaned down and kissed him. "I wish I had the courage to leave Harold when I first fell in love with you. Even though I was afraid to leave, I knew in my spirit we were meant to be."

"I wish I knew it was fear. *That* I could've resolved easily. And quickly."

He smiled and I turned away. "Is something wrong, Shiree?"

"No, Kendall. I just wish I'd done things differently."

"Me too, Shiree. I wish I'd done things differently too."

We were quiet for a moment. Then he chuckled. "Why are you so sure we'll have a daughter?"

I laughed too. "I think because you and Aleece love each other so much. And how sweet it would be for you to have *another* little girl.

Although, I'm not sure how Aleece will feel about it. I think she'll be quite jealous."

"Alysiya will always be my first little girl."

We both smiled. He asked, "Are you aware that oftentimes in vitro results in multiple births? We might have another set of..."

He paused and closed his eyes. I looked down at him and a tear escaped his right eye. My mouth was suddenly dry, and I couldn't swallow. I embraced him and looked up at the beautiful blue sky.

I quietly mourned with him the loss of our children. My own tears fell as I silently asked God to allow me to endure his pain. "It's okay, Sweetie. It's okay."

I used the hem of my blouse to dry his face. I leaned down, kissed his forehead and held him close to me.

It was a sad, yet precious moment for us. I eventually joked, "Kelly will kill us if she has to carry more than one child!"

He forced a smile. "They'll have two great mothers."

I smiled and kissed him again. We began making out like teenagers when we heard voices and Kelly's laughter. The back door opened, and three women came out with Kelly and her mom.

Kendall and I stood, and he went over and embraced two of them. He motioned for me join him. "Felicia. This is my Aunt Jean and my cousin Wendi."

Then he turned to them. "This is my fiancée, Felicia."

I smiled and said, "It's so nice to meet you."

We all hugged, and Wendi said, "I'm happy to meet you too, Felicia. This is my bestie, Monique. She's visiting from D.C. She used to live here."

Both of us shook her hand. She was clearly mesmerized by Kendall. They all sat, and Kelly and I went in and brought out iced tea and snacks. Mom insisted they stay for dinner.

Miss Monique seemed to hang on Kendall's every word. When he became aware of it, he motioned for me to come back and sit next to him. He rubbed my cheek and kissed me. He smiled and asked, "Are you okay?"

"Yes. I'm fine, Kendall."

He whispered, "Go upstairs in about five minutes. Okay?"

I turned and everyone was watching us. Especially her. Kelly said, "He can't keep his hands off of her. We've had to endure that ever since she got here."

Aunt Jean said, "He's always been lovable. So, Felicia? When is the wedding? Your ring is lovely."

I smiled. "Thank you. We haven't set a date yet. Maybe in a year or so."

Kendall looked at his aunt and said, "It'll be soon, Aunt Jean."

I leaned over and kissed him. Then I turned to his family. "Please excuse me."

I walked into the house and waited for him. I was watching through the window when his dad came up behind me. "She seems captivated by him."

I turned, and he laughed. "Both of my sons have always had that problem. Girls have tripped over themselves since they were twelve and ten. Keenan would tell them to buzz off, but Kendall was always nice to them. Believe me, he's crazy about you. I'll send Keenan out. He'll sweep her off her feet."

"That means I should trust him, right?"

"It *means* you should trust that he's nuts over you. And that he'd never intentionally do anything to hurt you. But it doesn't mean he won't have an oops. Are you ready for that?"

He smiled. "I hope so. Thank you, Mr. Montgomery. I really appreciate that."

He touched my shoulder. "You'll be fine, Felicia."

He walked away, but then he turned back. "By the way. Call me Dad."

We both smiled and he left. Kendall came in and asked, "Were you watching me, Shiree?"

"No, Baby. I was *waiting* for you."

He reached for my hand and we went out into the front yard. He kissed me and showed me his mom's beautiful gardens.

We slowly made our way around the house. "Kendall. Will you expect me to be like Juanita?"

"Are you interested in women?"

"You know what I mean."

"Shiree. I will not share you. Am I not enough for you?"

I rolled my eyes. "That is not what I asked you. You like variety, remember?"

"I will not cheat on you, Shiree. We've had this discussion."

"I know I've told you in the past that I didn't expect your fidelity. But if we get married, I *will* expect it. Are you ready for that?"

He looked down at me and smiled. "Is that all you need from me? Because that'll be easy, Shiree."

"I worry that things will change if we get married. Do you remember telling me you could never be just someone's lover or just someone's husband? Will you promise to tell me, and not show me, if you want more?"

His gaze was intense. "What are you, Shiree? An elephant?"

"Do you deny saying it?"

"First of all, that is the second time you said *if* we get married. Secondly, I was so much younger when Juanita and I got together. I'm settled now. In three and a half years, I have never wanted another woman. I've looked and admired, but none have brought me to attention but you. You're it for me."

"Kendall..."

"You're afraid to marry me, aren't you?"

I laughed and turned toward his family. Unfortunately, I got their attention. I said quietly, "Of course, I am. You're whorish, Kendall. I can't compete with that. So, if we get married, like you, I refuse to share. Are you sure you're ready for this? Because I will *whip your ass* if you cheat on me. I'm not playing with you, Doctor."

He smiled and leaned toward my ear. "And how do you plan to do that?"

"I'll find a way. Maybe I'll tie your ass up while you're sleeping and get a belt and beat you."

He laughed and embraced me. "Shiree. I've been sure about you since that day I gave you formula, and you took my breath away an hour later. Besides, it's natural for men to admire women. That doesn't put me on an island."

"Admiration and having sex with them are two different things, Kendall."

"I'm well aware of that, Shiree. The latter feels *so much better*."

"I'm serious, Kendall. I'll leave you in a New York minute."

"I guess you'll just have to wait and see just how much I plan to love you. I was such a fool to ruin your trust in me."

"I never trusted you."

He glared at me. I laughed and stepped back. He reached for me, and I ran. He caught me and threw me over his shoulder. I screamed, "Put me down, Kendall!"

He hit my behind and sat me down. Keenan and Dad had joined the group, and Dad said, "Kendall. I told you to stop making her scream."

Everyone laughed. Kendall said, "Dad. No more embarrassing my wife. She screams because she loves it when I..."

I rubbed his arm, and said quietly, "Stop talking, Kendall."

Miss Monique continued to stare at him, even with his mirror image sitting next to her. Kendall noticed it too. He stood and said, "I'm sorry for being rude, but I promised Felicia a brief tour of Durham. Will you all excuse us?"

Mom said, "Stop and pick up a few tomatoes for my salad, Son. You will be back for dinner, right?"

"Yes, Mom. We won't be long."

During our ride, I turned to him. "That wasn't nice, leaving your family like that, Kendall."

"We were both uncomfortable, Shiree. She was clearly...determined to get my attention."

"I know how to handle that. You treat me like I'm a child."

"Honestly, to use your words, I was afraid I'd say something ugly to her."

I faced the window. "If the tables were turned, you would've punched the guy. We can't help it when someone is attracted to one of us. It's not fair that you take over and handle it. Whether it's someone attracted to you or to me."

"Do I do that?"

"Yes. You treat me like I'm all body and no brain. I don't like it, Kendall."

"Why would you say that, Shiree? You know that's not true."

"It *is* true. There are women in your face all the time. But like your dad told me, I have to trust that you love me."

He laughed. "When did Dad tell you that?"

"When Miss Thing was drooling all over you and I was in the kitchen."

"That's why Dad was trying to push Keenan on her. Dad likes you, Shiree."

"He told me to call him Dad, not Mr. Montgomery."

He cracked up. "Wow. He *really* likes you."

"You think?"

"Yeah. And that's huge. He doesn't like many people. He didn't like Juanita."

"Why?"

"He felt she was too uppity."

I laughed. "I always knew why you loved her. She has a sweetness that's hidden from most people. I first saw it the night my babies were in the accident."

He smiled. I asked him if he missed her. "Juanita and I will always love each other. I knew her secrets and she knew mine. Like you and Todd. And truthfully, the romance was gone long before I met you. She's so in love with Vonni. She said she kept me balanced, but you are my dream come true."

"What does that mean?"

"She believes you're the same sexually. But she thinks you're submissive, so she's convinced you treat me like a king, and you put my life before your own."

"Do you think that?"

"Yes, to you being my dream come true, and treating me like a king. No, to you being the same sexually and the submissive part. If you were a true submissive, you would not have had an affair with me. It takes a strong woman to do what you did for over three years."

Dr. Morales said the same thing. I asked him, "Do you remember saying Shiree never says no to you? And me saying I didn't like saying no to you?"

"Yes."

"You don't think that's submissive?"

"What I *think* is that we need to end this conversation. Because I call those things love."

"What have you asked of me that I've denied you, Kendall?"

"You made me beg you for three months to take me back."

We both laughed. "I could ask you the same question, Shiree. There's nothing I wouldn't do for you either."

"But I rarely ask anything of you."

"That's true. But you expect *many things* from me. Just like I expect many things from you."

I wasn't paying any attention to the tour of Durham. I was concerned about being submissive. Was that a bad thing? A good thing? I didn't know.

I remembered telling Juanita that I loved doing things that made him happy. It was easy to love him like that because he loved me like that.

His sister said she'd never seen two people more in love. Maybe what we have is so rare, people mistake it for something else.

When we pulled into the driveway, he grabbed the tomatoes and I sat there. "Shiree. Please don't over think this."

"I do expect things from you, but you still do whatever you want. Like the way you beat people up or threaten to. Or have other women. Or insist..."

"What other women?"

I turned toward him. "Don't act like it didn't happen, Kendall."

He reached behind my head and pulled me toward him. He brought his face toward mine. "Shiree. What's really wrong? Is this about the other night?"

"I don't know. All of a sudden, I feel like a fool."

"Our love and devotion to each other is the same, Shiree. There are things you do for me I'm not capable of doing for you. You cook, clean and keep things in order for me. Even when I asked you to stop, you insisted those were other ways you love me. You said it was your joy, remember? I take care of you and indulge you with pretty things, because that's *my* joy, and other ways I love you."

I looked up and began to cry. "Sweetheart. I couldn't love you like I wanted to before. I look forward to giving you love's icing. Isn't that what you called it?"

I smiled. "Yes."

"You've always been my princess, Shiree. And although you'll soon be my queen, I guess I'll always see you as my princess."

I smiled. He was the sweetest man I'd ever known. Harold never treated me like Kendall does. "I'm sorry, Kendall."

"I know what it is, and it's my fault. You have no control over my dumb ass. You're right about me taking over. And you feel trapped. Like when you told Kelly you don't like to go out with me. That was news to me. I'm sorry too, Baby."

I looked straight ahead and said nothing. He was right. I *did* feel trapped. Between wanting to keep him happy and fearing I wouldn't. I continued to want and need to be exceptional. I was sorry he ever told me that.

He turned me to face him, and he kissed me for a long time. He smiled and asked, "Do you remember our first kiss?"

"Yes, Doctor."

"Not like I do."

"Oh, yes I do. But I bet you don't remember kissing my cheek that first night at your club? I thought I was gonna faint."

He laughed. "That day in my office while nursing Alysiya, you leaned down to watch her, and your hair fell over your face and blocked my view. I moved your hair, and you looked up at me. My mouth watered because I was stunned by your beauty and the desire in your eyes. And when I kissed you, your taste overwhelmed me. Your response almost made me lose my cookies."

We both laughed. "Let's take Mom her tomatoes and get through this dinner. Then I'll take you out on the town tonight, and *I promise*, I'll be good. Okay?"

"Okay, but let's bring the others with us. I feel terrible that I've taken away their time with you. Okay, Baby?"

He smiled. "Okay."

I was worried about all the changes occurring in my life. What if Kendall decided he no longer wanted me? Or found someone else? And I was still scared Harold would run away with my kids.

I was nervous about walking away from my security with Harold. God knows I hated to admit that. I also hated to admit that now, Kendall has the reins.

They were both guilty of needing to control me. And I was guilty of letting them. When would I learn to stand on my own two feet?

I was trying really hard to keep what I'd learned about Harold from Kendall. It took Simone's comment about Kendall drinking my bath water to make me see a lot of things clearer. She was right.

I finally understood that I felt more indebted to Harold than in love. Not from a financial standpoint, but because he stayed after my trifling behavior with Sam. I felt I owed it to him. But no more. I'd paid my debt in full.

I also felt Harold was prouder of what he created me to be, versus who I was. He acted as if I was some acquisition he could brag about or show off. His obsessiveness became his priority. Not me.

But with Kendall, like Simone said, I believed he *would* drink my bath water. Harold always gave me what *he felt* I needed, or what *he* wanted me to have. Whereas, Kendall did things *he knew* made me happy. And if he had to, Kendall would roll up his sleeves and dig in the dirt for it.

I was finally over my guilt. Well, most of it.

Although Monique still seemed to be crushing on Kendall, it appeared that Keenan had successfully gotten her attention. After dinner I asked Wendi, "Do you guys have plans for tonight?"

"We're thinking about going out for a drink. What are you guys doing?"

Kendall glared at me and said, "Shiree, let's find a quiet spot so I can look in your eyes and fall in love with you again. Like I did in Jamaica."

I thought that was odd. He told me earlier he was okay with us hanging out with his family. Wendi said, "I know the perfect spot, Kendy. It's hidden away downtown. The two of you will love it."

Monique turned to me and asked, "So, you guys have been to Jamaica?"

"Yes. It was magical. We're going again on Monday."

Aunt Jean said, "That's so romantic. Lorraine tells me you have four children, Felicia."

Monique sat up and asked, "You have four kids?!"

"Yes. I have three sons and a daughter. Kendall and I plan to have more."

Miss Thing sucked her teeth, and Kendall began to fidget. "Kendall is my kid's doctor, which is how we met."

Monique turned to Kendall's mom. "Wow, Mrs. Montgomery. You must be very proud to have a doctor in the family."

"We're proud of all of our children. They all followed their dreams."

Dad and Kelly came out of the kitchen and joined us in the living room. I said to Kelly, "We're thinking about going out for a drink. Wanna join us?"

"I told Wendi I would hang out with her and Monique. Why don't you and Kendall spend some time alone?"

I turned to Kendall. "What do you want to do?"

"Whatever you want to do, Baby. I don't care."

I stood and said, "Excuse us for a minute, please."

I took his hand and made him follow me upstairs. We went in our room and closed the door. "Kendall, you should spend more time with your family. We have all of next week together. Let's go with them."

He stared at me and then turned away. "Okay, Shiree. Whatever you want."

"What is it, Kendall? Earlier, you assured me we'd go out with them."

He sighed. Then reluctantly, he went in his pocket and handed me a card. It was a business card with Monique's contact information on it. "I could fill a room with the number of cards and napkins and notes I get. With phone numbers and messages of love or sex. I have no interest in them or her."

I wanted to go downstairs and slap the piss out of her. "That dirty bitch!"

"I can handle this, Shiree. I'm used to it. I just hate it happened here."

"This is different, Kendall. She has blatantly disrespected me. I'll handle it."

He reached for the card, and I snatched it back. "What are you doing?"

"I was *going* to tear it up, Shiree."

"I'll take care of it."

I put it in my pocket. "So, we're not going?"

"Yes, we're going. Give me a minute. I'll meet you downstairs. And, Shiree?"

"Yes?"

"Be kind."

Once I was downstairs, Kelly asked what we decided to do. "We've decided to go with you all. Kendall will be down shortly."

Everyone was gathering their things and preparing to go. I went over and began to chat with Monique. I eventually asked, "So, what do you do?"

"I'm in IT."

"What a coincidence. So am I."

"Really? We're in the same field?"

"Yes."

I went in my pocket and showed her the card. "Sharing the same field is one thing. Sharing *my husband,* is something I *will not* do. He gave this to me, and he asked me to be kind. But there is nothing *kind* about what you did. I'm obeying my husband, because that is what *I do*. But if you *ever* approach my husband again, the girl from New York won't be so kind."

I smiled and handed her the card. Kendall and Kelly were standing in the doorway watching me. His parents, aunt and Keenan were also watching.

Wendi had her head down and her hands over her face. I got up and turned toward the doorway. I smiled again and asked, "You guys ready?"

When we got in the car, I turned to Kendall. "That woman almost got hit in her mouth. But your parents would've been done with me for sure."

We were in Keenan's new car, and he was watching intently because Kelly begged him to let her drive. Kendall and I were in the back, and Kelly said, "I can't believe that chick. She gave you her business card, Kendall?"

"Yes. When Mom and I were in the kitchen after dinner, she came in there and gave it to me while Mom's back was turned."

"What did you say?"

"She handed it to me and walked out."

Kelly shook her head and said, "I can't imagine that she's still coming out tonight."

Kendall turned to me and said, "Shiree. I thought we agreed you wouldn't say anything to her?"

Keenan was laughing at us. I said, "No. I told you what she did was blatant and disrespectful. And you know if some guy came on to me right up under your nose, you'd knock his teeth out."

"You made me promise not to do that again."

"I know. But will you keep that promise?"

"Between my parents, Kelly and you, I don't have a choice."

Kelly said, "I told Dad what you said, Felicia. We all laid into him."

"I guess your parents are done with me now."

Keenan was still laughing when he said, "Dad was laughing when we left. He told Mom he thought you were gonna hit Monique like you hit him."

We all laughed. When we arrived at the club, that heffa had the nerve to be there. Wendi came over to us. "Felicia. I swear I didn't know. I knew she was admiring him, but I didn't think she would do anything like that."

Kendall said, "Don't worry about it, Wendi. Felicia is okay."

I said, "Wendi, I'm used to women crushing on Kendall. I'm fine."

Wendi turned to Kendall. "Kendall, I'm so embarrassed. She said you were smiling at her, because I asked what the hell made her do it."

Kendall laughed. "Honestly, Wendi. I would never look twice at someone like her. She's not..."

I touched his arm. "Kendall Montgomery. Stop talking."

"She's lying on me, Shiree. I don't want you thinking I was looking at her."

"You look at everybody. I'm not worried about that. Come on, let's get a drink. I think I'll buy her one."

Wendi and Kelly looked at me, and Kendall said, "That's my wife. Always taking the high road."

I walked over to Monique. "Hey, Girl. What are you drinking?"

"What?"

Wendi said, "We both drink lemon martinis."

I turned to Kendall. "Three lemon martinis, please. Thanks, Baby."

Then I looked at his sister and said, "Go with him, Kelly. We're good."

I turned to Monique and extended my hand. "We're good, right?"

She shook my hand and said, "Yes. I apologize."

"And I accept."

I smiled and sat down. The three of us made small talk until Kendall and Kelly came back. After we had our drinks, Kendall reached for me and we danced to a slow song. "I have a surprise for you."

"What surprise, Kendall?"

"We're staying downtown tonight. I packed and made reservations while you were telling Monique off."

I laughed, and he shook his head. "You mean to tell me you're not gonna fight me over this, Shiree?"

"No, Baby. Are you gonna make me scream?"

He pulled me closer. "Umm-hmm. If you promise to do the same."

"Under one condition. That we get up early so your parents won't know we stayed out."

"No, Shiree. I can't remember the last time we've laid in bed together."

"I want to cook breakfast with your dad in the morning. And I have to apologize for telling Monique off in their home. I feel terrible. But I swear if they weren't there, I might've slapped her ass."

"You're always calling me a thug, but you're the damn thug, *Felicia*."

"So, if Felicia is a thug, what is Shiree?"

He held me close and started laughing. "I'll answer that while we're lying in each other's arms until checkout tomorrow."

"We're leaving at eight a.m."

He whispered in my ear, "Let's go."

We walked over to the others and Kendall said, "We'll see you guys in the morning. Shiree and I are staying in town tonight. Where's Keenan?"

Kelly said, "He's on the dance floor. Don't worry. I won't let him leave me."

We all laughed, and Kendall said, "You know your brother."

We laughed again and Kelly said, "No worries. We'll see you guys tomorrow."

When we checked in, the room overlooked the city and the moon was full. Before going up, we stopped at the hotel bar and brought up drinks.

He put on a jazz CD and held me close as we danced slow and had a quiet moment in each other's arms. I laid on his chest and enjoyed the steady pace of his heartbeat. My heartbeat.

I realized that day that Kendall would be more of a handful than Harold ever was. I'd need to be around him more. Juanita told me he was too gorgeous to be trusted. That may be true, but what was also true was that he loved and adored me.

I looked up at him and he kissed me. He picked me up and sat me on the bed. He got on his knees and removed my shoes and looked at my anklet. He had it repaired and insisted I never remove it.

He kissed the bottom of my foot and tickled me. I pulled away and got on the floor with him. "I'll need clothes for Jamaica, Kendall. I bought a few things when Kelly and I went out, but not enough for a whole week."

"I bought you panties, bras and two dresses."

"Really?"

"Yes. But whatever you need, I'll get for you."

I turned my lip up. "Probably just a few more things. I don't need much."

"I know that. It's unnerving at times, but I'm used to it now."

We finished our drinks and got in bed. "I can't wait to spend next week together, Shiree. It's like going back to where it all began. Sort of began."

"Gosh. I remember being so scared to love you."

"I remember walking in your room when you had that tear in the corner of your eye, and I promised myself I'd never make you cry. I lied."

"I'm not crying now. I'm happy, and so in love with you."

We kissed and made love all night. I cried twice…

The following afternoon, I knocked on her door. Kendall, his dad and siblings were outside looking at Keenan's new car. "Come in, Felicia."

I was nervous as hell, but I walked in. "Have a seat. I see you got my note."

"I owe you an apology for last night."

She glared like Kendall. "No apology needed, Felicia. You handled it better than I would have."

I wanted to laugh, but I decided against it. "Kendall's looks draw a lot of attention, so I've gotten used to women doing things like that, Mrs. Montgomery."

"My husband is handsome too. So I know what you're going through."

We both smiled. "My son is the apple of my eye. I always thought Juanita was right for him. But, it was more like she was *good* for him. She loved him and pushed him, and she was hard on him when he needed it. But I soon saw that something wasn't being fulfilled in him. You make him happy, Felicia."

"He makes me happy too. My current situation was very stressful and controlling. Kendall became my soft place to land."

She smiled again. "Kelly told me you prefer not to speak about Kendall's breakdown."

I closed my eyes. "When I had the miscarriage, his heart shattered. And I knew he needed me...for so many reasons. But I was healing from surgery, and..."

"He knows that, Felicia. Don't beat yourself up over that. Kendall has always loved and cared for people more than most. That's why he became a doctor. Some of his patients can't afford to pay him. But he refuses to turn anyone away."

I nodded as I recalled some of his stories. She added, "He saw children lack medical care when he was younger. He emptied his piggy bank once when a childhood friend fell and cut his leg. Justin's parents couldn't afford stitches. Kendall watched Justin almost bleed to death, or so he thought, being only nine years old. He was horrified. So, they walked to emergency, and Kendall gave them his bank."

"That doesn't surprise me at all. He loves his kids so much."

"Felicia. Kendall has wanted to be a father for a while now, but Juanita couldn't have children. And honestly, I figured you wouldn't want any more."

"It's true I have my hands full, but I want this for him. For us. I have a habit of spoiling him."

She and I both laughed. "He's always been adorable, Felicia. He told me that he never imagined love like what he has with you."

I closed my eyes, and a tear rolled down my face. "Mrs. Montgomery. I feel the same way."

She embraced my face, and I looked up at her. "I know what happened when your husband found out. About the pills. I know how much you love him. You've both given everything. I pray constantly for both of you."

She reached for her tissue box and gave me one. "I've been as concerned about you as I am about my son. I was gonna come up there soon."

I was moved by her genuine concern for me. "About the eggs, Felicia? What if your plan doesn't work?"

"We're going to exhaust every way possible. Even adoption."

She smiled and closed her eyes. "Thank God. I'm delighted to hear that. Juanita wouldn't consider adoption."

"He knows there's nothing I won't do for him."

"I admit, I was afraid for him when you all told me about the eggs. But I now have peace that God will see it through."

"Me too. I believe one way or another, we'll have a child."

She smiled again. "Take care of him. He has a tendency to feel invincible at times. Insist that he rests more."

"I assure you I'll do just that."

She embraced me and kissed my cheek. "I'm glad you're going to be my daughter. Will you call me Mom?"

"I'd be honored. Thank you, Mom. I can't wait for you to meet my parents. They love Kendall. And about the wedding, I'll probably just have something simple with immediate family and close friends. I've been married twice already."

"Whatever you want is fine. We'll be there. And I'm looking forward to meeting your parents. Your mother called him a couple of times when he was here. It meant the world to me and I never forgot it."

"She adores Kendall. She gave both of us a hard time at first. But she knew I was so sad in my marriage, and that Kendall gave me so much joy."

"Kendall didn't think you'd come here, for fear of being judged. I never felt that way, Felicia. These things happen."

"Thank you, Mom. I appreciate that. Maybe we'll have the ceremony in your backyard. It's so beautiful. But it won't be for another year or so. I have a lot of mess to clean up with my current husband."

"That would be wonderful, Felicia. I'd love…"

Kendall knocked and walked in. He looked at both of us. "Mother, have you kidnapped my wife?"

"She and I are just chatting."

"Shiree? What have you told her?"

"I'm not sure, Kendall. Although, I did tell her how much I love you."

He came closer. "Is it this much?"

He opened his arms wide and I laughed. "A little more than that."

Mom said, "Leave her alone, Kendall."

He pulled me up in his arms and kissed me. "Mom. Didn't I tell you how precious she is?"

"Yes, Kendall. And I agree."

Dad walked in asking, "Has the party moved up here?"

Mom said, "Felicia and I were talking. We're done now."

He sat next to his wife, and I saw what a stunning couple they made. I thought, "No wonder my Kendall is so gorgeous."

Dad pointed his finger at me. "You two are good for each other. Don't ever let anything or anyone come between you. You hear me?"

Kendall smiled and nodded. I said, "Yes, Dad."

He turned to Kendall. "Your mom and I allowed misunderstandings and ugly words to break us up, remember?"

"I remember, Dad."

"So never say anything that can cause a wound. And try to be as honest as possible, without being hurtful. Mom and I agreed to always say sweet things, even when we're upset."

Kendall said, "After all these years, she and I have never done that."

Then Kendall laughed and looked at me. "Although that night we reconciled, you had a few choice words for me."

I looked at him and remembered. Kendall looked back at his father. "Thanks for the words of wisdom, Dad. Shiree and I will always be mindful of being kind in word *and* in deed."

Then I added, "Yes, we will, Dad. Thank you for yesterday too."

He nodded. "Good. And ask Momma here about that screaming. She learned how to be quiet. All women scream with Montgomery men. They can't help it."

He hollered laughing as he walked out. Kendall also laughed loud and walked out too. I stood up, and Mom said, "He's terrible, Felicia. Please get used to it. Okay?"

I was so ashamed. She chuckled and said, "Don't be embarrassed. Keenan still makes me scream. That's why I don't allow him near me unless no one's here. But I did learn how to keep quiet."

"You did?"

"Yep. I'll email you. Unless you're not too embarrassed to talk about it."

I paused. Of course I was embarrassed. But I sat back down and looked at my hands. "Kendall loves that I scream. But I always wanted to control it better."

She got up and closed and locked the door. "Try breathing through your nose. Some women hold their breath, but that destroys the moment. Continue breathing but close your mouth and breathe through your nose. You still might moan, but it'll be a lot quieter. Okay?"

I got a visual and realized it might work. "Okay. I'll try it. Thanks, Mom."

She waved her hand. "Don't mention it."

She sat in front of me and held my hands. "Keenan and I separated for a long time. I wouldn't take him back, so he got another woman. It almost killed me."

"I'm sure. I'm so sorry."

"He begged me to take him back. Even though I loved him to pieces, I refused him for a long time."

"When Kendall and I broke up, I did the same thing."

"My mother used to say that everyone should experience at least one serious heart break, Felicia. Not only does it soften your heart, but the cracks serve as doorways allowing new love, or forgiven love to flow easier."

I smiled at that. "I love the wisdom of our mothers. I'll remember that."

"Keenan really likes you. He told me he knew right away you were right for Kendall. Plus, you're one hell of a cook. He admires your willingness to help in the kitchen and around the house. And he'll never forget you hitting him."

We both laughed. "Dad is a sweetheart. You all are. Dad told me to forgive Kendall if he…ever cheated. He said as much as Kendall loves me, men sometimes have…moments."

She nodded in agreement. "That's true, Felicia. Sex doesn't usually affect the love people have for their spouses. It feeds our flesh. Because we're human, we sometimes make bad decisions. Whatever you do, don't let pride cause you to miss even one moment of Kendall's love. Or allow it to cause him to miss a second of yours. I regret it now."

I smiled at her. We both stood and she put her arm around my waist. We went toward the door and she turned toward me. "By the way. If Kendall is anything like his father, you scream as often as you can."

I looked at her, and we both laughed.

Chapter Seven

The entire weekend, I opted to text versus talk to Harold. I told him I would talk to him on Monday when he returned. But Sunday night, he sent me a text saying he knew I wasn't in Miami. He wanted to know where I was.

I forwarded it to Simone, and she and I agreed he still had someone following or tracking me. I quickly deleted the texts so Kendall wouldn't know what we learned. I also asked my parents to tell Harold I was in Miami if he asked.

When we landed in Miami, I was so happy to see Simone and Stew. She and I went to the ladies' room so we could talk privately. "Do you think he actually has someone following you, or just having you tracked?"

"I don't know and I don't care. I'm finally done, Simone. I regret waiting this long to spend my life with Kendall. I was so concerned about devastating Harold, yet he cared nothing about me."

"Please don't cry, Felice. I can't have a sad matron of honor."

"I'm gonna be your matron of honor?"

"Yes. Thursday."

We both screamed. She said, "The divorce is final. Thank God!"

"I thought you were gonna wait."

"I was, but he's so adamant, Felicia. And waiting seems silly now."

I agreed and we went back to the bar area for the hour's wait for our flight. We were all excited about the upcoming wedding.

Kendall and Stew were talking low and smiling at us. Simone asked, "Why are you two whispering?"

Stew asked Kendall, "Should we tell them?"

Kendall said, "We might as well."

Stew turned toward us. "We have the house you all rented last time."

We couldn't believe it, but we were both excited. I asked, "How did you get it, Stew?"

"I still had the address in my GPS. So I inquired and it was available."

Simone said to Stew, "We'll use Annette's old room with the balcony like Felicia's. This is wonderful!"

Kendall said to me, "We're gonna live on the beach again, Baby."

He was so happy. I kissed him and said, "Thank you, Sweetie."

After landing, we rented two cars and were on our way. Kendall said, "That house is really *our* house. No one else stayed there but us."

"I know, right! I wanna get some of those chicken wings."

He laughed at my excitement. Before going to the house, we stopped at the grocery store. Kendall and I went into the produce section. I wanted to grab a container of tea, so I told him I'd be right back.

While perusing the tea, I was approached by a man who asked me what tea I preferred. "I like green tea, but I'm not partial to any particular brand."

"I understand it has lots of good properties."

"Yes, it does."

I eventually chose one. I turned to leave but he stopped me. "Would you join me in a cup of tea sometime?"

"Thanks, but I'm married."

"Oh. Are you happy?"

I saw Kendall coming toward us. "Yes. I'm incredibly happy."

Kendall slowed down and began observing us. The guy offered me his card. "Just in case you decide you'd like...a cup of tea."

"No, but thank you. I hope you enjoy your tea."

I walked toward Kendall, who was burning holes in the guy's back. "Look at me and breathe, Kendall."

His eyes eventually met mine and he said, "I heard your conversation. I went down the next aisle looking for you and heard him ask you about tea."

"Okay. You okay?"

"I'm not a lunatic, Shiree. I only intervene when someone is too persistent."

"So you trust that I can handle it?"

"Of course."

We saw Simone and she had plenty of bacon and eggs. Stew had bread, butter and milk. Kendall had fruit and veggies. I only had tea. So, we grabbed snacks, water and everything else we needed and put them in Simone's cart.

During check out, we saw him again. I told Stew what happened and Kendall said, "As long as he doesn't try again, I'm good."

We managed to escape any drama, and finally we were at our house. We were so happy to be back there. We asked the guys about having the wedding at the house. Stew said, "Sure, Simone. I'll find someone to marry us here."

We smiled at each other and went up to her room. I said, "We need to shop for the wedding."

"I know. What should we wear?"

"All white would be beautiful. Especially on the beach. Or do you want to wear white and we wear another color?"

"Maybe you all can wear tan, and Stew and I will wear all white."

"I love it. I wonder how hard it'll be to find white at the end of November?"

"I don't know. We're not in the states, so it might not be a big deal here."

We heard the guys outside. We looked out and saw them out back with drinks. I whispered, "Harold should be back by now. I need to call him, but I don't want Kendall around. Do you think I have time?"

She looked out again. "Yes, but don't be long. They'll want us out there soon."

When I called, he answered with a chuckle. "Are you home yet, Harold?"

"Yes, we've been here for a while. I see you've done some snooping."

"You know what? I have no interest in talking about that right now. I called to tell you that I've extended my vacation and I'll be home Friday."

"Where are you?"

"Miami."

"I guess you're really pissed with me."

"I would like for you to stop having me followed."

"He stopped a month ago."

"I'll talk to you later in the week."

"Did you keep the tapes?"

"Which ones?"

"The ones the PI gave me."

"Oh. I thought you were referring to the ones from our bedroom."

He got quiet. "Yes, I found those too. And no, I no longer have any of them. I destroyed everyone I found. You're filthy, Harold. You never loved me."

I hung up.

I was shaking. My nerves were twisted, and I knew I'd never be able to hide my anger from Kendall.

Simone and I went down and stopped to get a drink at the bar. I poured a shot of vodka. Simone went outside and I went in the kitchen to compose myself. I walked out to join them and dropped my glass on the patio.

The glass shattered and Kendall quickly got up to help me. The others got up to help too. I went back inside, and Kendall followed me. "Shiree. Is something wrong?"

"No, Baby. I just dropped the glass."

"You seem uneasy. Are you sure?"

I smiled. "I assure you. All is well, Kendall. I could use something to eat though. Aren't you guys hungry?"

"Yes, I'm a little hungry. Come on back outside."

"Okay. I'm gonna get another drink."

"I'll get it. Go and sit."

I went back out and Simone said to me, "I was thinking about just staying in tonight. How do you feel about that?"

"I love that idea. I'm more tired than I thought."

Stew said, "Ken and I will go out and get dinner. You two rest."

After the guys left, we each went to our room, unpacked, showered, and dressed comfortably.

Later while in the kitchen, I turned to Simone and shook my head. "Every time we go away, something happens. I pray the worst thing was that conversation with Harold. And I *pray,* that Kendall doesn't find out what he did."

"At some point, you should tell Kendall. Not about the tapes, but everything else. And not now, but soon."

"Why?"

"Your need to keep peace and trying to hide your anger and hurt isn't working. He's bound to notice, if he hasn't already."

"As painful as my breakup with Todd was, we never hated each other. We even found a way to love each other. But over the years, Harold has eaten away at my love for him. And now this. I don't think I'll *ever*...get over this."

"And you shouldn't. But you can't let it turn you into something you're not. And don't let it ruin your vacation, Felicia. Because we both know if Kendall finds out, he'll murder Harold."

The following day after breakfast, Kendall asked, "What time are you and Simone going out to shop?"

"In about a half hour. That reminds me..."

I paused. "What is it, Shiree?"

"I'm not sure how to do this, but I need money or a credit card."

He laughed. "Why is it so hard for you to ask me for things? I *want* you to ask me, Shiree."

"I don't want him knowing my whereabouts, so I can't use my card."

He went in his wallet and gave me his American Express card again. He saw the anguish on my face and glared at me. "What the hell is wrong, Shiree?"

"Nothing, Baby. I don't like asking you for money. It's weird."

"I'll call the bank and request a card sent overnight with your name on it. That way you won't have to ask me anymore. You'll have your own card. Okay, Baby?"

"I didn't know about Jamaica, or I would've brought my other debit card. The one he doesn't have access to. I don't have any credit cards. Well, I do have one, but I only use it for emergencies and its home..."

I paused. I thought about the hotel charges and got mad again. I opened my mouth to speak again and he stopped me. "You're babbling, Shiree. You do that when you're nervous."

I reached up and kissed him. "I promise not to spend too much."

"Spend as much as you want, Shiree. It's fine."

"Thank you, Baby."

While shopping, Simone handed me her phone and showed me a text. Kendall asked her what the hell was wrong with me and if Harold did or said something.

She replied she hadn't noticed me acting differently. Then she got in my face. "Felice. I told you he would notice. Come on. You have to shake this."

"You're right. There's no way I want him to know what we learned."

I began to realize I'd been waiting for the other shoe to drop. It always did. Every time we went away, something happened.

But maybe this time...maybe not. And admittedly, my dream was dancing around in my head. I had an uneasy feeling that Harold would show up in Jamaica.

When we returned, I announced I would be cooking dinner. Kendall said, "Baby, we want to go out. Are you okay?"

"Yes, I'm fine. I can cook another night. You're right. Let's go out and have a good time."

He walked over to me. "Come upstairs with me for a minute please."

Simone and Stew watched us go upstairs. I looked back at Simone, and she shrugged. Then she nodded as if to say, go on and tell him. I looked again and she confirmed it. That was the last thing I wanted to do.

He closed our bedroom door, and I tried my reverse psychology I'm so notorious for. I turned to him and asked, "What's the matter, Baby? Aren't you feeling well?"

"Don't try it, Felicia."

"Kendall. My name is Shiree."

"Tell me what's wrong."

I turned to walk away, but he stopped me. I sighed. "I learned recently that he..."

I paused. He sat me down. "He what, Shiree?"

"I saw the credit card statements where he's been whoring around all over the country. I rummaged through his files and found all sorts of evidence that he's known for *two years* about us! There's a picture of you and me at the Black and White Ball...over eighteen months ago, Kendall! That..."

The cleft in Kendall's chin was twisted. He was fit to be tied. "I suffered for so long with guilt and concern for him, and he..."

He held my arms and looked at me. "Shiree. Listen to me. It's over. You will no longer be under the same roof with him."

I looked up at him and tried not to cry. He embraced me and assured me it would be okay. "Let's go back to that spot on the beach we went to when we were here before. Remember we did shots of tequila and got drunk?"

"Yes. Okay, Kendall."

"When did you find out?"

"Before I left. I didn't want to tell you until we got back home because I didn't want it to ruin your vacation."

"Shiree. It's *our* vacation. I'm good. Please don't worry about me, Baby."

He held me close. "From now on, it's you and me, Shiree. Understand?"

"Yes, but..."

"No buts. I'll take care of you and the kids. Okay, Baby?"

He kissed me and we went back downstairs. But that cleft was still twisted, and I knew by his calm that he was plotting to kill Harold.

During dinner, we told the guys we had everything we needed except the shoes. Kendall asked, "Simone, will you have another wedding later?"

"No. I don't think so, Kendall. I've had enough of those."

I said, "I feel the same way, Simone. Been there, done that."

Kendall glared at me. "I want a wedding, Shiree. I want to see you come down the aisle in a white dress."

I laughed because I assumed he was joking. But he wasn't. "Kendall. I'll walk all over the house for you in a white dress."

"No, Baby. We're having a wedding."

"I told your mom maybe we would have it in her backyard."

"I like that idea a lot. It's settled."

Simone groaned, "Damn. We gotta go to country ass North Carolina for the wedding?"

Stew and I laughed. Kendall said, "Durham is not country. Raleigh/Durham is in the heart of the state and very progressive. Your Florida ass is country!"

Stew and I laughed again. Simone said, "Kendy, go back to the woods where you were hatched...little girl."

Kendall opened his mouth, but all he could do was laugh. We all hollered laughing. He said, "Okay, Sister. That was a good one. I see my wife has been telling family secrets. She must be punished."

"I had to balance the scales, Kendall. It was only fair."

After dinner, we found the place on the beach where we bought the shots. The fruit stand wasn't there, but we had a blast doing shots of Tequila.

Simone and I had on shorts and waded in the water. It was so nice not worrying about schedules and being seen. I finally began to relax.

Until I saw Kendall and Stew make eye contact. I didn't think much of it at first. Then I saw it again. They suggested we go, and then they chased us to the car.

But they didn't seem very interested in catching us. As a matter of fact, they each turned around and ran in different directions.

When Simone and I turned and saw them, we looked at each other and began to go back. I asked Simone, "Did you notice them looking strange?"

"No. Did you?"

"I saw them..."

We heard someone screech in pain. Simone and I looked at each other and she laughed. "They're playing, Felicia."

"I don't know. Slow down, Simone."

The guys ran toward a rundown shack. They went around it, but in different directions. Simone went in the direction Stew took. I said, "Simone. Wait for me."

I was scared, but she was going with or without me. We held hands and heard Stew say, "Man, why the fuck are you following us?"

We looked at each other and proceeded to the back of the shack. The guy from the grocery store was under Stew's foot. Simone and I were horrified. She said, "I'm calling the police."

Stew said, "Simone, we're good. Right, Brother?"

Sitting with his back against the shack and bent over, he said, "Yes."

Kendall squatted and looked at him. "Is Benson paying you to follow us?"

"Yes."

I walked over and wanted to kick him in his face. Kendall asked Stew to let him up. The guy had several bruises on his face. Kendall asked, "What's your name?"

"Jim Johnson. Of J&J Investigations. You're welcome to take my card."

He gave Kendall his card and it had James and Jeffrey Johnson on it. Kendall asked, "Does he know she's here?"

"Yes, I told him."

"How much is he paying you?"

"Two fifty a day plus expenses."

Kendall and Stew looked at each other. Stew said, "You have three options. We could dump your ass in this water, and your family would never see you again. Or...we could take you to our place and tie you up for the next week so you can hear us fucking our wives while you starve to death."

Then Stew squatted next to Kendall. "Or you could get your ass on the next plane and explain to Benson you became deathly ill and had to leave."

"I'll be on the next plane."

Kendall asked, "Where is your report? Where are you staying?"

He answered all of Kendall's questions and told him he'd gladly give him all of his reports. The three of them were headed toward his car when I stopped them. "Excuse me. How long have you been following me?"

He turned to me. "Including others we employ, for over two years."

I walked closer. "So my husband has known for over two years?"

"More or less. We weren't sure at first, because you and your friend were both going to the house on East Ave. But within a few months we saw you at The Doctor's Lounge. Then it was clear who you were seeing."

I paused. "Why did you hit on me in the store?"

"Because I'm a man, Mrs. Benson."

He turned back toward Stew, and Kendall hit him so hard, *I* saw stars. He hit the ground and didn't move.

Stew grabbed Kendall because he was about to hit him again. Kendall looked down and said, "I'm a man too. And her *name* is Mrs. *Montgomery!*"

I yelled, "My God, Kendall! You killed him!"

Simone put her hand over her mouth and looked down at him. She said, "Naw. He's still breathing."

She turned to Kendall. "What the fuck, Brother?!"

Then she started laughing. That's when I realized she laughs when she's scared. My crazy ass laughed too.

The guys escorted Jim to the airport the next morning, but not before they scanned his driver's license, passport and credit cards. Stew told him if there was any evidence of him telling Harold anything else, he'd pay him a visit.

Simone and I went shopping. We were still outdone about the previous night. I shook my head and said, "Girl, that was some crazy shit last night."

"Crazy as hell, Felice! Did you know Kendall held him while Stew beat him?"

"Yes! Kendall said he was suspicious when the guy didn't have an accent while he was talking to me at the store."

Kendall and Stew saw him at the restaurant, but we didn't see him. The guys didn't mention it to us because they didn't want him to suspect they were on to him. So, when they saw him on the beach hiding behind the shack, they ambushed him.

"You said something was gonna happen, Felice. I'm like you now. I pray we've seen the worst of it."

We sat at a shaded table outside of a souvenir shop. Simone said, "You need to accept that Kendall is probably gonna whip Harold's ass. Did you see him knock the shit out of that guy?"

I closed my eyes. "Damn, Simone. How can someone so sweet and gentle be so...wow, Girl? I thought he hit *me*."

She hollered laughing. "Last night in bed, I was still upset. So Kendall gently made love to me like nothing happened."

"Stew did the same thing. I told him I couldn't believe he beat that guy like that. He kissed me and asked me if I was jealous."

"What?"

She laughed. "I like it a little rough sometimes. Just a little. I'm not crazy, Felicia. Stop looking at me like that."

I sucked my teeth and shook my head at my sister. We both fell out laughing. Then I asked, "Did you two have that threesome?"

She laughed again. "How did you know about that? I don't remember mentioning that to you."

I thought about it. "That was in my dream. Remember the dreams I had after the accident?"

She laughed. "That's eerie. We *did* talk about a threesome, but we couldn't agree on a man or a woman. Then neither of us wanted to share."

"Do you think he's ever cheated?"

"Sometimes I do. Because he looks at kitty cats all day long and he's handsome and around tons of women at both jobs. But most of the time I don't, because he loves me so much. Either way, he loves me *so* much, Felice."

I smiled. "That would be true, Sis. So, are you gonna give him a baby?"

She leaned her head back and laughed. She seemed prettier than ever and her hair had grown a lot. "I stopped using protection a while ago and my period is late."

I reached for her hand. *"You're pregnant??* Is that why your ass is so wide?"

"I'm almost sure I am. That's the main reason I agreed to get married now. I wasn't having a baby out of wedlock."

I got up. "You and your secretive ass! You should've at least told *me*, Simone! Let's get a test."

"I have it. I bought it while you were in the beauty supply store."

"How do you feel?"

"Actually, I feel pregnant. Swollen and sore breasts, nauseous and I threw up once in Pittsburgh."

"Does he suspect?"

"No. I threw up when I landed in Pittsburgh. He doesn't know about it. And I haven't mentioned any of it to him."

"It's still early. Let's go to the house so you can take the test."

She was already complaining that she had to pee. I remembered Stew asking me how many times I'd peed that day before he tested me. I begged her to hold it.

When the test appeared positive, she sat and stared into space. The first thing she said was, "Curtis wanted a child so bad. Lord, Felicia. I never felt good about that. But this feels so right."

She bent her head and cried. We both had tears and I gently removed the vial from her hand. "We'll box this and wrap it for Stew. Okay?"

She nodded. I put my arms around her and then I slapped her hand. "Simone! You've been drinking."

"I wasn't sure, Felicia. And if I didn't, he would've been suspicious."

"We'll put diluted ginger-ale in a bottle for tonight. They'll think we're drinking Moscato."

We finished our shopping and had his gift wrapped. We also bought a few bottles of Moscato and ginger-ale. Then we hid our clothes in one of the other bedrooms, and decided we'd use that room to dress the next day.

Stew found someone to come to the house to marry them. The forecast for Thursday was sunny and eighty degrees. Everything was coming together beautifully.

The guys asked us to dress up really pretty, because we were going out later. When they returned, they had smirks on their faces and secrets behind their eyes.

They brought salads and sandwiches for lunch, and Simone looked at the food and crossed her eyes. The scent of the feta cheese turned her stomach.

When I saw her face turn colors, I asked her to go upstairs with me and she politely emptied her stomach in my bathroom. "We'll say you have a nervous stomach about getting married."

"I don't think it'll work. I can't go out. I have to tell him, Felicia."

"Let's try one more thing. Instead of telling him you're throwing up, I'll tell them you've been on the toilet all day because of something you ate. It excuses you from eating right now and drinking later. And by tonight, you'll be ready to eat something light. Stay here and I'll get you some crackers."

I went downstairs and the guys were looking at me. "Simone is not feeling well, so I told her to stay up and rest for a while. I'm gonna take her some crackers and ginger-ale. She ate something earlier and it's not agreeing with her. She'll be fine."

Stew got up. "I'll go up and take care of her."

I put my hands up. "She'd prefer some solitude right now, Brother. I put her in one of the guest rooms and forced her to rest for about an hour. We had a breakfast sandwich with who knows what on it. I was sick earlier. It just needs to pass. She doesn't want you watching her sit on the toilet."

I smiled and he sat back down. Earlier, I'd put two bottles of the ginger-ale on the counter. I picked up one of them along with the crackers, and I went back up.

She was in Carla's old room and I went in and closed the door. "Okay. You're excused for lunch. And I think Stew is going to stay away for a while. I told him you were on the toilet."

She laughed. "I think it's passed, but I'll chew on the crackers."

"I need to get back down there before he decides to come up. Rest for at least thirty minutes."

By six-thirty we were dressed and ready to go. The guys were both dapper in their suits and ties and still wearing smirks on their faces.

Simone appeared to be okay, but I was a nervous wreck. When we left the house, a beautiful white limousine awaited us. We went into the heart of Montego Bay and stopped in front of a beautiful restaurant. We got through dinner fine and then we went to a great jazz club.

While at the club, Stew and Kendall told us more about Jim Johnson. They said he gave them a copy of all reports over the last two years. Kendall said, "Your home phone is also tapped, Shiree."

I shook my head and marveled at Harold's need to control me. I almost felt like he got what he deserved.

But my focus was on Simone. She used her upset tummy as her excuse not to drink. So I drank enough for both of us. Kendall asked, "Is something wrong, Shiree?"

"Not a thing. I'm happy and excited about tomorrow. By the way, my card came. The name on it is Felicia Montgomery."

I showed it to him and he smiled. "That's your name. It's just not official yet."

"If I get caught using it, I could get arrested."

He leaned over and kissed me. "Then I'll bail you out. Or go in with you."

My leg began to dance under the table. The room started spinning and Kendall began to laugh. "Shiree, you're drunk."

I could taste his cognac and I suddenly wanted to taste a lot more. Simone began giggling. "Felicia. You need to get home and in the bed."

Stew laughed too. I asked him, "Why you laughing? I'm not drunk. Just tired. It's been a long day and I spent most of it trying to keep Simone..."

Simone stood up and said, "Felicia! Be quiet!"

I put my hand over my mouth. "I wasn't gonna tell, Simone."

She looked at the guys and took my hand, wanting me to come with her. "I was gonna say Stew shouldn't see you until the ceremony. You shouldn't sleep together tonight."

Stewart stopped her and asked, "Tell what, Simone?"

"It's about your wedding gift. It's a secret."

"Are you sure? Nothing's wrong, is it?"

"Nothing's wrong, Baby. I promise you."

I giggled and Kendall said, "Let's go. She's smashed."

We agreed that Simone and I would meet in Carla's room at eight a.m. Stew said he did not come all the way to Jamaica for her to be in another bed.

That night in bed, I was completely out of character. Not just because I was tipsy, but the reality of my last four years was starting to overwhelm me.

And Kendall recognized immediately that something was wrong. "Relax, Baby..."

He pulled out. "No, Kendall. Why did you do that?"

"Sweetie, what's wrong?"

I didn't answer right away. "Please tell me what's going on, Shiree."

"You don't really want to know."

"What does that mean?"

"It means…I feel really stupid, but at the same time on the edge of being heartbroken. I've been trying so hard to look past it, but I can't. I wish you could begin to understand what the last four years of my life have been like. Two days after my wedding, I collapsed and was determined to leave and get an annulment. But I believed him. I *believed* him, Kendall. I forfeited my opportunity to be with the man of my dreams for a man who treated me like one of his possessions. He kept telling me he couldn't live without me. And I believed that too…"

"Come here, Baby."

He brought me in his arms. "I have an idea what you went through, Shiree. Remember, I was there for most of it."

"But there was so much I never told you. Things I was too ashamed to admit I was enduring. I knew he was sleeping around. I also knew he was aware of us. He made it his business to know every move I made."

"I promised myself I wouldn't force you to do anything, Shiree. But I really think you should move in my house and legally separate from him. Soon, Baby."

"I think I should get my own place for a while, Kendall."

"Shiree…"

I touched his face. "Kendall. Please don't be upset. It's time for me to grow up and start making my own decisions."

"I'd be worried sick about you. And I would miss you terribly."

I smiled. "No, you wouldn't. You'd be there all the time. I don't want you out of my life, Kendall. I need time to repair it. Without being influenced by anyone."

"You mean me."

"I *mean* I'm thirty-two years old and I've always had someone making decisions for me. Molding my life into something that worked for them. My parents, work, Harold…never Todd. Todd accepted me just as I was."

I thought about how different Todd was. Maybe because we lived simply, and we grew up simply. We weren't expected to attend balls or live in grand homes.

Kendall got up and went to the bathroom. He then went out on the balcony and sat on the loveseat. I put on a robe and joined him.

I sat next to him and he put his arm around me. "Shiree. I just want to love you. Not mold you into something unrealistic or something that is no longer you. *You,* is who I love. I feel as though you regret loving me."

I felt terrible because I'd clearly hurt his feelings. "Not true, Kendall. Loving you was the best move I've *ever* made. Harold pretended to be something he wasn't. And it was too late when I realized how manipulative, selfish and narcissistic he was. The true love of his life is himself. He kept saying to me over the last two years how glad he was that I seemed so much happier. Who does that?"

Kendall chuckled. "I could never do that. About eight months after Juanita and I were married, I had a fling. She found out, but she didn't mention it right away. She decided to have one too. With a guy she cared nothing about, but she and I both knew he was crazy about her."

I put my hand on my chest and dreaded hearing how this ended. "Then she left me a trail of crumbs so I could find out easily. I was livid. She told me every time I put it inside anyone that wasn't her, she would do it again."

I hollered laughing. I also made a mental note to call her soon. "I can't believe you didn't hit the guy."

"She told me if I did, she'd nurse him back to health."

Juanita is a mess. I laughed again. "But the two of you figured out an arrangement that worked for both of you. Right?"

"Yeah. For a while. But it's too dangerous. I would never agree to anything like that with you. Never."

We sat and talked on the balcony for a long time. I told him things I never had about my marriage with Harold. He was very quiet. I finally said, "I wanna finish making love."

He got up and took my hand. He was still totally naked and we went back inside. I sat on the bed and he stood in front of me. "Kiss me, Shiree."

I did what he asked. He played in my hair and enjoyed me loving him. I learned he liked his toes kissed. I insisted that he lay down and I went to his feet.

I kissed his toes and inserted them one by one into my mouth. He enjoyed it immensely. Then he sat up and said, "Stop before you kill me. Damn, Baby..."

He laid me down and kissed me. He opened my legs and his first touch was like a bolt of lightning. I instinctively closed my legs. "Open your legs, Baby."

He laughed and began to kiss my tummy and my breasts. He whispered in my ear, "I know you want it, Shiree. I need to taste you. Let me lick your pussy."

I moaned as his words caused my legs to shake. He went back and opened them. "Put your fingers in your mouth and rub your clit."

I continued to struggle touching myself, but I did it for him. He licked me and moaned. He reached for my hand and put my fingers in his mouth. He put them on my clitoris and massaged it.

He raised my legs and put his tongue inside of me. I came and groaned so loud. He removed my hand and he sucked me. I surrendered and let go of the pain that four years of abuse had done to me. And I embraced in totality, the love and pleasure I got from Kendall Montgomery.

He moved on top and inside of me. His thickness almost paralyzed me. I whispered, *"I love you so, so much."*

He went so deep that tears formed in my eyes. My whole body raised up off the bed. We came together, and the pleasure of it mixed with all of the pain.

He held me close and told me to cry all I wanted to. After a while, he released me and moved my hair away of my face. He kissed my entire face and smiled.

He then got up, went in the bathroom and returned with a washcloth. He sat on the bed and cleaned my face. "Thank you, Kendall. I'm sorry I got so emotional."

"Don't apologize, Sweetie. It's perfectly understandable. I admit I almost cried too. I was reminded of that night at Gary's when we both cried. Remember?"

I nodded. "And I was thinking that maybe you're right. Maybe you should take some time to get things in order. I don't want you to have regrets, Shiree. Just please stay at our place. Before you say no, please think about it."

He sounded so sad. "Okay, Kendall. I'll think about it."

While lying in his arms, he asked, "Shiree, will you marry me?"

"What, Kendall?"

"Answer me."

"Yes, Baby. Why are you asking me again?"

"Marry me tomorrow."

"Kendall. You know I can't do that."

"I know, Shiree. But we can commit or pledge to love each other forever."

"Okay. If that'll make you feel better about us, I'll do that for you. I don't want anyone else but you, Kendall."

"How will it make *you* feel? Am I pressuring you?"

"I think because I've been married twice already, I feel a little uneasy about it. Not about you, but the whole idea of doing it so quickly. But when we begin the process of getting pregnant, I believe we should be married. She deserves to be legitimate. So, I will not be asking Harold for a separation."

"Shiree..."

"I'm getting a divorce."

I got up at seven o'clock the next morning and quickly showered and brushed my teeth. I tried to be quiet so Kendall could sleep longer. But when I came out, he was sitting up and asked me to turn the shower back on for him.

I asked why he was getting up so early. "I think I'll take Stew out for breakfast so you all can do what women do on your wedding day."

I smiled and remembered his request that we also get *married*. When he came out of the bathroom, he came over and kissed me. "I'm glad we talked, Shiree. I didn't like it, but I do understand how that can be heartbreaking."

"Thanks, Kendall."

He smiled. I watched him getting dressed through the mirror. "Kendall?"

"Yes?"

"Are you planning to kill Harold when we return?"

"That's the plan."

"Sweetie…"

"I always suspected he was abusing you. And I know you didn't tell me because you *knew*…I would've beat his ass unrecognizable. He's lucky…"

"Kendall…"

"That bastard didn't deserve you! I might not either, but I love you with all of my heart! *All* of my heart, Shiree. He doesn't *have* a fucking heart! So yeah, that's the plan."

The cleft in his chin was deep and crazy looking. Again.

I walked over to him. I reached up and embraced his face. I touched the cleft with my thumb. It began to relax. I continued to massage it and I smiled at him.

I looked into his eyes. "I know, Sweetie. And I'm so blessed to have you. For some reason, even though we did a lot of foul things, it's like we were each sent to save the other. I love you so much. Tell me again how much you love me."

He exhaled and began to calm down. His body wasn't as rigid. He leaned down and whispered in my ear, "I love you…more than my life. And beyond."

We held each other close, as if letting go would somehow change something. We soon gazed into each other's eyes, and I said, "I want you to promise me…*promise me,* you'll not lay a hand on him."

He looked at me a long time. I watched him through slanted eyes. He finally leaned down and kissed me. "Okay."

I watched him closely. The cleft was still relaxed. He continued to dress and soon turned back to me. "So tell me. What's Stew's wedding gift?"

I wagged my finger at him. "Oh no, Doctor. I'm not telling. Shame on you for asking me that. You'll tell Stew."

"I swear I won't. I was intrigued last night when you almost spilled the beans."

"I did not. I was in complete control."

He laughed. "I don't think so, Shiree. I had to help you walk out."

"I just like being in your arms. I was fine."

I grabbed my purse and a tablet I'd been jotting some notes on. He came over and looked at it. "What's all this?"

"Because Simone is going to be nuts today, I had to make some notes so I wouldn't forget to remind her of certain things."

Then I looked up at him. "We didn't get a gift for them. I thought of it yesterday, but she was with me."

"Actually, I forgot to tell you I reserved a suite at the Half Moon. I arranged it yesterday, along with the limousine. We'll all have dinner near the hotel and the limo will drop them off, bring us home and then pick them up tomorrow morning."

"That's great! I'll get a card and a token gift so they'll have something to open and save from us."

He came closer. "So, what's the secret?"

"What secret?"

"Stew's gift?"

"I'm not telling you, Kendall. You'll know when he tells you."

"I won't know until tomorrow. Then everyone will know except me."

"I'll tell you tonight. After we leave them. Okay?"

He glared. "I'm your husband. You're supposed to be more loyal to *me*."

I laughed at him. "It's not working, Husband. I'll find out if they plan to exchange gifts privately or with us there."

He continued staring. I asked, "So, what's *her* gift, Doctor?"

"A house. In Gates."

"Get the hell outta here! For real?"

"Yes. Not far from our house, Shiree. He bought it about a month ago for her. He was gonna surprise her and have it renovated first, but now they'll do it together."

I was like a child. I was jumping up and down. "That's great, Kendall! I'm so happy for them."

"Now will you tell me?"

"You're so spoiled. But I really can't, Kendall. When you see it, you'll understand why."

I turned to leave, but I went back and kissed him. "This might be the last time I see you until the wedding. I'm gonna miss you, Kendy."

"I'll get you back, Licia. You..."

I put my finger up to my lips and whispered, "Listen."

We both went to the door and listened. We heard them arguing. Stew said, "I really need you to tell me the truth, Baby."

"You're wrong, Stewart. I really want this. I just ate something in that sandwich and didn't feel well yesterday. But I'm fine today."

Their voices got closer, so I opened the door. "Good morning. How are the lovebirds today?"

Simone said, "We're fine."

Stew asked, "Has she mentioned being nervous or having cold feet, Felicia?"

"No, Stew. Not at all. Actually, I'm the one who's antsy."

Kendall said, "I believe my wife offered you two a good morning."

Stew laughed and said, "Ken. Felicia. Good morning."

Simone kept going into Carla's room. I was about to follow her, but Kendall grabbed me. He said, "Stew. Felicia has agreed to illegally marry me today."

Stew bent over laughing. "I like it. And Simone will be thrilled. We both said how cool it would be if we could get married together."

Then Stew turned to me. "Felicia. Please tell me about Simone. I'm afraid she's not feeling good about this. I need you to tell me the truth."

"If you only knew how much she wants this. Just yesterday she said this feels so right. Better than any time before."

He smiled. "Honestly, Felicia? You're telling me the truth?"

"I swear, Stew."

Then he turned to Kendall. "So what do we do until three o'clock?"

"Let's go and get some breakfast and buy our wives some pretty things."

I said, "Don't overdo, Husband. What time is the minister coming?"

Stew said, "I told him about two forty-five. We'll be here to receive him."

"Good. I'll need to be with Simone. Like now. You guys get outta here."

When they finally left, Simone came out and I asked her how she felt. "I just emptied my stomach. That's why I was trying to get away from Stew. I feel great now. Stew thinks I have cold feet."

She laughed and we went downstairs. I was going over my notes and began to tell her our morning schedule. "We need to leave at nine for manicures and pedicures. I was gonna schedule a massage, but I decided against it. Have you taken your shower yet?"

"Yes, but I didn't get a chance to lotion and stuff."

"Go and finish and I'll fix you something light to eat. Can you eat or do you want to wait?"

"What are you fixing?"

"English muffins and eggs."

"That sounds calm enough. Actually, no eggs for me. And coffee?"

"We really need to get some decaf, Simone. After today, he's gonna be all over you about that. When do you plan to exchange gifts?"

"I don't know. I want to tell him right after so he'll stop worrying."

"Thank God. Kendall has been bugging me about what you're giving him."

"Really?"

"Yeah. He couldn't believe I wouldn't tell him."

We both laughed.

By two o'clock, I think everyone was on edge except Kendall. They were in Simone and Stew's room and we were in Carla's. Simone was completely ready except for her dress and shoes.

Her favorite colors are black and white, and it took all I had to convince her not to put something black on.

She had on two garter belts. A blue one and a white one. She wore the ring that belonged to her grandmother as something old. Her outfit was new, and she wore my diamond earrings as something borrowed.

She was clean, manicured, pedicured and made-up. So was I. I decided to surprise Kendall and I bought another dress. An all-white calf length dress that he dreamed of seeing me in. It was sexy but not inappropriate.

Except for Simone's garter belt, the four of us were in all white from head to toe. The guys got white tuxedoes and shoes, and even the limo was white.

Simone and I were claustrophobic because Carla's room didn't have a balcony. We didn't want to be seen, so we sat and waited. I asked for the tenth time, "How's your tummy?"

"Felice. Please stop asking. I'm fine."

I made sure the small gift box was in her purse along with a few crackers in a paper towel. I wanted a drink, so I called Kendall. "Hi, Baby."

"Hey, Baby. You okay, Shiree?"

"Yeah. Are you guys nervous?"

"I'm fine. My brother here is worried she won't show up for the dance."

I laughed. "Tell him she's all dressed and pretty for him."

He told Stew what I said. Then he laughed. "Stew's smiling and I think he's blushing."

"Good."

"You okay, Shiree? You're not getting cold feet, are you?"

"No, Kendall. I'm a wreck though. Could you fix me a drink and put it outside the door?"

He laughed again. "What about Simone?"

"What about her?"

"Should I bring her one too?"

I turned toward Simone. "Simone, you want a drink?"

"Yes, please."

"Yes, Kendall. Two glasses of Moscato please."

I drank both of them.

At five minutes after three, we heard the music the pianist was playing. Stew hired him along with the minister.

The plan was that I would come out first and Kendall would escort me down the stairs and outside. Then he would go back and escort Simone down the stairs and out to Stewart.

I looked at Simone and she was perfect. I twirled around and she said I was also perfect.

There was a tap on the door. I opened it, and Kendall was standing there waiting for me. He gave me his arm and I held it until we were at the bottom of the staircase.

He kissed my cheek. "You're breathtaking, Shiree. I love your dress."

"Thank you, Husband."

We went out and I stood on the other side of Stew and the minister. Stew came over and kissed my cheek. "This is it, Sis."

I smiled and rubbed his arm. "Yes, it is."

When we turned, we saw Simone and Kendall coming down the stairs. Kendall was making her smile. Then she looked up into Stew's face.

Poor Stew's eyes watered. And I'm sure his mouth also watered. Simone was absolutely stunning. We actually found a bridal boutique, and it was funny that the dress Simone fell in love with was on the clearance rack. A girl after my own heart.

It was beautiful. It was a sleeveless lace dress that fit her curves perfectly. It was lined from the waist down, but just lace from the waist up. She found a beautiful white bustier to wear underneath, and wow, it looked fabulous!

The love that was obvious between them seemed to replace the air. Neither of them looked at anything or anyone else. Only each other.

I feared Stewart was gonna cry. I looked in Simone's hand and the single sunflower was there along with the hankie. I exhaled because I knew someone was gonna cry, if not all of us.

The ceremony was quick. They both said *I do* and the minister asked that we change places.

Kendall and I held hands, and the minister simply asked us if we loved each other. We both said yes, and he said our declaration of love before man and God was now sealed.

The next hour was spent laughing and crying and drinking. Well, almost drinking. We had champagne and Simone had ginger-ale dressed up like champagne.

She and Stew were so happy. And Kendall was acting as if we were really married. Kendall raised his glass and toasted them. Then he raised it again and motioned for me to stand next to him. "On behalf of my wife and me, we would like to present you with your wedding gifts."

I went into the kitchen and got them out of the drawer I'd hid them in. I handed the bag to Simone and the card to Stew. He read it and learned about their room at the hotel, dinner, and the limo.

They were both happy and Simone opened the bag and found a silver bridal frame. I said, "When we get home, we'll get it engraved."

While they were out earlier, Stew bought a camera and had the pianist take several pictures before they left. Simone kissed both of us, and Stew said, "Thank you both. Simone wants us to exchange our gifts now. She asked that I go first, but I really want her to go first."

I intervened and said, "You go first, Stew!"

The guys looked at each other, and Stew said, "Okay."

He went upstairs and Simone asked, "Do you know what it is, Felicia?"

"Maybe."

She punched my arm. "You've known and haven't told me?"

"Girl. If you don't stop hitting me…"

Kendall said, "So, of the four of us, you're the only one who knows what both gifts are, Shiree."

I smiled and did a dance. Kendall laughed, and Stew came back and handed Simone a small box. He kissed her and said, "Simone Greer. I believe I've loved you since the day I first laid eyes on you. You've made me sooo happy."

She smiled at him and was teary eyed again. She looked up at us and opened it. Inside was a key. He said, "There's a small card at the bottom of the box."

She took it out and read it out loud. It read: This key opens the door to our new home and new life together, Simone. I know you will fill it with more love and joy than I've ever known. I love you so much.

She turned it over and there was a picture of the house. She put her hand up to her mouth and cried. Stew said, "It has four bedrooms and…"

She jumped up and down and said, "I know it's perfect! Thank you, Baby!"

She held him a long time and kissed him all over his face. "I love you so much, Stewey."

They kissed each other passionately, and Kendall and I smiled.

She went in her purse and gave him the box. I jumped up and down, and Kendall looked at me and laughed. Simone said again, "I love you, Baby. More than I would've ever imagined I could. I hope the contents of this box will finally put to rest any doubt you may have."

He smiled and opened it. Kendall came closer and we all stood there waiting for him to move the tissue paper over.

He removed the vial and knew exactly what it was. But he couldn't seem to put it together at first. Kendall said, "Stew. It's positive, Man."

Stew said very slowly, "Simone? Are you playing with me?"

"No, Baby. You're about to be a father. So we're gonna need that house."

He took her by the hand, and they ran out on the beach. Kendall and I looked at each other and we both had smiles from ear to ear. He laughed and said, "That was one hell of a wedding gift."

They soon walked back in, and both of them had tears in their eyes. Kendall went over to his brother and hugged him. "I'm so happy for you, Brother. Come with me."

They went over to the bar and Kendall reached underneath. "This calls for something special."

He pulled out their favorite imported cognac and they went out on the patio. I went into the kitchen and got a bottle of water. "Time to flush, Sis."

She hugged me. "Thanks for everything, Felice. He's so happy. We both are."

We held each other a long time. Then she said, "Let's call our sisters."

We ran upstairs and went to my room. We got Annette's voice mail, but Carla answered. I pushed speakerphone and asked Carla, "Where's Annette?"

"At work. I'm on my way home. What's up, Sistas?"

We looked at each other and Simone said, "Do us a favor. Ask Annette to call us as soon as possible. And you need to be there so we can tell you guys what happened. It's not bad so don't worry."

"Hell no. Tell me now, Simone. Come on, don't make me wait."

"Please, Carla. We need to do this together."

Annette was calling in. I said, "Hold on, Carla. It's Annette."

When we finally got both of them on the phone, Simone said, "Ladies. I have great news. Stew and I got married today."

They both screamed, and Simone and I did too. We already told them we were coming to Jamaica, but then I said, "You guys! We haven't had the chance to tell you that we're in our house again. Our house on the beach!"

Annette said, "Get the hell outta here. Are you serious?"

"Yes. I have my old room and Stew and Simone have your room, Annette."

Then Simone said, "There's more news, Ladies. Stew and I are having a baby. I think I'm somewhere around eight weeks."

We all screamed again, and Carla said, "Nette. Didn't I tell you somebody was pregnant? I dreamed about fish twice!"

We all screamed laughing. Annette said, "That's why your ass and hips have spread so much. Why didn't you say something?"

I said, "Because her ass is too secretive."

We all hollered laughing and Simone said, "We're keeping this info under wraps for a while, Guys. Please don't share, okay?"

They both understood. Then I said, "Simone got a house for her wedding gift. She doesn't know it yet, but it's in Gates near all of us."

Simone looked at me and screamed again. Everyone was so happy.

I wonder why Carla dreamed about fish twice?????

Kendall came up and said, "Our ride will be here in a half hour. Simone, I assume you and Stew need to pack something."

"You're right. Bye."

She ran out and I yelled, "Stop that damn running!"

I began putting my hair up, and I noticed Kendall staring in the mirror. "Is something wrong, Baby?"

I turned toward him, and he asked, "Why are you putting your hair up?"

"I need you to get used to it. I'm planning a short haircut soon."

"Why, Shiree?"

"Because I'm ready for a change."

"Okay. Then we'll both cut our hair."

I turned back toward the mirror. "You're not gonna cut your Locs, Kendall."

"Would that upset you?"

I opened my mouth, but nothing came out. He was behind me and rubbed my behind. He smiled and looked at me through the mirror. "You were saying?"

"No, Kendall. I mean, maybe. I never thought about it. I just assumed..."

"I assumed too, Shiree. I love your hair. You said you love mine too."

I smiled again and faced him. "Yes. It's very sexy."

He removed my clip. While putting his hands through my hair, he kissed me. "Yours is too, Shiree. Don't take it from me. I love that it's natural and all yours. And how it cascades down your back when I kiss you. I'll always remember the day you were feeding Alysiya, and how it fell over your face. *So sexy,* Baby."

"If it means that much to you, I won't cut it. We have to go."

He kissed me and smiled. "Thank you, Felicia Shiree."

I rolled my eyes. "You're welcome, Doctor."

Dinner was great, but Simone began having nausea after every meal. She got up and went quickly to the bathroom. She threw up and I helped her clean up.

Stew was outside the bathroom begging to come in. I let him in, and he helped his wife. I left and suggested to Kendall that we go back to the house. When they returned, we told them we called the limo service.

Once the limo arrived at their hotel, I embraced Simone. "Congrats again, Sis. I'm so happy for you two. Please take it easy."

Then I turned to Stew. "I know this is your wedding night, but don't overdo, Brother."

He hugged me tight. "Thank you, Felicia. For taking care of her while she waited to surprise me. I'll make sure she's okay."

The guys also hugged, and Kendall gave Stew the card for the limo service. Kendall told him they'd be expecting to hear from him the next day and they'd bring them back to the house.

On the ride home, Kendall began kissing me. I couldn't help but remember how hot the sex was with Harold in the limo.

I wanted to suggest something, but I didn't want him to know. Ironically, he asked, "Have you ever thought about having sex in a limo?"

I reached over and picked up my glass of champagne. "Actually, I have...thought about it."

"Will you be okay?"

"Yes, I think so."

He took off my panties and raised my dress. "Your dress is so beautiful. When we make it official, will you wear it again?"

"If you really want me to. You like it that much?"

"I love it."

He took it off and set it aside. He cupped my face and kissed me again. Then he laid me down and put his hand between my legs.

He got on the floor, inserted two fingers inside of me and began kissing my sex. I held on to the seat and tried not to stab my husband with my heels.

I put one foot firmly on the floor and reached for his hair. He sucked me while his fingers were torturing me. I groaned loudly and whispered, "*Kendall...*"

My body convulsed and the motion of the car sent me spiraling. I managed to do it quietly and Kendall was soon helping me up.

He whispered, "Shiree, I can't wait to get you home."

"We're waiting?"

"You wanna make love now?"

I put my tongue in his ear and whispered, "Yes, Baby."

I unzipped his pants and removed them and his boxers. I got on the floor and enjoyed the taste of him. He leaned his head back and began to moan...a lot.

I got up and straddled him. I slowly took every inch of him. "Don't move, Shiree. Please."

I sat there and kissed him. I ran my fingers through his hair while he composed himself. I began squeezing him and I whispered in his ear, "It's okay, Baby."

I moved against him and continued squeezing him gently. His moans became louder and he grabbed my behind and finally moved with me. I moved faster and his release was incredible.

I held him close and continued to gently squeeze him. He whispered, "I love you so much. I pray I'm never without you."

We didn't go out our last night there. They finally allowed me to cook dinner. I fixed Simone baked chicken, and Stew and I had lamb chops. I also made wild rice and a big salad for all of us.

The men had smirks on their faces again. After dinner, Kendall and I cleaned the kitchen while Stew helped Simone. Her nausea was getting worse. Stewart said, "Ken, I think we should tell them soon. Simone needs to get some rest."

Simone and I went toward Stew, and I asked, "Tell us what?"

Kendall was behind me and said, "We have one last surprise for you."

We turned toward Kendall. Simone asked, "What is it?"

Stew said, "Ken and I put an offer on this house."

Simone and I looked at each other and hollered. I stopped and said, "Wait. An offer means you don't have it yet. Right?"

Kendall said, "That's right. The owner is hesitant. It's not really for sale."

Stew said, "But we offered more than its worth, so we're hoping to entice him with more money."

"How much is your offer?"

The guys laughed and Kendall said, "I'm not telling you that, Shiree. It's a gift for you and Simone."

I went over to Stew. "We understand that, Stew. But another fifty thousand might sweeten the deal. Let me do this."

Stewart put his hands up. "Felicia. Don't put me in that. Kendall will shoot both of us."

Kendall said, "Shiree. That money is for the kids' education. If any of them decides to go to medical school, it'll cost a fortune. We are not touching it except to invest some of it."

"Okay, Kendall. I trust whatever you say. I just wanted you to know I don't mind helping."

He laughed and kissed me. "Okay, Baby. But we're good."

I turned to Simone. "Can you imagine this house being ours?"

"I know, Felice. It's unthinkable."

Stew said to Simone, "Come on, Baby. Let's get you off your feet."

After making sure our things were packed and in order, I rejoined Kendall downstairs. It was about eight-thirty, and Kendall reached for my hand. "Come with me, Shiree. I have a surprise for you."

I laughed. "Doctor. Why do you continue to surprise me when you know I don't like surprises? I really don't like them."

He smiled. "Just come with me."

I took his hand, and we went out on the beach. He began tickling my hand and I ran away from him. He glared for a moment and then began chasing me.

I headed in the direction of *our* spot and he slowed down. When I reached the clearing, I saw a blanket and basket. As I got closer, I saw wine and a bowl.

I turned to him and he was smiling. He began taking off his shirt. Then he took my hand and we sat on the blanket.

He kissed me and smiled while looking in my eyes. "Shiree. I never thought in a million years we'd ever come back here."

"Me either, Kendall. It's like a fairy tale. And to think we might soon own it. It's unbelievable."

He unwrapped the bowl. It was full of fruit. He laughed while reminding me, "The first time we made love out here, you were drunk. Do you remember?"

"Wasn't that the night I cried?"

"Yes. I had no idea what to do with you. It was the first time I saw you cry during sex. You begged me to make you come. I was beside myself."

"I did not, Kendall."

He laughed again. "Yes, you did, Shiree. I'll never forget it."

We drank wine and fed each other fruit. "Do you plan to make me come, Doctor?"

"I plan to, Shiree. Stop teasing me."

He pulled me close and we laid next to each other. He reached for a slice of pineapple and fed it to me.

The night was perfect. He reached in the basket and removed four candles. Together we lit them, then he removed his and my clothes.

He then laid down behind me and made love to me soothingly. Just for me. It drove me insane. He was gentle and patient. He spoke so sweet to me and refused to let me escape.

I began to wonder what I did to deserve such a prize. We made love for hours.

We eventually went to our room and went to bed. He soon fell asleep, but I was wide awake. I looked at him and smiled. Even in sleep, he had me trapped. He moved slightly and pulled me closer.

He loved me so much, I thought. I made a good choice. Although he wasn't perfect, I finally accepted I wasn't either. And it was okay.

And although both men loved me, (yes, I believed Harold loved me), I honestly believed Kendall's love was pure. Whereas, Harold's was perverted, and more *need* than love.

Not need *of* me; but need *for* me to be that perfect wife and mother and whatever else I am or was to him.

I ignored every text and call from Harold since I hung up on him. I spoke to Mom regularly, and she assured me all four of my children were fine.

I'd finally gained the strength to leave him. After pouring my heart out to Kendall, I was much stronger. And watching Simone and Stew so happy, I got strength from them also.

And seeing Kendall's joy about a baby, I really wanted to do this. I wondered if the private detective really stopped tracking me, or if he actually went home and pressed charges against them.

How awful it would be for us to land and they put handcuffs on Kendall and Stew. I blocked that out of my mind and cancelled it out of the atmosphere.

I also planned to give Kendall what he wanted. I decided to move into his house. I made a second mental note to call Juanita.

The following morning Simone was terribly ill. We all took care of her and made her sit and chew crackers. She kept saying she wouldn't be able to fly.

We assured her it would be okay. Stew decided to check and see if four first class seats were available. After successfully securing them, he told us he requested seats near the bathroom.

Later, I walked in Stew and Simone's room and Stew was packing her things. "Stew let me do it. We're really particular about how our stuff is packed."

He looked at me and smiled. "Felicia. I realize you love Simone and me, but your care and kindness moves me to tears. I'll never be able to completely tell you how much I appreciate you."

"You're right, Stew. I love you both to pieces. But I know you guys would do the same for Kendall and me. I'm told you took care of Kendall day and night for a while last year. Please leave before you make *me* cry."

"Okay. I'll leave before we're both crying."

We both laughed and he left.

Minutes later, Simone came in. "Mrs. Greer, what are you doing up here?"

"I was scared Stew was gonna have my shit all over the place. Thanks for doing this for me. I feel better, so I'd like to help."

"You sit and tell me what to put where. Okay?"

"Felice. What are you gonna do? I mean, about Harold?"

"I've decided to move out, Simone. As soon as I get back. I will no longer live under the same roof with him. And although I know I should get my own place, I think I'll go on and move in the house with Kendall."

I waited for her reaction. She smiled. "I'm glad, Felice. You need to be with Kendall. And you no longer owe Harold anything or have any reason to believe anything he says. With his lying, conniving ass."

She got up and was clearly pissed as hell. "And whatever you do, *do not tell him* you're moving. Just let his ass come home and find out."

I shook my head. "Don't worry. I've learned my lesson. He told me Monday that no one was following me anymore and that guy was on my ass then. What a liar. And don't tell Kendall my plans. I want to surprise him."

While checking the kitchen, Kendall came up behind me. He grabbed my hand and brought me out back. "What is it, Kendall?"

"Let's take five minutes and go to our spot."

I smiled and we ran to it. There was a small box sitting there. It was gift wrapped and I turned to him. "Kendall..."

"It's your pretend wedding gift."

"Oh, Kendall. I didn't get you anything."

"Of course you did. Open it, Shiree."

I bent down and picked it up. Inside was a rose gold charm bracelet. It had two charms on it. One with the initials FSM and the other one had the initials KM. I turned to him. "Baby, I love it. Thank you so much."

He helped me put it on. "Shiree. When we get home, will you put your wedding band on?"

"Soon, Kendall. Give me some time to tie up some loose ends. Okay?"

"Okay, Baby. Have you noticed my left hand?"

I looked at his hand and saw he was wearing the ring I gave him. "Kendall. I never expected you to wear a ring. You never wore one before."

"Actually, I did. But when we became free spirits, we both removed our rings. But I never denied being married."

I reached up and put my arms around his neck. "I love it. And I love you, Doctor Montgomery."

"I love you too, Felicia Shiree Montgomery."

Chapter Eight

During the two weeks after returning to Rochester, I learned a little more about my...Harold. I also learned a lot about Felicia Pierce.

I hired a mover and had most of my things taken to Kendall's house in Gates. I succeeded in surprising him.

I packed the kids up and brought them with me too. I hired an attorney and had Harold served. It was heart wrenching, but I knew I had to do it right away or I wouldn't have the nerve to do it later.

I never told anyone my plans except my parents. I felt better doing those things on my own without being told how to do it or having someone do it for me.

I learned through Lenora that Harold had given two weeks notice. I was sad and relieved at the same time. I knew how much he loved his job.

Harold called me and sent me texts constantly until he was served. Then his silence had me on edge. Until we were finally face to face.

It was one of the few days I had to report to the office. I was sitting with Trina after a meeting. We were at her desk and she was about to leave for lunch. "I really wish you would reconsider and come to the Christmas party, Felicia."

"Girl, that man would insist on being on my arm and I would have to do too much explaining."

"But Harold's leaving. What difference does it make now?"

She looked at her phone and said, "I gotta go. My ride's here."

We hugged and she left. I went into the conference room to get my coat and work bag. When I turned to leave, Harold was standing in the doorway.

He came in and closed the door. I went around the conference table intending to leave, but he asked me to stay. "I just need a few minutes...please?"

I closed my eyes, but I nodded and said okay. He pulled out a chair and motioned for me to sit. He sat across from me. "I realize no amount of apologizing will make up for what I did to you, Felicia."

He looked up over my head, obviously avoiding eye contact. "I'm ashamed about so many things. I could tell you why, but I'm sure it still wouldn't make sense. I've been consumed with the fear of losing you since before we were married. That Sam situation caused me to lose all sense of common sense."

I felt sorry for him. "Felicia, I always knew you lied about only being with him twice. But I also knew you were trying to spare my feelings."

"What's the point in all of this, Harold?"

"I'm stepping out of the ring, Felicia. I admit defeat."

"All I was to you was a challenge?"

"No. Of course not. But that was my fatal mistake. I didn't want to lose you for the right reasons. But also for a lot of the wrong ones."

He paused. "There's so much I want to tell you, so hopefully, one day you'll no longer hate me."

"I'm more disappointed than anything, Harold. In you and in me. What I *hate* is what this turned us into. Of course, I could've remained faithful and forced myself into that mold you created for me. But I would've never been a good mother or daughter or wife or anything of value."

"I know that now. I was delusional to expect any of that from you. I need you to know that I intentionally used credit cards for hotels and restaurants to make you think...so you could see them. The truth is, I lied about cheating. I did cheat after I learned of you and him. But never before that, and definitely not during your pregnancy. I loved you so much, Felicia. And I realize now I need help."

He got up and looked out at downtown Rochester. A single tear slowly rolled down my face. "Harold..."

"I removed everything of mine from the house and it's now on the way to Detroit. I took some of the pictures, but I made sure you had duplicates of everything I took of the kids...and you. My attorney assured me the divorce will be swift and I believe I was generous about everything. But please, go over it with your attorney."

He went in his briefcase and handed me a manila envelope. "I decided to keep the house in Detroit and live there. I hope you're okay with that?"

"Of course, Harold. I'll have my name removed from it right away."

He turned back toward the window. "And unless you want child support, I'll continue to maintain the house expenses and the account for your parents."

"That's fine, Harold. I know you'll always be fair. Thank you."

Because my parents would never take anything for keeping the kids, Harold set up an account for them. He deposited five hundred dollars a month in it, but it had my name on it.

That way they didn't have to claim it as income. He gave it to them annually. "I hope I'm not keeping you, Felicia. I should've called first."

"No. We needed to talk. When are you leaving?"

"Tomorrow. I think I've covered everything. But I couldn't leave without seeing you and saying some things to you. And I know Kendall wants my head after the Jamaica fiasco and everything else. I plan to call him. To apologize."

He came over to me. "As crazy as it sounds, I'm happy to know you're with someone who loves you so much. And will love our children and take care of them. Especially since he's known them for so long."

He smiled and it was nice to see. "I know this also sounds crazy. But today is the fifth anniversary of that Christmas party. Five years, Felicia."

I looked at him and more tears fell. He looked at me and had tears too. I turned away and couldn't speak. He walked over to the window again. "I went to see your parents this morning and thanked them for always being so kind to me. And I spoke with the guys and we promised to always keep in touch."

"Your mom called me. She told me you finally told them everything. She assured me I would always be her daughter, and that she understood."

He faced me again. "Yes. I finally did. I have a doctor in Detroit that I've set up a few appointments with. Karen asked me to tell you to please call her. She misses you and is so worried about you."

I nodded and went toward the window and stood next to him. "Thank you for loving my children, Harold."

"Oh, no. *Our* children, Felicia. All four of them."

I smiled and said, "The boys were sad about us. Thank you for telling them you'd be back to take them to Yankee Stadium next summer. They also said you promised they could go to Detroit for a visit."

He nodded and smiled. "I hope we can be friends. Like you and Todd are."

"Me too. It's easier."

"Are you still okay with me coming back for the kids for Christmas? I know how hard that'll be for you."

"Yes. I also know how much you love and need them now. We'll share them lovingly. I never want us to fight over them."

He turned toward me. "I want that too."

We looked at each other for a moment. He touched my shoulder tentatively. "If you ever, *ever* need anything, don't hesitate to call me. I may have been a lousy husband...but I will always love you and care about you, Felicia."

"Thank you. Same here, Harold."

The sadness in his eyes was overwhelming. I guess mine was too. "You know what, Harold? I need to go. Are you still taking the kids out for dinner?"

"Yes. Where should I pick them up at?"

"My parents. And I'll pick them up from there afterwards."

I gathered my things and put the envelope in my work bag. I turned toward him and was at a loss for words. But I managed to say, "I guess I'll see you later."

"Yes. And I'll see you in a week when I get the kids."

I paused. "Actually, it just dawned on me. Why don't you see if they can go with you tomorrow? There's no need in you coming back."

"Really? That would be great. I'll check and let you know."

It was hard, but I managed a smile. "Okay. I'll let you work on that and I have a lot to do, so maybe I'll see you later today."

He came over to me. "I really appreciate this."

I opened my arms and we hugged each other. I closed my eyes and tried hard not to cry. But I failed. I put my head down and walked out.

When I finally got to my car, I laid my head on the steering wheel and cried for what seemed like forever.

I eventually drove to my house. It felt hollow and empty and void of love. I sat on the stairs and cried again.

My phone vibrated and I reached in my pocket to get it. It was a text from Harold saying he'd successfully changed the kids' reservations. I replied I would have them ready at nine tomorrow morning.

I went up to their room and realized my kids had clothes at three different houses. I called Mom and asked her how many clothes were there. She laughed and said, "They have tons of clothes here."

I told her they were leaving tomorrow, and she was sad. "Bring them each a suitcase, and I'll take care of it."

"Thanks, Mom."

"Are you okay?"

"I guess so. Harold and I had a moment, and we both sort of cried. It was heart wrenching."

Mom was quiet. "Mommy. I wish this could have been different. It's nothing like me and Todd's break up."

"Harold came in our lives and was a blessing in so many ways. I've cried too, Felicia. And I'll continue to check on him. Jackie and I were beside ourselves. But she and I will remain friends, and the four of us are planning a cruise for next year. Life goes on, Daughter."

After hanging up, I walked into our room. So much was missing. I walked into his closet and saw where he had the wall repaired. No signs of a hole. I never told Kendall.

His closet was completely empty. I went in mine and most of my things were still there. And hanging on the wall was the armoire with all of the jewels.

I realized there were many things that would always remind me of him. I went back into the bedroom and noticed he took a few of the pictures but left the one of me in the bikini. That saddened me too.

I also noticed an envelope on the dresser. I opened it. He wrote me a letter. I didn't want to read it, but I needed to get it over with. I sat on the bed and read it:

Dear Felicia,

I hope to see you before I leave, but if not, I need to say this to you. I'm so sorry about the way things ended with us. I would've never thought I could hurt you like this. I take responsibility for all that happened and how my obsession caused you to do things you may not have done. I was never unfaithful until I learned about you and Kendall. I lied about that, hoping to make you as jealous as I was. I was far more devastated by the Sam incident than I let on. And I turned it into a war I had to win. Then I was determined to keep you away from all men. Who would've thought taking the kids to the doctor would result in you meeting someone?

I learned about you and Kendall by accident. Your laptop bag was on the table and your other phone apparently slid out of it. I saw calls and texts to and from him. I then hired the PI and learned exactly who it was. For two years I watched you, but I could not bring myself to say anything. I was embarrassed at first. My ego was destroyed and I was hurt. I blamed everything and everybody but me. But I now realize I was wrong. So wrong, Felicia. I pray you will find a way to forgive me. And yourself. I know how you felt when you found out about my knowledge of Sam. Please don't beat yourself up. I just wish I'd been what you needed. I always loved you. Just too hard, as you told me recently.

One last thing. It's important to me that you know I will always be here for you. Whether you need help with the kids or anything else, please don't hesitate to call me. I worked it out so that you should always be financially secure, and I will always take care of you and the kids. I assume you and Kendall plan to marry. I'm not asking that you have him sign a prenup, but I opened an account with the kids and my name on it, with you as guardian. For them and you. I admit I did a check of Kendall's assets, so I know he's also a millionaire. But I assume you know that.

Please let's be friends through this. That will give me peace. Thank you for all you gave, Felicia. I will always love you.

Harold

The letter was covered with my tears. I tore it up and flushed it down the toilet. I didn't want Kendall to somehow find it.

Why, why, why did this have to happen? I could've been so happy with him. I admit some of his jealousy was flattering. But it became my prison. And now I have this house. Maybe I'll sell it.

That evening, Mom and I were getting the kids' stuff together. I was quiet and in my own little world. Mom touched my arm and said, "Baby, please don't grieve too long. It could make you sick. And then I'll worry myself sick about you."

"I know you're right, Mommy. I just need some time to pass I guess."

"Kendall will help. He loves you better. Right?"

I tried to laugh. "I hope so, Mommy. He's had his moments too."

"Have you seen him today? I'm surprised he's not here."

"No, I told him I needed to prepare the kids for their trip and he said he would see us at home. Harold said he'd be back here by eight."

Mom went in the living room and brought four gifts back. She had tears in her eyes. "These are their gifts."

"Mommy, please don't cry. Would you like them to stay with you tonight?"

"Then you'll miss them."

"I *will* miss them. But...I think you and Daddy should have them tonight. I'll have plenty of time with them when they return, now that I have so much free time."

About fifteen minutes later, Harold and the kids walked in. Then Kendall. I stood up and looked at all of them. "What's this?"

Harold smiled and said, "I invited Kendall to join us for dinner, Felicia. He and I needed to call a truce. And as the father of these kids, I needed to be a man and face him."

Mom and I looked at each other shocked and open mouthed. My father came out and the men all spoke and shook hands. Kendall said, "Together, we told the kids that a lot of things would be different. And we agreed to talk once a week once the kids get back. Just for a while and I'll update him on the kids."

Harold said, "He and I will both be fathers to them. Like when Todd and I shared the boys. Todd taught me a lot back then."

I was floored. Daddy said, "I'm really proud of both of you. There's been enough pain. Now we can all heal and start anew on a positive note. For the sake of these kids, if for no other reason."

I went in the kitchen and leaned over the counter in tears. Someone was rubbing my back and I looked up and saw my father. "No more tears, Shiree."

I smiled at him calling me Shiree. On occasion he called me that, but it had been many years since he'd done it. "Shiree, Daddy?"

"When you were born, I wanted your first name to be Shiree. But your mother was adamant about Felicia being first. I called you Shiree until you were about a year and a half. Your mother made me stop because she was afraid you wouldn't know what your name was."

We both laughed. "That's why when I hear it, my heart smiles. Do you know that Kendall calls me that?"

"Your mother told me. She says he says it with so much love."

I smiled and hugged my father. I heard the door close and I released him. I thought out loud, "I wonder who left?"

"Harold. He's gone."

I went back in the living room and Kendall looked at me. "You okay, Shiree?"

More tears fell. He dropped the toy he and Benny were playing with and came over and took me in his arms. "Please don't cry."

Aleece came over and asked, "Mommy, why you crying?"

I looked down at her and she smiled. "Dr. Ken will make it better, Mommy. He's gonna take care of us."

"Okay, Baby."

Benny came over and said, "Mommy. I'll take care of you too. Daddy said it's a man's job to take care of you."

I bent down and embraced my twins. My two reminders of a time I so loved their father. The very reason they even exist. I realized it wasn't in vain after all.

It wasn't in vain.

I went to the restroom and I learned later that Daddy and Kendall had a conversation. Mommy told me Daddy said to Kendall, "I see you choose to call her Shiree. I always preferred it too."

Kendall laughed. "Honestly, Mr. Pierce. The moment I knew I loved her, I began calling her that. It's such a pretty name. And whenever I say it, it's like me saying I love you."

"I agree. Take care of her. She's sad now, but I believe you're better for her. Help her through this gently. Okay?"

"Yes, Sir. She means everything to me. I assure you I'll be patient. I know she loves me, and I'll do whatever is necessary for her and the kids."

Chapter Nine

That night Kendall bathed me and brought me tea. He tried to get me to eat, but I just couldn't. I hated to think what he must be thinking. But I was grieving for so many reasons. He finally said, "Maybe we should've brought the kids."

"I'm really gonna miss them, Kendall. But my mom cried when I told her they were leaving. I felt terrible for her."

"I've been thinking about something. How would you like to go and visit Kelly for Christmas? That way we could see the kids."

I thought about that. Then I said, "I don't think I'm ready for that yet."

"Harold could bring them, or we could get Kelly to get them and take them back. No one has to see you. I already told Harold that my sister lives there."

"Give me a day or so to think about it. I don't want my parents to be alone."

The following day, I had a lot to keep me busy. Kendall set up my office in the den downstairs so I didn't have to go to my house anymore for work.

Lenora called me and tried to persuade me to attend the Christmas party. She finally admitted, "The big wigs are giving us an award, Felicia. I wanted to surprise you, but you forced my hand. The troubleshooting trio had a higher percentage of resolving and preventing issues than any group in the region. We're sort of famous."

I laughed. "Okay, Girl. I'll be there. What time tomorrow?"

"Seven o'clock at the Convention Center."

"I assume you want me to keep this from Trina."

"Girl, yeah. I wanna see the look on her face."

"Me too. It'll be priceless."

I stopped by to check on my parents, but I waited until the kids left. I couldn't bear to look in Harold's face or endure another scene like the day before.

I knew I'd miss Harold. I already did. Especially his cooking and doing the grocery shopping. He taught me to love cooking. And Kendall taught me how easy it is to eat without meat.

Harold finally changed bank accounts, so only my salary goes in the old one. But he never removed any of the money already there. When I checked my balance, there was over eleven thousand dollars in my account.

I asked Harold if he wanted to split it. He said no, but he asked me to please buy my parents and the boys each a nice gift for Christmas. I told him I would.

I looked at the texts between us over the last few weeks and wondered if the day would come when I didn't feel so horrible. Our behavior caused two people in love to divorce. Maybe when Harold finds love again, I'll feel better and feel more comfortable with our new relationship. Like with Todd.

Kendall and I hadn't stayed overnight at the downtown apartment since returning from Jamaica. I talked to Simone every day, but I hadn't seen her.

It was Friday, and Kendall and I agreed we would stay downtown. After grocery shopping, I pulled in the garage and Kendall came out to greet me. "Hi, Shiree. How was your day?"

"Better. How are you, Hun?"

He stared at me. "I'm good. You called me Hun."

"I've called you that before. Stop tripping."

He laughed. "Okay. It's all good. You still love me?"

"I'm thinking about it. I'll really love you if you help me with these bags."

The Greers came out and we all greeted each other. I asked Simone if she was feeling better. "Girl, this is madness. I went to the doctor yesterday and she confirmed I'm between eight and ten weeks and doing fine."

"Do you still feel up to going out?"

"I'm looking forward to it. I know how to bring my ass home if I start feeling bad. Today has been a good day."

She and I walked into her place and I asked her, "So, when are you moving into your house?"

"After the holidays. Shayna is going to Texas and Stew and I are going back to Pittsburgh for Christmas."

I was looking out of her window. "Felicia. Did you hear me?"

I looked up at her. "I'm sorry. Just trying to find my place in the world."

She came over to me and said quietly, "Felicia. Please don't sink into depression. Isn't this what you wanted?"

I put my head down. "Yes, Simone. It is. In part. But the other part is why I fought it for so long. Look at what it cost. My family is obliterated. Kids everywhere. Husbands all over the place. I've really fucked up my life. And my parents in tears because they're worried to death about me and missing their grandbabies."

I shook my head, got up and opened her refrigerator. "What else can I do to hurt my loved ones?"

Simone looked out and saw they were still taking in the groceries. She took me into her living room. "Listen to me, Felice. I also have two ex-husbands and my daughter is all over the place. My mother is constantly on her knees praying and begging me to come down there with her. Our troubles may be slightly different, but they're basically the same."

I turned away and she grabbed my arm. "My mother insists on calling me and I have to stay on the phone with her while she prays for me. She cries and prays, Felicia. It's unbearable."

"I'm sorry for being so dramatic, Simone. I just can't seem to get over it. And poor Kendall has to endure me grieving, and he probably thinks I'm grieving Harold."

"Are you?"

"No, Simone. I mean, I'm sad that I hurt him. And I'm sad for my kids. But mostly, I'm sad about my bad choices. I have so many regrets."

I was falling apart, and she held me. "Kendall and Stew asked me to talk to you. Ken wants to marry you now, Felicia. He's afraid you'll decide to move on without him. Why would he think that?"

"That's just *him* being dramatic. I have never said anything like that. The only thing I said was that I should get my own place for a while, just to clear my head. But I moved in with him instead."

"He thinks you regret loving him. Is he one of your regrets?"

I opened my mouth but couldn't say anything. I looked at her and started to cry again. I finally asked, "Can we go upstairs? I don't want to be heard."

"You go over and cook dinner. When they leave, we'll talk. Okay?"

I agreed, got myself together and walked over to our side. Stew and Kendall were discussing something regarding the club. I said, "You guys don't mind me. I'm gonna start dinner. Would you and Simone like to join us, Stew?"

"No thanks, Felicia. We're having leftovers."

About ten minutes later, Stew left and Kendall came in the kitchen. "What are you cooking?"

"I'm sautéing veggies and potatoes. You want a drink while you wait?"

He came closer and put his arms around me. He moved my hair and kissed my neck. "You smell so sweet, Shiree. I love you, Baby."

I leaned back into him and felt at home in his arms. "I love you too, Kendall."

He put his hands under my breasts and gently squeezed them. I could feel him harden behind me and I closed my eyes and enjoyed him.

He turned me around and kissed me. He reached over the food and turned off the stove. He carried me up the stairs and stopped halfway up. He sat me down and kissed me passionately.

I went in his sweatpants and I removed him. He moaned. "Oh, Shiree... I've missed you so much."

I took him in my mouth and sucked him hungrily. He soon stopped me and stepped down. His hand was under my skirt and he felt how wet I was.

He put his finger in his mouth and brought my legs up. He pulled off my panties and opened my legs wide. He devoured me and was soon inside of me.

I wrapped my legs around his back. "Oh, K. I need you so bad. *Please make me feel better.*"

He kissed me and went deeper. I held him tight, as I came and convulsed in his arms. I leaned my head back and moaned, and I felt like

I was emptying myself of all of the pain. He whispered, "Say it for me again, Shiree."

I choked on the words he needed to hear. "*I love you so much, K.*"

He growled as he also appeared to rid himself of the pain. I said in a whisper, "I'm so sorry, Baby."

Simone and I met in the garage. She was hot in her heels and jeans. "Excuse me, Mrs. Greer. Are you gonna be okay in those heels? Although I must say, you're looking good."

She looked at my outfit and shook her head. "First of all, Kendall is gonna send your ass home when he sees you in that pink dress. Didn't he tell you not to wear that damn thing in public?"

"Girl, I've only worn it once."

"And you are *wearing* that diamond choker, Felice. Damn, Girl. You *must* let me borrow that. I know it's real."

I laughed at her. "Yes, it's one of many diamonds Harold gave me. Do you think it will upset Kendall?"

"He knows you have jewels."

"But I've never worn this before. I don't want him to think..."

"Stop it, Felicia. Wear it and deal with it. He'll be fine. He probably won't even notice it with all your ass and legs hanging out."

We got in my car and Simone asked, "Okay. What's going on?"

"I was starting to blame him for my woes. We hadn't had sex in over a week because I slept with the kids before they left for Detroit. One night he came and got me. He told me to come with him because he needed me."

I was looking straight ahead and remembering. "I got in bed with him, but I was afraid they might wake up. So I left him there. He was so upset with me."

"Oh no, Felicia."

I shook my head. "I know, Girl. He hasn't touched me since that night. But an hour ago..."

"I know. We heard. Stop doing it on the stairs. Although Stew and I were happy for him. He's been so blue."

"That's why the sexy dress, Simone. I want him hot for me all over again. I might stay there tonight. I'm hoping he'll be so hot he can't wait."

"Okay, Girl. We do have to heat it up sometimes. I'm feeling you."

"Ever since the kids and I moved in, I've felt so guilty. And poor Kendall has tried everything to ease my pain. I can't seem to get over the look on Harold's face. I've destroyed him."

"You did no such thing! He wanted to take your life, Felicia. No one has that right. No one. You promised Kendall to love him forever. Can you honestly say you still love Harold?"

I thought about that. "Honestly, I don't think so. And I don't think I've ever loved him like I love Kendall."

When we got there, our table was waiting for us and the waitress came over right away. She had a glass of cranberry juice and a glass of Ciroc over ice. She sat them on the table and looked at us with a smile. "Felicia and Simone. Right?"

Simone said, "Yes. What's your name?"

"Debbie. I started last week. I was told that you are Stew and Ken's wives. I'm your personal waitress for the night. You want something to eat?"

Simone frowned. I said, "Hi, Debbie. I'm Felicia. And yes, I'd like an order of wings."

"Yes, Ma'am. Nothing for you, Simone?"

"Some pretzels, please."

Debbie smiled and left. I had on a long wrap and I sat with it still on. I didn't see Stew, but I saw Kendall. He was surrounded by women as usual.

I sat back and observed, and Simone cracked up. "Girl. Kendall is too nice. He charms those hoes."

"Simone. Stop calling our sisters those names."

She sucked her teeth. "Every one of them would sleep with our husbands. You better recognize."

"I know that. But would our husbands sleep with *them?*"

She smiled at me. "Probably not. Stew likes big boobs."

I laughed and slipped out of my wrap. I put my legs under the table and continued watching Kendall, who still didn't seem to see us.

One of the women was awfully friendly. She put her hand around his waist and whispered in his ear. I turned to Simone. "Who the hell is that?"

"I've never seen her."

"Well, she's about to see all of me."

Simone cracked up.

I got up and walked over to him. He finally saw me and froze. Miss Thing asked him something, but he ignored her. He walked toward me and I smiled at him. "Don't let me interrupt you."

He glared at me, then leaned down and kissed me. He put his hand on my waist, turned and said, "Pam, come here."

She came over to us smiling. "Baby, this is Pam. She's visiting from Durham. We went to high school together. Pam, this is my wife, Felicia."

I extended my hand and she shook it. Her girls came over and she said, "This is Ken's wife. What's your name again?"

Kendall laughed and said, "It's Felicia, Pam. Damn, Girl."

I laughed too. Kendall turned toward me and said, "Ladies, excuse me a minute. I need to whip my wife's ass."

He took me aside. "Shiree? What the hell?"

He looked at my legs and then at my chest. I stood in front of him and pressed against him. "Don't you like this dress? You bought it for me."

He slanted his eyes and his dimples were dancing. "I feel like I did that day Juanita caught us in Atlanta, and you and Simone walked through the hotel lobby looking like new money."

I laughed and pressed against him again. "Stop teasing me, Shiree. And please don't get up again. I can see your kidneys, Baby."

He picked me up and carried me to my seat. Simone said, "Kendall, you're such a bully. Stop being so dramatic."

"Simone. How did you let her come out looking like that? Damn. I'm gonna fight tonight."

I asked, "Are you seriously upset about my dress, Kendall? Because I'll go home and change. I'm sorry, Baby."

He glared at me. "Don't move, Felicia. I mean it."

When he left, Simone and I cracked up. She said, "Girl, he'll be back in less than five minutes. It worked."

"Yeah, but it never dawned on me that he might get mad and hit somebody. Plus, he called me Felicia. He's pissed."

"Do you have something you could change into in the back bedroom, Felice?"

"Actually, I do have clothes here. Do you have anything here?"

"I might have something. You want me to go check?"

"Not yet. Let's see what happens next."

Five minutes later, he and Stew came over and sat with us. Stew kissed Simone and said, "You look great, Baby. You feeling okay?"

"Yes, I'm fine."

Kendall sat next to me. Stew said, "Felicia. You look great too."

Kendall rolled his eyes at Stew. Stew said, "Man, she wore it for *you*."

I leaned toward him. "Kiss me, Kendall."

He glared at me. "If you don't kiss me now, I won't kiss you later, Doctor."

He leaned over and whispered, "I'm going to whip you with a belt, Shiree."

Then he put his hand on the back of my head and brought my face to his. He kissed me really sweet and said, "Give that dress to Goodwill tomorrow. I can't believe how fabulous you look in it. But it's too short for my wife to wear in public."

"Okay, Kendall. I won't wear it again."

"No you won't because after today, you won't own it."

"I'm not giving away the prettiest dress you've ever bought me. I love it."

"That dress is too small for Shayna. Get rid of it!"

We all laughed and he did too. Debbie brought the wings and pretzels, and Stew and I ate the wings. Simone cringed and Kendall watched.

He loved to watch me eat wings. It was erotic to him, which was why I ordered them. I asked Kendall, "You wanna try one?"

"No, Shiree. But you enjoy yourself."

"Are you gonna watch?"

"Um-hum."

I whispered, "Can I put my foot in your lap and feel your erection?"

I looked at the wing in my hand and licked it. He said, "Stop, Shiree."

I fell out laughing and he shook his head. I looked over at Simone and she was laughing behind her hand. Stew was too busy eating the wings. Kendall continued watching me. "I'm full, Baby."

He laughed. "You ate two wings. How are you full?"

"I only ordered them to arouse you. Did it work?"

He stared for a moment and then he leaned over and whispered, "I want you to get your pretty ass up and go to the bathroom. I'll follow you."

"Okay, Baby."

I picked up my purse and walked in front of him. I heard Simone laughing and I turned toward the ladies' room. He grabbed me and took me to the back.

We went through the lounge and into his bedroom. He closed the door and pushed me against the wall. He kissed me and I could feel his raging erection. I went to my knees, unzipped his pants and took it out.

He grabbed my hair and brought me closer to him. I took him in my mouth, and he moaned and moved in and out. "Shiree. You play dirty, Baby."

After a few minutes, he pulled me up and took off my panties. He removed my dress and I stood there naked. Except for my diamond choker. "No bra, Wife?"

I didn't answer. He went lower and parted my legs. He raised my left leg and buried his tongue in me. I let out a groan and he sucked me and moaned as I gave him what he wanted.

He stood and kissed my breasts. Then he moved me away from the wall and removed his pants and boxers. He told me to lean over the bed. He came up behind me and slapped my behind. "You've been a bad girl, Shiree."

He entered me and we both moaned. He went further inside of me and chewed on my shoulder. "I've always wanted to do this. Now that you're all mine, I can."

He sank his teeth in my shoulder, but it didn't hurt. He bit me and licked me at the same time. Then he did the same thing on my neck. It drove me nuts.

He went so deep. He growled and asked me not to move. He reached around and massaged my clitoris. He squeezed my nipple with his other hand, and I came again. "How much more can you take, Felicia Shiree?"

"No more, Kendall."

"You shouldn't tease, Shiree. I've told you not to do that."

He went deep again. And again. He was moaning in my ear and I squeezed him. Hard. He groaned and came quickly.

He eventually slumped on my back and I laughed. "Don't mess with me, Negro. I have a few tricks of my own."

We both brushed our teeth and did a quick wash. He went in my drawer and gave me a pink bra and panty set. "The bra will show, Baby."

He glared at me like he didn't care. I chewed on my lip and I said to him, "Kendall. I'm sorry about my behavior lately. I needed time to adjust to… I don't do change well. Do you forgive me?"

He stared at me at first, then he walked over to me. "Of course, Shiree. I was worried that I'd somehow…that you had regrets."

"I told you before that's not true. But I do regret other things and decisions I made before meeting you. I wish I'd known you five years ago."

"Me too, Baby."

"And about going to Detroit. Not this year. But thank you for offering it. I love you."

He smiled. "I love you too, Shiree. And don't ever come in here dressed like that again. Yes, I like you to dress sexy, but never like that."

"I won't do it again, Kendall. I just wanted to get your attention."

He glared at me and went in the closet. "Come in here please."

I walked over to the closet and he held up two pair of jeans. "Can you wear jeans under that damn dress?"

I laughed and looked further and found a top. "I'll change. Go on and I'll meet you out there."

He embraced me and kissed me. "You always have my attention, Shiree. I saw you when your pink ass came in the door."

He kissed me again and walked out.

When I returned to Simone, she was talking to Pat. Pat had sort of eased her way into our space, but I wasn't sure if I trusted her. Simone felt she was harmless. I said, "Hey, Girl. How you doing?"

"I'm good, Felicia. It's good seeing you. You don't come out much."

"I have small children. But they're with their father until after the holidays."

"I'm always teasing Kendall about you. You have really enchanted him."

I laughed and asked, "Do you have children?"

"No. Didn't Kendall tell you I'm Gay?"

"No, he didn't."

"I've always been open about it, but for some reason most people are surprised to learn it. That's why he didn't want me near you. I asked him who you were, and he told me you were already taken."

Simone said, "I would've never guessed you were Gay."

Pat laughed. "It's always funny to me that some straight people assume we look a certain way. It's true that some Gay people express themselves in their dress or the way they act. Straight people do too. But for the most part, we usually look like anyone else."

I picked up my drink and said, "The reality is, it's nobody's business what a person's sexual preferences are except who they're doing it with. And don't we all have sexual preferences?"

Simone said, "I know I do."

We all laughed, and Pat said, "You're right, Felicia."

I added, "I've always thought *some* people who look down their noses at Gay people are envious of the fact that they have the nerve to do what the hell feels good to them."

Pat nodded and said, "So many people walk around sexually deprived or simply afraid to admit what does or does not feel good to them. Sex isn't that difficult. But some people are so hung up about it, they live a lifetime never grasping it, let alone enjoying it."

Kendall came over and spoke to everyone. Then he leaned down and said, "Pat. Get away from my wife."

She laughed and said, "So, now you're claiming her? What changed?"

"None of your business."

He kissed her cheek. "How are you feeling?"

"Better, Ken. That flu really had me down. But I'm much better now. And why didn't you tell Felicia about my lifestyle? Were you scared?"

He laughed. "Damn right! But not so scared that I won't whip your ass."

We all laughed, and Pat got up and punched Kendall's arm. She said, "My friends are here. I'll talk to you all later."

She went and sat with her friends and Kendall sat next to me. He kissed me and asked, "You okay, Baby?"

He rubbed my cheek and kissed me again. "Yes, Kendall. I'm fine. Are you hungry?"

"No. I'm still full from dinner."

Simone asked, "Where's Debbie? I need something to eat now."

Kendall said, "She might be gone. What do you want?"

Simone said, "Hmmm...let's see."

Kendall laughed at her. "When you figure it out, let me know."

I leaned over and asked, "Are you feeling okay, Simone?"

"Yeah, I'm just so hungry all of a sudden."

"I'll go in the kitchen and have them fix you a salad."

"I don't want a salad."

"You need to start loving them. I mean it, Girl. You are too gorgeous to let this ruin your figure. We both need to go to Curves. A couple of days a week. We're gonna start next week."

She rolled her eyes at me. I asked Kendall if there was someone in the kitchen to make a salad. He said he wasn't sure, but probably not. I decided to go and check.

I got up and went toward the bar. There was a guy there and I tried to get the bartender's attention. The guy looked at me and asked, "What are you drinking?"

Without looking at him, I answered, "I'm not drinking."

He got up and came close to me. "What's your name?"

"I'm married. To the owner."

"Umm...that's too bad."

He sat back down and I exhaled. The bartender told me the kitchen just closed. Stew came over to me and asked. "What do you need, Felicia? I'll get it for you."

"I was hoping someone was available to fix Simone a salad."

"I'll fix her one."

"I know you're busy, Stew. If you trust me in the kitchen, I can do it."

He kissed my cheek. "My wife is so lucky to have someone like you who loves her. Anyhow, you own the damn kitchen. This *is* your husband's place, Felicia. Go on and do your thing. And thanks again."

Kendall told me recently that he owns the club. I always thought he and Stew owned it together. But they agreed to share the profits as well as the work. Like the house on East Avenue. Stew owns it, but they split everything.

I went into the kitchen and turned the light on. I looked around and tried to reacquaint myself with it. I'd been in there a couple of times before, but it was always when Kendall and I were drunk and hungry.

I washed my hands and looked in the fridge. When I got what I needed, I closed the refrigerator door and Kendall was standing there. He scared the shit out of me. I screamed and dropped a tomato. "Baby, I'm sorry. I thought you heard me."

I rolled my eyes at him. "What do you want, Kendall?"

"I saw you talking to that guy at the bar. Simone dared me to sit and watch. She owes me a lobster dinner."

We both laughed. "I told you I could handle it."

"I know that. Although, he came damn close to touching you."

I laughed and continued washing the veggies. "Are you sure you don't want something, Sweetie?"

"No, Baby. Unless you're referring to your sweet pussy. I always want that."

He licked his lips, and my woman parts began to dance. "You have a hickey, Shiree."

"I'm well aware of that, Kendall. But it's not the first time you've given me one. You've done it before between my legs. Several times."

"Really? He never saw them?"

"I *assume* I hid them from him. But I also thought I'd hid *you* from him too."

He was leaning against the counter and he laughed. "I love having you here, Shiree. I'll be so happy when we're married."

I walked over to him and leaned against him. "I enjoy being here with you too. It's hard to believe we're finally free to love each other openly. As much as I hate what Curtis did, I guess one day I'll look at it as a good thing."

"Don't forget Harold has known for two years. We don't know how long he would've sat on that information."

I went back and finished the salad. "Wow, Kendall. Can you imagine that?"

"Hell no. I would've whipped your big ass, Miss Felicia."

I looked at him cross-eyed. "You said you'd never hit me."

"I won't. But I'd find some way to straighten you out, Woman. Don't you dare cheat on me again!"

"What, Kendall?!"

"That...guy. You didn't think I'd forget, did you?"

"That wasn't cheating and you know it. I thought we were done."

He sucked his teeth and glared at me. I put my hands on my hips and said, "But you *did* cheat on *me*, Doctor."

"I told you I never touched her, Shiree."

"You've said that a hundred times. But you *did* touch her. You may not have put your, *you know what* in her. But you *definitely* touched her. And you would've *fucked her* if things had been different."

He was looking down at me through slanted eyes. Then I said, "And I'll never know if there were, or are others."

I walked toward the door and he grabbed me. "You're really pushing the envelope tonight, Mrs. Montgomery. You know I haven't cheated on you. And your language is unbecoming of a lady that's so pretty."

He smacked my behind. "Okay, Doctor. I love you anyhow."

He squeezed my behind and rubbed it. "Did I hurt you, Shiree?"

"No, Kendall."

"Did you like it?"

I rolled my eyes at him and he smiled. We took Simone her salad and she frowned again. "Girl. If you don't eat this food, I will hurt you."

She said in her little girl voice, "I don't like salads."

"I can see now these are going to be seven rough months. Eat your food!"

Pat and her friends were at our table. And Pam and her two friends also came over. Pam asked, "Felicia. Did Kendall really make you change clothes?"

I laughed. "I wore it as a joke. I wasn't gonna keep it on."

"Girl, that dress was hot."

"You can have it. Do you want it?"

"I sure do. Where is it?"

"I'll get it cleaned and send it to you."

I turned to Kendall. "Make sure to get her address, Hun."

He glared at me and didn't say anything. I wondered what his problem was. While everyone else was talking, I leaned closer to him. "What's wrong?"

He never looked at me. "Later, Shiree. And you called me Hun again."

I looked at him confused. "Do me a favor and don't call me that. I know you called him Hun."

"Okay. But for the record, I called him other things too."

He smiled and leaned over and kissed me. "I just don't like that one. Okay?"

"Okay. Is something else bothering you?"

He looked over at Pam and her friends. "We'll talk about it later. In the meantime..."

He raised my chin and kissed me again. He tugged on my ear and whispered, "Let's go away after Christmas, Shiree. To Europe."

My eyes got big. "Europe?"

"Yes. I've wanted to take you away for years. Think about it."

"Kendall. I have to work. I've already taken too much time off this year. Oh my God. That reminds me. I have to go to the Convention Center tomorrow night. Our group is being recognized."

"Really?"

"Yes. Damn! I really don't want to go, but Lenora is depending on me."

He looked straight ahead and continued to watch Simone frown over her salad, and Pam and Pat talk. He finally asked, "Are you going alone?"

I looked at him and didn't know how to answer. "No. I mean, I was hoping you'd take off an hour or so and escort me. Could you?"

He continued looking away from me. "Are you sure?"

I put my arms around his neck. "Kendall, look at me."

He turned. "Why would you ask me that?"

He was glaring and quiet. I whispered, "Stop being so spoiled. I'd be honored to have you escort me. We have to get used to it, right?"

He smiled. "Okay, Shiree. I'd love to."

After closing, Pam and her friends were still hanging around. I noticed one of the girls trying to close in on Stew. Simone drove my car home and I hung around making sure Miss Thing was clear I had my eyes on her.

I decided to go to the bedroom to get the clothes I took off earlier when I heard Pam and the other one in the ladies' room. The other one said, "Pam, you said your man would put us up. Then we get here and find him married."

"He's not married to her. He just fucks her. He'll take care of us."

I went to the bedroom and gathered my things. On my way out, Kendall came in and asked if I was ready. I rolled my eyes at him. "Kendall. I need to know if you're involved with Pam. And please don't bullshit me."

He laughed. "You can't be serious. Are you, Shiree?"

"I just heard her say she came here to see *you*. Why is she in Rochester?"

"She told me she came to help her sister with her son. He's attending RIT and he's going home for the holidays."

I rolled my eyes again and grabbed my purse. I checked my phone and began walking out. He stopped me. "Shiree. You and I need to talk about this. We really have to establish whether we trust each other or not. I'm standing here telling you that I have never been involved with Pam and you're trying to decide if I'm telling the truth. We're both in fucked up places."

Pam knocked on the outer door and asked if she could come in. He said, "Stay here. She doesn't know you're back here. Watch and listen."

He went out into the lounge area and she and her girls came in. Pam asked, "Where is Felicia?"

"I think she's gone. What's up?"

"I was hoping we could crash with you tonight. We'll make it fun."

He laughed and shook his head. "Pam. Didn't you meet my wife? What makes you think you can crash and have *fun* with us?"

She moved closer and said, "Just you, Ken. I know you've always liked me."

"Pam. Why would you think that? I never gave you that impression."

"I know. But when I saw you last month, I felt a connection. So, I thought I'd come up here and...see you."

"I wasn't alone, Pam. Felicia was with my family. Keenan and I were just grabbing something at the store."

I went in my purse and I walked out. I went over to Pam and said, "Here's two hundred dollars. That should get you a couple of nights at a decent hotel."

Then I turned to Kendall. "I'll see if Stew's ready to go."

I headed toward the door and Pam said, "Felicia, I..."

I threw my hand up and said, "Don't forget to give Kendall your address."

On the way home, Kendall and Stew were still dying laughing over crazy ass Pam and her girls. Especially funny, was when Kendall snatched the money out of Pam's hand.

He told her she almost got him in serious trouble. And just because his wife is kindhearted and giving, and felt sorry for them, he didn't. I said, "You two are terrible. Kendall was so mean to her, Stew."

Stew was cracking up. He said, "And the ugly one had eyes for *me! What?!*"

He and Kendall were crying laughing. Kendall said, "You were gonna kill me over her, and then you turned around and gave her money. Who does that?"

"You could've let her keep the money, Kendall."

"Hell no, Shiree. And she's not getting the dress either. People like that will come back two days later looking for something else to get from you. You've got to stop being so easy, Baby. Some people are just users."

The following morning, Kendall and Stew went to the gym and Simone took Shayna skating. I was at the apartment alone and I picked up the phone. When she answered, I was pleased to hear her voice. "I've been thinking about you so much. How are you?"

"Felicia! It's so nice hearing your voice."

"Believe me, I feel the same way. Is this a bad time?"

"No, not at all. I admit I've been thinking a lot about you too. Yvonne is out and I'm just relaxing."

"Juanita, so much has happened."

"I know some of it. I understand you and Harold have separated. Ken also said you told him about the eggs."

"And Kelly has agreed to carry the baby."

"I know. That's wonderful."

She and I apologized for our lack of communicating. She explained that she and Yvonne hit a bump in the road, but all was well now. That's why she and Kendall stopped sleeping together. We talked for an hour and caught up on everything.

The second call I made was hard. When she answered, she said, "Sister. I've been worried sick about you. Are you okay?"

"Yes, Karen. I'm fine."

"The kids are so precious. It's like looking at you and Harold. I hate this happened. But I saw it coming."

"Let's talk about you. How is Eric?"

"He's Eric. My sweetheart and my thorn. I love him and want to shoot him at the same time. But otherwise, he's good."

"Are Mom and Dad doing okay?"

"They're fine. They're saddened by what's happened, but they're okay. Did you know they invited your parents here for Christmas?"

That threw me. "Did they accept?"

"I don't know. Our mothers were talking recently, and they were both crying on the phone."

I got choked up. "Felicia, I probably shouldn't have told you that. I'm sorry for upsetting you."

"No, no it's okay. I don't think I'll ever be able to face your parents, Karen. How much did Harold tell you?"

"Just that his horrendous behavior drove you into the arms of another man. And that you told him he made you feel worthless."

I was quiet. I sometimes wished I was dreaming again. "This is really hard for me, Karen. I love you all so much. And honestly, I'll always love him too."

She choked up too. "I'll always love you too, Sister. Tell me about him."

"Excuse me?"

"The doctor. Tell me about him."

"Are you sure? I mean, I wouldn't want you to share it with Harold."

"Of course not. I promise, Felicia."

"He came on to me and wouldn't stop. Harold had become so manipulative and hard to live with, that at first, Kendall was a pleasant distraction. Then he became my soft place to land."

"We met him and his wife when you had the accident. I can't believe my brother was so controlling. He realizes now that he made a huge mistake."

"Did he tell you what happened while we were dating?"

"You mean the guy you had the fling with?"

"Yes. He never got over it, Karen. He treated me like he needed to create a barrier between me and the outside world. It was terrible."

"So how long have you been seeing him?"

"Harold didn't tell you?"

"No."

"A long time, Karen. We were seeing each other when I had the accident."

"Wow. That's deep, Felicia. Did his wife know?"

"Yes. She found out early in our relationship. Believe it or not, she and Kendall had an open marriage, so she wasn't a problem."

"I asked Eric about an open marriage. He hit the ceiling. I need variety. I've cheated several times."

"Really, Karen?"

"Girl, yeah. I love Eric more than anything, but I like a little more freak in my man. I've concluded that one man isn't enough for me. So every now and then I get a little strange."

I laughed and she did too. "We don't think badly about you, Felicia. Honest. And we don't want to lose you, Sister. Promise we'll always be sisters."

"Of course, Karen. Let's get together when this is over. You and me."

I heard children in the background. "I'd like that, Felicia. Harold and the kids just came in. You wanna hang up?"

"No. Could I speak with him?"

"Okay, but don't hang up."

She gave him the phone and I said, "Hi. How's it going?"

"Good. Is something wrong?"

"No. I finally returned Karen's many calls. I couldn't face her."

He laughed. "I know the feeling. You okay?"

"Yeah. How about you?"

"Getting better. Having the kids is great. Thank you for giving me this time with them."

"I think I'll feel better when you find someone. Is that silly?"

"Yes, because I don't plan on doing that anytime soon."

We both laughed. "I'm glad we're friends, Felicia. It helps a lot."

"I'm really proud you confronted Kendall. That was extremely big of you."

"I had to. I admit I didn't want to, but my kids mean everything to me. He's a good guy, Felicia."

Needing to change the subject, I asked, "So they saw Santa today?"

He laughed. "Yes. Again. They went yesterday too. Everyone misses you, Felicia. You…"

"Harold. I can't talk about that."

"I'm sorry. It's hard for me too. Here's Karen."

I wiped the tears from my face and Karen said, "I'm glad you and Harold are civil. He really misses you, but he's trying to put up a brave front. He told me he'd give his right arm to have you back."

"I tried repeatedly with him, Karen. You know that."

"I know, Felicia."

"And I even slept with him until he left. We always had great sex."

"Girl, that was obvious. The temperature would rise when you two were together. But a person needs more than great sex. We need to be free to live our lives, and hopefully we'll make the right decisions. But we're not perfect."

I smiled and remembered why I loved her so much. "Thank you, Karen. For loving me at my ugliest moment. I'll always love you and the family."

"Me too, Felicia. Let's talk again soon."

"Yes, let's promise. And please kiss Mom and then kiss Dad and tell them it's from me with love."

"Will do, Sister."

Kendall came in about thirty minutes later and took a shower. I prepared his lunch and brought it up to him. When he came out, he was smiling. "What do you think of a Valentine's Day wedding, Shiree?"

I stared at him. "For whom?"

"Don't get smart, Woman. For us."

"Why are we rushing, Kendall? That's so soon."

He sat in front of his food and turned to me. "You spoil me so much. Are you gonna stop when we're married?"

"I've been spoiling you for almost four years. Why would I stop? I love you more now than ever."

"You've made me so happy, Shiree. I just want to be your husband now."

"You *are* my husband. I have the white dress to prove it."

We both laughed and he asked me why I wasn't eating with him. "I made a salad for Simone, and I want it there when she gets back. I suspect she's gonna be very difficult the next seven months. She must eat better, Kendall."

He smiled and I went next door. Stew thanked me and I grabbed my plate and went up with Kendall. While eating my salad, I informed him that I needed to go home and find something to wear to the Christmas party.

He smiled and didn't say anything. "What are you smiling about?"

"Because you said you have to go *home*. That was music to my ears."

I shook my head. "What are you wearing tonight, Kendall?"

"I have suits here, Shiree. But I'll go with you if you want me to. Or, I could take you shopping for a new dress. I like that idea better."

"It seems strange that we can do things like shop together now, doesn't it?"

"Yeah, it does. I'm looking forward to it."

When we walked into the mall, at least two women tripped over themselves looking at my husband. I couldn't help but remember his dad telling me little girls did the same thing.

One very nice woman recognized him and thanked him for forgiving her bill. By the time we reached Lord and Taylor, I was shaking my head. I told him, "I don't think I'll shop with you that much. This is nerve wrecking."

He laughed. "Shiree. Women are drawn to the Locs. Not me. Would you feel better if I cut them off?"

"No, Baby. I told you in Jamaica I didn't want that. And believe me, they're drawn to you, Kendall. Locs or not."

"Are you ever jealous, Shiree?"

"Sometimes. But most of the time I'm not."

He smiled, brought me close and kissed me. "Don't be. There's no need, Baby. I promise you."

He rubbed my cheek and kissed my forehead.

When we reached the dresses, he looked at the mannequins. "I always choose something the mannequins are wearing so I can get an idea how it will look on you. Although they're not shaped like you, I'm able to determine if it will flatter your figure."

"I'd like another pink dress."

He smiled. "That's a good idea. Let's look for one."

All we could find was a fuchsia colored dress, but it was very pretty. I looked at the price tag and he hit my hand. "What are you doing, Shiree?"

"Looking at the price. I never pay more than a certain amount for a dress."

"You're not buying it. Stop that."

I tried it on, and it was very flattering and appropriate for the occasion. It was simple and slightly form fitting. Kendall loved it.

After he paid for it, I thanked him and suggested we leave. "You don't want shoes and a bag to go with it?"

"No, Kendall. I have those things. Especially after you just paid over two hundred dollars for it."

He laughed at me. "No make-up or hairdo?"

I rolled my eyes at him. "What are you saying, Kendall? Do I need make-up and a hairdo?"

"No, Baby. I'm just used to women going all out for these things."

"Well, I went to the salon earlier this week and I usually do my own make-up. It's just a party."

We left the store and he was taking his time. "Are you hungry, Shiree?"

"Not really. Are you?"

"Yeah. Let's go to the food court and cheat a little. I feel like a slice of…"

"No, Kendall. Then you won't feel well and I'll end up going alone. Or, I'll have to stay home to take care of you. Absolutely not."

"Come on, Shiree. I want a slice of pizza."

"No, Kendall. Come on."

Behind us we heard laughing. We turned around and saw the Greers. Simone was bent over laughing, and Stew said, "Felicia. I guess Simone isn't your only challenge. Kendall always eats crap. He just hides it from you."

I turned to Kendall. "Doctor? Is this true?"

"Well…I mean, I do sometimes."

"Kendall. You need to know that will be changing."

He pouted and Stew was dying laughing. "We can have a salad, Baby. And you too, Simone."

"Hell no, Felice. I already have a boat load of that shit at home. I appreciate you making it, but I will not be eating that mess twenty-four seven."

We all argued all the way to the food court. Shayna and Veronica were in another store, so Simone called them and told them where to meet us. I asked Simone, "So what brings you here?"

"I needed to Christmas shop. Shayna is leaving soon, so I need to get it done now. And Big Daddy wanted to get her something she wanted. So, he met us here."

I looked at Stew and asked, "So you're Big Daddy?"

He laughed and asked, "What can I say?"

We all laughed, and Simone said, "He bought her so much stuff, she doesn't want to go to Texas now. She's looking forward to moving to the new house, and she's in love with Stew."

I turned to Stew. "Brother, you better not spoil her."

He just smiled. I saw them approaching and Shayna ran over to me. "Hi, Aunt Felicia!"

"Hello, Sweetie. Hi, Veronica."

Veronica said, "Hey, Girl, you look great. How are you?"

"Good. You look great too."

Kendall walked toward the pizza and I glared at his back. Veronica said, "Dennis is a personal trainer on the side, so we're both very active."

Veronica whispered to Simone, "You feeling better?"

She nodded yes. Veronica looked at Stew and said, "Take care of my sister. She can be a handful."

He smiled at Veronica. "I know. In many ways."

We all laughed, and Kendall came back with pizza. Veronica said, "I need to go. You good, Sis?"

Simone said, "Yep. I'm good. I'll call you later."

After she left, I turned to Kendall. "You want a bite, Shiree?"

"Yeah, give me a little."

He put it toward my mouth. "Bite it."

"Let me hold it."

"No. I don't trust you."

I opened my mouth to bite it and I snatched it out of his hand. I ran around the table and Shayna was cracking up. I was in front of a trash can and I held it over it. "Shiree. Don't do that."

I walked over to him and asked, "Kendall. Do you believe I love you?"

"Yes, Shiree."

"Do you believe I want you healthy and feeling your best?"

"Shiree…"

The Greers were watching us and laughing. "Eat the pizza, Kendall. Just know that when you eat that junk, it breaks my heart."

I turned to Simone and said, "We have to go too."

That night, it was rather drab at the party. Lenora was with her husband and Trina was with a new guy she was dating. I had to remind Kendall that Trina didn't know about the award. Poor Trina couldn't keep her eyes off of Kendall.

When we went to the ladies' room, Trina said, "Damn, Felicia. I'm gonna dream all night about what that's like. Please don't be mad at me."

Lenora laughed and said, "He *is* fine, Girl. I can't believe you've been doing him for three and a half years."

Trina said, "What gets me, is that she was doing him back when we went to the ball. Whoda thunk it? Some women have all the damn luck."

We were still laughing as we left the restroom. Kendall was at the bar, and of course, some chick was in his face. I thought out loud, "This is getting on my nerves."

Lenora said, "That's the downside of having a gorgeous man."

They went back to the table and I went to the bar. Kendall put his hand on my waist and smiled at me. "Mrs. Winston. This is my fiancée, Felicia."

She stared at me as if she knew me. "Aren't you...Harold Benson's wife?"

"Ex-wife."

She looked at my left ring finger and I smiled. "I had no idea...I'm sorry. It's nice meeting you. Dr. Montgomery has been my son's doctor for two years."

"It's nice meeting you too."

When she left, I asked, "What the hell did she want, Kendall?"

He looked at me and smiled. "Her son is my patient, Shiree. She was just saying hello. She might've said more if you hadn't rescued me. She's been a flirt since I met her. Now she knows she has to deal with you."

He raised my hand and kissed it. I rolled my eyes at him and he chuckled. "How long are you gonna be mad at me? I gave the pizza to Shayna."

I smiled as I remembered him saying in the car, "You almost made me cry, Shiree. I never want to break your heart ever again."

Near the end of the evening, the VP of our department went to the podium. Lenora and I winked at each other. He introduced the VP of our region and he began to explain why he was in attendance. "I had to be here to meet the people responsible for our awesome year and to present them with a token of our appreciation."

He began by giving our entire division credit for their great work. Then he said, "But there are three people I'm told are known as the Troubleshooting Trio."

Trina looked at us with her mouth opened. We all smiled, and he continued. "Their numbers are unlike any we've ever seen. So I would like to ask Lenora, Felicia and Trina to please join me up here."

Everyone stood and applauded us. He presented Lenora with a plaque and congratulated each of us. Poor Trina cried. We were the belles of the ball.

By the end of the night, it was obvious to everyone who we were. Many people came over and kissed and hugged us. That didn't go over well with Kendall. At all.

We went to the ladies' room again and did our dance. We told Trina we knew, and she couldn't believe we kept it from her. Lenora said, "Felicia. I continue to fear you won't be with us much longer. Please stay as long as possible."

"I know, Lenora. I've had so many things happen. But this is what keeps me going. My job is the one thing I do well without question. I need this. And I definitely need you guys."

We all had a moment. Later, as we were preparing to leave, Kendall was clearly feeling some kind a way. "What's wrong, Baby?"

He stared at me. "I can't handle watching men feeling all over you. I'm not that crazy about women doing it either."

I laughed. "Come on, Kendy. Let's go to the club and have some fun."

Before getting out of the car at the club, Kendall embraced me. "I'm really proud of you. You and your girls really did your thing."

I smiled. "Thank you, Doctor. That means a lot to me."

"Once things get calmer in our lives, I hope you'll reconsider and go back to work fulltime. I understand better now not only how fabulous you are at your job, but how much you love and need it."

I looked in his eyes and couldn't help but think of Harold. He would never have said anything like that to me. "Thank you, Baby. But with us preparing for another child, we need to cross that bridge when we get to it."

He smiled and kissed me passionately. "Umm… I've wanted to do that all night."

When we walked in, the place was packed. We got a lot of stares, or I should say Kendall did. The women were frozen in place. They all seemed to be shooting daggers at my poor husband. Or were they shooting them at me?

He was gorgeous in his navy suit and I admit my dress was fabulous. I looked over at someone waving our way. It was Simone sitting at the bar.

Kendall had his arm around my waist and I turned to face him. "Baby, Simone is at the bar. I'm gonna go over there."

"You're gonna leave me alone?"

"Yep. But I'm sure you won't be too far away, Sweetie."

He leaned down and kissed me. "Never."

As soon as I reached Simone, she said, "The hounds are all over him."

I turned and shook my head. "Why aren't they all over Stew like that?"

"He doesn't spend a lot of time out here like Kendall."

I noticed all of the barstools were taken. A few minutes later, Stew came out and kissed my cheek. "How was the office party?"

"Pretty boring, but we were recognized by the big wigs, so it ended with a bang."

Simone laughed and asked, "Were people shocked to see you with Kendall?"

"Yes. About as shocked as people are to see us together here. But that's not stopping them from swarming all over him."

Stew said, "Kendall is being a good host, Felicia. We have to be nice to keep them coming. And that's how we keep you and Simone happy and well taken care of. Did she tell you I finally talked her into leaving her job?"

I looked at her shocked, and she said, "For now, Felicia. But I can't promise anything after the baby is old enough to be with a sitter."

Stew frowned and I laughed. I was still standing and someone came up behind me and embraced me. "That better be my husband."

He leaned down and said in my ear, "Your ass is so pretty, I need to stand behind you before someone mistakes it for something to sit their drink on. Damn, I can't believe it's mine."

I leaned down and laughed. Then I turned around, put my arms around his neck and I kissed him. He played in my hair and asked, "Do you know your friends and their husbands are coming out?"

"What friends?"

Simone said, "Kendall, you have a big mouth."

She turned to me. "Annette and Carla are bringing Tony and Earl out tonight. To meet our new husbands."

"Oh, *hell* no! I'm not ready for that."

"We knew you'd feel that way, so we arranged it behind your back. The guys are ready to move on, Felicia. We all need to."

Someone got up, so I sat at the bar. "I know you're right. I just..."

I looked up and saw Tony and Earl. Both so handsome. Then Carla and Annette. Stew said, "We have a table reserved for all of us. Let's do this."

Everyone walked over to greet them except me. Kendall turned and came back to me. "Shiree. Don't be like that."

Tony and Earl came over to us. Tony said, "You must be Kendall."

"Yes. It's a pleasure to meet you."

Tony smiled and they shook hands. "I'm Tony, Annette's husband. And this is Earl."

Earl shook his hand too. "Glad to meet you, Man."

Kendall said, "Same here, Earl."

I was facing the bar and Tony came over to my left side and Earl on the right. They each kissed my cheek, and Earl said, "Girl, get your ass up."

Tony laughed and said, "We came to have some fun. Come on, Little Sis."

I put my head down and laughed. I finally turned around. "For somebody who can't stand surprises, you all love to surprise me."

Kendall extended his hand, and I took it. We went to our table and the waitress brought champagne. I rolled my eyes at my sisters and they laughed at me. Earl said, "Simone. Carla says you're moving to our side of the world."

"Yes, and I'm so excited. And...Stew and I are expecting a baby."

The guys were clearly surprised, and they congratulated Stew. Simone's face started changing colors and I jumped up. "Come on!"

We got her to the bathroom just in time. Carla said, "No more greasy food, Simone. What did you eat?"

"Well, I had chicken and fries earlier."

"*Fried* chicken?"

"Well, yeah. My mother told me to eat what I want."

Annette said, "Your mother is old school like our mothers. They think it's okay to gain a hundred pounds during pregnancy too. We know none of that is good, Simone. We will have to cook for you for the next few months. Baked foods and fresh vegetables. I'm surprised Stew lets you eat like that."

"He doesn't know. He would have a fit."

I walked over to her. "Simone. We are not playing with you. I understand how food can be comforting, but we will not allow you to get fat and make yourself sick and the baby sick too. You must change your thinking. Now, Simone."

"Okay. I promise. No more fried food or junking out."

We all scowled at her and Annette said, "Okay. Let's get back out there before someone calls my husband Gary by mistake."

We all laughed, and I said, "You guys were wrong for crashing me like that."

Carla said, "Again, I thought you should be told. But these two threatened to whip my ass."

We all laughed and went back out. Kendall winked at me from across the table. I shook my head and looked the other way. Earl said, "We've been invited to come over during the playoffs. They have an all men's night."

Annette said, "Except for the waitresses, I'm sure. Are they nude, Kendall?"

"No, Annette. They have…some clothes on."

Earl rubbed his hands together and Carla asked, "They're topless, Kendall?"

He laughed and said, "No, Carla. I'm just kidding."

Stew said, "They're bottomless."

The guys hollered and Simone said, "You do that, and you'll be bottomless. If you know what I mean."

We all laughed and enjoyed the remainder of the night. And although I didn't like the way it was done, the guys got along really well, and I was glad we were back together like a family again.

Chapter Ten

Kendall and I had a problem. We wanted to spend our first Christmas together, but he needed to be in Durham to present his parents with the house.

But I didn't want my parents to be alone. Keenan informed Kendall that everything was done and even the furniture had been delivered. What to do?

Kendall asked if I thought my parents would go to Durham. I told him I didn't think so. We eventually decided to go to Durham five days before Christmas, and then return to Rochester on the twenty-third.

They were thrilled to see us. We didn't tell them we were coming, so when we walked in, Mom dropped the book she was reading. Dad wasn't home.

When Dad came in, Mom and I were in the kitchen cooking dinner. Kendall had driven to Raleigh to meet Keenan so they could finalize everything with the contractors.

Dad reminded me of Harold's father, because he loved me so much. He also teased me a lot. The first thing he said was, "Kendall must not be here, because you're not screaming."

I hit his arm and then I hugged him. "Dad, you're terrible. How are you?"

"I'm good, Felicia. What brings you all here? Are you staying for Christmas?"

"Well, I'm gonna let Kendall answer those questions. But, I can tell you there's a surprise for you and Mom."

He looked at Mom and she was smiling. She said, "Kendall told me they're surprising us with something tonight. It's something from all the kids."

He glared at me like Kendall. I laughed so hard. He said, "Maybe I should tickle you. I believe then you'll tell me."

My eyes got big and he came after me. I ran behind Mom, and she and I were cracking up. Kendall walked in and I screamed, "Kendall! Dad's trying to make me tell the secret!"

Keenan also walked in and went to the powder room. I marveled at how alike they were. Although they each had their own distinct personalities, they looked alike and had similar mannerisms.

Dad laughed and said, "That girl screams every damn time she sees you!"

We all laughed, and Kendall walked toward his father. "Is it true you're trying to force my wife into telling the secret?"

They laughed and hugged each other. Kendall asked, "How are you, Dad?"

"I'm good, Son. And yes, it's true. If you hadn't walked in, I'd know by now. I threatened to tickle her."

They continued talking and I went back to the stove. Dad asked, "What are you cooking?"

"Comfort food. But nothing greasy or fried. Baked chicken smothered in gravy and onions, and veggies over brown rice. And baked sweet potatoes."

Mom said, "I'm making the lemonade. That's all she let me make."

I reached in the oven and pulled out the homemade rolls Kendall likes. He came over and kissed me. "Shiree. You did all of this in two hours? It looks great."

Keenan returned and came over and kissed me too. "Hi, Sister-in-law. How are you?"

"I'm good, Keenan. Here. Take these for me."

He picked up a towel and I passed the rolls to him. He sat them on the counter and started looking in the pots. I hit his hands and said, "Wash your hands, Brother! You know better."

He laughed and said, "I see you're still a pistol. I just washed my hands."

We both laughed and the front door opened. A familiar voice said, "Hello!? Anybody home?"

Keenan went toward the door, and Mom and Dad looked at one another. They both smiled and Kelly walked in. She greeted her parents, and Mom asked about Terrell. "He stayed with friends of ours. I'm only staying two days."

Dad asked, "Okay. Why are you all here?"

Kendall and Keenan both greeted and kissed their sister. Then she and I hugged. Kendall asked Kelly, "Are we all set?"

"Yep."

Keenan said, "Mom and Dad. We're taking a ride."

After making sure the stove and oven were turned off, the six of us went out and were greeted by a limo. Once we were all in, Kelly reached behind her and gave each of us a glass of champagne.

The driver pulled off and Kendall said, "Growing up, we always knew we were blessed to have great parents."

Keenan said, "We also knew we weren't rich by a long shot. But look at us. We're all college graduates. Kendall's a doctor, and Kelly and I both have business degrees. Your sacrifice has not gone unnoticed."

Kelly said, "We also know you've been saving for Terrell's education too. You both worked so hard for us. Mom, you were always there when we came home from school. And Dad, you made sure we had everything we needed. And a lot of what we wanted."

Mom was in tears and Dad was smiling, but his eyes were misty too. I was a wet blanket. Kendall said, "Nothing we could do could begin to compare with your sacrifice or the example you set for us. You were both strict and demanding, but we agree that we're all better for it. And I have a side note. Dad, thanks for taking that second job when I was in med school."

Dad looked at his wife, then back at Kendall. "Yes, Dad. I knew."

We were all silent and tears were everywhere. Kendall composed himself and said, "Thank you, Mom and Dad."

Keenan and Kelly also thanked them for sacrificing for them too. Keenan raised his glass and said, "Keenan and Lorraine, we salute you!"

The limo driver was told to drive around the block a couple of times. We couldn't see out, so they had no idea where we were. We finally stopped, and Kelly said, "It's time!"

We all smiled and she pushed the button. The chauffer opened the door and we all got out. We were greeted with a big red bow on the front door.

Mom's hand was on her chest and Dad was glaring at us. On the porch was a pretty box and everyone agreed I could present it to them. I picked it up and turned to them. "Mom and Dad. On behalf of your children, we are excited to present to you your Christmas gift. Merry Christmas!"

I gave the box to Mom and she took the keys out. She looked at Dad and gave one to him. He looked at us with that Montgomery glare. "I wondered who was doing all of this work over here. You guys bought this house? For us?"

Keenan laughed and said, "Kendall bought it, Dad."

Kendall said, "We all contributed. Keenan took care of all of the contractors and oversaw the entire project. It was priceless."

Kelly said, "And Felicia and I chose the fixtures and the furniture and stuff."

Mom smiled at all of us and said, "Lord have mercy! I don't know what to say. Thank you all so, so much! Let's go in!"

We all laughed. We went up on the porch, and the first thing they saw was the doormat that read: Montgomery. Mom covered her mouth and turned to her husband.

Then she saw the beautiful landscaping and walked along the porch admiring it. Dad said, "Bae, I thought we were going inside."

Dad removed the bow and opened the door with his key. He turned to Mom and motioned for her to go in. Dad followed her in, and they were both stunned. It was unrecognizable.

Both of them had been in there before. It was always a simple home in need of repair. The transformation was incredible. Everything was new from floor to ceiling.

It now had an open floor plan, so the living area, dining area and kitchen could all be seen. Mom immediately went toward the kitchen. She was as excited as a little girl in a toy store.

I watched Kendall watch her. He was loving how happy she was. Keenan and Dad were talking at the fireplace, and Kendall went over and joined them. Kelly and I joined Mom in the kitchen.

She turned to face us, and she had happy tears. She hugged both of us, and said, "This is incredible. I feel like those people on HGTV!"

We laughed and the guys came over to us. We went through the whole house and they both marveled at all the updates. The bedrooms were left unfurnished, but the other rooms were done.

We went outside to see the backyard. Dad stood there and enjoyed the view. Kendall knew he would love it. Kelly said, "So, Mom. We figured you guys would rent this out for extra income. But Dad just said you guys would love to live here."

"Absolutely! Dad and I have been saying we didn't know how much longer we could endure those stairs. So, maybe we'll rent the other house. Right, Keenan?"

Dad turned to his children and said, "Yes. But instead of renting it, I'd like to keep it available for you all. So, when you visit, you can have your own space."

Kelly said, "We thought about that. So…"

Keenan stopped her and said, "Let's go back home and eat that food. We can finish this discussion at the table."

We all laughed and left the house.

While we were enjoying our dinner, Kendall turned to his father and said, "We set aside a few dollars from the renovation budget for *this* house, Dad. We were thinking about maybe creating a master suite down here. Or whatever you want. Also, your final surprise is a new kitchen."

Keenan said, "We realize it's a lot all at once, so you can think about it. We can talk again after the holidays."

Dad looked at Mom and she nodded. Then Dad said, "Your mom and I are so proud of all of you. And thankful for all of this. It's so generous. Thank you."

We all smiled and then Dad asked, "So, why aren't you guys staying for Christmas?"

Kendall looked at me and I said, "My ex left Rochester, and I agreed to let the kids spend the holidays with him. It's been hard for my parents, so I don't want them to be alone."

Mom said, "Of course not. I'm sorry, Felicia."

"Thanks, Mom. I'm an only child, so…"

"No explanation needed. You're a good daughter. We're looking forward to meeting your parents."

Kendall and I enjoyed our time there. We got through Christmas and the New Year. Harold brought the kids back and was back in Detroit starting his new life.

Kendall and I had all four kids *and* Zack for a couple of weeks. But with me home, we got through that okay too.

By the end of January, we'd met with the doctors to discuss the in vitro process. Kelly had also seen her doctor and had all of the tests necessary for the procedure. The in vitro was scheduled for the first week of February.

Kelly agreed to take a week of vacation in February. She had a guy she'd been dating for about a year, and Terrell stayed with him. By the end of February, Kelly's period was late.

It was Thursday the twenty-seventh, and she called me while I was cooking. It was about eleven-thirty in the morning. "Is Kendall there?"

"No. Is everything okay?"

"Yes. I'm fine. My period is late."

I dropped the spoon in my hand and sat down. "You okay, Felicia?"

"Kelly. How late?"

"Just a week. But I'm never late. I'm so excited."

I couldn't think straight. I asked, "What should we do?"

"I'm gonna call my doctor and ask him. I'll call you back."

I paced and drank wine. Last week I was notified that my divorce was final. That was much quicker than I anticipated. Harold asked me if I'd gotten something in the mail. I told him I did, but neither of us mentioned it again.

For some reason, I didn't tell Kendall I'd gotten my divorce papers. I promised to marry him once Kelly got pregnant. But now I wasn't sure if I was ready.

But I was already behaving as though we were married. I told him to handle all of our money together. He was hesitant at first, but I insisted that I didn't have a head for such things and he finally came around.

He invested a portion of the money Harold transferred. The rest was put into CDs. He refused to put it together until we were married. He also insisted on paying for all of the medical bills and expenses for the in vitro with his own money.

I guess that's a man thing. So far, it's cost him over twenty-five thousand dollars. I took one of the CDs and put it in Kelly's name. It was one hundred thousand dollars and I made her promise to put it aside and not tell Kendall.

Then I gave her another hundred thousand to pay off her mortgage, which only had forty-three thousand left on it.

I told her to pay off her other bills with the balance, and that freed up a huge chunk of her income. I told her, "Save, Kelly. All you can. You'll be out of work for a long time once you become pregnant. Kendall already has a college fund for Terrell, but he'll need so much, so we'll all help."

The phone rang again and I jumped. Kelly said, "He wants to see me at two-thirty."

"Lord, I wish I could fly out and be there with you."

"I know. I'll call you after I see him."

"Kelly, I was thinking. If it's positive, let's tell him for his birthday."

"Okay, Felicia. I'm praying so hard. I really want this for all of us."

That night I was beside myself. We had four days to wait to tell him. The test was positive. She was instructed to come here and see the doctors who performed the in vitro procedure.

We arranged for her to see them on Tuesday. I got through that night, and the next day we reserved a flight for her to come to Rochester on Sunday. "Kelly, I still can't believe it. I don't know what to do with myself."

"Me either. And Felicia?"

"Yes?"

"Thank you for everything. I appreciate you so much."

"Listen. You've done more than I could even measure. Let's not fight about that again. This will bind us forever. Sisters forever."

"Sisters forever."

The next day I went to Simone's. She lived exactly five minutes away. It was cold and snowy, but I didn't feel any of it. I was still numb from the news.

Annette also came over. When I got there, I could see many of the changes they'd made. "Simone, I hope you haven't done all of this yourself."

"No, Felicia. Stew helped me a lot."

I sat down. "You guys are not going to believe this."

They were both staring at me. "The in vitro worked. Kelly is three weeks pregnant."

They both sat there with their mouths opened. Simone said, "Felice. You're about to have another child."

"I know. And she'll be twins with yours. They'll be four months apart."

Annette asked, "How's Kendall? He must be somewhere receiving oxygen."

We all laughed. "We haven't told him yet. Monday is his birthday, so we're planning to surprise him. Kelly will be here Sunday, so I have two days to figure out how to hide her. I don't want to put her in a hotel by herself."

Annette said, "She could stay with one of us or your parents."

Simone said, "She can stay here. She knows Stew and I wouldn't mind."

"I hate to put you out, but that does sound ideal."

"Don't even go there, Felicia. I'd love to have her."

I poured a glass of wine and Annette asked, "So, how are things going? Have you adjusted to being his wife full time?"

"Yes, I think so. He's had to adjust to having the kids all over the place. But the boys are with Todd most of the time. And my parents would be lost without the twins, so they spend a couple nights a week with them."

Simone said, "Felicia. Kendall is so happy. He talks about you so much that it gets on my damn nerves. Shiree this and Shiree that."

I laughed. "He's a prince. He's different from Harold because he loves me gently. And genuinely. Now that I don't have to sneak to see him, I don't have much to keep me busy. But I don't dare go back to work full time until Kelly gets through this. And then I'll have five kids. Or more."

Annette asked, "What do you mean *more*?"

"It's not uncommon for in vitro to produce multiple births. There's a good chance she could have two or more babies."

Simone scratched her head. "I would shit a brick if I had more than one baby."

Annette said, "Girl. You should have seen Felicia when she found out she had twins. She almost lost it."

Simone said, "Girl. Don't be putting those thoughts in the air in here. Neither one of us needs more than one child."

I high fived her and said, "Lord knows that's the truth. By the way, I need you all to start preparing to go to North Carolina in the spring. I promised him we could have a private ceremony in his mother's garden. It's beautiful."

Sunday afternoon I picked Kelly up from the airport and we went to Simone's. Stew was there to help and laughed that he had two pregnant women to take care of.

I left them to get back to Kendall and the twins. When I walked in, he was on the floor doing a puzzle with them. Toys were everywhere, and he looked like he needed a drink.

I laughed. "Daddy. You all right?"

"I'm fine. Come here."

I went over and Benny said, "Mommy. Dad is doing it wrong. He don't know how to do a puzzle."

"He *doesn't,* Harold. Say he *doesn't.*"

He looked at me and said, "He doesn't know how, Mom."

I leaned down and said, "Give Mommy a kiss, Son."

He reached up and kissed me and hugged my neck. Alysiya was busy combing her doll's hair. She was a real girly girl. "Aleece. What are *you* doing?"

"I'm trying to make her hair like mine. But her hair ain't big enough."

I laughed. "Alysiya. We don't say ain't. Say isn't."

"Okay."

I leaned down and kissed my daughter and then my husband. "Thank you, Baby. Would you like me to fix you a drink? I'm gonna throw something together for dinner soon."

"No, I'm good. Go on and get dinner. I'll take care of them."

I smiled and he went back to the puzzle. About twenty minutes later, he came in the kitchen. "I put a movie in for them. It's amazing how they sit still for those movies. Even the ones they've seen a hundred times."

"I know. It's like a babysitter. You know they'll be four in a week. I'm planning to find a preschool or daycare for them. It's that time."

"That's gonna be hard for your parents."

"I know. I was thinking that maybe I'll start them part time and wean them away from Mom and Dad. Remember the day we met? They were two months old. It's so hard to believe almost four years have passed."

"I know. And I'll be thirty-eight tomorrow. How scary is that?"

"You do have a birthday tomorrow, don't you?"

He glared. "Like you didn't know. What did you get me?"

"I'm gonna have to go out and buy you something. But first, Stew and Simone invited us over for breakfast at nine tomorrow morning."

He glared again. "What are you all up to?"

"Nothing, Silly. They're doing breakfast for your birthday."

After dinner and baths, we managed to get the kids down by eight thirty. He asked me if I'd talked to Harold lately. "No. Why?"

"When I spoke with him last week, he mentioned having the kids for Easter. You didn't know?"

"No. I haven't talked to him in a few weeks, Kendall. I leave that up to you."

"I think we should take them. And see Kelly."

"Let's talk about it later. I need to think about that. Okay, Baby?"

"Okay. Are you feeling okay? You seem a bit distracted."

I walked into our bathroom. "I'm fine. What makes you think I'm distracted?"

"Especially the last couple of days. What's going on, Shiree?"

I laughed. "Nothing, Kendall. All is well. I assure you."

He brought me in his arms and looked into my eyes. "You sure?"

"Yes, Baby. I would tell you if something was wrong."

He glared at me a long time. "You know what, Kendall? I don't like how you're looking at me. I feel like you think I'm lying to you, and that is *not* a good feeling. Don't do that, Sweetie."

"I know you're not lying to me. I'm sorry, Shiree."

I walked away from him. "I admit that I have a birthday surprise for you. And that's all it is. Okay?"

He came toward me and I put my hands up. "It felt too familiar, Kendall. Please don't do that to me. If I ever keep anything from you, it's not because it's something bad or foul. I need you to trust me. I can't handle that."

"Felicia Shiree, I'm sorry. I just know when something is going on with you. I wasn't thinking anything bad or foul, to use your words. Honest, Baby."

I walked out and went downstairs. He came behind me. "I'm really sorry."

I turned to him and had tears in my eyes. "I've spent the last...almost four years lying because I love you so much and couldn't stand being away from you. Now I realize you probably look at me and don't know when to believe me. You see a liar when you look at me.

I turned back and attempted to prepare my tea. I dropped the tea bag in the sink and cried. He turned me around and brought me in his arms again. "I can't believe I've upset you like this. And believe me, Shiree. I do *not* think you're a liar. Never, Baby. I was there all those years and I know what you went through. *For me.* How can I fix this?"

"Until I give you a reason not to trust me, believe me. What did you think was going on? Another man?"

"No, Baby. I never thought that. I just thought something had upset you, and you wanted to keep it from me. Or you weren't feeling well. Please believe me."

He sat me down and fixed my tea. Then he kneeled in front of me. "I hate when you cry. You give me so much and I get so greedy sometimes. I really do trust you more than anyone I've ever known."

He touched my face. "Yes, it's true that I watched you lie for years. For *me*. But you don't have any reason to lie *to* me. You had many reasons to lie to him."

He stood and brought me up with him. He held me tight. "I feel awful when I remind you of him, Shiree. I'm sorry for making you cry, Baby. I love you so much."

"There's nothing and no one that could ever make me betray you. Ever, Kendall. We've been through too much, Baby. And for the record, I love you more."

He kissed me and I saw that look. He carried me upstairs.

The following morning was bright and sunny, but very cold. There was still snow on the ground, and honestly, I wanted nothing more than to crawl further under the covers.

But, I decided to get up and get the kids dressed. As soon as I moved my feet, he grabbed me. "Don't leave yet. It's so early, Shiree."

I looked at the clock and it was ten minutes to six. He rolled on top of me. "Are you feeling better?"

I smiled. "I do, Kendall. Thank you. Happy Birthday, Sweetie."

He leaned over and pulled something out that was under the bed. "Thank you, Baby. I wanted to give you something today because my birthday could never mean this much without you in it. This time last year I was so sad and missing you so much. Remember when I showed up at Network?"

"My God, Kendall. That was only a year ago? It seems like eons."

"I know. I wanted to run Phillip over. If you weren't so close to him, I probably would have."

"You're so silly, Kendall. No man could ever replace you. I remember wondering how I was supposed to live the rest of my life without you."

"Thank you for giving us another chance. And for being the best thing that has ever happened to me."

He gave me the gift-wrapped box. "Kendall. That is so sweet, Baby. Do you mean that or did you sneak out and buy this because I cried last night?"

He laughed. "I'm not *that* good, Shiree."

I also laughed. I got up and turned toward the bathroom. "Open your gift first, Baby."

"I have to pee and brush my teeth. You brush yours too."

He smirked at me. "It's *your* pussy, Shiree."

I threw a pillow at him. "I'm gonna somehow stop you from talking like that."

He followed me in the bathroom. After we cleaned up, he motioned toward the bed. "Let's get back in. I want some early morning, birthday loving."

I smiled at him and dropped my robe. He looked at me as if I'd surprised him. He reached for his manhood and moaned.

I put my hand between my legs and massaged my honeypot. I had goosebumps and began to shiver. "Hurry up, Kendall. I'm freezing."

After we made love, he gave me the beautifully gift-wrapped box again. "Open it, Shiree."

When I removed the gift wrap, I was holding a Gucci box. I asked jokingly, "What could this be?"

"Something I don't think you have."

I raised the cover and saw the most beautiful watch. It was very simple, but very nice. A gold bangle watch, with a mother of pearl face and a single diamond where the twelve should be. "You can wear it every day, Shiree."

"I love it, Kendall. Thank you, Baby."

I leaned over and kissed him. "I hid your gift in the room with the kids, Kendall. So, unless you want them in bed with us, I'd advise you to wait and not wake them up."

We slid back under the covers and he clicked on the TV. He wrapped himself around me and I dozed off.

When I woke up, he was gone. It was seven-thirty, and I heard the kids. I walked in their room, and he was in there. And he had his gift in his hand.

I almost fainted. I was scared his surprise was ruined. "Really, Kendall? I can't believe you couldn't wait for me to give it to you."

"I didn't open it, Shiree. And I didn't look for it. Aleece gave it to me."

I looked at my daughter. "Did you do that?"

"Yes, Mommy. It's his birthday!"

I looked at her and couldn't do anything but laugh. She crawled up beside him and played with his hair. I shook my head. She was such a flirt. He noticed it too. "She's gonna have me fighting more than her mother."

"That might be true. But you have to wait to open your gift."

Benny asked, "Dad, can we make another snowman?"

"There's not enough snow, Benny. The other one is still out there, so maybe we can find something to dress him up with."

Kendall looked at me. "Maybe later, Benny. Right now, we're going to Aunt Simone's for breakfast. Let's get dressed and get over there."

After getting the kids dressed, I went in the bathroom and sent Simone a text. She replied: Kelly and I are cooking. We're both fine.

I told her we were on time and we'd be there shortly. Then I sent Mom a text and she replied she'd just gotten there. Annette and Carla were also coming.

My nerves were on end. When we finally got there, Kendall said, "I see we have guests. I'm surprised you all went with breakfast instead of dinner."

I laughed, grabbed the gift and we went in. As we were removing our coats and boots, everyone was telling Kendall happy birthday. We went into the dining room and Kelly was hiding.

When everything was calm, I turned to Kendall. "Open your gift, Baby."

He looked at me confused. "*Now*, Shiree?"

"Yes. Just this one for now."

Aleece said, "Open it!"

Benny asked, "Dad, want me to open it?"

Everyone said, "Aww..."

"I think I do need help. Would you help me, Benny?"

Benny smiled and grabbed it. When the paper was ripped to shreds, he handed the box to Kendall and asked, "Can you take the top off?"

Kendall laughed. "I think so, Lil Man. Thanks for helping me."

Anyone could see that Kendall really loved my kids. He removed the top and moved the paper. Underneath was a baby tee shirt. I had it made. It read: I'm on my way, Daddy...

He laughed at first and looked at me. He didn't get it. "Shiree, what does that..."

He got up and looked at my mother. She shook her head yes, and Kelly walked in from the kitchen. "In about eight months, your daughter will be here."

He put his hand over his mouth, and Kelly took her crying brother in her arms. Stewart and I took both of them into the kitchen and everyone else remained in the dining room. There wasn't a dry eye in the house.

I pulled out a chair and got him to sit. I sat on his lap and wiped his tears with a towel Kelly handed me. He held me tight and reached again for his sister.

We all laughed, wiped tears and finally he spoke. "Wow! I don't even know what to say. *Kelly*…"

He shook his head and had tears again. Then he looked at me. "And *you!* I've cried more since knowing you than in my entire life. I love you so much."

"I love you more."

He kissed me. He looked back at Kelly. "So…you're really…pregnant?"

She nodded and smiled. She leaned down and kissed her brother. It was a precious moment. He then asked, "Girl…when did you get here?"

She laughed. "Yesterday. I stayed here with Stew and Simone."

"I love you, Sis. So much. Thank you."

She kissed his forehead and I said, "We need to get back to our friends."

Aleece came in and asked, "Dad. Why you crying? You don't like your present?"

He motioned for her to come to him. She went to him and raised her arms. He picked her up and she said, "Dad. I think your shirt is too little. Mommy can fix it."

He hugged her tight and kissed her. "Okay, Aleece. Let's eat."

After breakfast, while Kendall was opening his other presents, I went over to Kelly and asked, "How are you feeling?"

"Physically, I'm fine. But my emotions are all over the place. I'm really happy for Kendall. And I'm a little scared."

I hugged her. "I know. But we're all committed to travel this journey together. You won't ever be alone."

She hugged me back really tight. We held hands and I laughed. "I have to keep reminding myself that I'm about to have a new baby. A little girl."

Kelly laughed too. "What if it's a boy?"

"Then we would have another Kendall. I would love that too."

We smiled and the girls came over. Kelly said, "You have such beautiful friends."

She and Simone hugged, and Simone said, "Kelly and I had a ball last night. We were both saying we must be crazy as hell to be this old and having babies."

Kelly said, "Felicia. I've thought about it a lot and I think I'm going to move here now instead of waiting. Terrell agreed to come this summer and to go to school here for a year. Then he'll go back and be with his friends for his senior year."

"Really, Kelly? I would love that."

"I could afford a nice apartment because I checked, and I'm eligible for disability."

I laughed. "Kendall and I both have places you could stay for free. My house is less than ten minutes away."

I motioned for Kendall to come over and we told him her thoughts. He said, "Kelle, Felicia's house is bigger than my house. And the apartment is so far. Let's think about it some more and see what makes the most sense."

Mom came in with a cake and Daddy walked in. He asked, "Felicia. Can I see you?"

I looked at him and feared something was wrong. We went in the foyer and he said, "Kendall's parents know about the baby."

"I know. Kelly told them yesterday. We're planning to call them when we get back home. How did you know that?"

"His mother called us yesterday. She and your mother talked a long time and she's flying in today at noon. I assured her I would pick her up, but I thought you'd appreciate knowing."

"I sure do appreciate it. I'm starting to think we need to move into my house. Kendall's is getting crowded."

"I wish you would. It was nice being so close."

"That's true, Daddy. Do you think Kendall will live in another man's house?"

Kendall walked out and spoke to Daddy. After pleasantries, Daddy turned back to me. "That was never his house. It was always your house."

Kendall said, "That's what he told me too. And it might make sense for us to move there."

"Were you eavesdropping?"

He laughed. "I heard you ask if I'd live in another man's house. I admit my pride is hesitant, but I'm thinking that makes a lot of sense. There's enough room for all of us to live there."

Mom called Kendall and we all followed and sang happy birthday. The kids were thrilled and soon Mom and Dad left for the airport.

Kendall was *really* gonna be surprised. Again. Stew and Kendall went into the study, and I whispered to Kelly, "I don't know if I should tell you this, but your mom is on her way here."

"She told me she was coming, but I didn't think it would be today. She wants to meet your parents, Felicia."

"My parents just went to get her."

She smiled. "That's so kind of them. Mom and Dad really love you and they were hoping to meet them. Dad is having some dental work done tomorrow, so he couldn't come."

"How would you feel about staying at our other house? I just spoke with Kendall and my father, and we all feel it makes more sense for all of us to move in my house. It has six bedrooms."

"Wow. Really?"

"Yes, but let's talk about it later. We need to leave soon because the airport is only fifteen minutes away and we need to get home to surprise Kendall. Again."

Mom called after we got home and asked, "Where are you?"

I told her we were home and she asked, "Can you talk?"

"In a minute. I was about to put them down for a nap."

"We're coming there. And Dad is coming too."

I smiled. "That's great, Mom! I'm so glad about that!"

I turned to Kendall and asked him if he'd take the kids up for a nap. "Okay, Baby. Anything else you need?"

I smiled. "No, but thank you, Baby."

Once he was gone, I turned to Kelly smiling-. "Your dad came."

She smiled too. "Kendall is gonna faint. I've never seen him so emotional before. He's so happy. We have to pray all goes well."

I nodded and touched her arm. "Yes, we do."

When the doorbell finally rang, I asked Kendall to please get it. Kelly and I pretended to be busy and he went to open it. We heard them say, "Happy Birthday!"

We snuck into the larger foyer and heard him say, "Oh, My God! This is the best birthday I've ever had!"

Once they were in the house, we came out and greeted everyone. His mom went right to Kelly and held her a long time. "Baby, how are you feeling?"

"Great, Mom."

Then she looked at me. "Felicia. Come here."

She hugged me tight and I hugged her too. She said, "This is such a beautiful day. We're all so happy and excited. Your parents have been so nice to us."

She and Mom had a moment. Kelly was talking to her dad when he looked over at me. He came over and asked, "How's my other beautiful daughter?"

My heart melted and I smiled. He opened his arms and brought me in. He held me tight and I was reminded again of Harold's dad. "How was your flight, Dad?"

"Great. The flight attendants weren't that pretty though."

We all laughed, and Kendall said, "Dad. That's enough."

Kendall took the men into the family room. The moms, Kelly and I went into the kitchen and Kendall's mom asked, "So, where are those precious children?"

"I put the twins down for a nap. And my older sons are with their father. I usually see them on weekends."

Kendall walked into the kitchen and hugged his mother again. "Mom. It's so good to have you here."

"It's good to be here, Kendall. Felicia, your family has been so kind and welcoming. I wish it was warmer here."

Kendall laughed. "I've been here for years, and I'm still not used to the snow and cold."

We heard our fathers laughing, and Kelly said, "Our dads are getting along great."

Kendall said, "They're both Panther fans and both are Army vets."

My mother said, "Lorraine and I are going to the store. We're going to cook dinner."

I said, "Mom, I can go."

"No. We've already talked about it. We want to go."

"Let me give you some money then. Please, Mom."

She looked at me and I said, "Okay, Mom. I won't mention it again."

Kendall laughed and said, "Shiree. You had a lot of secrets to keep. Now I really understand your behavior. Do you forgive me?"

I looked at him and rolled my eyes. I went to the fridge and got a bottle of water. I asked if anyone else wanted one. Kelly said, "I'll take one. Thanks."

Kendall came over and took the bottle and opened it for his sister. Then he took mine and opened it. He raised my chin and said, "I love you, Shiree."

I rolled my eyes again. His Mom asked, "What did you do to her, Kendall?"

"Well...I sort of accused her of keeping something from me. She got upset and cried."

His mother came over and popped him on the head. We all laughed, and she said, "Kendall. Don't do that."

He rubbed his head. "Mom! It's my birthday! You almost knocked me out."

I laughed again. He turned to me and stared. He picked me up and kissed me. He twirled me around and said, "I'm sorry, Shiree. Okay?"

"Okay. Put me down!"

His mom said, "He's never loved anyone like that, Barbara. Not even Juanita."

Mom said, "Same with Felicia."

While the mothers were cooking, I went up and got the kids. Aleece went in the kitchen and Benny wanted to be with the guys. Aleece began asking a million questions.

Mom finally said, "Alysiya. No more questions until tomorrow."

She pouted and went into the family room with her brother. I laughed and asked, "Was I like that, Mom?"

"Lord, yes. I had to pop your mouth many times. You were determined to know people's business."

We all laughed, and Mom said, "I see another you, Felicia. I see a girl."

"Really, Mom? It's so early."

"I know. But I see a girl as clear as day. I can see it because it's yours."

Kendall's mom said, "I see the same thing. I hope his heart isn't set on a boy."

Kelly and I looked at each other and cracked up. Kelly said, "Your mom does it too I see."

"She was never wrong with any of my kids. When I had the twins, she told me I had a girl. Then a boy. Then she said I had one of each. Daddy and I thought she'd lost it. I was ready to have her put away."

Kelly laughed and asked my mom, "It's a girl, Mrs. Pierce?"

"Yep. It's very clear. And call me Mom. Please."

Kelly smiled and said, "Yes, Mom."

That night we had a great dinner and discussed our plans for the next year. We decided that we would move to my house. All of us. And if Kelly's friend came to visit, they could spend time at the other house, the apartment, or a hotel.

Terrell would finish this school year in Detroit, and then go to school here for his junior year. Kelly agreed she would move here the end of March. She would live here for a year or so.

We also agreed to have the wedding around Easter. That way the kids would be with Harold and we could do it privately and quickly.

Chapter Eleven

Just before we moved into the house, Kendall insisted on buying all new bedroom furniture. I expected that.

We moved in mid-March, just before Kelly came to live with us. And the second week of April we all went to Durham, North Carolina.

I agonized over telling the Bensons my plans. I finally decided not to. I wore the pretty white dress.

I couldn't decide who to ask to be my matron of honor, so I asked my mother. My four sisters stood with us as well.

And on April nineteenth, two thousand thirteen, almost four years after we met, we finally became Dr. and Mrs. Kendall Montgomery.

Stew and Kendall were informed in February that the owner of the house decided to accept their offer. So, Simone and I became the owners of the beautiful house in Jamaica.

Shortly after returning from the wedding, Juanita and I had lunch. She was thrilled about our nuptials and the baby. She told me she was secretly seeing a man. "I missed having the love of a man. I can only hope she never finds out."

"Do you love him?"

"No, I don't think so. But I do love how he makes me feel."

I laughed. "I remember telling you that about Kendall."

We both laughed.

We began preparing for Terrell to arrive. He was getting the entire bottom floor. Kelly had the bedroom on the first floor with the en suite.

We moved the twins out of the nursery and put them in TJ's room. We put twin beds in their new room and also in Marcus' room, so when the boys were here, although they had to share a room, they wouldn't have to share a bed.

Kelly's boyfriend came to visit a few times and they stayed at a hotel. Terrell was staying with him until he moved here.

Kendall allowed me to postpone our honeymoon. He wanted to go to Europe, but I wasn't feeling being so far away because of Kelly.

Everyone seemed settled in the house except Kendall. The first thing he did was call Harold and insist that he stop paying the bills. They both laughed because Kendall told him he felt like a kept woman.

But something else had him troubled. I couldn't quite put my finger on it. I found him watching me sometimes. And periodically, he would ask me about the time we were apart.

Otherwise, he and I were transitioning smoothly. He continued to be loving and patient, and I continued spoiling him. He and I both spoiled Kelly.

Kelly had her ultrasound in May. She had one child. A girl. I told them I didn't want to know, but Kelly slipped and mentioned it. Twice.

At that point, she'd only gained twelve pounds and was doing very well. Simone was also having a girl. All of the women were thrilled. We weren't sure how the guys felt.

Just before Memorial Day, I asked Kendall about the parade. He laughed at my excitement, but he agreed to go with us.

While there, Benny and I were walking toward a hotdog vendor. I looked up and saw Mitchell. And he saw me. I almost peed on myself.

He was coming toward me, and I was looking around for Kendall. He and Aleece were fighting over her cotton candy. I turned back around, and there was Mitchell. Right in front of me.

And before I knew what was happening, he hugged me. "Shiree! It's so good to see you. How are you?"

He hugged me tight and long. He smelled wonderful. "Great, Mitchell. How have you been?"

"Good. Diane and I are home for the holiday. Is this your son?"

I looked down at Benny. "Yes. Benny, say hi to Mr. Mitchell."

He reached up and shook his hand. "Hi. I'm Harold Benson."

"And I'm Felicia's husband, Kendall Montgomery. How are you, Mitchell?"

Kendall stepped in front of me and extended his hand. Benny said, "Dad. Mommy is gonna get us hotdogs."

Kendall didn't hear a word Benny said. Mitchell shook Kendall's hand and said, "It's a pleasure to meet you, Kendall."

Then Mitchell turned to me. "Your name is Felicia? I thought your name was Shiree?"

Once we got home, Kendall grabbed my hand and literally pulled me up the stairs. I'm almost certain I saw smoke coming out of his ears.

He insisted I remove my clothes. He also removed his. He started the shower, and I pointed toward the door, "Kendall...the kids?"

"Kelly has them. Come here, Felicia."

"Don't you dare call me that!"

"I'll call you Felicia..."

"And I will *not* respond!"

I put on my robe and started out of the room. He came out and grabbed my arm. He was naked and pissed. "You will do what I say, Fe..."

"Say it, Kendall. Say it, and I'll slap the shit out of you!"

"You're not gonna hit me, Felicia."

I slapped the shit out of him. He stood there. I slapped him again. Harder. He walked back in the bedroom and sat on the bed. I went into the bathroom and turned off the shower.

I sat next to him. I knew he was hurt, and I prayed for something, *anything* to make him feel better. I picked up his hand and kissed it. "I'm sorry, Kendall."

I touched his face and gently rubbed it. I put my forehead on his cheek, and said, "If you stop calling me Shiree, my heart will stop."

He finally looked at me. "Do you still love me? Have you stopped loving me, Kendall?"

He sighed. "No, Baby. But...why did you do that? How could you give him the one thing that was mine? Who is he?"

When Mitchell asked me about my name, Kendall said, "Her *name*, is Mrs. Montgomery. And you can say goodbye to her. Mitchell."

Kendall took Benny's hand, and then mine. We went back to our spot, where Kelly and Aleece were sitting. Terrell had also come, but he was somewhere with his friends.

Benny was complaining about his hotdog, so Kendall looked at me with fire in his eyes. "Stay right here, Felicia. Do not move."

He took Benny and Aleece for hotdogs. Kelly looked at me with her mouth opened. "What the hell was that?"

"Lord, Kelly. I ran into an old friend and Kendall lost it."

"I know. He saw that guy hug you. I never saw him move so fast. I thought he was gonna go over there and kill him, so I reminded him I had Daddy on speed dial."

We both laughed, but I knew I was in deep trouble. I had to figure out some way to explain it. No one ever called me Shiree except him and Daddy. So, I could never convince him it was some old friendship. What was I gonna do?

Then Todd and the boys came over, and we all continued watching the parade. But I knew Kendall was mad as hell.

As scared as I was to do it, I decided to tell him the truth. I realized this was my chance to finally get it off of me. He was waiting for me to answer his question. "Mitchell is...he's the one I...dated. He said he and his wife are visiting for the holiday."

Kendall got up and ran his fingers through his hair. He couldn't face me at first. He went in the bathroom and turned the shower back on. "Please join me, Shiree."

I slowly got up and removed my robe. I obeyed my husband and got in the shower with him.

As I walked in, he opened his arms and embraced me. He turned the showerhead on me and wet my hair. He reached for the Summer Grace and shampooed my hair and cleaned me.

While rinsing me off, he kissed my forehead. "I knew that was Mitchell, Shiree. I also know about James and Bill. I don't remember the names of the others."

I felt as though my brain was spinning right out of my head. And he knew it because he held me up. "I also know you didn't sleep with all of them. Based on the report, you could've only slept with Mitchell and James. You never saw any of the others privately."

As soon as Kendall went to work Tuesday, I called Simone. "Girl, you will not *believe* what happened."

"Wait. Let me grab my coffee."

"I'm gonna get Annette and Carla on too, so take your time."

Before she returned, I managed to get both of them on the line. "I didn't want to repeat this. Do you guys remember that guy Mitchell I was seeing?"

They all said yes. "I ran into him yesterday at the parade. He hugged me, and Kendall saw it and lost it. He came over to us and told Mitchell he was my husband. Then...Mitchell called me Shiree."

Simone screamed and Annette said, "What the hell?! Did Kendall kill him?"

Carla said, "Damn, I always miss the good stuff."

"No, he didn't kill Mitchell. But he *damn sure* wanted to kill *my ass*. But the worst was yet to come. Kendall later told me he knew all about Mitchell. And the other guys too."

Simone asked, "Are you calling for bail money? I'm not believing this. There's no way Kendall didn't kill *somebody*."

"Simone. Remember in Jamaica when that PI gave Kendall his reports?"

"Yes."

"He gave him *everything*. Two years of reports. *And* pictures."

"You're shitting me! What did they say?"

"Well, all of my activity was tracked, even that. So Harold *also* knew about those guys. *Do you believe that shit!*"

Annette said, "Harold is whack. Who the fuck does that?!"

Carla said, "Girl, your life is a soap opera."

We all laughed. "Kendall and I fought something terrible yesterday. I even slapped him twice because he wouldn't call me Shiree anymore."

Annette said, "Damn. He really *was* mad. And you too, Licia!"

Simone said, "I told you Kendall would lose it if he ever learned some other guy called you Shiree."

"When he asked me who the guy was, I told him the truth. He was outdone that I didn't lie to him. And because he has pictures, he knew *exactly* who Mitchell was."

Simone said, "Damn. That's a different Kendall."

"He told me he chose to accept it for what it was. He said he fully expected me to lie about it because in my mind, there was no way he could know the difference. He couldn't get over my honesty."

Annette asked, "So, all is well?"

"Pretty much. I came clean about Mitchell, but I never admitted to sleeping with James. He said he never took the time to read the report completely at first. It was too long. But after we moved, he saw it again while unpacking and began to read it again. About six weeks ago, he got to the part that tracked my activity during our separation."

After hanging up, I began to understand Kendall's strange behavior lately. I also wondered what else he knew. I didn't need another Harold.

A few days later, Kelly and I were in the kitchen. She asked, "Are you and Kendall okay?"

"I think so. He was really upset when Mitchell called me Shiree. I explained to him that I thought I'd never have anyone call me that again. In my sadness, it was my way of having some part of him back."

"Gosh. The both of you were a mess. I'm sure you missed him terribly."

I shook my head and remembered. "Kelly. It felt like he'd died. And honestly, that guy couldn't begin to replace my Kendall. And even though he called me Shiree, nobody says it like Kendall Montgomery."

Later in June, we had a double baby shower. Simone's mother came and finally met Stew. She fell in love with him and stopped bothering Simone so much. She told Simone, "The other two were wrong. This one is right. He loves you from his soul."

The week of July fourth, Harold, Todd and the three boys went to New York City. This time they went to Citi Field and saw the Yankees at the Met's new stadium.

They saw two games. Harold still hadn't gone back to work. I wasn't sure if it was by choice or what. I suspected he was preparing to take over Benson's.

Aleece was very upset that her father left her because she's a girl. So Kendall took her to a local baseball game. She's now a Rochester Red Wings fan.

On the nineteenth of July, Simone gave birth to a precious, beautiful baby girl. She looks like her daddy and Stew named her Brooke. It took him a month to stop crying. He adored her.

In August, Terrell was enrolled in a parochial high school here, and the twins were enrolled in preschool. I was still working off site and

Kendall's practice was busier than ever. So was the club. The trio rarely had time to play anymore, so they began hiring live entertainment.

Kelly's due date was November twenty eighth, but the middle of October she gave us a scare. I was in the kitchen preparing to take the kids to preschool.

Kendall bought Terrell a used car to drive to school. He was very smart and helpful, and no trouble at all. Just before he left that morning, Kelly came out of her room looking worried. "I think I need to call the doctor. I'm spotting."

I had Terrell take the kids to school. I insisted Kelly get off her feet while we waited for the doctor to return her call. I remember biting three of my nails off.

She was put on bed rest. She and the baby were doing fine, but they were concerned that she might begin labor too early. They figured the baby to be about four and a half pounds. At that point, she'd only gained twenty-three pounds and was enjoying great health otherwise.

Kendall was beside himself. I feared he was gonna pass out from worry too. I told him to remain calm around Kelly, because she fed off of our energy.

A week later, Stew and Simone were visiting and I was holding Brooke. She was a fussy baby, and I laughed because she was just like her mother.

Brooke was adamant about being held, and I warned Simone and Stew about holding her so much. Kendall said, "I'll be glad when my little Kelley is born."

I hit his arm. "Kendall. Be quiet. It's supposed to be a surprise."

Kelly came out of her room. "Are you really naming her Kelly?"

I smiled. "Yes. Her name is Kelley Shiree. Spelled with 'e y' on the end."

Kendall took Brooke and began to make her laugh. Kelly began to cry. I said, "No, no, no. None of that. Don't upset yourself, Kelly."

Simone said, "She's right, Kelly. We all love you for your sacrifice."

She sat, and my front door opened. My mother walked in and asked, "Kendall? Are you here? I need your help."

He gave Brooke to Stew and ran to help her. I walked out of the kitchen and saw him kiss her cheek and relieve her of the cake in her hand. He said, "Thanks, Mom. But Shiree will have a fit."

"She'll get over it."

I crossed my arms and spoke to my mother. When they walked into the kitchen, I asked, "Who's the cake for, Mom?"

"Everyone. I thought we could all use a treat."

Everyone greeted Mom and started rubbing their hands together. I said, "No cake for the women. And I'll slice a piece for the men."

They all looked at each other, and Kelly said, "I just want a little."

Mom said, "And you will have it. Felicia, go and sit down somewhere. I will slice a piece for everyone."

I rolled my eyes and worried, because Kelly was getting off of her routine. I realized it was okay sometimes, but she'd been doing it a lot lately. I looked at Simone and she sucked her teeth. "Don't look at me like that. I've lost my weight."

And she had. She was as gorgeous as ever. Kendall came over to me and embraced me. "Sweetie. You take such good care of us. But every now and then we like to have something special. Don't upset yourself over this."

I nodded and said, "Okay, Kendall. I suppose one slice is okay."

That night, Kendall and I lounged in our room on the loveseat. He didn't want chairs in front of the fireplace like Harold and I had. He asked me to please get a loveseat. So, I did.

I was doing laundry and waiting on the last load to dry. He said, "Baby, I can't get over how much work it takes to keep this house in order. You're constantly cleaning and cooking and washing clothes. It's a full-time job."

"I know. But that's with any house. There's just more of it here because it's bigger. But Terrell does a great job keeping the bottom floor clean. And although Kelly is moving slower now, she always helps too. But I won't let her do much now."

"Have you ever thought about hiring help?"

I laughed. "No, I never thought of it. But when I was carrying the twins, he wanted me to. I refused. I don't need it."

He smiled and looked at me lovingly. "I still fear that one day I'll wake up and learn you're not really my wife. I'm so happy."

"I'm happy too, Kendall. Come here. I want to show you something."

I took him to the nursery and showed him what I'd done. I decided on a combination of white and pastels. With balloons sprinkled throughout the room.

I brought down one of the cribs and one of the cradles from the attic, which I still had.

I opened the closet and showed him all the pretty clothes for little Kelley, some of which were Aleece's old things. There were diapers and blankets and drawers full of undershirts and socks and bibs.

On the wall hung the undershirt I gave him for his birthday. I framed it, along with pictures of Kelly throughout *our* pregnancy. "Shiree. This is so surreal. I still can't believe this is happening."

"I know, Kendall. It's really starting to become real for me too. It's weird to watch my child grow across the table from me."

We both laughed. "Come and help me get the clothes, Kendall. I wanna talk to you about something else."

After we finished with the clothes, we went back to the loveseat. I turned and smiled at my husband. "I did something just before Kelly moved here. I hope you won't be too mad at me."

He crossed his arms. "What was that, Shiree?"

"We, you and I, we paid off her mortgage."

He looked at me and said nothing. "Say something, Kendall."

"That was very kind, Shiree. I was planning to do that anyhow."

He was about to get up. "Actually..."

He stopped and looked at me again. "Actually??"

"I also gave her one hundred thousand dollars in a CD. To put aside for Terrell. I know you all are also preparing and saving for his education, but I...I have never known anyone to be so selfless, Kendall. I was moved to tears for weeks over her sacrifice. Please don't be too mad..."

He leaned over and kissed me. I pulled away to speak. "I..."

He put his finger on my lip. "Be quiet, Shiree. I know how generous you are. And I also know how deeply you love. I'm not mad. But like you said to me some time ago, trust me. I know I'm stubborn, but I don't want you thinking you have to hide stuff from me."

"Kendall. I wasn't planning on keeping it from you. I just had to find the right time to tell you. You know I'm not a spender. I buy as needed. And I give when my heart is moved to. People like our children, our parents, our families. I'll always make sure they have all they need. I'm sorry I kept it from you."

He brought me in his arms. "When the baby is here, will it be hard for you and Kelly?"

"What do you mean?"

"She'll need to be with Aunt Kelly so much. Will you be okay with that?"

I got a visual of my daughter in Kelly's arms. I opened my mouth and paused. I eventually said, "I hadn't thought of that. I need to prepare for that, don't I?"

He nodded. "Maybe you can share the feeding. Breast *and* bottle."

"She might be a breast baby and not like the bottle. Or like the twins, need to be breast fed to avoid ear infections."

He held me closer when he saw my anguish. "Don't get upset, Shiree."

"I need to get the other cradle out of the attic and put it in her room. I'll get it cleaned up and...and..."

I began to cry, and I realized I was going to miss so much. I was getting my first dose of jealousy and I hated even admitting it to myself. I suddenly wished I had my uterus back.

On November second, Kelly went into labor. It started slowly, but four hours later, things began to move quickly. Little Kelley decided to come three weeks early.

Our daughter was born just after eight o'clock that night, and I was there to help her into the world and to cut the cord. No pun intended.

I looked up at Kelly and smiled. "She's here, Kelle."

They whisked our daughter away and I walked over to my sister. She and I hugged, and we were both laughing and crying at the same time. We heard her cry, and it was music to our ears.

I closed the curtain while the nurses attended to Kelly. I knew Kendall would be coming in soon. Trish smiled at both of us and someone tapped on the door.

Kendall came in wearing scrubs and reached for my hand. We walked over to our daughter. He watched every move anyone made toward his daughter. Her scores were high, and he smiled and spoke medical lingo with them.

He said almost to himself, "She's fine. She's perfect."

Finally, they wrapped her up and handed her to him. He brought her to his face and touched her cheek with his.

He closed his eyes, and tears fell from them. I rubbed his back, and we both looked at her through tears. I watched as he looked in her face. We both saw it. He whispered, "*Shiree...*"

His gaze never left her. She had his dimples, but everything else was me. He continued to hold her and watch her until I reached for her. He reluctantly handed her to me. We both laughed.

I looked at my daughter and held her close. She looked so much like me. He put his arm around me, and I kissed her face. I turned to Kendall and said quietly, "We did it, Sweetie. We have a baby!"

"Thanks to God and you, Shiree. There's no way we could've known so much would happen since that day I asked for your eggs. I'm so thankful."

He and I kissed each other and then our daughter. I whispered to her, "You're our little miracle, Kelley. Come and meet your other mommy."

"Actually, Shiree..."

I looked at him and he was staring at her. He turned to face me, and he also whispered, "I'd like her name to be Shiree Kelley instead of Kelley Shiree. Please?"

We moved further away, and I said quietly, "But we agreed it flowed better the other way around. Right?"

"I know. But look at her. She's the spitting image of you. Please, Shiree?"

I looked at her and smiled. "Okay, Kendall. Let's just call her Shiree for now. I know I told you to name her, but I think I have another idea. I'll tell you later."

She started forming her mouth to nurse. I turned to Kelly, and the nurses were preparing her to go to recovery. I stopped them and said, "Before you go, please hold her."

She smiled and reached for her. When Kelly held her, little Shiree nuzzled up to her and started fussing. Kendall and I watched them, and Kelly said, "Brother, I need to feed her."

He smiled and stood there. He finally said, "Oh...I'll go out."

When he left, I went over to her and opened her gown. She'd never nursed before, so I helped her through it. Little Kelley took a minute, but soon latched on. Kelly said, "Let Kendall in. It's okay. We can cover most of it."

I smiled and went and got him. He came in and we held each other as she and Auntie Kelly began their second phase of bonding.

Kendall asked me to use the name, Felicia Shiree Montgomery. He loves to call me Mrs. Montgomery and rarely calls me Shiree anymore.

He was adamant about his daughter being named Shiree. I was too, but he and I agreed that we also wanted her to have his sister's name.

The day after she was born, he and I took a walk and discussed it. "Kendall, we agree that Kelly will be her Godmother, right?"

"Of course."

I paused. I had no idea how he would react to my suggestion. "What, Shiree?"

"Well, I was thinking that maybe we shouldn't use the name Kelly. Being her Godmother is already honoring Kelly, right?"

"I suppose. You have another name in mind?"

I smiled. "Yes. Just like you want her named after me, I want her named after you too."

He glared. "What name, Shiree?"

"Kendall."

"Are you serious?"

"You don't like it?"

He walked away and turned toward me. He seemed to be trying to absorb it. Then he laughed and said, "I went to school with a girl named Kendall. At ECU."

I walked over to him. "Do you like it?"

"So, her name would be Shiree Kendall Montgomery?"

"I like Kendall Shiree, but whatever you prefer."

Two days after they came home, Kendall's parents came to visit again. It seemed we had a thousand people at our house, and my parents and sisters, including Gina were running around helping with everything.

Lenora and Trina were there, along with everyone from Kendall's practice.

Poor Shiree was getting passed around and spoiled royally. All of my kids were there, and the twins were amazed that they had a little sister.

The boys weren't impressed, but they continued to ask how the baby ended up in Aunt Kelly's tummy. Terrell went over to his Uncle Kendall and wiped a tear from his eye. He said, "You do realize I'll never let you forget that I saw you cry."

Kendall ran after him and Stew said, "His day will come, Ken. We all cry when we become fathers."

Kendall went over to his mom. "Mother. May I hold her please?"

She was sound asleep and Kelly said, "We really should put her down. She's going to be spoiled rotten."

The Bensons sent a beautiful bouquet congratulating us on the arrival of our daughter. It had been a year since Harold and I ended our marriage.

I sometimes couldn't believe we were no longer together. And being in that house didn't help.

Karen told me confidentially that Harold was seeing someone seriously. I actually felt a twinge of jealousy.

I wondered why I continued to feel pulled by Harold. It was as if our separation was just temporary. I didn't feel like that at all with Todd. It was very unnerving.

A week later, Harold's number showed up on my cell phone. I was in the kitchen and I told Kelly I'd be right back. I went upstairs.

It was about ten in the morning, and I walked in our room and answered. He said, "Hi, Felicia."

"Harold. How are you?"

"You seem in a good mood. I first want to congratulate you on the birth of the baby. You gotta send a pic."

"Thanks. She's really precious."

"So, she's actually your child too?"

After explaining, he said, "That doesn't surprise me at all. You loved me like that."

"Are things going okay for you?"

"Yeah. Very well, Felicia. I'm now CEO of Benson's and it's keeping me very busy. Listen. I know the kids spent Christmas with me last year, but I was wondering…"

"Of course they can. When will you come for them?"

He laughed. "That's so generous of you. And happy belated birthday by the way. I thought to send you a card, but I decided it wouldn't be appropriate."

"Thank you. And happy early birthday to you. Are you dating?"

He laughed again. "A little. Here and there. Are you still worried about me?"

"Not worried. Just hopeful you'll soon find love again."

He was quiet for a moment. "I had a moment with someone, but I pulled back. I'm not ready. Plus, I continue to compare them to you."

I opened my mouth and immediately closed it. I was truly speechless. He laughed again. "I think I just embarrassed you. I'll check flights and let you know when I'll come and get them. According to Ken, Aleece is finally writing her name. I worried about her."

"Yes, she's doing great."

"Don't worry about me, Felicia."

"And you shouldn't compare anyone to me, Harold. I did some foul things."

"You did what you did because I was such a jerk. I honestly believe that if I had been a better husband, it would have never happened. Am I right?"

I paused, but then I said, "You're right, Harold. I know I wouldn't have done any of it. I…I loved you so much."

He and I were both quiet. "I need to go, Harold. Let me know…when you schedule their flights."

My hand was shaking when I hung up. I went in the bathroom and put water on my face. I looked at myself and wondered what the hell was wrong with me.

I walked downstairs and said to Kelly, "I need to run to Mom's for a minute. Will you be okay?"

"Of course."

Sitting at Mom's table, I was eating her pretzels like they were gonna fly away. She laughed. "What is *wrong*, Felicia?"

I shook my head. "Mommy. I just talked to Harold."

"How is he? Jacquie told me last week that he finally seems happy again."

"He's fine. I'm the one that's a mess. I still can't seem to get completely over him. I still feel something for him."

"Felicia, that's normal."

"But I didn't feel like that with Todd. I actually miss Harold sometimes."

"You'll get past it. Stop worrying about it. It's because of the way things ended. There was so much deceit and pain between the two of you. With Todd, he was the villain. With Harold, you feel like you were the villain."

I looked at her while crunching on the pretzels. "You think?"

"Yes. Absolutely."

On occasion Kendall calls me Shiree, but he seemed to have settled on calling me Mrs. Montgomery. When he first saw our daughter, he was so happy she looked like me. And she does. A lot.

Alysiya began showing signs of jealousy because she always had that distinction. Both of them have complexions lighter than mine. But Kendall so far is a mini me. I'm glad they look like sisters.

Both of the twins are jealous of the attention Kendall gives her. But Aleece is especially disturbed by it.

Exactly one week before Christmas, Kendall and I were getting ready for bed. It was a few days after Harold came and got the kids for the holiday. Kendall was coming out of his closet and I was sitting on the bed.

I watched him as he went about his normal routine of preparing for the next day and checking his phone.

He went over to the cradle and looked at his daughter. She was sleeping peacefully and although she was more spoiled than any of my other kids, she slept through the night and did well with me bottle feeding her part time.

He was so attached to her. He leaned down and kissed her. Then he smiled and touched her bushy hair.

I smiled and asked him, "Have you ever wished you had a son?"

He seemed to be thinking of how to answer. "At first I thought I wanted a son. But you gave me many reasons why a daughter would be so precious. And you were right. Why do you ask?"

"Typically, men want sons and women want daughters. I was just curious."

"Do you want another one?"

I laughed. "No, Dear. We have enough kids."

"Shiree, you seem tired. Are you feeling okay?"

I smiled and put my head down. I guess I have a certain look when something is on my mind. "Yes, I feel fine. Kendall can be a handful during the day because she wants so much attention. I guess she got that from you."

He sat next to me. "I've missed our regular love making. Is this what it's like having kids and being so busy?"

"Yes, it is. I noticed you called me Shiree. I've missed that."

I got up and began turning down the bed. "You don't like Mrs. Montgomery?"

"I love it. But you calling me Shiree has always been so sweet to me."

"Does it bother you when I call our daughter Shiree?"

"No. I love that too. But I miss being your first Shiree."

He came over and kissed my neck. I was sitting on the side of the bed and he kneeled in front of me and looked up in my eyes. "I'm sorry, Shiree. I just realized I've been neglecting you. Everyone's had my attention except you."

I turned away. He gently caressed my chin and turned my face back toward his. "I can't imagine that I've done that. You miss me, don't you?"

"I do miss you, Kendall. I need you to touch me more. I wonder if we made a mistake getting married and living together."

He got up and sat next to me. He cupped my face in his large hands. "Please don't say that. I pray you don't really feel that way."

"No, I don't feel that way. I'm saying maybe we made a mistake. When we lived separately, you and I missed each other so much. I remember nights I would wake up and want you next to me so bad. Now when I wake up, I fear I'll disturb your much needed rest. I miss you wanting me like you used to."

He seemed to panic. He looked at me as if he was suddenly afraid. "Shiree. You don't believe that, do you?"

I looked in his eyes again and I felt sad. "Kendall. You don't look at me the same. I guess I was delusional to think I'd always have that. Am I no longer pretty to you? Or sexy? That would kill me."

He pulled me to my feet and kissed me. He held me close. He stepped back and looked at me. "What have I done? I'll fix it, Baby. I'm sorry."

"I just need assurance that you still love and want me."

He kissed me again. He removed my robe and cupped my face again. "My gorgeous Shiree. I will love you…forever. I love you more today than I ever have. I've allowed things to come before you and I'll never forgive myself for it."

He went to his knees and kissed my stomach. He rubbed my legs and opened them. He kissed me there and then stood and laid me down.

He removed his boxers and laid next to me. "I think of you so much when I'm sitting in my office or driving in my car. In the trunk of my car is another collection of Philosophy and Vicki's newest bras and panties. I've been so busy, I forgot to give them to you. That will change, Shiree. I promise."

"I realized recently that as much as I spoiled you, you also spoiled me. I guess I've been feeling sorry for myself."

He made love to me all night.

The next morning, he was up earlier than usual. I saw that Kendall was out of her cradle. I went to the bathroom and then put on a pair of sweats and one of his University of Rochester hoodies.

I was headed downstairs when I saw him coming up with a breakfast tray. I smiled. "Kendall. This is so sweet. I'm sure Kelly helped you."

"She showed me how to do most of it. I'm getting better."

We went back into the bedroom and he kissed me. "How are you feeling?"

"Very good. Thank you, Doctor."

"I hope you'll give me the chance to make it up to you, Shiree."

"All is forgiven, Kendall. I know you love me."

He sat the tray down. "I'm staying home with you, and Kelly has agreed to take care of little Shiree all day. I want us to spend the day together in each other's arms, and then I'll take you out for a fabulous romantic dinner."

"That sounds wonderful, Kendall. But it's not nece…"

"It is necessary."

He insisted I get back in bed and we had our breakfast. We laid in each other's arms and we both dozed off. When we woke up, we showered and dressed and got back on the bed.

I again laid in his arms. He played in my hair and said, "When Shiree was born, I looked at her and saw our love as a living, breathing thing. I saw what your love for me looked like. It looks like you, Shiree. That's why I can't help but call her Shiree. My Shiree. I love you both so much."

I smiled at that. "Kendall. That is so beautiful. Just like you. You're such a beautiful person."

Although he was behind me, I could sense he was smiling. "I don't think anyone's ever called me beautiful before."

I laughed. "I first realized it that day you played and sang for me. Do you remember when I told you I couldn't see you anymore? And you played and sang Jaheim's, *Finding My Way Back to You*?"

"I do, Shiree. That was the first time I thought I'd lost you. I've done many foolish things."

"But you always found your way back to me."

We both smiled and I laid back in his arms. There was a knock on the door and Kelly asked, "Can I come in?"

Kendall got up and let her in. She walked in with little Kendall and smiled. "I just wanted to ask you guys if I could have some time to talk to you later. Terrell and I have been talking and we would like to share some of what we've discussed. I don't want to interrupt your time together now, but Kendall is missing her mommy."

I got up and took her. She smiled and I kissed her. Feeling my cheek on hers, she turned toward it and attached to my lip like Aleece used to do. I allowed her to nibble on it and her daddy laughed and said, "I remember Alysiya doing that."

Then he turned to his sister. "What's on your mind?"

"Terrell told me about a week ago that he'd love to live here in Rochester. He's made friends and has a silly little girlfriend."

We all laughed, and she continued. "I've also enjoyed my time here. I was thinking I might be able to work for GM here. I figure with my connections and Simone's, it should be easy for me to get in."

I was thrilled, but I looked over at Kendall and he wasn't. I asked, "What do you think, Kendall?"

"What if we decide to leave Rochester? I would hate to leave you, Kelle."

"I thought about that too. I'm ready to leave Detroit, and this could just be a stop on my way to wherever. I'm okay with that."

Kendall smiled and said, "Then I love it. And I can keep my eye on Terrell. At sixteen, I feel better knowing I'm close to him. I would love to have you all here."

Kelly also smiled. She reached for her niece and said, "Okay. Little Kendall has visited long enough. I'm gonna order pizza because Terrell did so well in his classes. I'm so proud of him. After tests this week, he's out until after the New Year. He's smart like you were, Kendall. You are."

We all cracked up. Kendall said, "You didn't do too bad yourself, Kelly."

"I did all right, but it came natural for you. I had to work hard to stay on the honor roll. Terrell is more like you."

Little Kendall made a mess in her diaper and I took her into the nursery while they continued to talk. Kelly soon came in behind me. "I can clean her."

"No. You go on and talk with Kendall. I'm so happy you'll be living here. And we insist that you and Terrell stay in the other house."

She smiled and hugged me. "Let's go shopping and to lunch tomorrow, Felicia. The guys can take care of Kendall."

"Okay, Kelle. That sounds like fun."

She smiled. "You look better today. I sensed some sadness lately."

"I was missing Kendall. He's been so busy. And this time of year is always non-stop at his practice."

She giggled and looked behind her. "I think you scared him. He started barking orders and the next thing I knew he was trying to cook."

We both hollered laughing. "I was afraid he was gonna burn the damn house down, so I took over and finished it."

He came in and asked if we were talking about him. We both said, "Yes."

Then I said, "I told Kelly that she and Terrell could stay at the other house."

"Of course. That would be perfect, Kelle. You'd be close by and it wouldn't be sitting there vacant."

The following day, Kelly and I went to the mall. We remembered the day we met and how we were dealing with the same madness then.

We were both done Christmas shopping, but I suspected her reason for going had to do with something else.

Kendall and I agreed to only one token gift for one another. We also agreed that Christmas would always be for the kids.

Kelly and I sat in the food court and had lemonade. "So, what are Glen's thoughts about you relocating?"

She turned and looked at the kids in the train passing by. She smiled at them. "I haven't told him. I've…sort of been getting to know someone here."

"What?! Who, Kelly?"

"You'll probably have a fit and so will Kendall."

"Who is it, Kelly?"

I couldn't imagine who it could be. She was looking at her hands and finally looked up. "Jim. I mean, Dr. Reynolds."

I continued to look at her, trying to make it make sense in my head. Jim Reynolds worked at Kendall's practice. He was in his late forties and white. "Kelly? Are you sure?"

She hollered laughing. "He and I got to know each other when I would go over and see Kendall or take the kids for their appointments. And when he came over to see little Kendall, we began communicating through Facebook and email. He really likes me, Felicia. And I like him too. He's not the first white man I've dated."

I tried to swallow but my throat was too dry. "Felicia. I need your support here. Your husband is gonna freak the hell out and I'll need someone on my side."

I sipped my lemonade and found my voice. "Have you two been dating?"

"We did lunch once. But we felt like felons. We're both afraid of what Kendall will say, but I'm not ashamed of our friendship. And no, I have not slept with him."

Still trying to grasp it all, I looked up trying to find the right words. I wished I'd never done that. The devil himself was looking right at me. And smiling.

I froze. Then I quickly looked back at Kelly. "We have to go. Now, Kelly."

"Come on, Felicia. I really…"

"Do you remember Kendall said he beat up a guy for harassing me?"

"Yes."

"He's looking at me and we need to get out of here."

We went toward the exit and I sensed they were following. Sam *and* Jonathon. I took out my phone and said to Kelly, "I think they're following us. We can't go to the car. They'll…"

"What do you mean *they*?"

"Let's go to the ladies' room."

We quickly turned right and went into the ladies' room. When we got in there, I told her about Sam and Jonathon, the calls and Kendall beating him up.

Kelly was livid, so I put my finger on my lip to shush her. "They might be waiting on us. If for no other reason, to get back at Kendall. What should we do?"

"We should call Stewart."

"No way. He'll end up in jail."

"Annette or Carla? Then we can go to the police station."

I sent Annette a text. She replied: I'm coming right now. Meet me outside of Sears facing Long Pond Rd. I need ten minutes. I replied: We'll be there.

We walked out of the bathroom and saw no signs of them. We agreed to act as normal as we could. We were a good distance from Sears, so we casually walked and talked and laughed. I said, "About Jim. I'm happy for you. But how do you plan to tell Kendall?"

"I was kinda hoping you'd tell him."

I cracked up. "Why me?"

"You can say anything to him and he'll listen."

Sam walked up to me. "Hi, Felicia. I can't believe my luck. How are you?"

I forced a smile. "I'm good."

Jonathon walked up behind us. "Felicia. You are a sight for sore eyes. Just beautiful. Who's your friend?"

We were still in the mall, but right outside the entrance into Sears. Ninety seconds from being outside. I said, "We have to go. Our ride is waiting on us."

Sam stood in front of me. "Would that be your husband?"

"You wanna find out?"

He frowned and turned to Kelly. "She and I used to be an item."

Kelly rolled her eyes and we started going through Sears. We saw Annette and she came over to us. "Girl, I've been waiting on you two."

She looked at the guys and we continued outside toward her car. She parked it right in front of the store.

Sam grabbed my arm. "Felicia. I wanna see you."

I looked at his hand on me. "I'm not interested, Sam. Should I call my husband?"

Jonathon came up behind me. "We know you don't mean that. We had such a good time the last time we were together. Maybe we *should* call him and tell him how hot is wife *really* is."

"Let me go, Sam."

Annette came over and went in her purse. She did what she'd been threatening to do for years. She took out a gun. "Check this out fellas. I think she said she wasn't interested. Now, if one or both of you would like to taste what comes out of this bitch, keep messing with her. If not, I'd advise you to get the fuck on."

They both backed up and Kelly and I got in her car. Annette stared at them and said, "Leave my sister alone. I can't tell you how much pleasure it would give me to pull this trigger. If I ever see you near her again, I *will* kill you."

When we pulled off, Annette said, "I wish that bastard would have tried me. I've wanted to shoot his ass for years."

I yelled, "Annette, where did you get a damn gun??!!"

"I told you I had one."

Kelly said, "Oh My God, Annette! I almost pissed my pants when you pulled that damn thing out."

W circled around the mall parking lot and eventually pulled up next to my car. Annette asked, "Are you going home?"

"Do you think they're following us?"

Kelly said, "I doubt it. Between the gun in their faces and this mall being so big, chances are slim that they're anywhere near us. Plus, they probably think Annette really is our ride. So they think we're long gone."

Annette said, "Let's go to my house and have a drink."

Once at Annette's, she opened a bottle of Moscato. Kelly said, "I pumped enough for two days. I want a drink too."

I made them all swear not to tell Kendall or anyone else what happened. Kelly asked, "Are you trying to tell me my brother got on a plane and whipped that man's ass for calling you?"

"Yes. I told Kendall what they did and he was furious. I felt it was safe to tell him because Sam was long gone to Richmond and I didn't think I'd ever lay eyes on him again."

I told her everything. Kelly asked, "So, if he and his buddy did this without your consent, why do they think you'd want anything else to do with them?"

"Kelly, I..."

I couldn't answer. Annette said, "Because she loved it. And they know it."

"My God, Felicia. You did?"

I nodded my head in shame. "It wasn't violent or by force. They tricked me. I was in bed with Sam. And during sex, Jonathon came in. He came up behind me and whispered in my ear and was touching me and... It was...indescribable. Please don't ever tell Kendall. It happened way before I met him, but it would devastate him."

"Girl, I'm not telling his crazy ass nothing. Hell, we've all done things we're not proud of. We may not regret them, but we're not trying to advertise it."

Annette said, "Hell yeah! I've got stories that would shame a hoe in the street."

We all laughed and Kelly said, "Girl, me too. Especially in college."

My phone rang. Sam had me so spooked, I thought it was him. But it was Kendall. "Hey, Baby. Are you still shopping?"

"No. We're at Annette's. What are you up to?"

"Not too much. When are you coming home? I have a surprise for you."

I laughed. "You do not. Your daughter is wearing you out, right?"

He hollered laughing. "No, Shiree. She's sleeping. She's been very good."

"Kendall, why do you want us to come home? We're visiting with Annette."

"Okay. Just let me know when you're on your way."

"Okay, I will. We won't be long."

After hanging up, I said, "I pray Sam is just here for the holidays. I couldn't bear the thought that he and I live in the same city."

Kelly asked, "Do you think you would see him?"

"Hell no. I am so over that. I'm afraid for Kendall. His temper could really get him in trouble. Or hurt. What am I gonna do?"

Annette said, "Don't worry about something that hasn't happened, Licia. Sam has no idea what your last name is or where you live. Kendall and Stew gave bogus names, and Kendall doesn't even know that prick is in town. You and Kelly need to go home and pretend all is well."

"Kendall can always tell when something is wrong. I can never hide it."

Kelly said, "Today is a good day to start hiding it. Neither of us wants him to know."

Before we left, Kelly laughed and said, "I'm sorry, but I have to say this. Both of those guys are fine as hell. Any woman would be drawn to them. So don't beat yourself up, Felicia."

Annette hollered. "Girl. That man was crazy about Felicia. We had to hire a friend of mine to spy on Sam. He was obsessed with her."

Annette and I looked at each other and we both yelled Benny's name at the same time. I said, "Annette, call him. He can keep an eye on him for us."

"Damn. I don't know if I still have his number. Do you know I haven't seen another man since I met Gary? I never thought one man could satisfy me, but Gary has proven me wrong."

Kelly looked at Annette and laughed. She asked, "Gary?"

"I meant..."

"I knew it. Every time we're all together, he always looks at you like you're a Porterhouse steak."

We all fell out laughing. Annette went through her phone and screamed, "I have it! I still have his number."

We watched as she called him. While talking to him, she said, "Negro, I still have my evidence."

She laughed and asked him if he still had his information about Sam. He said he did, and she told him what we wanted him to do. She looked at me and asked, "Do you remember his sister's name? He still has her address."

I thought about it. "Cynthia or Cheryl. Something like that."

After hanging up, she told us he wanted her name in case she moved. He remembered Sam spent a lot of time there. "He'll check out her old address tonight and look for Virginia plates or rentals."

Kelly said, "Let's get back home. And I want you to fix yourself a drink and get intoxicated. That way maybe you'll relax and not be so obvious."

Annette said, "And act horny."

We all laughed at Annette's crazy ass.

The garage door was barely up when he came out. He helped us with our packages and took my hand. We went up to the bedroom and he closed the door. "What is it, Kendall?"

"Juanita and I have been selected by our peers as Philanthropists of the Year. Montgomery Pediatrics, Shiree!"

By the time we were in bed, I exhaled regarding Sam. We spent so much time talking about the award, that Kendall wouldn't have noticed an atomic bomb. Unfortunately, he soon dropped a bomb on me.

I snuggled up to him. "Baby, I'm so proud of you."

"Don't forget, Juanita deserves a lot of the credit. She did a lot with the women's shelters."

"I know. I can't wait to call her tomorrow."

"She told me you two had lunch a while ago. She said you wanted her to tell me. Why did you keep it from me?"

"I wasn't keeping it from you. I know the two of you are very close, Kendall. I don't feel threatened by it because you've always been able to love both of us. And I needed her to know that it's okay."

"I no longer love her like that, Shiree."

"I know, Kendall."

"She told me about her lover. She's afraid she's in love with him."

I laughed. "I knew she was in love with him when she told me. Do you know him?"

"She never told me his name. I think he's married."

"Do you remember when Harold wanted us to continue living together?"

"Yes."

"Do you also remember saying to me that you knew I had slept with him?"

"Yes. I remember."

"When did you really stop sleeping with her? Or do you two still have sex?"

"Shiree..."

"It's okay, Baby. I just want the truth."

He raised my chin and looked in my eyes. "No, Shiree. It's *not* okay. What is this about?"

"I just want to know. Or would you rather not tell me?"

"I have not touched her since we've been married. No one but you, Sweetie."

"But?"

"Once, Shiree. Long ago. It happened once. *I'm sorry.*"

I was quiet. He sighed. "She was really upset one night. She called me crying and I felt terrible for her. It was...at least two years ago. Well before you left Harold."

"Don't tell me anymore, Kendall. I don't even know why I asked."

"I stopped when I said I stopped, Shiree. It was a one-time thing. I told her to come over, but she refused. Funny, but she couldn't disrespect you in that house either. So, she got a hotel room and I met her there."

I attempted to get up but he wouldn't let me. "I was scared she was gonna harm herself, Shiree. I didn't go to have sex with her. I was afraid for her. It just happened. I swear to you, Baby."

I realized he didn't have to tell me. I had the option of getting upset or simply accepting it. I decided some of the things I'd done were worse. "It's okay, Kendall. I know you didn't mean to hurt me. And if something had happened to her, it would have been devastating for both of us."

He got up and walked over to my side of the bed. He sat next to me and put his arm around me. "Please look at me, Shiree. I want to tell you more, but it would sound cruel."

"It's okay, Kendall. I'm fine."

He kissed me and held me close. I said, "I think because it was Juanita, it's not that upsetting. Were there any others?"

"No, Baby. Never."

"I believe you, Kendall. We're okay."

"Shiree. It means so much to me that you're happy. I know how hard you work to keep me happy. Todd and Harold blew it. I pray I never hurt you again."

"What don't you want to tell me?"

He put his head down and looked at his hands. "I no longer wanted intimacy with Juanita long before we stopped. She became so promiscuous, that I didn't know her anymore."

"How do you know that? Did she tell you?"

"Vonni told me. I know, she hates me. But she was worried about her and called me. She asked me to talk to her. When I did, Nita told me everything. I never told Vonni...everything."

"There's more?"

"Yes. Yvonne was caught sexting with someone and Juanita was so hurt. So, she joined a sex club, unbeknownst to Yvonne, and became...terrible. She'd talked about joining one for years."

I sat there with my mouth opened, trying to keep up with it all. "Was Yvonne cheating?"

"Apparently she was. With one of her students. She told Juanita that the girl had a huge crush on her. And she begged Yvonne to let her...you know."

I was dumbfounded. "Kendall. Not another word. I can't take anymore. And about you and Juanita, let's agree to forget it. Okay?"

"I prayed I would never have to tell you. But I couldn't lie to you, Shiree. Especially after you came clean with me."

I stood up and straddled him. "Thank you for also being honest. I'm sure it was hard to tell me."

The next few days were calm, and the news about Sam was interesting. Benny found out that he and his *family* appeared to be staying at his sister's place.

He learned that Sam is now married and has two children. Aysia and a three-year-old son. Jonathon is staying at a hotel with *his* family. A wife and daughter.

Benny assumes they're here for the holiday. I asked Annette to tell Benny to continue watching him and I'd pay whatever it cost. Then I told Annette I never believed she had a gun. "Is it real, Nette?"

"Yes, Ma'am. Tony and I both have guns. The Fraziers don't be playing."

"But it's so dangerous, Nette. Don't you worry about little Tony?"

"Of course. We keep them in a wall safe inside of our closet. He doesn't even know it's there. We both have permits and we're both trained."

"Wow. Did Benny say anything else about Sam?"

"Yeah. He said Sam is now the owner of two Popeye's franchises. Well, he and his wife own the second one."

Then she laughed. "Benny said the wife is absolutely nothing to look at. He described her as funny looking."

I laughed. "Get the hell outta here, Nette!"

"I had to know what Miss Thing looked like, so I asked."

I was surprised. "Maybe she has money."

"My sentiments exactly. So I asked Benny to check."

We both laughed. "The good part is he no longer has my number, so I don't have to fear him contacting me."

"You just need to learn how to keep that look off of your face when you're up to something. It would not be pretty if Kendall finds out you've hired Benny."

I paused. Since I knew she had some time alone, I decided to tell her what happened recently. "Annette. I have to tell you something.

I've kept it to myself for as long as I can. You're gonna be shocked, so prepare yourself."

"Licia. I know you didn't tell him about Benny and Sam."

"No, Nette. I'm not crazy. It has to do with Harold."

"Harold? What about him?"

I told her the story exactly as it happened…

When Harold arrived to get the kids, the twins and I were downstairs at my parent's house. I insisted they get their books and toys up before leaving.

Harold came down and they were all over him. Mom called the kids and told them to come and get the gifts they'd made for their dad and grandparents.

I began picking up toys, and Harold said, "I was hoping to see your daughter."

"She's with Kendall's sister."

"I can't believe you have five kids, Felicia. Is it overwhelming?"

"At times, but they all have great dads."

I smiled and continued putting books back on the shelf. When I turned back, he was right in front of me. I instinctively looked up, and our noses almost touched.

Scared, I stepped back, but I was against the bookshelf. He shook his head and handed me a book. Then he turned and walked away.

I stood there shaking like a leaf. He said, "Felicia. I never realized until just now how much my behavior affected you. You had a look of terror on your face."

I looked down. "Harold…"

"You were afraid of me, weren't you?"

I looked up. "No. Sort of, but…"

"I can't believe you were scared of me. Felicia, I would never have hurt you. Please believe that."

"I never thought that, Harold. I thought you were about to…touch me."

"That's just as bad."

He sat on the sofa. "I felt I had to do whatever was necessary to keep you. I was manipulative and conniving, and many other ugly things. I turned love into something no one would want any part of."

He shook his head and sighed. "But all it got me was a sad, hopeless wife. My behavior turned you into something..."

"Harold. We're passed that now. Let's not go back there."

"I was told six months ago that I need to apologize to you. But I had to tell you everything, so you would understand why."

He walked over and stood in front of me. "I told you most of it, but I never told you that I saw you and Kendall together a couple of times."

He continued pacing. "Or that you called me Kendall numerous times. Usually after sex."

I closed my eyes. "I saw you many times on East Avenue and at his office. I even saw you...in his arms."

I put my hand up to my mouth and turned away from him.

He walked back across the room. "You never knew I had access to a company car. I learned you spent most of your Thursday afternoons with Kendall. So I would park near the house on East Avenue and wait for your arrival."

Listening to that made me want to cry. I found myself back in that place of grief for him. "But I also went to his practice sometimes and I'd just sit there. I wanted to kill him, Felicia."

"Stop it, Harold. I don't want to hear anymore."

"I need you to know why you don't have to worry about me touching you. One day you pulled up and went inside. I walked around the building and saw you and him in his office."

"Please, Harold..."

"I didn't stay long, because I saw Kendall kiss you and then put his head between your legs."

I was floored! I put my hand up to my mouth again, and I remembered that low feeling I had when he confronted me.

I turned toward the bathroom, but he came over and stopped me. "It was about two months before Curtis told me what he knew, and that's why I had no interest in sex near the end. Knowing it was one thing. Seeing it killed something in me."

He admitted he had sex with me to try to win me back or get me on tape. His plan was to threaten to send it to Kendall. But I was able to destroy them just in time.

He swore he was never going to do it. I'll never know. He also told me he knew Simone and Stew had been together as long as Kendall and me.

I asked him what else he knew. He crossed his arms and asked me what else was there to know? We stared at each other for a moment and I said, "I'm sorry I put you through that, Harold. It was foul and terrible and...I'm really sorry."

"I know, Felicia. I'm really sorry too. I sometimes wonder if I'd exposed my knowledge of Sam and Kendall right away, if things would have been different. I don't know."

I wondered too. "Honestly, Felicia. I'm glad you're happy and your life is easier now. You didn't deserve to be tortured. I'll always regret that."

Annette had been listening quietly. Until then. She said, "Girl that is some deep shit. I would lose it if I found out Tony has known about Gary all this time."

"Honestly, Nette. There's a very good chance Harold knows about you too. But unlike Curtis, he chose to keep it to himself."

"I bet you're right."

When I hung up with Annette, I looked at the phone and shook my head. I chuckled and said to myself, "I wonder what she'll say when I tell her the rest..."

Harold asked me to forgive him. "I forgive you, Harold. But honestly, it was easy for me to blame you for my indiscretions. You did what you did out of love and obsession. I did what I did out of pain and the need to feel worthy. We were both wrong. I pray you can forgive me too."

He nodded his head yes and looked at his watch. "Felicia. There's one thing I always wanted to know."

"Oh Lord, Harold. I don't like going back there."

"I really need to know something. Okay?"

"All right."

"Why the others?"

My smile turned upside down. It pained me to face him with that. "Harold, I was so heartbroken over losing Kendall. And I..."

"I just need to know why you didn't leave me, since I no longer satisfied you."

"It wasn't sex, Harold. It was Kendall. I was trying to replace *Kendall*. I didn't sleep with those guys, Harold. I'm sorry."

"I just wondered. I honestly didn't think that was your style. I have another confession."

"Must you tell me? This is not very comfortable for me."

"I know. But I don't want you feeling like you're the only bad person here. Do you remember when I went to Boston? That time I called you about the alarm going off?"

"Yes. You already apologized for that."

"What I didn't tell you was that I really went to Baltimore. I'd been seeing a woman named Maria. She had an abortion that Friday. She told me it was my child."

"My God, Harold."

"I know. I'll never know if it was mine, but the condom *did* malfunction, and she *was* pregnant. The good part was she had no idea I had money. I told her I had to scrape up the money, but I wanted to take her to a private doctor. They confirmed her pregnancy and aborted that day."

"We should have gotten the annulment, Harold. Don't you think? And we could have shared the kids, just like we're doing now."

"In hindsight, I suppose you're right. I was too selfish to see it then."

"One thing I will tell you is this. I realized I couldn't stay with you, without him. Even before I met him, there were times I never wanted to come home. Kendall filled the voids and never made me feel like I didn't measure up."

"But you stayed. Was he content with you part time?"

"He asked me to leave you repeatedly, but I always believed it would kill you. And even though I believed that, I was selfish too. I wanted my family *and* Kendall. I'm not proud of it, but it's true."

"Really? Hmm..."

"It was also easier than facing you with my secrets. Another truth is that somewhere deep in my gut, I always knew you knew. And later, I believed if Curtis hadn't told you, you would've gone on like that forever."

"There's some truth to that. I can't tell you how many times you called me Kendall. But the thing that shattered my resolve was seeing you in his arms. Sex with you wasn't the same. And I can identify with you wanting both of us. Except in my case, I was willing to deal with the affair, have a part of you and keep my ego intact. We both demonstrated excess in our own way."

We looked at each other and nodded. Neither of us had any more to say it seemed. I finally asked, "Don't you need to go?"

He looked at his watch again. "I still have about thirty minutes."

He walked over to me. "That night I told you I knew about Kendall and you took those pills, I wished I'd been the one who took them. I finally understood how much you loved him and didn't want to live without him."

I closed my eyes in pain. "When I unlocked the door and found you, I was sure you were dead. I admit there was a part of me that hoped it was me you couldn't live without, but when I found your phone and read the text you sent him..."

I went to the toy box and picked up one of the balls. "I could never admit to you that I was in love with Kendall. I just couldn't form the words to say that to you, Harold. I never wanted to hurt you."

"I know, Felicia. And truthfully, if I'd never found that phone, and if you never called me Kendall, I would've never known. You never missed a beat when it came to taking care of us."

"I can't believe I had two husbands for so long. I struggled for a long time after you left."

"I guess we both did."

He walked over to me and smiled. "It's true that time heals. I feel so much better now. And my sessions with Dr. Dennison have helped tremendously."

"I'm so glad to hear that, Harold."

"And...I think I may have found her, Felicia. Do I have your permission to let the kids meet her?"

I smiled. "Yes. Who is she?"

"Her name is Sheila and she's a chef. Her father was African, and her mother is French. She's beautiful."

"How did you meet her?"

"I'd heard about this awesome chef in France from different people. On paper, she had it all, so I wanted her for Benson's South. I contacted her and made her an offer. She laughed at me and said, *"Sir. I would need twice that amount to live in America."*

He laughed and continued. "I asked her to come for an interview and she came with her mother. I expected some stuffy French woman with her aging mother to appear. When she walked in my office, she took my breath away. We've been dating for a couple of months."

"I'm really happy for you."

He laughed again. "She's so bossy that she would never allow me to control her. I guess I don't have what it takes to appreciate a beautiful submissive wife."

I couldn't believe he referred to me that way. I suppose it's true. "Are you talking about me? Am I really submissive??"

"That's what made me so crazy. I knew you would conform to whatever I wanted. Within reason. I just took it too far."

"Wanting to please my husband, that makes me submissive?"

"Not just that. You don't bitch and moan like many women. You usually did anything I asked of you and I can't remember you ever complaining until I made your life unbearable. I have never met a woman as easy to love as you. You don't spend money like most women and don't get me started about how great you are in bed. You are any man's dream come true, Felicia."

I didn't know whether to be flattered or what. Then he said, "Kendall has his hands full with you."

I stared at him and wanted to slap him. I almost felt like he was calling me a whore. "Are you saying I'm loose?"

"Not at all, Felicia. But if Kendall ever messes up, he's a fool if he thinks you won't cheat on him too. You're a prize, Felicia. I honestly hope he succeeds at what I failed at."

"I can't believe I'm that different from other women."

"You are. Believe it."

I stood there with my mouth opened. We looked at each other and appeared to be at a loss for words. Again. I know I was.

And I realized that even after all of the confessing and baring our souls, I still had my secrets and I assume he did too. "Do you ever miss me, Felicia?"

"Huh?"

I was so deep in thought, he had to ask me again. "Absolutely. Many things I miss, Harold."

He came closer. "You know what I mean."

I felt like my face was on fire. Benny came downstairs and said, "Daddy, we wanna go and get on the plane. Come on, Daddy."

Benny came over to us and I hugged my son. "Mommy. You should come too. You and Dad."

Harold frowned and said, "We'll be up in a few minutes. Go on up and get your coats on."

I looked around the room trying to find something to do. He laughed and asked, "What's the real reason you keep asking if I've found someone?"

I turned to him. "It's still difficult for me to be happy, knowing you might not be. I think…"

He came over to me. "Do you still want both of us?"

He picked up my hand and kissed it. The front door opened, and I heard Aleece say, "Hi, Dad!"

I heard Kendall's booming voice and I pulled my hand back. Harold laughed and went toward the stairs. He looked back at me. "I'm just teasing you, Felicia. I'm glad we had this talk. I'd like to talk again. It's therapeutic."

He went up the stairs and left me there.

I was scared as hell Kendall would see it written all over my face. Mom came down and said, "Kendall's here."

"Yeah, I heard him come in."

I looked around again, trying to find something to clean up. Mom was looking at me with narrowed eyes. "He rattled you, didn't he?"

I nodded and went into the bathroom. Mom came in behind me. "Erase that look off of your face, Felicia. Now!"

Kendall called down. "Shiree. The kids are about to go."

"Okay. I'll be right there."

I went upstairs drying my hands. I looked at the kids and said, "Mommy wants you guys to be really good. Okay?"

They both smiled and said, "Yes, Mommy."

I kneeled down and hugged both of them. Kendall reached down and got me because I started to cry. "Shiree. None of that. Come on, they have to go."

I got up and went toward the kitchen. I turned back and said, "Harold. Please call when you get there."

I heard my parents and Kendall hug and kiss the kids, and I finally heard the door close. Mom came in the kitchen and I was going in the fridge for something to drink.

She stared at me and I grabbed the juice. I sat down and Kendall came in. "Don't upset yourself like that, Shiree. You almost made me cry."

I looked up at him and he started laughing. I picked up an apple and threw it at him.

Two days before Christmas, my parents came over and informed us they'd decided to fly to New York City for the holidays. I was stunned. "Mom. You guys are always home for Christmas. What made you decide to do this?"

Daddy said, "Every year, your mom and I watch the ball drop on New Year's Eve. We've said for decades that one year we would go. We're both in good health and in great shape, Felicia. So last night, we searched for a hotel that has a view to Times Square. It's costing us a fortune, but we want to do this."

I looked at them shaking my head. Kendall said, "Good for you. And Felicia and I insist on paying your hotel costs."

Daddy said, "Oh no, Kendall. We've got it."

"Oh yes, Calvin. As much as you all do for us, and the way you help us with the kids, it's our pleasure to do it."

I said, "Absolutely. But I'm gonna miss you, Daddy."

Mom smiled and said, "I'm so excited, Felicia. We're gonna be there for nine days."

Daddy went out to the car and brought in several presents and put them under the tree. Kendall and I reached in and found theirs. I said, "Mom, you guys be careful. And we'll keep an eye on your place for you."

Soon they were gone, and I looked at Kendall and shrugged. Then twenty minutes later, Kelly walked in. But not alone.

Kendall and I were in the family room and Terrell was downstairs. Neither Kelly nor I could muster up the nerve to tell Kendall about Jim. So Jim told Kelly he'd do it. But I assumed he'd take him out to lunch or something.

Kendall and I discovered last year that both of us were closet *Rudolph the Red Nosed Reindeer* fans. I watch it every year and he does too. We hollered laughing when we found out.

So we'd planned to pop some popcorn and go to the media room to watch it. But Terrell was in there watching something, so we grabbed the popcorn and went to the family room.

When Kelly came in, neither of us noticed she wasn't alone. So when we heard a man's voice, it quickly dawned on me and I panicked.

When they walked in the family room, we both sat there surprised. Well, I was surprised. Kendall was tongue tied and stunned. He asked, "Jim. What brings you here? Is everything all right?"

"Yes, Ken. All is well. I was…"

Kendall turned to Kelly and asked, "Did you two pull up at the same time?"

They both smiled and I said, "Jim, please sit."

Kendall got up and went over and shook Jim's hand. He asked again, "Is something wrong, Jim?"

Jim smiled again and Kelly went over and sat next to him. Jim said, "Ken. Your sister and I went to dinner tonight. She and I have become close. We felt it was time to tell you."

I went to the bar and poured Kendall a shot of cognac. A large shot. I hurried and gave it to him.

Then I poured wine for Jim and myself. I looked at Kendall, and he hadn't said a word. He was standing there dumbfounded. With his mouth opened. And frozen in place. I said, "Jim, that's great news!"

Then I turned to Kendall, who finally sat down. I turned off the DVD player and said, "Kendall. Isn't that great news?"

He turned to Kelly and asked, "How did this happen?"

She laughed and asked, "What kind of question is that, Kendall?"

Jim said, "Ken. I know you're shocked. Kelly and I were shocked too, but we found we really like each other."

Kendall reached for his glass and leaned back. He looked at Jim and said, "I'm clearly the last one in the room to know. And it's unfortunate that you and my family felt the need to hide it from me. I admit I'm shocked, but I'm not upset. I'm thrilled for both of you."

My husband put his arm across the back of the sofa behind me. He began tapping on my shoulder. Jim smiled and said, "Because of the age and race differences, and the fact that I work for you, we were uneasy."

Jim looked at Kelly. "But we've been drawn to each other for a while now. During her pregnancy, she and I got to know each other and became close. I continue to be blown away by her beauty and the heart of this woman."

Jim was still looking at Kelly. Kendall had his index and middle fingers on his lip, as if pondering something. We both watched Jim and Kelly as they seemed to be speaking to each other without words.

Kendall finally broke the silence. "So what are your Christmas plans, Jim? Is your son home or did he stay on campus?"

"James went to Tampa to be with his mother, so I don't have any plans."

Kendall said, "Then it's settled. You'll have dinner with us. Come and join me at the bar. For a real drink."

I asked Kelly, "Would you go with me to check on little Kendall?"

When we were safely in Kendall's room, she and I laughed hysterically. "Girl! Why didn't you warn me??"

"Because you said it yourself. You can't keep anything from Kendall. I was afraid if I told you, you'd be a bumbling mess all day. He was determined to tell him today."

"Did you see the look on poor Kendall's face? He was stunned, Kelly."

She was still laughing. "I thought he was gonna pass out. But then he recovered okay. Do you think he's sincere about being happy for us?"

"Yes. He seemed genuinely happy for both of you."

Little Kendall began to stir, and I sent Kelly back to her date while I changed her. I smiled at my daughter. "Your auntie has herself a new boyfriend. It'll be different. But as long as she's happy, we're happy. Right?"

Kendall began kicking her legs and cooing away. I laughed and picked her up. "Come on, Mini Me. Let's go and see Daddy."

With Mom gone and Kendall inviting Jim for dinner, that meant I had to cook. I was gonna do something anyhow, but not anything too extravagant.

The next day was Christmas Eve, so we'd need food for the next few days. That morning, Kelly and I got up early and went to Wegman's. We filled two carts with Christmas goodies. I talked to Gina, and she and Todd also agreed to come with the kids.

When we returned, Kendall and Terrell were in the front yard cleaning the snow away. About an inch of snow fell overnight, but otherwise it had been a pretty mild winter.

While getting out of the car, Kendall came over and said, "You won't believe who's coming to visit."

Kelly and I both shrugged. I asked, "Who?"

"Keenan. He's a few hours away. He's driving. He said he was going to surprise us but thought he'd better call."

"Is he alone?"

"Yes. He decided to come here since Mom and Dad are gone on the cruise until after the New Year."

Kelly smiled and said, "That's great, Kendall. It'll be nice having him here for the holidays."

With everyone off from work, Stew and Simone came over for brunch. Everyone was thrilled to see Keenan. While eating he said, "So sister-in-law, I'm sure you have a single girlfriend or two I can meet."

I looked at Simone. "Do we?"

"I can't think of anyone off the top of my head. But I'm sure our husbands know a lot of single women."

They both pretended to be clueless. We laughed and Stew said, "The good news is that I'm sure the club will be a meat market. We're reopening the night after Christmas."

It dawned on me that Trina was single again. I got up and grabbed my phone. "Excuse me a minute."

I went upstairs and called her. "Hey, Girl. What are you up to today?"

"Not a thing. I was gonna drive to Cleveland to be with my cousins for Christmas, but my car is acting up. I'm afraid to take the chance and rentals are either unavailable or way too expensive on Christmas Eve. So I'm gonna just stay in town."

I smiled. "Guess who's visiting?"

"Who?"

"Kendall's brother."

She screamed. "Stop lying, Felicia. Do they look alike?"

"Yep. Except he doesn't have Locs."

"Is he single?"

"He sure is. And he wants a little company. Come on over."

"I'll be there in an hour."

We decided to do an impromptu Christmas Eve gathering. Surprisingly, Annette and Carla and their husbands agreed to come. They were able to take the kids to Carla's mother's house, because she was making cookies with all of her grandkids.

When Trina walked in, Keenan was instantly taken with her. He was in the kitchen with us helping us prepare finger foods for our guests. So after introductions, Trina joined us.

Kelly was telling Keenan about Jim and he barely heard anything she said. I said to Kelly, "Let's leave them to do it."

I waved goodbye to Trina and she smiled and continued talking to Keenan. I turned back and asked them to also clean the shrimp.

Keenan and Kendall are the same height, but Keenan is slimmer. Trina is slim and tall and chocolate. While watching them, I thought they made a great couple.

Kendall had apparently already told Keenan about Jim, because the only thing Keenan said to Kelly was, "Kelle. As long as he's nice to you, I'm good. I guess that'll teach you not to comment on the women in my life now."

She punched him and left it alone. Kelly really liked Trina and we both hoped they would hit it off.

Jim came over that afternoon, so Keenan got to meet him that day. The guys went downstairs to play pool. Harold took his pool table to Detroit, so Kendall replaced it with a new one.

When the Summers and the Fraziers arrived, the party was in full swing. We put the babies in the living room until Kendall went to sleep. Then we put her in Aunt Kelly's room and left Miss spoiled Brooke in the playpen.

She was spoiled rotten. And little Kendall was trying to catch up with her. Brooke refused to allow Simone out of her sight. Keenan suggested to Trina that they go up and rock Brooke to sleep. She smiled and said, "That sounds like a good idea."

We all watched as they went up with Brooke screaming for her mother. I went up behind them and told them they were welcomed to go in our room. I opened the door and said, "No one can hear her scream in here."

Stew was laughing as the screams suddenly stopped. Simone was antsy, worried that something was wrong with her. Kendall brought me aside and said, "We have two more guests coming."

"Who, Kendall?"

"Juanita and Yvonne."

"You're kidding, right?"

"No. I'm not kidding. She called to update me on one of our patients. So, I told her about Kelly and Jim, and that Keenan is here. She asked if it would be okay if they stop by because she has something for little Kendall."

I laughed. "I guess the more the merrier. But next time would you kindly ask me first."

I walked away and went back to helping Annette and Simone at the bar. Kendall came over to me. "Shiree. May I please see you for a moment?"

I rolled my eyes at him and we went downstairs. Jim and Terrell were at the pool table, so we went into the media room. "Shiree. What was that?"

"What was what?"

"That look on your face I've never seen before. What was it?"

I looked at him real hard. "Nothing, Kendall. I would simply like a little notice when you invite people over."

"I didn't invite her. She asked if they could stop by. There's a difference."

He stepped back and looked at me again. "I don't believe that's what's bothering you. Tell me, Shiree."

I walked up to him and got as close as I could. "When I answer you, stop asking me to elaborate. Just stop it, Kendall."

I walked back upstairs and left him there.

About twenty minutes after arriving, Yvonne asked me about little Kendall. She said, "I'm dying to see her."

"Come with me. Let's see if she's still asleep."

We went into Kelly's room and my daughter was gone. I looked at Yvonne and said, "It looks like someone beat me to it."

We left Kelly's room and I didn't see her with anyone. Big Kendall was also unaccounted for. "Maybe Kendall took her up to change her. I'll go up and check, and then I'll bring her down."

I went up to the nursery and Kendall was sitting in the rocking chair with his daughter. She was asleep and he was quietly watching her. He didn't even hear me come in. Or so I thought. He eventually asked, "Why were you so cruel to me, Shiree?"

I stood there wondering the same thing. Although I knew the answer to his question, he didn't deserve to be treated that way. I'm to blame for who and what I am.

I reached down and took her from him. I looked into the face that looked mine and I laid her down. "I'm sorry, Kendall."

He got up. "I've never felt so terrible in my life, Shiree. I've been sitting up here trying to figure out what the hell I did."

Little Kendall appeared to be waking up, so I began to change her. "It was me, Kendall. You didn't do anything. I'm really sorry. I love you so much, and..."

He finished changing Kendall while I stood next to him in tears. "I thought you'd be okay with them coming. I don't think sometimes. I always felt you were secure regarding Juanita. I'm sorry..."

"That has nothing to do with it. I love Juanita. I'm just tired. Let's get back to our guests."

We went back downstairs. I gave Kendall to Yvonne and she fell in love with her. Juanita went over to them and they fought over who would hold her. Kendall said, "You two are like two kids fighting over a toy. Am I gonna have to take my daughter?"

Little Kendall was enjoying it. She seemed to be laughing at them. Brooke was now in Kelly's room downstairs sleeping away. I went upstairs to my room and sent all of the girls a text except Kelly. I asked them to come up right away.

They eventually made it up and I closed my door. I turned to them and said, "I know this is not the time, but I need help with something."

I told them what Harold said. Carla said, "Felicia. I'm the same way. So I'm not the one to ask. I enjoy doing everything for Earl."

Annette said, "Licia. I can't believe you're just now realizing that. Anyone who knows you could see it."

"Nette. To me there's a difference between being good to your man and being submissive to him. To me, submissive means bowing down to someone in a negative way."

"In some cases, it's true that it's negative, Licia. But that's not how it is with you. You submitted to men who were worthy of your attention and your best. Giving a man your all isn't a bad thing in this case."

I looked at Simone and asked, "Well??"

She laughed and said, "I always warned you not to give people more than they deserved or had earned. But I agree with Annette. Your husbands were different. I don't really know how your relationship with Todd was, but I would bet that you were different with him."

Carla said, "She's right, Licia. You weren't that way with Todd. Right?"

"That's true. I loved Todd like he loved me. Our love was simpler. Easier. We worked and paid bills and raised our kids."

Dr. Morales pointed out that I allowed Harold and Kendall to control me. But they also *took care of me*. Todd wasn't able to do the things financially that they did.

Maybe I felt indebted to Kendall, like I did with Harold. Maybe it was because I didn't feel I measured up. "I wonder if it's because I feel like I'm not good enough, so I try to make up for it by being submissive."

Simone yelled, "That's a damn lie! Don't you dare believe that shit, Felice!"

Annette asked, "Why now, Licia?"

"Because I just jumped all over Kendall and tore his nerves up. And mine too. I feel terrible because I can't make being submissive a good thing."

Annette said, "Submissive is only bad when it makes you feel bad. You've always enjoyed taking care of Kendall. He adores you, Felicia. And you adore him. If it makes you feel better, then call it something else. Call it adoration. Or love. He's just like you. If you're submissive, so is he. Honestly, I've never seen anything like what the two of you have."

Carla said, "You said Harold admitted he couldn't appreciate you. Kendall does. And it shows."

Simone said, "Do not let crazy ass Harold destroy your vibe with Kendall. Besides, I need everyone in a good way when I tell my husband that he's about to have a son soon."

We all sat there with our mouths opened and Simone said, "Some might call me submissive, Felice. But Stewart has loved me like no one *ever* has. I would give him anything. And even though he hasn't asked for another child, he *has* said he would love to have more. So, I heard his heart and decided to give him just that. The desires of his heart. It's okay to love like that when *you're* loved like that."

I smiled. We all did. We hugged and cried and wrapped ourselves around Simone. She was almost three months pregnant and doing very well. She planned to tell Stew the next day on Christmas morning.

When the house was quiet and the crackling of the fireplace was the only sound in our bedroom, I looked at my sleeping husband and gently woke him up. I nuzzled up to him and held him close to me.

I began kissing his chest and managed to roll him over so I could lie on top of him. He embraced me and held me close to him. "You okay, Shiree?"

"Baby. I'm sorry for waking you up, but I need to say something to you."

He opened his eyes and rolled me off of him. "What happened, Baby? Did something happen?"

I sat up and he did too. "Kendall. I've struggled for years with something and it finally came to a head today. Unfortunately, you were in the line of fire. I will never forgive myself for taking it out on you. I'm so sorry."

"Tell me, Shiree."

"It's about a conversation I had with Harold recently. He told me that one of the reasons he married me was because I'm submissive."

"You're kidding, right?"

"No, Kendall. I *am* submissive and you know it too. Just like Juanita and Yvonne said years ago. I just need to figure out how to feel good about it."

"Shiree. I don't know how you define it, but I see a beautiful, strong and loving woman when I look at you. To me, a submissive person is someone who is weak and needs guidance. They're unable to function or think for themselves. They're also unfeeling and rote, like a servant. They *need* to be told what to do. None of that is you, Baby."

I thought about that. "I occasionally have these moments when I feel foolish for being this way. Like I'm not normal. And although Harold was trying to be nice, when *he* said it, it was the last straw."

Kendall tilted his head. "When did this conversation take place, Shiree?"

"The day he picked the kids up. He asked my permission to introduce them to his new girlfriend. He described her as bossy, and that she would never allow him to control her. *Then* he said he never knew how to appreciate a submissive wife. I was floored!!"

Kendall laughed. "Baby, that's ridiculous! At least it is to me. I see you as a rare jewel. Do you realize I have never been so in love as I am with you? Those things you might think are submissive are to me your charm. You are the most genuine and giving person I know. And the way you love is indescribable. You taught me how to be transparent and you've seen me cry more than my mother."

I caressed his face and looked into his eyes. "Thank you for saying that, Sweetie. That makes me feel so much better about all of this. And Simone and my other sisters helped me with it today too. I told them what I did to you, and they helped me to see it better."

"What did they say?"

"They helped me see that I love you like I do because you love me the same way. You and I are true examples of people who love each other with our actions and not just our words."

"I feel sorry for Harold. He still doesn't get it. I pray he learns if he plans to marry this woman."

"Me too. Can you find it in your heart to forgive me, Sweetie?"

"Of course, Shiree. Just promise me you won't ever change."

I smiled. "I promise, Baby."

I straddled him again. "It's two-fifteen on Christmas morning. Merry Christmas, Husband!"

"Merry Christmas, Wife. Are you truly feeling better?"

"Yes. I feel better, Kendall. And again, I'm so sorry about earlier."

"You know I can't go back to sleep unless I make love to you. You can make it up to me if you..."

I looked at him sideways and sat next to him. "I remember when Harold and I got married, we discussed sexual fantasies. You and I have never done that. Do you have any unfulfilled fantasies?"

He tensed. "No, Shiree. I don't."

I laughed. "What's wrong?"

"I remember having that conversation too. With Juanita. And we were never the same."

He and I both laughed. "Please don't tell me you desire something I can't give you."

I laughed again. "You don't even like naughty movies or toys?"

"Shiree. After all these years, you must know I don't own any naughty movies. I do however enjoy using the vibrator with you. Although, even that makes me jealous at times. So no, I have no interest in any other toys. Do you?"

"No, Baby."

He tugged on my ear. "Actually...I would like to see you masturbate without assistance."

"I'll do that for you. I probably won't climax, but I don't mind doing it."

"I don't think I've ever met anyone who couldn't give themselves an orgasm."

"I think I over think it. But that night in Jamaica was so hot. Like when I climaxed without trying. Remember those times on the phone with you?"

"So you really had orgasms?"

"I sure did. But the one in Jamaica was by far the hottest. I wonder why?"

He smiled at me. I smiled back. Then I asked, "Do you want more kids?"

He laughed. "No, Shiree. Where did that come from?"

"Are you sure? Because if you want a son..."

"Do you actually want more kids?"

"I want to know how you feel. Tell me the truth, Kendall."

"I *feel* we have enough kids, Baby."

"But you only have one. This is your opportunity to tell me, Kendall."

"I'm quite content with one of my own and our other kids. Honestly."

I smiled. "Okay. I know a secret. But you have to promise to act surprised when you hear it later."

He stared at me. "Okay, I promise."

"Stew is about to be a daddy again."

"*Really??* That's great news! When is she telling him?"

"Today. For Christmas. She's due in June."

"I'd love to witness her telling him again. My brother cried like a baby. And I know he wants more. He's gonna be so happy."

"Speaking of brothers, I wonder if Keenan is back yet?"

"He sent me a text saying he'd see us tomorrow."

"You're kidding, right!?"

"No, Shiree. They almost did it up here in our room. Once Brooke went to sleep, they were all over each other. You really made a good choice."

I punched him. "You mean to tell me she let him spend the night after knowing him a few hours? He was supposed to make sure she got home okay and look at her car. Would you respect a woman who did that?"

"Times are different, Shiree. Trina is clearly a respectable woman. But she's not held back by old standards. It's not like she's...you know."

"No. I don't know, Kendall. Why don't you tell me?"

He looked at me and laughed. "She's not...a whore, Shiree. They like each other and want to be with each other."

I stared at him and he laughed again. "I asked you if you'd respect her."

"Shiree. You seduced me and I always respected you."

"I guess we'll never agree on who seduced who, will we?"

We both laughed and he asked, "So do you think Stew will get a boy this time?"

"Simone thinks so. She said she hasn't had any morning sickness. She's convinced it's a boy."

Chapter Twelve

We got through the holidays very well. My parents returned in one piece, and Keenan left a happy man.

It was April of 2014. Kendall and I had just celebrated our first wedding anniversary. Kelly and Terrell moved into the other house, and life for the Montgomerys settled into a simple existence.

Kelly was able to transfer to GM in Rochester and a friend of hers was renting her house. Little Kendall had to get used to not being in Aunt Kelly's arms and Aunt Kelly had to get used to it too.

Kelly and Jim continued to date and they both seemed to be happy. Terrell was set to graduate in June, and he decided to follow in his uncle's footsteps and become a doctor. He wasn't sure what he would specialize in yet.

We were so proud of him. As Salutatorian of his class, he had several offers and scholarships to choose from.

The twins were flourishing, and Aleece loved taking care of her baby sister. Benny was extremely close to Kendall and it seemed the two of them were always together.

My other sons transferred to a parochial school and were doing very well. Todd and Gina bought a new house and were closer to us, so I got to see my boys a lot more.

Simone and Stew were anxiously awaiting little Stewart. We all were. She was doing well and decided to remain home and be a stay-at-home mom. Brooke finally settled down and was no longer so spoiled.

I never heard anymore from Sam. We successfully kept it from Kendall, and Benny said he would track him periodically in case he came back. He and Jonathon and their families left Rochester shortly after New Year.

Benny refused to take a dime from me. I always wondered if Annette paid him. *Her* way.

A few weeks ago, Tony caught Annette. It was awful. He apparently suspected and followed her. He caught them leaving Gary's place.

He left her and took TJ. She was completely devastated and absolutely heartbroken. It was too painful for her to live in the house alone, so she moved in with her mother.

Over the last few months during some of my down time, I began to realize something...

In January, I had a dream. It was about those dreams I'd had after the accident. I dreamed the six of us were back in Myrtle Beach.

When I woke up, I laughed about the absurdity of it. But days afterwards, I began to journal something. So much of what I dreamed actually came true.

In my dream, Kendall told me, "Be careful. Harold knew about Sam and you didn't know he knew."

He told me that after I came home with no underclothes on, and I thought Harold busted me.

And Carrie. The fact that Harold actually slept with her. I made it up in my dream to protect myself, but it was true in my dream *and* in reality. So strange.

And the conversation outside of the hotel, when in my dream Harold came to Myrtle Beach. The things he said. He actually said most of it later in reality. Like how he knew about Kendall but was unable to face me for fear of losing me.

And who could forget him saying that I called him Kendall many times.

One funny thing was the morning I cooked breakfast in Myrtle Beach in my dream, and the conversation we all had about me screaming. It was similar to the one we had that morning Stew knocked on our garage door, and later we all had breakfast together. Simone said I always exempt Kendall from helping in the kitchen just like she did in my dream.

And the sexy white dress. I thought when Simone told me she mentioned it while I was unconscious, that explained it. But Kendall and his need to see me in a white dress always made me smile. No, my wedding dress wasn't *that* sexy. But to him it was.

And he continues to talk about it. Hmmm...the sexy white dress. Maybe it was fate telling me I would marry the sexiest man alive in the dress of his dreams.

Also in my dream, I feared my father knowing because I was afraid he would confront Kendall. And sure enough, after I was released from the hospital and went to Kendall's, Daddy confronted him by phone and then Kendall voluntarily faced him at their house.

And Kendall confronting Harold. How he told Harold I was *his* wife in my dream and actually telling him that when he called Harold that day.

And that look on his face I saw in my dream. The one that was foreign to me. And then seeing it in reality that day when he and Harold were actually face to face in my parent's house. I actually saw it one other time. In Jamaica when he knocked that guy out on the beach.

Kendall told me in the dream that he wanted me to be his wife on my own, not because Harold no longer wanted me. He said the same thing that day at our place when I tried to sneak my stuff out after he'd called Harold.

But more than anything, how adamant Kendall was about me not sleeping with Harold. How he made a point of that after walking away from his confrontation of Harold in my dream.

So over time, I periodically wrote down everything I could remember from the dreams. Because it was so long ago, I sometimes had to go back and insert things as I remembered them or change the sequence.

One thing that stood out as not coming true, became the one thing that scared me the most. For some reason, even though he displayed it before the accident, it was Harold's crush on Juanita.

But then I discovered something that horrified me even more...

I discovered texts from Tara to my husband...

About the Author

Kendra Martin, the author of the Exes and Excess series, is from Rochester, New York. She now lives in Raleigh, North Carolina with her husband, and is currently writing her next book.

Visit her online at kendramartinltd.com

Other titles by the Author...

Exes and Excess, 2016

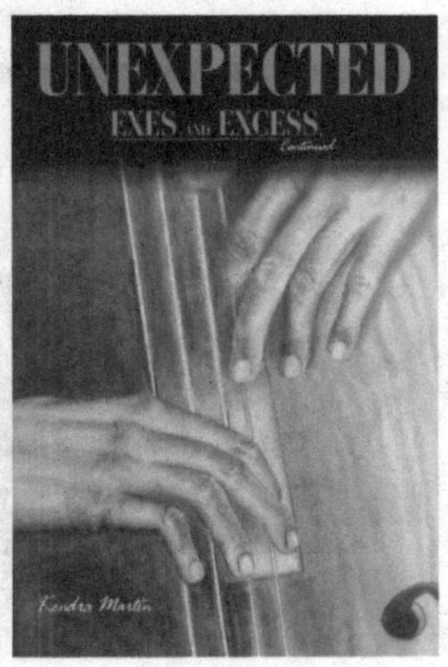

Unexpected, 2017

Embracing Shiree...An Exposé, 2020

With Love and Appreciation, I thank Sista-Love Book Club for supporting my work and encouraging me so much. Here's to You!